The Settlement

The Settlement

W. Earl Daniels

PART I

JOHN ROBERT DANIEL

CHAPTER 1

THE DRUMS OF WAR

It was late October 1860. The place was the farming community of Saulston, in Wayne County, North Carolina. The air was brisk, and most of the leaves had fallen from the trees that surrounded the little white plank board house that sat a hundred yards from the dirt road that passed to its front. On each side of the house was an oak tree with Spanish moss hanging from the limbs.

From the road, anyone passing the house might have thought, unless they saw a periodic puff of gray smoke rise from the head of the man sitting in the rocking chair, that the man was probably taking a late-afternoon nap.

However, anyone thinking that did not really know John Robert Daniel. Taking a light day nap was not his nature. John Robert was a tireless worker. If he was breathing air, his hands, legs, or both had to be moving. He had not acquired 150 acres of land and built the house with his own two hands, all done by his age of thirty-two, without lots of work before the sun rose and a lot after the sun set.

It was then—only then—that he felt prepared to ask seventeen-year-old Becky Newsome to marry him. He had known her most all her life, and to him she was the most handsome woman he had ever known. And, much to his surprise, she agreed to marry a man almost twice her age. She agreed because for as long as she could remember having known him, she had loved his most thoughtful and caring attitude toward others, especially for her. She admired him for his desire to be secure and independent before starting a family.

But this time, Becky would have been wrong. John Robert was thinking about his last trip to Adamsville.

In return, she gave him six children, three boys and three girls. Their eldest was William Henry, age fourteen; and the youngest was Rebecca, age six months. Becky had already told John Robert that with their family growing that it was time for him to start thinking about an addition to their house. She might have thought that was what he dwelling upon as he rocked on their front porch with his corncob pipe clenched between his teeth.

Adamsville was about six miles southwest of Saulston and, and at the time, about two miles east of the city limits of Goldsboro. Today Adamsville has been incorporated into Goldsboro, a town since World War II known as the home of Seymour Johnson Air Force Base.

Within the last week, John Robert had taken a load of sugar cane to Adamsville to be made into a barrel of molasses. While there he spent some time sitting on a wooden crate catching up on the recent news regarding the threat of war with the Northern states. Although the benefactor of much of the Southern states' farm production was the Northern states, it was primarily the Northern states that opposed the manner in which much of the production was achieved.

Slave labor planted and harvested the raw products the Northern states used in the manufacture of finished products sold not only around the world but back to the Southern states. The manufacturing and production in the Northern states was done without slave labor. And although slave labor had made a number of wealthy people both in the North and South, the North had become adamantly opposed to the Southern states' use of slave labor.

What John Robert gathered from the conversations was that should Abraham Lincoln be elected president of the United States, the war drums would beat much louder. And while neither John Robert nor any of his neighbors owned slaves or utilized slave labor in their farming practices, the very idea that Northern states could impose their beliefs upon Southern states was intolerable. There was a deep-rooted belief that individual states had the right to make their own decision with regard to slavery. If the Southern states caved to this imposition upon states' rights, what would be next? And he was convinced that before any state permitted an invasion of what it believed to be states' rights, states would start to secede from the union of states.

He departed Adamsville that day with three things weighing heavily upon his mind. And it was those three things that he pondered, on this day, in his rocking chair, as he periodically took deep drags on his pipe. First, it was his understanding and conviction that each state had to remain independent to its own convictions and make its own decisions regarding the economy of those who lived in the state. He did not agree with the idea of slavery, nor would he ever own another person as a slave. But in his mind, the manner in which the issue of slavery was resolved could be the first crack in the wall of states' rights. Should other states influence the right of states on this issue, would they next be telling the Southern states what crops they could grow? What would happen to Wayne County should, for some reason, other states oppose the growth of the county's major crop, tobacco?

Second, in preparation for a war, a company of Goldsboro Volunteers was already being formed by Captain Junius B. Whitaker. That company would become an element of the Ninth Regiment of the North Carolina Volunteers.

John Robert's second concern was that today, North Carolina was calling for volunteers, but what about tomorrow? If there weren't sufficient volunteers, would there be a conscription of men to serve? At the age of forty-three and with six children, John Robert did not suspect he would be conscripted. Nevertheless, he did worry about his son, William Henry. He remembered hearing his grandfather speak of boys as young as twelve years of age serving in the Revolutionary War, and that was not even a hundred years ago.

Finally, if he were to volunteer, could he do so with the understanding that his son would not have to serve? He thought he might be able to make a good case that his eldest son was needed to work the farm to provide for his mother and five siblings.

These were the concerns John Robert was pondering when he saw William Henry walking proudly up the path toward the house swinging a string of fish in his right hand.

William Henry was already as tall as his father. His shoulders were broad, and he had become as strong as an ox from the labor he contributed to the farm. This time of the year, in the mornings, he would walk to the pond, approximately a half mile from the house, to set his fish traps. In the late afternoon, he would return to gather his daily catch. Before going to bed, he would clean the fish, gut them, salt them, and place them in a barrel of brine to later be cooked by his mother.

There was no question in John Robert's mind that, if need be, the farm could be turned over to William Henry, who would look after it, and the family, as well as his father. As he waved to his son, he thought, "This is a matter I must discuss with Becky, and soon."

At the beginning of December 1860, John Robert still had not said anything to Becky about his thoughts or plans should there be a civil war. It was a difficult subject, and he still clung to the hope that this talk of war would soon pass. But all his hopes were soon to change.

South Carolina was the first state to take a stand against what it believed to be an invasion of states' rights. On December 20, 1860, South Carolina seceded from the Union. Five days later, the Union troops that had been stationed in Charleston relocated to a small island in the Charleston Harbor, known as Fort Sumter. At that time Fort Sumter was considered by the North to be property of the United States government. Nevertheless, secession by South Carolina set the stage for other states to soon follow.

During January, five other states, Mississippi, Florida, Alabama, Georgia, and Louisiana, followed South Carolina's lead. Before talking to Becky, John Robert had to make a trip to Goldsboro to discuss with Captain Whitaker the idea of trading his service for that of his son.

On February 1, unknown to John Robert the very day that Texas seceded from the Union, he said to his wife, "Becky, before I start to break ground for the spring planting, I need to go to the leather shop in

Goldsboro to acquire a new pair or reins for our mule, Dusty. I should return home by midafternoon."

"Will you be taking William Henry with you?" she asked.

"No! He will be filing the cutting edges on some of the breaking plows, but if you need him to do something, just let him know." With those words John Robert left the house to mount the horse that William Henry had already saddled for him. With a wave to Becky, who was standing in the doorway, he rode off down the lane toward the dirt road that passed in front of their house.

CHAPTER 2

THE AGREEMENT

William Henry had saddled John Robert's favorite saddle horse, Lucky Boy. Lucky Boy was a quarter horse that stood about fourteen hands in height. He was all brown except for a white blaze on his forehead and a white arrow head mark on his right side. The pride with which he trotted could cause any rider to convey the appearance of a well-experienced horseman.

As John Robert sat proudly in the saddle letting Lucky Boy trot with the grace of a horse taking care of business, he was dressed in trousers with a belt pulled tight and a checkered wool shirt that fit snugly enough to accent his broad shoulders and hardened biceps. The cold nip in the early February air had necessitated his wearing a leather duster, which he hoped to place behind his saddle as the day warmed.

He desperately wanted to convey the image of a man much younger than forty-three. At his age, he knew it was important for Captain Whitaker's initial impression of him to be favorable. He could not afford an impression of a man who could not do the job expected of him. He was fairly certain that Whitaker's first choice for men to fill out his company of volunteers would be those in their late teens to early twenties.

At the leather shop where he acquired a new set of leather reins, he asked the directions to the encampment of Whitaker's volunteers. He was told the encampment was located just a few miles south of the town, on the banks of the Neuse River. Raff, the owner of the leather shop, said, "You can't miss it because the area is dotted with hundreds of white tents." Laughingly, he said, "You'll think you have ridden into an Indian village."

After stowing the new reins into one of his saddlebags and swinging himself back into the saddle, John Robert nodded at Raff and said, "Thanks! I may be back soon for a pair of blinders after I see how that new mule works without being distracted."

Raff waved back and said, "Now don't you go joining up, ya hear!"

Raff was correct; John Robert had no problem finding the volunteers' encampment. Prior to entering the camp, he reined Lucky Boy to a stop, dismounted, removed his duster, and tied it behind his saddle. Although there was a cold, bitter nip in the air, which was made colder from the wind blowing across the river in his direction, John Robert needed to be seen as one tough enough to handle the elements that resulted from bad weather.

Back on Lucky Boy, John Robert entered the camp. Some of the men were marching with rifles on their shoulders, and others were marching with only sticks on their shoulders. He could hear rifle fire farther down the river. "Probably a few boys learning to shoot straight," he was thinking. As he passed a boy carrying a kettle, he asked, "Can you tell me where I might find Captain Whitaker?"

When the young boy looked up at John Robert, John thought, "He can't be more than sixteen years old."

"Yes, sir! If you will ride down by the riverbank, you'll see a tent with a flag in front of it. About an hour ago, he was sitting at a desk in front of the tent."

"Thank you! Have a good day," replied John Robert.

John Robert laid the reins to the right side of Lucky Boy's neck, and Lucky immediately turned and started walking in the direction of the river. Within a hundred yards, John Robert could hear the rushing of the river as it made its way east toward the ocean.

A number of tents lined the river, but a flag rising slightly above the tents marked where Captain Whitaker should be if he had not left since the boy saw him.

When John Robert was within a couple of tents of the flag, he spotted a young man sitting at a small desk without a coat, scribbling on a piece of paper. John Robert lifted himself out of the saddle, walked Lucky over to the nearest hitching post, and tied him. He then approached the studious man, who had not looked up.

Clearing his throat, John Robert said, "Excuse me, sir. Would you happen to be Captain Whitaker?"

Without looking up, the young man replied, "Depending upon who's asking." Then, looking up and seeing an older man with broad shoulders, a narrow waist, and arms the size of small tree trunks standing in front of him, he jumped to his feet, saying, "Sir, I apologize for my curt answer. Today has been a little stressful. How may I help you?"

"Understand you are looking for volunteers."

"Yes, sir. Do you have a son who might be interested?"

"Pleased to say that for now, that is not the case. However, I might be."

"No offense, sir, but may I ask your age?"

"No offense taken. And please do not consider me boastful when I say I can shoot the eye out of a squirrel at fifty yards and hit anything moving at one hundred yards. And after looking around your camp, I probably can whip about everyone I've seen. Furthermore, there is not anything you need built, from bridges to houses that I can't build. Now to your question, I have forty-three years, which include twelve to eighteen hours a day of experience. Have you got anyone here that can match that?"

"Don't know that I have. But I do know I need men with the agility of a cougar, the stamina of a hard-ridden horse, and the craziness to go wherever I tell them to go without questioning the order. And generally, that is found in men much younger and with less experience than you."

"Captain, while you know what you want, I can promise you two things: I, John Robert Daniel, will never question your orders, and at the end of any battle, I will be one of the last men standing."

A slight smile came across Whitaker's face, and he said, "I like and believe you, John Robert Daniel. But offering yourself, at your age, leads me to think there is more to your offer. Why would you volunteer when you are obviously an educated man who knows, at your age—and I suspect you have a family—that the likelihood of your being conscripted to serve is probably outside the realm of possibility."

"A little flattery never hurts," thought John Robert, and he began. "Captain, you are much wiser than your youthful appearance would suggest. There is a stipulation to my offer of service—which, by the way, is for the duration of the war, should a war come. I have a family of six children, and another may be on the way. My oldest boy is fourteen. I do not want him in the war as long as I serve. And should I die on the field of battle, I do not want him conscripted before he is sixteen years of age. Someone needs to provide for the family, and once he is sixteen, the next oldest son should be able to provide. These are my terms. If they are agreeable, I will report for duty immediately upon being called by you."

Captain Whitaker scratched the top of his head and then responded. "I understand that you are volunteering yourself in lieu of your son, and I understand why. But your request is not at my decision-making level. And how do I know you will honor your terms?"

"Do you have any boys here from Saulston? If so, ask them what they know about John Robert Daniel. I am confident that all will tell you I am a man of my word."

"Okay, I will make your request known to my superiors. Should we need your services and agree to your terms, I will send a Saulston boy to fetch you. Regardless of what you are doing, you are to stop and report immediately. Are we in agreement?"

"Yes sir, Captain. You have my word and my hand on that." John Robert extended his hand to Captain Whitaker. The two men shook hands.

John Robert turned and walked over to Lucky, unhitched him, and swung himself into the saddle as if he were twenty years younger. When he looked in the direction of Captain Whitaker, he said, "By the way, Captain, my son's name is William Henry."

Lucky knew it was time to go home; he turned without any command from his rider and started loping through the encampment toward Saulston.

CHAPTER 3

A CALL TO DUTY

While Texas was the only state to secede from the Union in February, there was one other major event that increased the gravity of a movement toward a war footing. Jefferson Davis was inaugurated as the provisional president of the Confederate States of America in Montgomery, Alabama.

On March 4, 1861, a second event happened that made war even more likely Abraham Lincoln took the oath of office as president of the Union. Lincoln had made it clear during his campaigning that he was opposed to slavery and that he would work toward abolition. However, no states seceded from the Union during March, and John Robert still had not told Becky of the commitment he had made in early February to Captain Whitaker.

On April 12, 1861, the divide between the Southern states and the Northern states became even wider when six thousand members of the South Carolina militia, believing Fort Sumter belonged to South Carolina, opened fire upon the small garrison of Fort Sumter. The fact that the commander of the garrison, Major Robert Anderson, was a former slave owner and native of South Carolina, was irrelevant because he had made it known that his loyalty was to the Union.

Historians would later say the hostile action by the South Carolina militia was the beginning of the Civil War. Some attributed it to fueling the actions of Virginia to secede from the union on April 17, 1861. With both South Carolina and Virginia seceding from the Union, pressure began to mount for North Carolina to join with its bordering states.

By now, the pressure within John Robert had built to the point that Becky had detected his worry, and to her he gave the appearance of what she considered to be abnormal behavior for her husband. He seemed unusually impatient with William Henry and was rushing him to complete some routine tasks that normally were not performed before early May. And whenever William Henry brought that fact to his father's attention, John Robert would snap, "Don't question my motive!" or he would remind his son that he was the one who made the decisions when things had to be done. A son's responsibility was to obey.

Her husband's actions, especially his blunt words with William Henry, were causing her much concern. He might be either having a health issue, about which she had not been informed, or worried that the possibility of a war might affect their economic situation. The time for her to confront him, which she rarely did, could not be delayed any longer. She had both the right and the need to know what was causing his irritable attitude and the rush with which he approached everything he did. Finally, his sudden need to rise earlier in the morning and go to bed later at night was most disruptive to their previous smooth way of life.

At the evening dinner, had there not been some talk between the girls, very little would have been said. Just before all were rising from the table, Becky said, "Nancy Ann, you are responsible for cleaning the kitchen and the dishes. All, with the exception of William, will help you." Looking at the other children, she said, "And I best not hear there has been any arguing over what Nancy tells you to do." Nancy Ann was two years younger than William.

"William is the exception because I know he has some chores Father wants him to do before bedtime." Turning to John Robert, who was already standing, she said, "John, you and I are going to take a walk."

All knew that when Becky became assertive, something serious was in the wind, and all hoped it wasn't about one of them. John quickly said, "I had plans to—"

Becky interrupted. "You have plans to take a walk with me."

John had come to know that meant there would be no further discussion in front of the children. Becky stood up; straightened her apron, which she had on unless she was going to church; and started for the back door. John obediently fell in behind her. Although she was only about five feet tall and weighed no more than 110 pounds, she could be one powerful woman.

She started across a field with giant strides. The sun was just before dropping below the horizon. The moon was already visible in the eastern sky. She wanted to be seated at her favorite spot, beneath a sycamore tree that was covered with Spanish moss, before the sun set. And while John's strides would have permitted him to pass her, he didn't dare do so. From her tone he knew it was time for him to listen.

Once seated on a wooden bench that John had built her shortly after they were married, she stared him in the eyes and said, "John, it is now time for you to tell me what is going on. And I don't want a long, stretched-out explanation before you get to the point."

John began. "I know I have waited way too long before telling you this, but I did so with the hope that with time, the matter would pass. But that has not been the case. Becky, you know that for some time now there have been rumors of a war between the Southern states and Northern states over the slavery issue. Should there be a war, there is a good possibility that William would be called to go or that he might feel an obligation to go. You and I know that neither of us could bear the thought of him having to go to war. I have taken action to try to preclude him from going."

"What have you done, John?"

"I have volunteered to go in his place. Now, before you say anything, Becky, please hear me out. I am forty-three years old; he has his whole life in front of him. And even though he is only fourteen, he can manage this farm and look after you and the other children as well as I can.

"I met with Captain Whitaker of the Goldsboro Volunteers with the hope of making a deal whereby if war breaks out, I will volunteer to go in

William's place so as to preclude his conscription. Should something happen to me, he would not be conscripted until he was at least sixteen years old. If I were to make it through the war, he would never have to go."

Becky sat there with a stunned look on her face. "Why didn't you discuss this with me?" she asked.

Looking at her with his heart filled love for her, he said, "Becky, you are a smart woman. I knew that once you thought through the alternatives, you would agree. You know that at my age, I will not be conscripted. But if the war does not go in our favor, William might have to go before he is fifteen. That is too young for anyone to die, not really understanding what they are fighting for."

"What makes you think Captain Whitaker will keep his word?"

"First of all, I do not have his word. He has to discuss my request with his superiors. If his superiors were to agree I would insist the agreement be in writing. There remains a very good chance that my offer will be declined because of my age. But, my dear, I had to try. I would not be able to live with myself if William was called and I had not done anything to prevent it. Becky, this is the right thing. You know I can take care of myself better than William could. He may be a man physically, but mentally, he is not prepared to make the decisions that would be necessary to keep him alive. Please know I did not want to hide this from you or hurt you in any way, but I am the better choice if one of us has to go to war."

As Becky looked down, she reached over, took John's hand, placed it in her lap, and then covered his hand with both of hers. Looking in his eyes with teardrops running down her cheeks, she said, "My dearest John, I have never and will never doubt that your decisions are in the best interests of our family. Your actions caused me to worry that you might be finding it difficult to share with me a health issue you were having, or the possibility of a war might be giving you concerns about our financial situation. And while the selfish part of me yearns for another alternative, I know you have thought this matter through for the both of us. So tomorrow morning after breakfast, I think you should share with the children the decision we have made."

John swallowed to squelch his emotions. He felt a great sense of relief when she said, "...the decision *we* have made."

He stood and pulled Becky to her feet and gave her a most grateful kiss. Together they walked back to the house, hand in hand.

$$\mathcal{Q}$$

It was April 30, and the rain continued to patter on the canvas roof of the tent that Captain Whitaker occupied. The rain had begun in the wee hours of the morning, and as of the noon hour, it appeared that it would continue through the remainder of the day and into the night. But just as the rain appeared to be endless, so seemed his finalization of the company's monthly training report to Governor Ellis.

Under normal military circumstances, his report would be submitted to a regimental commander. And although the Fourth North Carolina Infantry Regiment, consisting of ten companies from seven counties, had been designated companies A through K, the regiment existed only on paper. There was not a J company nor had a regimental commander been named. Iredell County had three companies, A, C, and H. Rowan County had had two, B and K. Wayne County had only Captain Whitaker's company, which was designated D Company.

The report was quite detailed in the training that had been conducted. The young men had learned the basics of formations, marching, and rapidly firing and reloading their muskets. They had learned how to maintain a barrage of fire by the first rank firing and then kneeling to reload while the second rank fired over the heads of the first rank. The second rank would then drop to reload while the third rank fired over both kneeling ranks. By the end of the third firing, the first rank was reloaded and could resume firing.

The men had been taught both offensive and defensive tactics. They had learned terrain assessment for its advantage to both offensive and defensive firing positions. And they had been trained in hand-to-hand combat where the only use of their weapon was its bayonet or its butt as a club. Throughout their training they displayed enthusiasm and aggressive bravado, damning the Yankees with every breath. And while the morale was courageous, Whitaker knew the true test of their courage would be when they came face-to-face with the opposing army.

This positive report was certainly one the governor would be interested in reading. Whitaker knew that one required phase of training had been omitted. The men had not been trained on how to secure and hold strategic targets once they had been acquired. To hold a strategic target such as a road, a bridge, or a town required the men to understand the importance of fortification and how to fortify a position.

Fortification required knowledge of how to identify whatever elements were available to construct a defensive perimeter and then actually construct a sound defensive barrier. The knowledge required for expedient results would come from experience—experience that would come from age and maturity. And while he was confident his men would do what they were told to do, he did not have anyone in his company equipped to address that requirement in a relatively short period of time. Whitaker did not want to order his men into combat without them knowing how to rapidly respond to a fortification requirement.

At the end of the report, there was a section that addressed what the company commander perceived to be shortcomings in order to become fully operational and what the commander planned to do to address those shortcomings.

Whitaker laid his pen down and stared through the slightly open tent door flap to the heavy downpour of rain, which, should it continue, might result in some rise in the Neuse River. He wondered if maybe he should have set the encampment a little farther back from the river. The thought of having made a mistake might have been avoided if he had had an engineer to consult, or maybe someone with fortification skills.

He was thankful for the section of the report that allowed for his assessment of shortcomings for which he had not provided training. Just as importantly, although he might not have the authority, he was going to tell the governor how he planned to address his shortcoming.

With his decision made, Whitaker called out, "Orderly! I need a messenger. And find someone familiar with Saulston." He slid the report to one side and began to compose a letter. "Mr. John Robert Daniel, regarding our conversation in early February of this year…"

Eight-year-old Mary Frances was leaning against one of the front porch posts when she saw a rider coming toward their house. She ran inside yelling at the top of her voice, "Mama, there is a man on a horse coming to the house!"

Becky knew in these times one could not be too careful when greeting guests. She had heard stories of some unsavory characters trying to take advantage of the uncertainties regarding the possibility of war.

"Nancy Ann, go fetch your Pa! And, if you see William Henry, tell him to come also. Now hurry, you hear me?"

Nancy nodded a quick yes to her mom and shot out the back door in a run. The last time she had seen Pa, he was working on a nearby tobacco barn. Passing the privy, she hollered, "William, you in there?"

William stepped outside the door. "Not now. You gotta go?"

"Naw! Ma wants you at the house. A man is coming down the road. I'm going to get Pa."

The family had had a discussion regarding some people who had recently appeared in the area without good intentions. As he ran through the back door, he grabbed the rifle that was positioned between the box of firewood and the wall.

Nancy saw Pa coming out of the barn and yelled, "Pa, Ma wants you to come to the house. A man is coming down the road."

John Robert struck out for the house in a dead run. He quickly passed Nancy. Upon entering the back door, he saw that someone had already grabbed the rifle. He hoped it was William and not Becky. Beck had a tendency to shoot before asking questions. He had told her more than once that her motherly instincts were overly active.

When John Robert exited the house to the front porch, he saw Becky standing in her authoritative position with William next to her holding the rifle. The rider reined in his horse about the time John Robert came out.

John Robert immediately recognized the boy. "You're Jake Hardy's son, aren't you?"

"Yes sir! I have a message for you from Captain Whitaker." The boy never got off his horse but extended the message in the direction of John Robert.

John took the message and said to the boy, "Get down and stretch your legs. I know you have had a long ride. Becky, why don't you get Hardy's boy something cold to drink?"

Having heard the message was from Captain Whitaker, Becky was not about to leave the porch. She turned to Nancy Ann, who was staring through the door, and said, "Nancy, you heard your Pa."

Nancy quickly turned and headed for the kitchen.

John Robert opened the letter and saw there were two pages. The first page made reference to his visit with Captain Whitaker and the offer he had made regarding his service in exchange for William Henry not having to serve.

The second page was an agreement. It read, "I, Captain Junius B. Whitaker, commander of D Company of the Goldsboro Volunteers, do hereby agree that for the voluntary services of John Robert Daniel, that his son, William Henry Daniel, will not be required to serve in the Army of the Confederacy so long as John Henry Daniel serves and is honorably discharged. In the event of John Henry Daniel's demise in the service of the Confederacy, William Henry Daniel will not be required to serve until his sixteenth birthday." It was signed, "Junius B. Whitaker, Captain, Company D, Goldsboro Volunteers." The executive officer, Lieutenant James Capps, had witnessed Captain Whitaker's signature.

John Robert peered over at the Hardy boy, who was sipping a glass of lemonade with his eyes fixed on Nancy, and said, "Is there anything more?"

The young man gulped, having been caught staring at Nancy. After clearing his throat, he said, "Yes sir! Captain Whitaker said that if you are in agreement with his terms, he requests that you enlist on or before May sixth."

"Anything significant about May sixth?"

"I don't know, sir. I am just the messenger."

"Tell him I will be there May sixth."

"Yes sir!" After taking one last quick look at Nancy, he swung up into his saddle, touched the brim of his hat with his forefinger, turned his horse, and galloped away.

CHAPTER 4

COMPANY D

May 6, 1861, came a lot faster than John Robert had prayed for. Every day since John had received the message from Captain Whitaker, he and William were up before daylight and were not in bed until long after nightfall. Fortunately, the days were now much longer, but still, many nights found them working by the light of lanterns. The result was that all fields were now planted with the exception of Becky's vegetable garden. She had assured John that once William found the time to plow the rows, she and the girls could do the planting.

William was in the barn saddling Lucky Boy for his father. He would be accompanying his father to the Company D encampment on his horse, Taz. His going to the encampment was necessary because his father wanted him to meet Captain Whitaker, and he was to bring Lucky Boy back home. Both horses were needed, along with the mules, to accomplish all the farm work.

Lucky was already saddled and waiting, and William was pulling the cinch tight on Taz as his father walked into the horse barn. From the glistening in his father's eyes, he knew Pa had already bid his goodbyes to Becky and the other children. Rarely did Pa show evidence of emotion.

As William was about to place his foot in the stirrup to mount Taz, his father said, "Son, have a seat. I need to talk to you before we leave."

Whenever Pa referred to him as "son," he knew it was a father-to-son talk, and it probably was not going to be easy for his father. William obediently took a seat on a metal bucket near Taz's hooves. Father leaned against one of the stall doors.

John began. "Son, first I apologize for not discussing my decision, which involved you. I know you were disappointed in me for that. I know because some of your friends have either already enlisted or are planning to enlist, and you feel you are not doing your part in this coming war. And in that regard, you might believe that you will be viewed by some as a coward. What is important is that you and I know differently. Physically you are a man. You are the only man I know who can take care of this farm—probably better than me—while looking after your mom, sisters, and brothers. Also, I know you have the courage to meet any challenge that is placed before you and our family. In short, son, you are the only one I can trust to do what needs to be done to care for and protect our family.

"I did not discuss my decision with you because I prayed something would happen that would cause this war to pass us by. Furthermore, I could not bear the thought of standing by and doing nothing while you, with a full life ahead of you, enlisted to serve in a losing cause…a cause that will cost the lives of many young men like you. I remain hopeful the war will be short lived and that I return home in a short time.

"However, if that is not to be the case, or if something happens to prevent me from returning home, you will have had two more years to observe the war and to think through the actions that will be required of you if you are conscripted. And while I believe you to be more mature than many your age, I know there are times you can be more reactive than thoughtfully active. I do not mean that to be negative, but I know when I was your age, I was the same. You may be surprised at the perspective you will acquire with only two more years of maturing. Please give some thought to what I have said and know that I believe the decision I have made is in the best interests of our family. Likewise, I would ask that for any issue for which there has to be a settlement, you place family before any one individual. Do you understand what I am trying to say?"

William stood up with tears running down his cheeks, embraced his father with the bear hug of all bear hugs, and with a choking voice whispered in his father's ear, "Yes, Pa, and I promise you I will not let you down. I love you, Pa."

John stepped back and placed a hand on each of his son's shoulders, and with his eyes once more glistening, he said, "Thank you, son. I love you. Now we must go in order for you to make it back here before sunset."

The two men, one a former young boy, mounted their horses and rode out of the barn. All the family was on the front porch to wave good-bye to pa and son as they rode together toward the road that would lead them to Goldsboro, home of Company D of the Goldsboro Volunteers.

Riding into Company D's encampment with his father, who was sitting tall in the saddle with an expression of self-confidence and purpose, could not have made William any more proud. His father surveyed the encampment in a manner that suggested he was inspecting the troops, some of whom were marching, and others were wandering in the ocean of white tents. Without any comments to anyone, his father rode directly to a white tent with a flag gently blowing in the breeze and its flap doors tied open.

In front of the open door, John lifted himself out of the saddle and passed his reins to William, who remained in his saddle. No sooner than John's feet touch the ground, a man at least twenty years younger than he was came out of the tent with his hand extended.

As John shook the man's hand, the man said, "Mr. Daniel, I am so glad we were able to finalize our agreement."

"I am also, Captain Whitaker. I want to introduce you to my son, William Henry."

William quickly came out of his saddle, and upon transferring Taz's reins to his left hand, which held Lucky's reins, he extended his right hand toward Whitaker.

"Glad to meet you, William Henry. Seeing that you are almost the size of your father makes me wish you were eligible to join our company."

"I'm honored, sir! But, my father has already assigned me my duties."

"Mr. Daniel, are you ready to sign your enlistment?"

"I am. But before I do so, and in my son's presence, I would like for you to look my son in the eye and tell him your understanding of our agreement."

Without any hesitation Captain Whitaker repeated, almost word for word, what he had written in his agreement to William's father. Then he added, "Our agreement has been forwarded to Governor Ellis. If for some reason he does not see fit to concur with our agreement, I personally will see the name John Robert Daniel is struck from our enlistment rolls. Is that fair, enough, Mr. Daniel?"

"That is fair enough. But until my name is added to your enlistment rolls, please just call me John. After that, I suspect it will be Private Daniel."

"Okay, John. Now if you will raise your right hand and repeat after me the oath of enlistment, I will then ask you to sign our enlistment roster."

With William Henry by his side, John repeated the oath and signed the enlistment papers. He then said, "Captain, sir, I have brought my own weapons, consisting of a Spenser M1860 repeating rifle and a Remington M1858 revolver. I did so because they have proven their worth to me in the past. However, my horse returns home with my son because he is needed on the farm."

Captain Whitaker nodded his approval and said, "I wish half our men had reported as well prepared as you. In addition to uniforms, mess kits, and horses, we are also supplying weapons. However, none of our weapons are of the quality or accuracy as those you have. Be sure to keep them with you at all times. Some of our men do have sticky hands."

John turned to his son, gave him one more bear hug, and said, "Son, you best get on back to your ma. Let her know that Captain Whitaker has reaffirmed our agreement. Hopefully, I will get to see you again before the company moves from this location."

William swung himself into his saddle, tied Lucky's reins around his saddle horn, and said, "Goodbye, and good luck, Pa. I'll be praying for you." Then, without looking back, he, Taz and Lucky started back toward Saulston. Pa could not help but notice how straight his son was sitting in his saddle with his attention focused upon his mission.

ॐ

Captain Whitaker told Private Daniel that for the next two weeks, he would train with other new recruits in the basics of soldiering. After that, the two of them would meet to discuss Private Daniel's future duties. He then directed his executive officer to escort Private Daniel to the supply tent, where he would be issued the essential items he would need while at the training encampment.

After receiving a mess kit from which he would eat his meals, a canteen, a shirt, a hat, and a somewhat dusty wool blanket, he was told that the uniform trousers were no longer in stock, but as soon as some arrived, he would get a pair. He was then escorted, on foot, about a quarter of a mile where he would be housed with three other new recruits. The executive officer never offered to help John carry any of the items he had been issued. This was John's introduction to the difference between an officer and an enlisted man. The officer gave the directions, and the enlisted man did the bidding.

When they were about twenty yards from the tent to which John was being assigned, the executive officer pointed it out. Then with a somewhat disgruntled attitude, probably from having been told to escort a private, he turned and without any comment returned in the direction from which they had come.

When John entered the tent, he observed three men about half his age in what appeared to be a serious conversation. Upon his entry, they immediately stopped talking and assumed what could best be described as a modified position of attention. John perceived that his weathered and aged appearance might suggest to the younger soldier that he might be an officer or a noncommissioned officer (NCO).

Looking around for the empty cot, John said, "Fellows, continue whatever you're doing. I'm just one of you."

A sense of relief suddenly emerged from all three, and one pointed to a cot against the back wall that was covered with various items of clothing and equipment. He said, "That cot is available. We'll get our stuff off it." The three scurried to the cot and started claiming their possessions.

Once the cot was clear so John could put down all he was carrying, one of the young men ventured, "My name is Paul, and I'm from Brogden, just the other side of the river. Aren't you a little old to be a private?"

John smiled and replied, "My name is John, and I think we'll soon find that this war is going to require every kind of soldier it can get, even the old ones. What is the news of the day?"

Another of the young men said, "I'm Jake, and this here is Luke. The news is that Arkansas has now seceded. If my count is right, that makes nine states that have declared themselves to no longer be part of the Union."

"You're right in your count," declared John.

The one identified as Luke asked, "Mister...I mean John...have you heard anything about when North Carolina will secede? We're ready to get this matter over with. The sooner we start, the sooner we can kick some damn Yankee ass!"

John took a closer survey of the young boys. A couple had never had a razor on their face. All stood wide-eyed with great expectations of a new adventure. Of course, none had given any real thought to what it meant to kill another man—or to, remotely the possibility of how quickly they might die if there was a war.

Finally, John commented, much in the manner he would have if talking to William. "Fellows, let's not be too hasty in our thoughts to kick ass. Just as some of you are thinking about kicking the ass of some wimp Yankee, you need to keep in mind there are lots more of them in the North, trained by military schools, who are thinking about doing the same thing to whom they consider to be rebels to our country. While I have never personally been to war, I have faced other men who were confident they could better me in a fight."

Luke quickly asked, "Did they?"

"Some did, and some of them I considered to be my friends. I would not like to think what they may have done to me had they believed I had betrayed our country. For one to believe you are a rebel is not a positive thought. Whenever you disagreed with your parents and got a strapping, it was because you rebelled against their expectations of you. It is my hope this war can be avoided and none of us are faced with the decision to kill another person in order to live. War is a matter of life and death. And even those who are right die."

John's words quickly dulled the anxious attitude for war. As he began to store the items he had received in his small designated area, the others, in a more thoughtful mood, sat down on their cots and began some busy projects. John paid little attention to what they were doing. His mind was on William's journey home and his family going about their daily chores without his presence. He knew Becky would make a special effort to keep all of them busy so they would not be worrying about him.

About 5:00 p.m. a bugle sounded, and Paul, who seemed to be the leader of the other two, announced to John, "That's the signal for us to get our mess kits and report to a formation of all the company. After instructions about tomorrow's schedule from the captain, we will stand at attention for the sounding of retreat. After that we will report to slop tent to get whatever gruel they will be feeding us tonight."

John thought, "At least for now we're not having to cook our own."

Seeing the others grab their hats and mess kits, John did likewise and followed them from the tent. Approximately one hundred yards away was a large open field where soldiers were beginning to assemble.

Upon arrival, John followed his tent mates to a smaller area designated for the assembly of all the new recruits. The more senior recruits assembled in a more organized fashion of ranks and columns, whereas the new recruits just stood around in a somewhat confused group. John estimated the confused group to total approximately 30 young boys and one old man. The old man was him. The more organized assembly amounted to about 250 young men. John suspected if he was not the oldest man there, he had to be at least one of the oldest, because he saw no others who looked near his age.

A man who appeared to be in his late twenties came before the small assembled group of new recruits and said, "Men, listen up! I am Sergeant Newell, your training sergeant. When the bugle sounds, I want all of you to stand like this." He then demonstrated standing at attention.

"We always stand at the position of attention for retreat. After retreat we will form a line to walk to where you will draw your evening rations. Tomorrow you will learn how to stand in columns and ranks and the fundamentals of marching. Now, all are to be quiet because Captain Whitaker is going to talk to you."

Captain Whitaker walked up the steps onto a wooden elevated platform. He began his remarks. "First, I again welcome all our new recruits, some of whom have been here for several days. You men will begin your basic drill training tomorrow." Looking in the direction of the larger group, he said, "You that have been here for a while will continue your training in tactics, particularly concentrating on fire and maneuver and how to charge our enemies with fixed bayonets. Pay attention to your trainer if you want to stay alive. Now, come to the position of attention for the sounding of retreat. And for you new recruits, the sound of retreat means the end of the training day and not a signal that we are retreating from battle." Some of the men could be heard snickering. But Captain Whitaker was not laughing. He then made one last comment. "For you who have not heard, Arkansas seceded from the Union today. And no, I cannot tell you when North Carolina will make that decision, but I think it will be soon."

Retreat was sounded, and all began to move toward the tent where they would receive their evening rations. John Robert Daniel had just completed his first day as a Confederate soldier.

CHAPTER 5

TRAINING

During the next two weeks, John Robert learned how to march in ranks and columns, and he proved he was the best marksman among the new recruits. With respect to marksmanship, much of his skill was due to using his own weapon versus the other recruits trying to master either the Springfield M1861 rifled musket or the Mississippi 1841 rifled musket. At fifty yards John Robert was consistently hitting the target dead center. Some, with their heavy and out-of-balance weapons, were having difficulty hitting any of the targets. Another factor that caused John Robert to stand out as a marksman was the fact his Spencer was a repeating rifle. He could get off at least four shots before some of the lads could reload their muskets.

John Robert also learned the technique for presenting a steady wall of fire. The men were lined in ranks in a manner where after the first rank fired, it would kneel to reload, at which time the second rank would fire over them and then take a knee for the third rank to fire. After the third rank had fired, the first rank was reloaded and prepared to start the drill all over again. Unfortunately, some were not as quick to reload as the others, thereby causing delays and disruption to the rhythm.

In addition to learning the various commands that would be used in combat, he learned how to prepare for an ambush and how to form a perimeter of defense, and he gained reassurance in his physical conditioning. He was somewhat surprised to discover many of the recruits were no match for his physical conditioning. He could outrun them and out lift them and do so without breaking a sweat. Hard farming work had kept his muscles toned and ready for any physical challenge that was presented to him. His performance soon earned the respect of not only the younger recruits but also his trainers.

Because of the rain, the training period was extended longer than initially planned. However, general basic training was considered to be complete by May 20. It was then that Private Daniel was told to report to Captain Whitaker for further orders.

When John arrived at the captain's tent, he found that the executive officer's attitude seemed to have mellowed some from the day when he had been John's escort. He gave John a hint of a smile as he glanced toward the open tent door and told John, "Go right in, Private Daniel. The captain is waiting for you."

John entered the tent as he had been trained. He halted, came to attention, saluted, and said, "Private Daniel reporting as ordered, sir."

"At ease, Private Daniel. I have just been looking over your training record, and it appears to me you should have been one of our instructors. I do have one question for you. Are you as good with that Remington revolver as you are with that Spencer rifle?"

"Might be a tad better sir," replied John.

"Well, I got to see for myself. Come with me."

John had never noticed there was a rear entrance to the captain's tent. The captain departed through the rear entrance with John close behind. They walked down to the riverbank, and the captain pointed to a small log floating near the far bank. Pointing to the log, the captain said, "You see that log with the turtle resting on it?"

"Yes, sir."

"Can you hit that turtle?"

"If you show me how you want him hit."

Whitaker pulled his Colt M1851 revolver and fired. The bullet stuck the log between the turtle's front leg and rear leg. But he missed the turtle completely.

John pulled his Remington 1858 revolver and fired his first shot. The turtle's head immediately disappeared. A second later John fired a second round. This time the turtle's body disappeared from the log.

Whitaker was stunned to see how deadly accurate John was with his pistol. Finally, he said, "Did you intend to take that turtle's head off with that first shot?"

As John replaced the empty casings with two more rounds, he said, "Sir, with the price of ammunition, I can only afford to hit what I shoot at."

"Well, when war breaks out, I sure hope you're standing next to me.

"Now, before I tell you why I wanted you here, I want to share with you the news of today, which I only received before you arrived. Today, North Carolina seceded from the Union. Tennessee is expected to soon follow. The window for the prospects of peace is closing. That makes the job for which I recruited you even more important."

John said, "For sure some of the troops will be pleased to learn our state has finally seceded."

"Which brings us closer to war. So, what do you know about fortifications?"

"I know that fortifications are a means by which individuals or buildings are made more secure. So in that regard, there are basically personal fortifications and garrison fortifications. But other than that, very little."

"You are correct. But in addition, there are what I refer to as 'strategic fortifications.' Strategic fortification means to secure a major road intersection, a railroad, or even a piece of land that gives a military advantage, such as high ground. Our men, while they have been taught the importance of following orders, have not been taught the concept of constructing fortifications with whatever is available, such as terrain, branches and limbs, or old ammunition boxes. I am looking to you to provide that instruction. Do you think you can do that?"

"Well, sir, I've never been to military school to learn the way the military might approach such a problem, but I am a product of survival school fortification. I know what to do to protect myself and my family."

"Good answer! This company is now your family, and I am looking for you to teach our family how to protect themselves on the battlefield, in garrison, and at points deemed to be strategic locations. How do you feel about taking on that task?"

"I'll give it my best, sir."

"Thank you. Plan for your class to begin tomorrow on personal battlefield protection. Your introductory class will begin at the assembly area for reveille and retreat. You will have the platform. Tell our supply NCO about any supplies you need. He has already been instructed to meet your requirements to the best of his abilities. And good luck, Sergeant!"

John stood there, somewhat stunned by the reference to "Sergeant."

That's right Sergeant Daniel. You have just received, to my knowledge, the first-ever pre-battlefield promotion. I don't want anyone to challenge your authority when you give them directions. On your way out, the lieutenant"—whom Daniel knew to be the executive officer—"will give you your new stripes. Get them sewn on quickly."

❧

For the last eight years, William Henry, unknowingly, was being trained for this day. Now the operation of the farm had fallen squarely upon his shoulders. He was surprised at how quickly his mother had withdrawn from offering him advice and was leaning confidently upon him to do all the right things.

After he left his father at the Company D encampment and rode home with Lucky in tow, he could not help but feel good about his father's confidence in him and the responsibility his father had bestowed upon him. And while he had hoped that one day his father would let him take over the farming operations, he had not imagined it would be this soon.

He pondered his tasks and the manhood role he now had to assume. However, because he had performed the routine so many times with his father, he knew exactly every step that was necessary to have a successful year. His only concern was the unpredictability of the weather. Even when there was a bad year, Pa always seemed to find an alternative that offset a poor growing season. Sometimes the alternative was drastic, but his father always retained the faith that the next year would offset the bad year. He had never seen his father panic, even when a severe hailstorm destroyed 75 percent of their tobacco crop. He prayed that under similar circumstances he could remain calm to the family, like his father, that all was going to be well.

Upon his arrival home, his mother only questioned if Pa's enlistment had gone as planned. William reassured her all had gone well and that his Pa had insisted the captain restate his agreement in his presence before Pa signed the enlistment roll. The other children listened, and like mom, they had no questions.

Each morning after breakfast, before taking to the fields, he made sure the shotgun Pa left behind was loaded and positioned just inside the front door. He also verified the other Spencer repeating rifle was in the corner next to the wood-burning stove close to the back door. Then he said, separately to both Ma and Nancy Ann, "Should a stranger coming riding up the path, or if I'm needed, fire one shot in the air, and I will be here as fast as Taz can bring me."

He had already decided that when he took the mules to the fields to work, he would also have Taz staked nearby. Unknown to his mom was that he carried his father's other revolver in one of Taz's saddlebags.

During the winter months when there was no land to work, his father had taken the time to make him as good a shot as his father. During his trips to the fields with the mules and Taz, he enjoyed recalling his father, saying, "William, I don't understand how you can be a better shot than I am with that revolver," And William would respond, "That's because I had a better teacher than you." His father would always laugh because he had been self-taught.

He hoped that before his father left the Goldsboro encampment, he would come home for a short visit. He thought his father would be proud of how he was measuring up to his father's expectations. He had thought about visiting his father, but he knew Pa would not approve of him leaving the family alone. Today, since he would be removing tobacco worms from the tobacco leaves, he did not need the mules. He rode Taz to a shady spot under a pine tree and then began hand plucking the worms from the leaves, breaking their heads off, and throwing both head and body to the ground. Then he would move to the next plant to repeat the messy job. As he walked along the long rows of tobacco leaves, letting his mind wander to the effects a war could have on the family and the farm, he heard the sound of one rifle shot. He immediately ran for Taz, who was tied under a pine tree about fifty yards away.

For Sergeant Daniel, his first day as a fortification instructor got off on a note of amusement, which he had to subdue for the time being. Standing on the wooden platform that was used daily by the captain for his announcements, Sergeant Daniel began his presentation.

Approximately twenty-five soldiers were standing on the ground, at attention, looking up at Sergeant Daniel. Noting that this had to be an uncomfortable position for the men, he said, "Stand at ease and take a seat on the ground. I will come down to talk to you."

Several of the men started punching one another and asking, "Isn't that the old man who was a private just day or so ago?"

Sergeant Daniel heard some of the questions regarding his quick change in status. So once on the ground, standing in front of the troops, he said, "I know some of you recognize me as the old private who was marching with you as late as yesterday and wondering how I could be made a sergeant so fast. Just let me say that you will soon discover that time passes faster when you are old."

His comment drew laughter from the group and instant respect. The word of his marksmanship skill had already spread among many of the men. So now he had their undivided attention, and his next comment became the highlight of his day.

"Our subject for today's class is fortification and its importance should we have to go to war. Before we start, are there any questions or comments?"

A young man whom Daniel would best describe as "still wet behind the ears" raised his hand.

"Great! A question I can use to start our discussion," thought Daniel. He responded, "Yes, soldier, what would you like to know?"

"With all due respect, Sergeant, I am a Southern Baptist, and I must tell you, the Good Book states very clearly that fortification is a sin. And I don't think it's an appropriate subject for discussion with regard to war fighting."

Working hard to stifle a chuckle from emerging, Daniel replied, "Soldier, you may have misunderstood the word I used. I said 'fortification,' not 'fornication.'"

This drew low laughter from some of the men, which Daniel put an end to by beginning his class.

He discussed how soldiers could fortify their positions by using terrain features such as hills, trees, and earthly depressions. After a couple of hours, he took the men on a terrain walk through a nearby forest. There they were required to point out terrain features that would provide them with cover and fallen limbs they could use to construct a fortified position. Last, he took them into an open flat field that provided no cover, concealment, or materials to construct a man-built fortification. They all looked at him dumbfounded when he said, "Fortify your positions!"

Finally, one soldier said, "How, Sergeant?"

"Dig yourself a hole in the ground large enough for you to get into."

"We don't have any shovels," one replied.

"What do you have?" asked Daniel.

The men looked at one another, and Sergeant Daniel said, "If you don't do something soon, you will all be dead."

Finally, one soldier dropped to his knees, removed his bayonet from his rifle, and began digging. Another had started digging with his hands.

Sergeant Daniel looked at his pocket watch but said nothing. Within thirty minutes all the men had dug a depression in the ground that would provide them some protection from an enemy's fire.

"Good job!" declared Sergeant Daniel. "You will note that you not only obtained some protection for yourself but that you have also created a depression from which you will have a good firing position. I can assure you of two things: with time, you will always be surveying the terrain for areas in which you can protect yourself, and you will get faster at digging. And I can guarantee you that if you are being fired upon, you will dig faster. We will spend another day on fortification on individual positions, then we will spend some time on fortifying a strategic location, and last, we will focus on how to fortify a location as large as our encampment. Now, we have just enough time to return to our assembly point for the captain's remarks and the sounding of retreat."

Upon reaching Taz, William opened the saddlebag and withdrew the revolver he had placed there earlier. He inserted it into his waistband, pulled the reins from the limb they were loosely wrapped around, and swung himself into the saddle.

From the urgent kick Taz received in his side, he knew he was not being geared from one pace to another but was expected to be at a full-out run in a matter of seconds. And probably there was nothing Taz liked any better than to feel the urgent kick and his rider lean forward in the saddle. Within seconds he was racing between tobacco rows with his neck stretched out and his hooves kicking up dust in a manner representative of a freight train blowing smoke from its stack.

When William exited the tobacco field and made for the house, he could see a rider within fifty yards of the house spin his horse around and start racing back down to the path to the main road.

Reining in Taz, he saw Nancy Ann on the front porch, holding the rifle and standing next to Ma, who was holding the shotgun. "Is there a problem?" asked William.

Ma replied, "Don't know. We didn't know the man. He appeared like he might be a drifter, and we felt like a man's presence might be needed."

Hearing his Ma refer to him as a "man" caused him to feel even more important with respect to his role on the farm. If Ma viewed him as the man around the house, he knew all his siblings did. It was important for him to confirm they had done the right thing by notifying him.

"Ma, you and Nancy Ann did the right thing by calling me. I think the closer we get to war, the more drifters we will see trying to avoid service to the Confederacy. And these drifters will be up to no good. So y'all continue to be vigilant in case that drifter decides to double back. I don't think he will now that he knows there is a man here. He's probably looking for a farm where all the men have joined the war effort."

Becky replied, "We will, and thanks for getting here so fast."

"There's no place on this farm that Taz can't get me back here from in just a couple of minutes. He's got to be the fastest horse Pa ever had." He waved to the family and turned to head back toward the field to continue his messy job. He didn't know whether Ma or Nancy Ann had seen the gun he had in his waistband.

CHAPTER 6

ORDERS

By early June 1861, Sergeant Daniel had completed the individual fortification training for all those designated for training. As he trained, he requested from Captain Whitaker any reading material he might have on strategic fortifications and encampment fortifications. From the reading material he obtained, he learned that any significant fortifications, such as encampments, were to be planned, organized, and directed by a trained construction engineer. In short, that was far above either his or a company commander's pay grade. Furthermore, he learned that strategic fortifications were dictated by the situation and the commanding officer. In other words, there was no standardized how-to. Guidance in that area was "at the discretion of the commanding officer by maximizing the availability of existing assets."

When he brought this to the attention of Whitaker, his response was "Practice some different scenarios that inspire creative thinking for strategic fortifications, and forget any effort to address encampment fortification. Hopefully, an engineer will be available when that time comes."

Accordingly, for the remainder of June, Daniel selected various local railroad and road intersections and river crossing points to teach his classes how to secure available assets to construct fortified positions. He soon discovered the men, when given the latitude to think through the problem, could devise creative schemes for fortifying the target.

The men encircled one road intersection with four large, deep holes, which they covered with tree limbs. Each hole comfortably accommodated four men.

At one railroad crossing, the men cut trees and constructed log walls on each side of the primary rail bed. The angle of the construction permitted the men to shift from one side of the wall to the other to defend against a train approaching from any direction.

And at a river crossing, they improvised by changing the route of the crossing point by felling trees in a manner in which the trees could not be crossed, and the moving force would have to go around the trees to either a deeper or wider crossing point. Then they created individual fortified positions from which to engage the enemy once the enemy had committed to following the route around the trees.

If the opposing force fell into the trap by trying to cross the river at a less-than-desirable location, they were slowed down by a crossing at a point that was either too deep or too wide. The delay permitted the fortified force to inflict maximum casualties.

Should the force try to retreat it would encounter a camouflaged fortified blocking force. Again, fallen trees were used to construct another fortified position.

Near the end of June Sergeant Daniel was able to report to Captain Whitaker his training was complete and he was confident the men understood the importance and were prepared to react quickly when found in a situation that called for them to be in a fortified position.

Captain Whitaker said, "Thank you, Sergeant Daniel, for undertaking an important challenge. I am confident your training will save many lives. As a reward for your efforts, I am looking to grant you a short leave of absence to visit with your family before we depart this encampment. Unless you have something you wish to discuss with me, you are dismissed for now."

"Thank you, sir. I hope my efforts have reaffirmed your confidence in me and reassured you that your agreement with me has made for a better company." Daniel saluted the captain and departed his tent without knowing what he had hoped to learn from Captain Whitaker, which was his future assignment in the company.

On June 28, 1861, in his nightly announcements to the company from his platform overlooking the assembled company, Captain Whitaker said, "Men, I congratulate you on your attentiveness, cooperation, and success in completing the fortification training provided you by Sergeant Daniel. From that training you know important ways by which you can protect yourself during combat. You will find the ability to fortify yourself especially useful should you become separated from the main body of our forces. When in combat, especially in a forest of dense foliage or on a pitch-black night, the odds of your being separated from the main body are very high. Every one of you should expect that to happen at some time or another. You may be alone or with just one or two others, but you are not with your company and possibly will be surrounded by an enemy force.

"Also, you have learned and gained self-confidence. Should the need arise and you are called upon to fortify a strategic point, you can draw from whatever nature provides, or you can scrounge to accomplish that mission. For that, I am very proud to know that should I ask that of you, you can and will deliver."

"Finally, I want to share with you that as of today we are now Company D of the Fourth North Carolina Infantry Regiment, and we have been mustered into Confederate Service."

With those words, a loud cheer rose from the assembled men. The cheer was Whitaker's prearranged signal for the artillery battery to fire a three-gun salute. The salute was limited due to the limited ammunition.

When the last shot was fired, the men spontaneously broke out with the words to the song "Dixie." The men were jubilant, with some even dancing.

Finally the XO yelled, "At ease! The captain has one more comment."

The crowd began to grow quiet as men punched one another, yelling "Quiet! Quiet!"

When Whitaker knew he could be heard, he said, "It is expected that within a couple of weeks, Governor Ellis will appoint a regimental commander. While I do not know this to be a fact, I remain confident that shortly after a commander is appointed, we will be leaving this location. On a rotational basis, I plan for those who have done well in their training to be given two to three days' leave to visit your families before we break camp. Now know this: should you be granted leave and you fail to return at your appointed time, you will be charged with desertion. Sheriffs and constables will be asked to seek you out and return you to the company. When you are returned to the company, you will be shot or hung as a deserter. No clemency will be granted. That is all!'"

At that time, the bugle sound of retreat resonated throughout the company area as the men came to the position of attention.

Eight-year-old Mary Frances, commonly referred to as Fannie, was playing in the front yard when she saw a man approaching the house on horseback. As she had been instructed, she immediately ran inside and reported what she had seen to her ma.

Ma, who was in the kitchen, quickly grabbed the rifle and ran to the front door. Yes, there was a man approaching on a black horse. She raised the rifle and fired it once to alert William, who was chopping weeds in the cornfield.

Upon hearing the rifle shot, William dropped his hoe and raced to Taz. Taz leaped into a run almost before William was in the saddle. William's right foot never made it into the stirrup. But by pressing down hard on the ball of his left foot and leaning over where his chest was almost on Taz's neck, he had sufficient balance to the house.

The man on the black horse was riding slowly, taking in the sights on both sides of the path leading to the house. The tobacco crop was one of the best he had ever seen, and the cornfield showed evidence of a plentiful harvest this year. Upon hearing the crack sound from the rifle, the man on the black horse came to a stop and looked around. In the direction of the cornfield, he could see a lot of dust moving above the tops of the corn rows and heading toward the house. He instantly knew the rifle shot was a signal for the man of the house to get there in a hurry. Obviously, the family was prepared for any situation.

Becky was looking down the path as the man on the black horse momentarily stopped but then continued toward the house with his horse in a gallop. There was something very familiar about the rider. It was how erect he sat in the saddle. He seemed to radiate a purpose for coming to their house, and short of a bullet, nothing was going to stop him. "Could it be?" she thought. He was dressed differently from any man she had ever seen. But he carried himself like the man she had known for the last fifteen years. Now he was waving his hat.

To the surprise of the children who now had gathered on the front porch and to William, who was now rounding the end of the cornfield, Ma, with rifle in hand, was running toward the man.

The black horse dropped his rear end to the ground as his rider reined him in hard for an instant stop. Before the horse came to a complete stop, the rider was out of the saddle and in Becky's embrace.

At that moment, the entire family recognized the man on the black horse was Pa, and they started running as fast as possible toward him. William, on Taz, passed the other children and was out of the saddle before Taz stopped. As he ran to his father, he felt his father's big arm reach out and pull him into the embrace with his mother.

Soon all the children were around John getting their hugs and kisses. There could not have been a better Fourth of July surprise. All the family was together again.

That Friday night around the dinner table, there was much laughter as John told of some of his more amusing training events, his unexpected promotion to sergeant, and the many naive young lads who should not have enlisted. He made a point to commend William on how he was managing the farm.

He said, "William, when I turned onto the path, I began to think maybe I had forgotten where I lived. You have done a Herculean job in getting the crops planted and prepared for harvest. You must be working day and night."

Becky said, "I'm afraid he is working too hard. But he wanted to ensure everything was done the way you would want it done, John."

John turned to William, and William stared back at his father with great anticipation as to what his father would say next. All the family had their eyes on John. He said, "William, I could not be more proud of you. While I always knew I could depend upon your ability to manage our farm and care for the family, I must admit you have exceeded all my expectations. From what I have seen, I am thinking that when this army term is over, I can sit back and let you continue. Maybe you will give me a job."

There was a little chuckle from the children. Becky had a big smile on her face.

Nancy Ann spoke up. "William, big brother, don't think for one minute I'm gonna call you Pa!"

John continued. "Now, all of you need to know I am only home for a couple of days. I have to be back in the camp by midafternoon on Sunday. Tomorrow I belong to William to help him with anything I can before I leave Sunday. I do not think we will be encamped in Goldsboro much longer, now that we are part of the Fourth Regiment. I believe as soon as a commander is appointed by the governor, we will get orders to move out. I have no idea where they may send me. But I will keep you informed the best I can.

"Finally, while I don't want any of you to be fearful of this war, I do want you to remain vigilant to any stragglers that may come around the farm. I am proud of the warning system you have established to get all to the house when necessary. When the war starts, you will probably see deserters and other scavengers trying to take from those who have something. Becky and William, be sure to never have on you any more money than you need when you go to buy supplies. And when you're traveling to and from the store, constantly be watching for anyone who might be following you. When William goes to buy supplies, I want the rest of you to stay in the house with a gun nearby. Don't let anyone in regardless of how down and out he may appear or act. And just as importantly, I want all to pay attention and do what William tells you when it comes to the safety of our family. A war can bring out the most common people, with only one purpose in their minds, and that is to take from those that might have something. Anyone have any questions?"

Fannie, with tears in her eyes, said, "Pa, you are scaring me."

"Honey, I don't want to scare you, but I just want you to be brave like you did today when you saw who you thought was a stranger riding up the path. You were brave and smart to tell your Ma. Stay brave and smart until I get back home. Now, we've talked enough on that subject. I'm thinking I best get to bed because William is probably going to work me hard tomorrow."

"Yeah! Pa, after tomorrow you gonna think getting back to the army is a vacation."

All were laughing as they departed for their respective sleeping areas.

None of the family could believe how fast the time had passed. Now John was just before swinging into the saddle of the black horse the company had issued to him. On Saturday, John had a fun day working with William making repairs to the horse barn. Several dividers within the stall area had either broken or come loose. When they were repaired, he and William climbed onto the roof to repair a few places where, several weeks before, a tree limb had come down during a thunderstorm and crashed through the right rear corner of the barn.

When all the work was done, Becky and the girls had a late-afternoon picnic planned under the tree where she and John had had some of their more serious discussions. But that afternoon it was only family fun on the agenda. William, along with his brother Frank, who was only four years old, decided they were going to wrestle Pa to the ground. Pa held his own until Nancy Ann and Fannie joined the game. Then John gave up and was taken to the ground.

After the kids had their frolic with their father, Becky said, "It took all of you to take him down, but I can do it by myself."

John, standing tall, replied "Prove it!"

As she walked toward him, he never took his eyes off her. That was what she was counting on because William slipped around behind his father and got on his hands and knees directly behind his father's legs.

Becky, with a seductive look on her face that had all of John's attention, walked close enough for her breasts to be touching his chest, and with one hand, she gave him a shove. When the back of John's legs hit William's body, his feet went into the air, and a giant surprised look appeared on his face. He hit the ground with a thud, and everyone, including John, had a great laugh.

Now the time for John to depart had come. All morning, when the children passed him, they would reach out for a touch and say, "I love you, Pa." And Pa would respond with "I love you also," taking care to call each by their name.

William stood at the head of the black horse, which his father called Bolt, holding the horse's reins. Pa once again gave all a hug. He reassured them he would keep them informed about any relocation he might experience, and he promised to be safe and come back home as soon as possible.

Once in the saddle, he took the reins from William, saying, "Son, thank you for looking after our family. I know I can count on you."

"You can, Pa!"

Without looking back, because he didn't want anyone to see the tears filling his eyes, John gave Bolt a kick in his sides and started to gallop down the path to the road.

All continue to watch until Pa turned onto the main road toward Goldsboro and disappeared from their sight.

Two weeks after John's visit with his family, Governor John W. Ellis appointed Colonel George B. Anderson, commander of the Fourth North Carolina Infantry Regiment. The date was July 16, 1861. By this time, all the men of the regiment had been provided a complete uniform with cap. This was with the compliments of Lieutenant Colonel John A. Young, who had been a clothing manufacturer prior to joining the regiment.

Within ten days of the appointment of the regimental commander, Captain Whitaker, during one of his nightly announcements, informed the men they would soon be breaking camp to join with other companies of the regiment. He stated, "I have received orders for our first assignment; however, at this time I am not at liberty to say where that might be. But you may now notify your families that we will be leaving Goldsboro in the near future. I remain confident that with your training, we are prepared to meet our enemy, engage him, and defeat him on the battlefield. You are to show pride in your Southern heritage because soon the North will know we do not accept dictates from the North, nor will we be under the heel of its boot. Men, know that I am proud of your accomplishments and even prouder to serve as your company commander." He then dismissed the assembly.

The men immediately started to hoot and holler, reveling in their commander's acknowledgment that the North was not their master and that he believed that soon the North would know they could not dictate the Southern way of life. Probably, John Robert was one of the few men who understood, that the country that fought so hard to achieve its independence was now on the precipice of another history-making event, not just for the South but for all of the country.

That evening John jotted off a short letter to Becky.

> My Dearest Becky and family.
>
> This evening we were notified that we will soon be leaving Goldsboro. I do not know where I am going. When I get there, if permitted, I will write again to tell you where I am. Remember what I told you about keeping the family safe. I love all of you, and I promise I will be coming home when this war is over.
>
> Your loving husband and father,
> John (Pa).

John then took his letter to the military mail sack and dropped it in. Tomorrow, a military courier would carry the mail to the Goldsboro post office. A mail carrier would then take the letter to Saulston, where it would be hand delivered to Becky. He returned to his tent to await further orders.

He did not have to wait long. Two days later the order was given to "strike tents, fold up cots, gather up cooking equipment, and pack them in designated wagons." In two days all would be marching to the train station in Goldsboro for a train ride to their next assignment—an assignment still unknown to the soldiers.

CHAPTER 7

THE NEXT ASSIGNMENT

Upon arrival at the train depot, the soldiers discovered they would not be riding in the comfortable coach seats, but, rather, they would be riding packed together in cattle cars. All the enlisted men took up several cattle cars, whereas the noncommissioned officers, or NCOs, had a cattle car to themselves, as did the officers. The NCOs took turns riding one NCO to each cattle car carrying the enlisted men. Their presence was to maintain order and discipline. The NCOs tried to rotate into the cattle car that was carrying the men for whom they served as their platoon sergeants.

Although John had never served as a platoon sergeant, he made a point to rotate into the car that carried the men with whom he had served. He was highly respected by the men, so there was never an issue that John could not resolve. Most of the situations resulted from the irritation from being packed into hot cattle cars, which caused some of the men to become confrontational with one another.

Since the train was moving north, there was much speculation among the men as to their final destination. Most of the speculation was that they were going north to launch a surprise attack on the Yankees.

And whenever there was a rotation of NCOs, the men always questioned them for the latest news as to where they were going. The standard response from the NCO was "Look, guys, we are as much in the dark as you are. The officers have not told us anything. As soon as we know something and have the authority to tell you, we will. So you can stop asking." But they didn't.

At each depot stop, the men would strain themselves peering through the spaces between the boards on the cattle car to read the depot signs, which provided notice of the name of the town.

In the NCO car, John noticed that one of the NCOs had apparently appointed himself the car conductor, because each time the trained slowed, from his vantage point, he could see the depot sign, so he would announce the station. First there was Wilson, then Rocky Mount and Weldon.

At Weldon, North Carolina, the train shifted to another track but continued to move north but at an unusually slower speed. Soon the train crossed a trestle, and the self-appointed conductor announced, "Boys, we are now crossing the Roanoke River. We'll soon be in Virginia. You can bet your bottom dollar we are going north for a surprise attack on those damn Yankees!"

Most of the men had never traveled any farther from Goldsboro than the neighboring towns, and some had never been as far as Raleigh, North Carolina. However, very few had ever been as far north as Virginia, which caused many to continue to stare between the slats to catch their first glimpse of the state.

But to their surprise, the trained continued its slow movement and made a shift to another track. It then seemed to be coming to a stop. That was when the conductor announced, "Boys, we are stopping in Garysburg. What in the hell is in Garysburg?"

Captain Whitaker swung into the open door of the NCOs' cattle car just as the train chugged to a stop.

"Listen up, men!" said Whitaker. "We are in Garysburg. Nearby is Camp Hill, our regimental headquarters. I'll be taking a horse and riding over there to meet with Colonel Anderson, our commander. I am expecting to receive additional orders from him. We will be spending the night here, so unload the men. Let them stretch their legs and find a spot to eat rations and sleep on the ground for tonight. At daybreak, we will reload to continue to our destination."

A voice said, "Where might that be, Captain?"

"I should know that after talking with Colonel Anderson. Now get busy and let the men get some exercise. Sergeant Daniel, you are to get our horses saddled. You will be coming with me. Are there any more questions?"

There were none.

"Good. If any of you need further instructions, see the XO. He will be located at our command post in the officers' car. Carry on!" The captain leaped out of the car, and Sergeant Daniel was right behind him.

When John's feet hit the ground, the captain said, "Sergeant, get our horses and come to the officers' car. I need to talk with the XO."

As John jogged past the cattle cars, he saw all doors were open, and the men were impatiently standing in the doors awaiting instructions. When he passed the car with the men from his platoon, he yelled, "Paul! Luke! Come with me."

There was some shuffling at the door, but soon the two sprang out. John had come to think of the two as his right and left hands. Whenever he had a task that he couldn't handle alone or that needed to be done fast, he called upon them.

When the two had caught up with John, Paul asked, "What's up, Sergeant John?" They both still wanted to call John by his first name but knew they needed to be respectful of his rank, so they put "Sergeant" in front of John.

"We are to get the captain's and my horses out of the horse car and get them saddled. I am going with the captain to the regimental headquarters."

"Where is that?" asked Luke.

"Camp Hill, but I have no idea where that might be."

The horse ramp was attached to the side of the horse car. While Paul and Luke put it in place, John went inside the car and positioned the captain's horse at the door so that when it was opened, he could be taken down and saddling could begin.

Paul took the captain's horse while John retrieved Bolt. Getting the two horses was not difficult since they were only transporting eight horses, which were sufficient for the two officers and NCOs that might need a horse.

As soon as Bolt was saddled, John swung himself into the saddle and took the reins of the captain's horse from Paul. He said, "Thanks, guys! I'll see you when I get back." He then started Bolt trotting toward the officers' car with the captain's horse in tow.

John could see the captain talking to the XO as he rode up. Without a word Whitaker took the reins from John and pulled himself into his saddle. Turning his horse due east, he started in a gallop. John was right beside him.

After about three miles, a large two-story white house appeared in the distance. John assumed it was a plantation house, but he could also see lots of white tents surrounding it and the movement of a lot of troops.

Whitaker slowed his horse to a canter and pointed toward the house, saying, "That's where we're going. You stay with the horses, and if I need you, I will send for you. You may be wondering why I brought you along. I figured if wherever we are going needs to be fortified, he might want to discuss our ideas for accomplishing that task."

John responded, "Yes sir."

As they rode up to the hitching post in front of the house, the sentry on duty came to attention and saluted Captain Whitaker. Whitaker said, "Captain Whitaker here to see Colonel Anderson, as ordered."

The sentry said, "Go right in, sir. He heard that your train had arrived."

John was already standing on the ground when the captain handed him his horse's reins. Whitaker then went inside, speaking to another sentry as he went through the door.

Around the noon hour, a soldier came out of the house carrying something on a tray. He walked over to John and asked, "You Sergeant Daniel?"

"That's right," replied John.

"Here's a bite to eat and some water. Your captain said he might be another couple of hours."

John took the tray, which contained a slice of beef jerky, a few boiled potatoes, a piece of bread, and a large metal cup of water. All looked good to him. Certainly it was going to be better than what the guys were having back at the train. As the soldier turned to walk away, John said, "Thank you."

Approximately midafternoon, the captain emerged carrying some papers rolled up under his arm. John speculated the papers were maps. Looking at John, the captain said, "No fortification requirements. They've already been done. Tonight we'll have a formation, and I will share with the men the information they've been anxious to hear."

John handed the captain his reins, and both men were back in their saddles heading toward the train. The captain appeared to be deep in thought, not sharing anything with John. His only comment was to say he hoped John's lunch had been satisfactory. John's only response was "Sure beat hardtack."

The evening, after Captain Whitaker's visit with Colonel Anderson, he had the men assembled around the officers' car. The door of the car was open, and Whitaker stood in the door so all the men could see him.

He began. "Men, today I visited with our regimental commander to obtain our orders to our final destination. You see, like you, I didn't know where we were going. I was just told to report to Colonel Anderson. Now I can give you the information you have been wanting to hear.

"We're bound for a garrison in Manassas, Virginia. There we will link up with some Virginia boys to wait for our next orders. I want you to eat and be loaded back on the train before daybreak. Promptly at daybreak the train will pull out headed for Richmond, Virginia. There we will off-load to march the remaining distance to Manassas. Now, try to get a good night's sleep and be aboard this train before daybreak. When we arrive in Richmond, we will off-load our horses, wagons, and supplies. All soldiers except officers will be on foot to Manassas. Officers will be on horseback. Sergeants, you are responsible for ensuring all our men have their weapons and the supplies they need for the trip. The distance is approximately one hundred miles. My hope is to average ten miles a day; that accounts for river crossings and some thick forest. While we could make faster time traveling by train or along some roads, I want you men to get some experience as to what you can expect once we make contact with our enemy. Then it will become necessary for us to avoid roads and use the forest for cover and concealment. Thank you for your attention! You're now dismissed."

The next day as the men scanned the landscape from the moving train, they discovered that southern Virginia was no different from North Carolina. Some appeared to be a little disappointed. They had been hoping to see something different. Others were glad Virginia looked a lot like home because any adjustment issues they might have experienced seemed remote now.

When the train arrived in Richmond, the NCOs had, among themselves, devised some detailed plans for carrying out the captain's instructions for off-loading the train and preparing for their trip to Manassas, but it still took two days. The day of arrival was spent off-loading, and the second day was spent securing everything that was to be transported by wagons and issuing rations and other supplies that were to be carried by the individual soldiers. Also, on that day John received instructions to report to the captain's quarters. The captain's quarters was a small building located in one corner of the stockyard that paralleled the train track.

In accordance with the captain's instructions before departing Goldsboro, Sergeant Daniel entered the captain's quarters without saluting. The captain had said, "Once we board the train, saluting of officers is suspended, unless you want to see one shot. Snipers shoot those being saluted, and if you salute me any place other than in garrison, I will assume you want to see me dead. Should I be forced to make that assumption, I will shoot you in self-defense."

"Come right in, Sergeant Daniel. I have a mission for you."

"Yes, sir. I will do my best to accomplish it. What might it be?"

"I am giving you one of the maps I received from Colonel Anderson. It's a map to our destination in Manassas. I want you to select a couple of good men to help you scout our route. Your mission is to remain three to five miles in front of the main body of our movement. You are to seek out any obstacles that might slow our progress. If possible, eliminate those obstacles, or send one of the men back to secure a sufficient number to accomplish that mission. You are to also locate points at which we can forge rivers. And finally, I want you to locate secure places for our company to bed down at night. Think you can handle that mission?"

"Yes, sir!"

"That is what I expected you to say. One other thing: be sure to secure the fastest horses our quartermaster has. Should you encounter anything detrimental to the movement of our force, I want to know it without any delay. So make sure the men you select to help you are also good horsemen. If you get any back talk from the NCOs of the men you select, you tell them to come to see me."

"I don't think there will be a problem, sir."

"The company will move out tomorrow morning at daybreak. When we break camp, you should already be three to five miles in front of us."

"I understand, sir."

When John departed the captain's quarters, he already knew the two men he wanted to join him. He wanted Paul and Luke. Both were excellent marksmen and horsemen. And while Paul was viewed by some as being too cocky, he was reliable, and he had proved himself during the fortification classes to be an excellent listener who would follow instructions without reservations or questions.

The quality that John had come to admire in Luke was that he was observant and had a great sense of direction. He thought he could put Luke in the middle of the woods on a dark night without stars or a moon and tell him to go any direction on the compass, and he could do it. In short, he had all the makings of an excellent scout.

Paul and Luke were honored to be chosen for such an important mission. Both liked the idea of serving with John because they knew John could hit anything he aimed his weapon at. More importantly, John was a thinker and not reactive. If times were to become difficult, John was the one man they wanted to be with.

The three departed Richmond at three o'clock the next morning. Paul and Luke were on horses the quartermaster said were the fastest he had. John knew what Bolt could do. Not only was he fast, but he was as strong as an ox.

It was late August 1861, and the traffic on the road in front of the Daniel house had increased. The locals were easily distinguishable from those just passing by. The locals normally were in a wagon, whereas those just passing by were on horseback.

Periodically, a rider would turn onto the path leading to the Daniels' house, but at the sound of the rifle fire, the rider would quickly reverse his course. Obviously, he had made a mistake by turning onto the path. But there was one rider who was not willing to accept a warning shot as discouragement.

Nancy Ann was on the front porch when she saw the rider. Ma was at least fifty yards from the back of the house working in her garden. William was harvesting corn in the cornfield on the west side of the farm. Nancy Ann believed that it was up to her to run the intruder away.

She quickly ran inside the house and grabbed the shotgun that was closest to the front door. After running back down the front porch steps into the front yard, she cocked one of the hammers on the gun. There was a hammer for each of the two barrels. Placing the butt of the gun on the ground to prevent receiving a kick from the gun when fired, she pulled the trigger on the cocked barrel. There was a loud explosion.

The rider stopped momentarily, but seeing it was a young girl who had fired the weapon with the butt on the ground, he knew she was not able to aim it. He started his horse into a gallop along the path in her direction.

Ma, hearing the blast from the shogun, started to run from the garden toward the house. Likewise, William ran to Taz, grabbed the revolver from the saddlebag, placed it in his waistband, and leaped into the saddle. Taz now knew the routine well and didn't wait for the kick. He was in high gear before William was settled in the saddle.

Nancy Ann stood her ground as the burly, bearded man rode right up to her. With the courage of her father, she said, "Mister, if you start to get off that horse, I will shoot you."

The burly man gave a smirking grin and replied, "Well, honey, I guess I best not get off my horse…right now." And as quickly as he had made his statement, he leaned over from his saddle and snatched the gun from Nancy Ann's hands. Then he said, "Now I'm gonna get off this here horse, and you and I are going to have some fun."

By now Ma was on the front porch, but she was running so fast that she ran past the rifle that rested next to the stove at the back door. All she could do was holler, "Don't you dare touch my girl!"

"What do I have here? Peers to me to be a two-for-one day." Then he let loose with a sinister laugh.

Because his focus was on the two women, he did not catch sight of William until he emerged from the corn rows.

William, seeing the man was holding the shotgun, retrieved his revolver from his waistband and was already pointing it in the man's direction.

Upon seeing the man on horseback racing toward him, the intruder cast the shotgun to the ground and pulled his revolver with his right hand. But his draw was not as fast as William's bullet.

The man was turning in his saddle when William's bullet struck him in the right arm just above his elbow. Later, when the news of what happened made it through the community of Saulston, folks would comment on how shooting the man in the arm was evidence of William's marksmanship skills. It was said, "He could have killed him if had wanted to."

However, William knew the truth, which was that he was aiming for a killing shot to the man's chest. But when the man turned to fire at William, William's round missed its target and hit the man in the arm.

The man let out a loud yelp as his arm went limp and his gun fell to the ground.

William did not rein in Taz. He gave him a kick to his side, and Taz crashed into the man's horse, sending the man to the ground.

The impact stunned the man, but not enough for him not to see his pistol lying about five feet from him. Using his left hand, he started to pull himself across the ground to get to his pistol.

Again, William's youth had him defeated. Just as he was about to grasp his weapon, the barrel of William's revolver jammed into the back of the man's head, and he heard the words "Mister, if you touch that weapon, I will send a bullet through your head that will blow you nose off the front of your face!"

The man slowly withdrew his hand.

Turning to his Ma, William said, "Ma, I want you and the others to go inside, lock the doors, and remain there until I return. I'm gonna take this deadbeat to the constable in Saulston."

"I will, but I'm going to keep this gun on him until you have him secured," Ma yelled back to William.

Looking down at the pain on the man's face, William thought, "Security will not be a problem. This fellow wants to get to the doctor before he loses too much more blood."

William got his rope from Taz and tied it around the man's neck. He then tied the other end to Taz's saddle horn.

"Why are you putting this rope around my neck?" asked the man.

"Well, the way I figure it, you are going to have to use your left hand to hold on to your saddle horn to prevent you from falling off. Should you think you are going to make a dash for freedom, the rope will jerk you off your horse, and then, since I don't plan to get off my horse, I will drag you by your neck to the constable. Should you die in the process, it will not be my fault."

When William pulled the man to his feet, the man moaned in pain. It was apparent to William that his bullet had broken the man's arm bone just above his elbow. William boosted the man onto his horse. The rope around his neck hung down the front of his chest.

William stepped into his stirrup and swung his leg across Taz. He hollered, "Ma, I'll be back soon." In his right hand, he had the reins to the man's horse. His revolver was back in his waistband, and the man's pistol was in William's saddlebag.

William started down his path with the man in tow. Becky could not help but notice how erect he sat in the saddle. It reminded her of how confident John sat in the saddle. She felt a stir of pride in her heart. She and John had done well with their son.

CHAPTER 8

DEPARTING MANASSAS

Company D arrived at the Manassas garrison on the tenth day after leaving Richmond. "The Biblical Trio," John, Paul, and Luke, as dubbed by Captain Whitaker when he saw the route the three had laid out for the company, continued to function as a three-man team. For every potential obstacle that could have slowed the company, the three had found a route around it. And they successfully found places or bridges where the company could cross rivers or streams.

At night, the camp sites were of sufficient size to accommodate the bedding down of the men and animals. Whitaker was surprised at the success the men had locating large sites that provided cover and concealment for the company. Although not necessary, he put out sentries and established perimeters of defense. The men needed to experience the importance of remaining vigilant even in safe zones. Once the fighting started, there would be snipers and potential Northern infiltrators.

By early September 1861, D Company was embedded with Virginia units of General Winfield S. Featherston's brigade. The brigade was a sea of white tents. John had been instrumental in advising the captain on how the encampment area assigned to Company D could be improved both in security and convenience for their unit.

It was during his moments with the captain that John learned the reason for their assignment to Manassas. The assignment had come about because the Fourth Regiment was still not completely organized. There was concern that when training was complete, if the men remained in Goldsboro with no mission, some would start to abandon the company to go back home to help with their farming. So as John now saw it, the assignment to Manassas was to give the men a feeling of purpose, at a distance from home so as to discourage anyone who might have walked away because home was so near.

John wrote a letter to Becky saying,

> My dearest Becky and family.
>
> Arrived well in Manassas, Virginia. Never heard of the place before we were told, just before departing Carolina. I have been training with the Virginia boys and doing some construction work around our garrison. Hope harvesting is going well with William and all of you are doing well. Don't worry about me. I am like on vacation compared to what William is doing. Can't give you my address cause don't know how long I will be here. Give my love to the children.
>
> Love you,
> John.

It was mid-October when John was told to report to the captain's office. John entered and saluted.

The captain returned his salute and said, "John, you're going to be taking a little trip. General Featherston sent out a request to all companies for names of men with construction knowledge for a special renovation project being done in Danville, Virginia. I nominated you, and you were selected."

"What is the project, sir?"

"Don't have any idea. Told it was classified for only those who needed to know. The ones who need to know will not know until they reach Danville. When you reach Danville, seek out the encampment of Major Ledbetter. You will give him these orders I have for you."

"How long will I be there, sir?"

"I have no idea. But when you're released by Ledbetter, you will report back to me. Take that black horse you've been riding and leave tomorrow morning at daybreak. Any other questions?"

"No sir." John took the papers the captain handed him. As John exited the captain's office, he thought, "Where is Danville? I never heard of Manassas before I got here, and now I'm going to another place I never heard of."

Once outside, John looked at the papers the captain had given him. One read that he was to report to Major Stafford Ledbetter in Danville, Virginia. The other—the captain must have anticipated his question—was a hand-scribbled map to Danville. It showed Danville to be southwest of Manassas near the North Carolina border. The captain had written a note: "The distance is about 200 miles. Take sufficient rations. Good luck. Whitaker."

Walking into Paul and Luke's tent, John said, "Well, boys, I'll be leaving you tomorrow morning."

Paul spoke first. "Sergeant John, we have an understanding. You don't go anywhere outside this garrison without Luke and me."

John chuckled. "Guess there is a first time for everything."

"Where are you going? What are you going to be doing?" asked Luke.

"Going to Danville, Virginia, and got no idea what I'll be doing. Captain nominated me for a special project, and the general selected me."

"Don't the captain know he can't break up our team? He made us biblical."

Again John laughed and said, "He didn't break us up. He just temporarily separated us. I'll be back as soon as the project is over. I just wanted to tell you to take care of yourselves while I'm gone because I won't be here to look after you."

"Thanks, Sergeant Papa John!" replied Luke.

"See you guys!" John departed to draw the rations he would need for his trip and to tell the quartermaster he would have Bolt for an extended period—Captain's orders.

After traveling a couple of miles in the direction of Saulston, the man William was taking to the constable started begging William to put a tourniquet on his arm; otherwise, he was going to bleed to death before they made it to a doctor.

From the pain William could see in the man's eyes, he didn't think he would have a problem with him trying to escape. He guided Taz to the nearest tree, got off, and tied Taz and the man's horse to one of the tree limbs. Then he grabbed the man by the back of his belt and started pulling him out of his saddle. This was the first time William realized how bad the man smelled. Obliviously, he had not had a bath this year.

The man started hollering, "Easy, boy. This here arm's killing me. And I don't want you to start it bleeding any more than it is now."

Once on the ground, the man was most cooperative as stood there holding his arm like it was the only valuable possession he had. William examined it, and while the man's sleeve was soaked with blood, he knew it wasn't life threatening. However, he thought, "The more disabled he thinks he is, the less trouble he will give me."

"Yep! Looks pretty bad. You probably do need a tourniquet." William started to unbuckle the man's pants.

"What the hell you doing, boy?"

"You need a tourniquet, and the only thing I see available is your belt."

"What about your belt?"

"Not my arm. Besides, the way I see it, without a tourniquet you could lose your arm or your life. Without your belt you'll only lose your pants. But since it's your arm, it's your choice."

"Take it!" yelped the man.

William pulled the man's belt out. The man turned loose his arm to grab his pants, but his arm hurt so bad he had to let go of his pants. And while the man might have felt like he was just before losing his pants, he didn't.

William pulled the belt tight just below the man's armpit. Once the tourniquet was secure, William boosted the man back into his saddle and got back on Taz. They then resumed their journey to Saulston.

Finally, the man said, "Boy, who taught you to shoot like that?"

"My Pa," replied William.

"Damn, he must be proud to have a boy who can shoot like you do."

"Naw, he would have been a bit disappointed. You see, I was aiming for your heart, but you had to go and turn, and I missed. If I hadn't missed, we wouldn't be making this trip to Saulston. What's your name, Mister?"

"Larson…Buck Larson. How old are you, boy?"

"Going on fifteen."

"Boy, I'm beggin' you not to let anyone know that Buck Larson was shot by a fourteen-year-old boy."

William smiled to himself and gave Taz a gentle kick. "We best get on to Saulston before you bleed to death."

Four days later Sergeant John Robert Daniel rode into Danville aboard Bolt. Bolt seemed to enjoy the journey as much as John. Both got to see sights they had never seen before. Now Bolt had his ears up, taking in all the sounds of town as well as listening for any commands from John.

Soldiers were everywhere, so finding Major Ledbetter was not difficult. The first soldier John stopped to ask the major's location pointed in the direction of a grouping of white tents and said, "Over yonder, to the right of that small bunch of tents is a white house. He's inside."

"Thanks!" said John as he pointed Bolt in the direction he was told. Bolt didn't need a kick as he started to trot in the direction John had pointed him. As Bolt went into his trot, John was thinking, "Horses in many ways are a lot like people. When a horse spends a lot of time with the same rider, both learn to anticipate what the other wants or expects."

About fifty yards separated the white house from the tents. John rode up to the house and tied Bolt to the hitching post.

When he walked inside, he saw a young soldier sitting behind a small table. John said, "Sergeant John Daniel here to see Major Ledbetter, as ordered." John then extended his hand with his orders.

The young soldier took the paper from John, looked it over, and then up at John. He asked, "Are you one of the special project men?"

"Yes," replied John.

"Okay, you're to go down those tents, find one with an extra bunk, and take it. Any of the men there can tell you where you can get food if you need it. There are two more of you due in tomorrow. When everyone is here, the major will talk to all of you at one time. Just take it easy until you hear differently." He then handed back his orders.

After finding a tent with an extra bunk, John moved his saddlebags and bedroll into the tent and claimed the bunk. From one of the soldiers walking by the tent, he asked where he could stable Bolt. The soldier gave John directions to a corral and told him there was also a place there for his saddle.

Once John had fed Bolt and turned him loose in the corral, he walked back to the tent to stretch out on the only vacant cot. There were three other cots, all showing evidence of occupants. Various items of clothing were scattered on and about the other cots.

The cot felt good to John's body. Sleeping on the ground for the last four days didn't agree much with his forty-four-year-old body. He had a birthday on August 17…there was no party. He purposely had not let it be known. He didn't need any more questions regarding him being too old to be in the Southern army.

John instantly fell asleep. Near midafternoon three other soldiers entered the tent. One said to the others, in a low voice, "Looks like we got our last tent mate."

Another commented, "Looks a little old to me. Suppose he's here by mistake?"

John never moved. He was in a deep state of sleep. He could have been sleeping on a railroad track with the training coming and blowing its whistle, and he would have not have heard it. However, when he heard a cannon fire—*or did he dream it*—his feet hit the floor.

Looking around, he saw six new eyes staring back at him. The owner of one pair said, "Sorry to startle you. My rifle accidentally fell over and hit that metal bucket."

"That's all right," replied John. "I needed to get up anyway. Didn't realize how tired I was."

"Where'd you come from?" asked another one of the men.

"Manassas. And you guys?"

One spoke for himself and the other two. "I came from Richmond. These two came from Petersburg. All of us in this area are here for some special project. That must be why you're here?"

"That's right," replied John. "You guys know anything about it?"

"No, but tomorrow morning, after breakfast, we are all supposed to get into some wagons for a ride to its location. There we are to meet with the major, who will tell us all about it."

"Thanks for telling me. By the way, my name is John Daniel." John made the point of not mentioning his rank. All already seemed a bit shocked at having such an older man with them. None of these boys were over seventeen.

The boys introduced themselves as Bill, Ray, and Zack. John could tell, from the looks on their faces, they were here for the adventure and had no idea what it would be like to shoot at someone else, much less be shot at.

The four had dinner that evening and breakfast the next morning together. When they left breakfast, they saw three wagons in the center of the road, between rows of tents. Zack turned out to be the talker in the group. "Well, there's our ride to the special project."

John could see the excitement on his face. Soon the mysterious special project would be revealed.

After about thirty men were gathered around the wagons, a sergeant stepped up into the back of the first wagon. He said, "Men, give me your attention. I am Sergeant Young. First, I am going to call roll to make sure all are here and accounted for. When I call your last name, yell out 'here' and hold up your hand."

When the roll call was complete and the sergeant was satisfied all were present, he said, "Now I am going to assign you to a wagon. When I call your name, get into your assigned wagon. An NCO is in charge of each wagon. I'll call the sergeant in charge of the wagon first, and they are to get on the seat with the driver. I have wagon number one. Sergeant Daniel, you have wagon number two, and Sergeant Winder, you have number three."

When John's name was called, he climbed into the seat next to the driver. The three boys looked at one another in shock. They had assumed that because John was in their tent, he must also be a private like them. The two boys from Petersburg were assigned to wagon number three, and Zack was assigned to number two with John.

Each wagon had nine men in the back and one NCO on the seat with the driver. When the wagons were loaded, Sergeant Young gave the command to move out. And the wagons started to roll toward the main section of Danville.

The wagon train went through Danville and to the other side of the town, where John could see three large brick buildings. All the wagons stopped in front of the first brick building. An officer on horseback was waiting for them.

When all the wagons were parked side by side, the man on horseback rode up and stopped where all could see him. He looked around like he was ensuring no one else was present. He then said, "Men, I am Major Ledbetter, and I want you to pay close attention to what I am saying, because these buildings are your special projects. These buildings were once tobacco storage buildings. They now belong to the Southern army. Your job will be to convert these buildings to the South's first prisoner-of-war facilities. This means the buildings will have to be gutted and the interiors rebuilt with cells that will contain at least fifty prisoners in each cell. An NCO will be in charge of the work in each building. The building you are assigned to work in is the same as the wagon you are currently assigned to. Now, I am going to walk the NCOs through building one and give them a briefing on their mission. You men can stretch your legs, but stay with your wagon.

"Sergeants Young, Daniel, and Winder come with me." Ledbetter got off his horse and tied him to one of the wagon wheels. He led the sergeants into the first building.

Upon entering, the men found it was stifling and pungent with the odor of wet or rotting tobacco. The only lighting came from small windows along the outer walls near the ceiling. In the shafts of light, John could see particles floating in the air.

As Daniel's eyes adjusted to the darkness, he could see several sets of stairs leading to the second floor. He could also see the interior was divided into a number of bins by wooden walls. Inside the bins were wooden baskets and barrels, which he assumed was where the tobacco had been stored. Sticky tobacco juice permeated the floor, and where a shaft of light hit the floor, he could see what appeared to be rats running through the light.

His assessment of what he was going to be faced with was interrupted by the major's voice. "Men, as you can see, there is a lot of work to be done, and the conditions in which you will be required to work are less than desirable."

John immediately thought, "Less than desirable is an understatement. These conditions are intolerable, and no man should be required to work in here."

The major continued talking. "For a number of years, tobacco was stored here before shipping to a processor or manufacturer of tobacco products. The owner, in his benevolence, made the buildings available to the Southern army to be used as needed, at no cost."

Again John's thinking jumped ahead of the major's talking. "Did the owner evermore get a good deal? We clean up his mess, and after the war, he gets them back with all the improvement the army made."

Ledbetter said, "Our job is to clear out the interior until we have one large open area. By the time your team has the interior gutted, I will have the lumber and bars for converting the interior to jail cells with a capacity of fifty men per cell. Also, I want us to construct some solitary confinement cells for those who may create some dissension or need for some other reason to be confined separately from the general population. For example, general officers will need to be separated from the general population.

"This afternoon you will receive a shipment of demolition tools that we knew you would need. However, if there is something more you need at any time during the time you are here, make me aware of the requirement, in writing, at the end of each day. I will try to get it for you. Now, when you get to your respective buildings, I want you to brief your men and walk with them throughout the entire facility so they can see the big picture. Also, there are some lanterns next to the wall near the entrance." He then turned back toward the entrance and pointed to a stack of lanterns.

Without asking for any questions, Ledbetter turned and exited the building. The NCOs followed. Once outside, John went back to his wagon thinking, "Why didn't he turn on a lantern while he was in there so he could see the full extent of the condition of the building?" When he reached his wagon, he told the driver, "Take us to building number two."

※

Back on the farm, William had hired two boys to help him complete his crop harvest. He figured it would take two strong boys to match his pa, but he was wrong. His pa could work rings around those boys, but they sure were a help, and he wasn't complaining.

He was thinking, "Ma hasn't heard from Pa in some time now. That either means he has moved again or has been too busy to write. Anyhow, there has been no news of any battles being fought in Northern Virginia, so I guess that is a good thing.

"Sure hated to see those boys leave today. Enjoyed having some fellows around to talk with. But Pa would agree that the sooner I could cut them free and not have to pay them any longer, the better for the family."

Turning to Lucky Boy, who was in his stall pulling hay from his hay rack, he said, "I know you miss Pa as much as I do. But it's good he can't see how fat you're getting. If he did, he would be on the both of us. Got to get to the house now, big fellow, or Ma will be yelling for me. The dark is beginning to slip in on us mighty quickly with the days getting shorter." With those words, William was out of the horse barn jogging to the house.

His timing was good; Nancy Ann had already come out the back door to call him. When she saw him coming, she waved and darted back inside. Days were getting cooler now, but that could be expected now in eastern North Carolina.

Becky was sitting at her end of the table, and the others were sitting on bench seats along the sides of the table. Pa's seat was empty. Becky looked at William and said, "Miss Reba came by in that cute little buggy her husband got for her. She says that now she can hitch it up whenever she wants and go wherever she wants without waiting for Herb."

Herb, or Herbert, was Miss Reba's husband. Both were older than Pa. They lived on a farm three miles away.

"Did she have any news to share?" William asked that question because he knew Miss Reba always had some news to share.

"She did. She ask me if I knew I had the most recent celebrity of Saulston living in my house. Course, I told her I didn't know what she was talking about. She looked shocked and said it was you, William."

"Me?"

"Yes. She said there was talk all over Saulston of how that Daniel boy brought in a wanted man for which there was a reward. Story is this fellow named Buck Larson, who is as evil as they come, thought he could rob the Daniels' farm. Seems he got surprised when fourteen-year-old William shot him in the arm, causing him to drop his weapon. Then William hog-tied him and took him into the constable. Said the whole town was talking about what a hero William was to stand up for his family while his Pa is off to the war."

"Oh, Ma, you know I'm no hero. Now, what was that part about a reward? Constable didn't say anything to me about there being a reward."

"According to Miss Reba, the constable just learned of the reward yesterday when he reported to the sheriff who he had in custody. I think tomorrow you might want to ride to Saulston and claim your reward."

"Just as much Nancy Ann's reward as mine. She was the first to stand up to him."

"Well, you plan on going tomorrow. Might be some money you can use to get you some more education."

William smiled because he was aware Ma knew how much he wanted to further his education. One day he would like to be a lawyer.

When John entered the building designated as number two, his nine men followed him. Turning to Zack, he said, "Zack, there are supposed to be some lanterns over next to that wall. Light some of them up for us. Couple you guys help him."

After the lanterns were lit, John could not believe the filth the men would have to clean out before any demolition of the interior could begin. John then gave the men the same briefing he and the other NCOs had received from the major. After walking through the entire facility while dodging unfriendly rodents and then adjusting to the shock of what was expected of them, the men decided to concentrate on the first floor before moving to the second.

While acknowledging the importance of the South having a POW facility, the men also expressed their disappointment at having been selected because they possessed special skills required for a secret special project. Probably Zack expressed the frustration of all the men when he said, "Why didn't they select about fifty eight-year-olds and put them in here and tell them not to break anything or take anything outside? In a week the demolition job would be done and the building cleaned out."

John, attempting to keep the men's spirits up, countered with "I know the demolition and cleaning of this building detract greatly from our assignment, but we must keep in focus where our skills are truly needed. That is in the construction phase. The tearing down and cleaning out is a necessity before we get to what we were brought here to do. And that is to build a good POW facility—one that if you were captured, you would hope to be put in."

During October and November, the men toiled and sweated at their job, even though the weather outside was getting much colder. To avoid some of the stench, the men wore bandannas over their mouths and noses.

However, that did not preclude some of the men from beginning to feel sick. The major criticized the men for being lazy and losing interest in the importance of their job. He also verbally attacked the NCOs for not properly motivating their men.

John's team was making good progress in spite of the fact that they were lucky to have six men working an entire week. It was in John's nature to try to personally pick up any slack resulting from men out sick.

As a result, John's team was able to start their construction phase by early November.

By mid-November John could feel his strength and stamina start to wane. He attributed his feeling to exhaustion brought on by the pace at which he was pushing himself. But lying on his cot at night trying to diagnose his own condition, he suddenly realized he was having more difficulty with breathing. He could not help but wonder if breathing in all the filth might be a contributing factor. He was not about to admit that age might also be a factor.

While he continued to push himself, he talked to others who were sick and found they all shared the same symptoms. He hoped now that the air was cleaner and fresher in the construction phase, his symptoms would soon pass.

Although he made it through November and most of December, on December 18, John was unable to get off his cot. Zack and one of the other soldiers physically carried John to General Hospital Number 1 in Danville, where he was admitted on December 19, 1861, with what the doctor wrote on his chart as an "unknown illness."

CHAPTER 9

HOME AGAIN–D COMPANY

On January 10, 1862, Captain Whitaker was sitting at his desk inside the Manassas garrison when a courier requested entry. Captain Whitaker acknowledged the courier's request with "Enter!"

The courier entered, stopped in front of Whitaker's desk, rendered a salute, and said, "Sir, you have a message from Major Ledbetter." He then handed Whitaker a message that had arrived via telegraph.

Whitaker accepted the message and began to read. "Captain Whitaker, I cannot understand why you sent an old man to do a young man's job. Your Sergeant Daniel was admitted to the military hospital with an unknown illness. His illness is known to me as old age. Send a more competent replacement immediately. Major Horatio Ledbetter, Special Projects Commander."

Captain Whitaker was known to be a calm individual who took each challenge with a great deal of measure before reacting. But this message pushed him beyond his calm demeanor border.

He arose from his desk with a face growing redder by the second.

Startled, the courier said, "Sir, do you want to reply?"

"Hell yes, I want to reply, but it will be hand delivered. You are dismissed." Almost in the same breath, he yelled, "First Sergeant, get in here now!"

With anger that was resonating from within the captain's office, the first sergeant felt hesitant to enter, but he did. "Yes sir," he said.

"First Sergeant, you are to find Corporal Paul…the boy from Brogden. Tell him to draw four days of rations, saddle his horse, and report to me within the hour."

"Yes, sir." The first sergeant did an about-face and disappeared as fast as he had entered. Whitaker sat back down and pull out a blank piece of paper and started to write.

Forty-five minutes later, Corporal Johnson was standing in front of Captain Whitaker's desk. Whitaker's face was still red as he folded and sealed a sheet of paper. Looking up at Paul, he said, "Corporal, you are to hand deliver this letter to Major Ledbetter in Danville, Virginia. Do you know where that is?"

"Yes, sir. I believe that is where Sergeant Daniel went."

"I know it has been snowing off and on for the last few days, but I want you to deliver this message as fast as possible. Then I want you to go to the military hospital in Danville, where you will find Sergeant Daniel. When he is able to ride, you get Sergeant Daniel and bring him home."

At first a happy expression appeared on Paul's face, and then it disappeared as he said, "Has Sergeant John been hurt?"

"Only know he is sick. If there are no other questions, you are dismissed."

"Yes, sir!" Paul spun around and exited without rendering a salute. In a matter of seconds, he was crouched in the saddle for his departure from the garrison. As Paul went through the garrison gate, with his horse kicking snow up with his hooves, one of the gate sentries asked the other, "Was that a pony express rider?"

In spite of encountering some deep snow drifts and with only a few hours of sleep each night, Paul rode into a snow-covered Danville within three days. He had no difficulty in locating Major Ledbetter's quarters—a little white house near about a dozen tents.

Paul bounced up the steps to the major's house and, without waiting for any challenge, stated, "I'm Corporal Paul Johnson from General's Featherson's Brigade with an urgent message for Major Ledbetter."

After Paul had passed the sentry, the sentry belatedly said, "Go right in."

Paul gave the door three hard knocks but waited for no answer. He just entered. After entering, his face turned red with anger when he saw Ledbetter sitting in front of a nice warm fire without his boots on or even jacket, paging through some papers.

Without even looking up, the man said, "Mighty arrogant of you to enter without an invitation."

Paul knew he had best get himself under control, or he might have a problem. He hastily said, "My apologies, sir, but I have an urgent message I am to deliver to you."

"Where are you from, Corporal?"

"General Featherson's Brigade, sir." Paul made a point not to say Captain Whitaker had sent him; because he had detected some anger in the Captain's voice when he directed the message to be hand delivered to the major. If there was any disagreement between the two, Paul did not want to be caught in the middle.

The name "General Featherson" got Ledbetter's attention, as he quickly dropped the papers he was holding and reached for the sealed letter Paul handed him.

Ledbetter carefully opened the seal with a wooden carved letter opener. He didn't want to tear the letter. It had to be important, assuming it came from General Featherson.

Ledbetter read, "Major Ledbetter, General Featherson is quite aware of the competence of Sergeant Daniel. He has been very kind to share with me your reports on your special project. In your report—and I refresh your memory—you state, 'The work progress on building number 2, under the skilled leadership of Sergeant John Robert Daniel, has been brilliant, as his progress is currently two to three weeks ahead of the other two buildings. I thank you for such an excellent choice to work on this important and special project.' How has his illness changed your mind, other than you expect his absence will cause what he has accomplished to be degraded similarly to the lack of progress of the other two buildings? Accordingly, I have ordered Corporal Johnson to escort Sergeant Daniel back to my company as soon as his health will permit it. With respect to his replacement, you will not receive one from my company. With all due respect, I suggest, unless you wish to entertain some questions from General Featherson, that you show some leadership by rolling up your sleeves, getting out of your office, and providing closer supervision. Captain Junius B. Whitaker, Commander Company D, Fourth Regiment, North Carolina Infantry."

While Paul did not know the contents of Whitaker's letter, he did know from the redness of Ledbetter's face and the angry look in his eyes that it was not what the major expected or appreciated.

Coughing and sputtering before he could speak, Ledbetter finally got his throat clear enough to say, "Corporal, get out of my office, go get your Sergeant Daniel, and get the hell out of Danville. And hope to God I never see either one of you again!"

Careful to show respect to a man so full of anger that he might do something irrational, Paul said, "Yes sir" and saluted, and without waiting for a return salute, he was out of the major's office before anything else could be said.

From the sentry he was able to get directions to the hospital. Upon entering the hospital, which for now had a small staff, he was told by one of the walking patients the ward where he could find Sergeant Daniel.

After entering the ward without anyone questioning his presence, he started to move down the center aisle, looking first to his right and then to his left. Near the end of the ward, on the left side, sitting up in bed, was Sergeant Daniel. This caused Paul to hurry toward Daniel.

Seeing Paul approach, John was the first to speak. "To what do my eyes owe this pleasant visit of great joy? Or am I dreaming again?"

"You're not dreaming, Sergeant Papa John. It's me, Paul Johnson! And your eyes are in debt to Captain Whitaker, who sent me to fetch you."

At this very moment, no more pleasant a message could John have received. It caused tears to swell in his eyes, as he wanted to say something but could not think of words to express his happiness. He was beginning to think he had been forgotten. He had not had any visitors, including Major Ledbetter.

Finally he was able to get out the words "Did I hear you right? You're here to take me back to Manassas?"

By now, Paul had leaned over and was giving John a hug. It was that love soldiers share with one another. Paul replied, "Yes, but before you swing your leg over any horse, I have got to get the doctor's approval."

"Forget the doctor. I'll get on my clothes…if I can find them. And we're not talking any horse. You get Bolt from that corral over by the small group of tents near the white house on the other side of the town."

"Hold on, Sarge. There is more than two inches of snow on the ground, and it's still coming down. I'm not taking you for a three-to-four-day ride in this snow unless I know for sure you are well enough to make such a venture. If I were to ride back into garrison with you draped over Bolt, I'm afraid the captain would shoot me instantly with no questions asked."

"It's good to know the captain thinks so much of me," thought John. "Okay, okay. Get the doc in here, and let's see what he has to say."

As Paul turned to go find a doctor, he heard Papa John say, "It's so good to see you. I missed you guys."

Hurrying down the ward, Paul was thinking, "You don't know how much we've missed you."

§

William was standing in front of the desk of the constable for Saulston. The constable was saying, "I bet I know why you're here. You heard about the reward money being offered for old Buck Larson, didn't you?"

"Yes, sir. Ma learned about the reward yesterday and sent me in here to see if what she heard was true, and if so, how I go about claiming it."

"Yes, it's true. Aren't you gonna ask how much the reward might be?"

"No, sir. I figure whatever it is, and if I am the proper person to get it, that you would see that I do."

"Son, I appreciate those respectful words, but one day trusting people is gonna get you in trouble."

"Sir, I only trust those who I know to be honest folk."

The constable smiled and said, "The reward is five hundred dollars, and yes, you are the proper claimant. I suppose you want it now?"

William smiled and said, "Yes sir, I do."

The constable spun his chair around and turned some dials on the small safe that sat on the floor behind his chair. When the door swung open, he reached inside and pulled out a stack of money. He then counted, out loud, $500 and handed it to William. He asked, "William, do you think you can get all this money home safely?"

"Yes sir," he replied as he pulled up his shirt, revealing the revolver he had in his waistband.

Again the constable smiled and said, "I think so also. Word is around town about how good you are with a gun. I hope no one shows up here wanting to find out for themselves."

William understood what the constable was saying and replied, "I hope your wish comes true because some days luck can be misinterpreted. I hope you will spread the word around, how lucky I was." John stuffed the money in a cloth bag that he pulled from his rear pocket, and then he put the bag inside his shirt. Turning to leave, he said, "Thank you, sir. Buck Larson may have just put another lawyer on the streets."

Within a few minutes, John spotted Paul weaving his way between beds with a doctor in a white coat following him.

When the doctor was beside John, he reached over and placed his hand on John's forehead and said, "I understand you want to get out of here?"

"That's right!" John replied.

The doctor replied, "While I think the cold fresh air might do you some good, you still have a low fever. And I don't like the idea of you getting wet. The snow has not let up. Furthermore, sleeping on the ground for three to four days could be the death of you."

"Doc, I can stay dry wearing my leather duster. It hangs to the top of my boots," replied John.

Paul said, "I can make him a hammock to keep him off the ground."

"While I will not stop you from doing what you want to do, I will insert in your medical records, should you decide to leave, that your departure was against my recommendation. I think you need to get your fever down before you leave. But I am not stopping you."

"Where are my clothes, Doc? Paul, you go get Bolt. Four tents from the horse corral is my tent. Ask Zack to show you my cot. Gather up my personal items, and make sure my duster is tied on my saddle. If not, you know what to do. I'll be dressed and waiting for your return."

Paul scurried out of the hospital. He knew what John meant when he said, "You know what to do." He meant take any other one Paul saw because someone had taken his.

When Paul returned, John had decided they would check into a local boarding house for the night and leave at sunup the next morning. That would allow one more night for John's fever to come down, which might be further helped by a meal better than the one he would have received in the hospital.

On the trail, the fresh, brisk air did seem to cause John to perk up some. He was quite interested in Paul filling him in all the happenings in D Company while he was gone. And while the duster did a good job of keeping his body dry, after several hours the wet cold began to penetrate the duster, John's winter coat, shirt, and long johns. His being warm was not helped by the snow that built up upon the top of his hat. By the time Paul had built a night cooking fire, John had to admit to himself that he was cold from his head to his toes.

When John was ready to go to bed, Paul constructed a hammock from a canvas tent side he had gotten near the horse corral. Once John was in the hammock, Paul covered him with a wool blanket from John's bedroll and placed another side of a tent over John so the snow would not penetrate the blanket.

After John was tucked in, Paul put John's boots beside the fire, and he slept in his bedroll beside the fire so he could keep it burning all night. This became the standard procedure for the next three nights.

The days found John more his old self in the mornings, but by late afternoon he would begin to show more weakness. Paul would suggest they stop for John to get some rest, but John insisted he was fine and they needed to push on.

On the fifth day, the two entered the Manassas garrison. John was slouched in his saddle. Paul took John directly to Captain Whitaker. Whitaker had another cot brought into his quarters, where there was some heat, and directed that Paul and Luke rotate daily in caring for John.

John was unaware of how he was being cared for because when he arrived, he was not in a state of awareness. The long trip had been hard on him. But when he came around to knowing where he was and who his caretakers were, his health started improving instantly.

One morning, about a week later, when the captain woke up, John was sitting upright on the edge of his cot. When the captain looked his way, John said, "Captain, thank you for bringing me home. I greatly appreciate your hospitality, but I think I am ready to rejoin the boys in their tent."

Whitaker replied, "Sergeant Daniel, I am sorry for what you have been through. Had I known the circumstances of your assignment, I would not have let you go. Know that you are welcome to stay here as long as you need to do so."

"Sir, again I appreciate your generosity, but I think the boys need me, and I need the boys."

CHAPTER 10

THE PENINSULAR CAMPAIGN BEGINS

By early February 1862, John Daniel's health had improved to where he was able to return to duty. In the interest of his continued health improvement, Captain Whitaker assigned John the responsibility of forming a carpentry detail of four men and himself to work on projects needed by the regimental staff. Such projects were to build shelves and tables and repair windows, doors, and roofs. Of particular interest to the staff was the need for more map boards. This was clear evidence to John that a lot of strategic planning was taking place, which meant an all-out war was imminent.

This became more evident to John when, in mid-February, he received a construction request that only he and one other trusted man could work on. He was permitted to enter a room within the regimental headquarters that previously had been off limits to everyone but certain designated officers.

He and his selectee, Corporal Young, were required to take an oath not to reveal anything they saw in the room, under the penalty of execution should they do so. Upon entering the room, he was met by General Featherson and three members of his staff. Featherson began by saying, "Sergeant Daniel and Corporal Young, I want you to construct a terrain box four feet by eight feet and about waist high. Do you know what I mean by a 'terrain box'?"

"No sir," replied John.

"Well, a terrain box is much like a large sandbox on legs. It is to have sides so that the men standing here with me can construct within the box a representation of the terrain we may have to fight on one day. Accordingly, after construction you will be asked to place dirt and rocks inside the box. These men will configure the terrain inside the box. Your job will be finished before they start. Do you have any questions?"

John's first thought was "A task this simple requires no questions" He replied, "No, sir."

During the construction of the terrain box, John got some insight as to what was on the horizon when he had to move one of the map boards he had built a week earlier. Attached to the map board was a large map labeled "The Peninsular Campaign." There not being anyone but him in the room at the time, he took a closer look. He noticed some of the places circled included Yorktown, Williamsburg, Seven Pines, and Mechanicsville. There were other places circled, but he heard footsteps approaching the closed door, so he quickly turned back to his work on the terrain box.

Within a couple of days, the terrain box was complete, with dirt and rocks inside as instructed by some of the staff officers. The most difficult part was getting the building materials. Fortunately, the brigade had its own sawmill, but it took a half day for the workers there to cut the materials to John's specifications.

After John and Young were released and reminded of their oath, they returned to D Company to await further instructions. It was during this time John found the time to write a short letter to Becky. He wrote:

> My Dearest Becky and family.
>
> Pray all is well with the family. I am doing fine and still in Manassas. Winter was much colder here than

in Saulston, and because of all the snow, I stayed inside most of the time. My job is mostly carpentry work. I know William is working much harder and currently preparing for planting season. Don't know how long I will be here, so don't try to write.

Love to all of you,
Your John.

Near the end of February, John began to see some increased activity by the officers. Captain Whitaker was spending a lot of time at brigade headquarters, and when not there, he was scurrying between the quartermaster, the supply depot, and the blacksmith. When he spoke, it was short and in clips. He seemed awfully anxious, which led John to believe the time for their first battle was drawing near.

On March 1, during the daily morning formation, Captain Whitaker, with a very stern look on his face, said, "Men, get prepared to move out of garrison on a moment's notice. Clean your weapons, ensure your bayonet will easily fix into place, and gather up your personal effects, including your bedroll and your personal cooking tin. You're not to break down your tents because where you are going, they will not be needed. Don't try to speculate where you're going, because you will probably be wrong.

"NCOs, make sure the men accomplish this order proficiently and efficiently. If a man is not prepared to move when I give the order, you personally will be held accountable. If you have any questions, be sure to ask me before noon because after that time I will not be available. I am confident you will not disappoint me. You are dismissed!"

Although the order had been given to dismiss, few of the men moved. They turned to one another and very quietly began to ask one another questions. All were confident that the day they had been expecting had arrived.

The general feeling among the men of D Company was mixed. Some were excited about getting to do what they had come together to do; others began to have feelings of doubt—not doubt as to whether or not they were prepared but doubt in their mental ability to do what was expected of them. The idea of marching side by side into a wall of gun-fire presented the reality that while it was hard to imagine they would be killed, certainly some of their friends would be killed.

Sergeant Daniel, speaking to the men around him, said, "Boys, you heard the captain. Break up this idle talk and start getting yourselves ready to move. After you get everything ready, I encourage you to take the time to write a short note home. You are not to mention anything about your movement. Within a couple of hours, I'll be around to see how you are doing."

John returned to his tent and began getting his gear together. Having recently written a letter home, he saw no need to write one now. After getting everything where all he had to do was grab it up and throw it on his back, he started his inspections.

John quickly discovered the men had taken the captain's orders seriously, and the extent of his involvement was to make some suggestions for securing their items in a better way. It was during his inspection that he saw a string of eight horses, including Bolt, being led out of the garrison. Following the horses were two wagons loaded with saddles, bridles, and other horse tack. John saw this to be evidence they would not be marching to wherever they were going; otherwise, the officers would be on horseback.

Midafternoon the captain called all the officers and NCOs together at his tent. His first question was "Are the men ready to move?"

All the officers and NCOs answered in the affirmative.

The captain continued. "I want the men assembled and in formation one hour before sundown. You are to give them one final inspection and correct any deficiencies. Under the cover of darkness, we will move to the train depot. There I want twenty men per boxcar. We are traveling by boxcar to prevent the movement of troops from being observed by any spies that might be in the area. You'll know the destination when we get there. Are there any questions?"

One NCO asked, "Captain, upon arrival, is there anything the men should be prepared for?"

"The men are expected, so food and a place for them to bunk are waiting for their arrival. Know that it is my understanding we will be arriving at a holding area, which means we will be there only temporally. That is all I know for now. If there are no more questions, you are dismissed."

One hour before sunset, D Company was assembled and in formation. The NCOs and officers conducted their final inspections. Only some minor adjustments were made, but all were present and prepared to move out upon orders from the captain.

As the sunset and the moon looked down upon D Company, Captain Whitaker gave the order "Forward, march!" and the formation followed the captain's lead. All were surprised to see Whitaker marching with them because he was normally on his horse.

After thirty minutes the formation arrived at the train depot. There the men of D Company saw men of the Virginia companies beginning to load into boxcars. Within the hour all men of D Company were loaded in. Each car had a couple of lanterns for light and a barrel in which the men could relieve themselves. Twenty minutes after the doors were closed, the men could feel a jerking of the car, causing some men to lose their balance and stumble into one another. The train was moving, and no one inside the boxcars knew their destination.

A few hours later, the men could feel the train shifting to another track, and shortly thereafter it came to a stop. All sat patiently waiting for the door to be opened. Some, anxious as to what might lie on the other side of the door, grasped their weapons a little closer. When the door was finally opened, it was still dark outside, and the men were more in the dark with respect to where they might be.

After all were unloaded, including the Virginia units, each company was designated a specific holding area. After the men of D Company were settled into their holding area, they were told to relax until daybreak and try to get some rest. As soon as the sun came up and they had breakfast, they would be directed to a more permanent location and begin a full day of work.

As the sun came up, the men could see, in the distance, the train still parked where they had unloaded. Then a buzz started through the encampment. The buzz was "We're on familiar ground. That's the same water tank we saw about seven months ago. We're back in Richmond."

Breakfast consisted of a bread roll, a wedge of cheese, and a strip of bacon jerky. Once breakfast was over, they moved to a portion of the encampment designated for D Company. Tents were already in place because they had been left behind by a Virginia company that had moved out four days earlier. There was also a corral for the horses, and there was a structure that from the ground to three feet above ground were four wooden walls. Above the wooden walls were canvas walls with a roof similar to a tent. This was to be Captain Whitaker's quarters and office.

The first day was spent settling in and learning the lay of the land. They learned the assembly area for their formations, and they found several outdoor showers and several privies with multiple seats. Most considered their accommodations to be better than those in Manassas. This caused some concern for John because any time things appeared to be too good, there had to be something he was missing.

What was missing began the next day and continued throughout March. The training was more intense than that done in Goldsboro, where it had been mostly basic combat skills. Here the emphasis was survival. One had to learn to more quickly load and reload their weapon. Fixing bayonets and charging into a line of straw dummies stressed that while using the bayonet to pierce one's enemy, they needed to use the butt of their rifle to feign off another attacker.

John soon discovered he might not have fully recovered from his December illness of unknown origin. The alternation of cold air and massive perspiration seemed to be weakening his physical conditioning. This was not recognized by the training officers and NCOs. When he stumbled or was unable to master a move with the same precision as his younger counterparts, he was berated by the trainers. They did not hesitate to remind him he was an old man and that if he wanted to stay alive, he would have to perform better than he was currently performing. John gave his all, but it seemed to him his condition was deteriorating.

John was not the only one who detected his weakening condition. Paul and Luke tried to convince him he needed to go to sick call. But for John, only slackers who were trying to avoid going to war went on sick call.

On April 2, John was called in by Captain Whitaker. Whitaker had been informed that John was in no physical condition to participate in any early battles, and because of his condition, he could easily get himself killed, and possibly others trying to protect him.

When John came in the presence of Whitaker, his face had an ashen appearance, and he seemed physically weak. The captain began by saying, "Stand at ease, Sergeant Daniel. Why don't you just take a seat?"

John replied, "I'm fine, sir. I can stand."

"Take a seat, Sergeant! And tell me what's going on. I know you haven't been measuring up to your own standards."

"Sir, I don't rightly know. There are days I feel like I may be having a relapse from my previous illness. But I know once the fighting starts, I'll be ready."

"Sergeant, I know you will give your best, but for now, your best is not your best. There is evidence that General George McClellan is on his way to lay siege to Yorktown, Virginia. It is believed that McClellan's forces could overrun General Magruder if Magruder does not receive reinforcements. Accordingly, tomorrow, under the command of General Joseph Johnston, we are leaving here to provide reinforcements to General Magruder. As you know, General Johnston is in command of all the Confederate forces. I think that to be an indication of the importance of this battle.

"Physically, I believe the trip will be too much for you. I am ordering you to report to sick call no later than tomorrow. You have done a good job for us, Sergeant Daniel, and I expect you to continue to do so, but you will only be able to rejoin D Company when you are fully recovered. Best of luck to you. Now you are to get out of my office. I have a lot to do before tomorrow."

"Yes, sir. I will obey your orders, but hold up on winning this war until I can get there to help."

The captain got up from his desk and walked over to John and put his arm around John's shoulders and said, "John, as soon as the doctor says you are well enough, I will be expecting you to report to D Company for duty. Understood?"

"Yes, sir." Sergeant Daniel saluted the captain, turned, and departed his quarters.

On April 5, 1862, General McClellan lay siege to Yorktown, Virginia, approximately sixty miles southeast of Virginia. This battle began the Peninsular Campaign. As McClellan was fortifying his positions and getting his big guns in place, General Johnston with his reinforcements moved from Richmond to Yorktown. McClellan quickly surrounded Yorktown.

When the siege began, John Robert Daniel was lying on his cot inside his tent. His fever was steadily rising. He experienced shakes from chills, his body ached, and he was finding it difficult to breathe. But he tried to continue battling through his sickness without admission to the hospital.

When he reached the state where he no longer could care for himself, he had no option but to seek admission to Chimborazo Hospital Number 2, in Richmond. He was admitted on April 10, 1862, and diagnosed with a serious case of pneumonia. The doctors expressed the opinion that his condition was brought on by the fact he had not completely recovered from the unknown illness he had experienced in December, combined with the strenuous training he was undergoing during March. He remained hospitalized for two weeks.

In the latter part of April, the doctor told John he was being released for light duty. During John's hospital stay, he learned that D Company of the North Carolina Regiment, along with a number of Virginia battalions, were engaged in a battle in Yorktown. Upon hearing he was being released from the hospital, John informed the doctor, "Doc, I have orders from Captain Whitaker to immediately report to him."

The doctor looked at John with an expression of "Sergeant, didn't you hear what I just said?"

As John hastily started to put on his uniform, the doctor said, "Sergeant, sit down!"

John continued to get dressed. The doctor then raised his voice and said, "Sergeant, as a superior officer, I am telling you to sit down."

Reluctantly, with his pants almost to his knees, John sat down on the edge of the bed.

"Now, listen closely to what I just said. I said you are released for light duty, and that does not include going into battle. You cannot leave this area for two reasons. First, you have to be where I can monitor your progress. At any sign of a decline in recovery, you will be readmitted to the hospital.

"The second reason is that Yorktown is under siege by McClellan's army. To translate that for you, it means if you were in perfect health, you could not get into Yorktown, just as those inside Yorktown cannot get out. From what I have heard, our forces are surrounded and are taking a severe beating. Any thoughts you have about going to Yorktown can be erased from your mind. I am having you assigned to a construction brigade here in Richmond. I want to see you at least for the next two Tuesdays, at which time I will make a decision as to any future assignment. Once you get dressed, report to my office, where I will give you a copy of your hospital release orders and your assignment orders. I see no need for any further discussion on this matter."

The doctor then got up and stormed out the door, leaving John somewhat bewildered as he sat on the edge of the bed. After getting dressed, he reported to the doctor's office and received copies of his orders. The doctor's only words were "I will see you next Tuesday morning, and don't be late!"

John departed thinking, "Well, I guess I just got a medical butt chewing." Reading his assignment order, he saw the doctor had him assigned to a construction company in the Virginia Engineer Brigade. He knew it was located on the outskirts of Richmond, where excavation and fortification construction was ongoing. He was to report to Major Applewhite.

That afternoon John retrieved Bolt from the corral and rode to the southern outskirts of Richmond and reported to Major Applewhite, who immediately assigned him to a lumber harvesting detail. His duty was to drive a team of four mules pulling a large wagon to a location a half mile out of the city. There he would leave the empty wagon and hitch the mules to a wagon loaded with cut tree trunks. He would then deliver that wagon back to a construction site to get another empty wagon. This he did for the next two weeks.

On Tuesday, May 6, 1862, John paid his final visit to the doctor. The doctor considered him to be completely recovered and able to return to full duty. With a copy of his medical release papers, John and Bolt made their way to brigade headquarters in record time.

Upon arrival at brigade headquarters, Sergeant Daniel reported to the senior NCO and gave him a copy of the doctor's release and return-to-duty orders. The senior NCO welcomed him with "I'm glad to see you back. Now let me see where I am going to assign you…"

Before the NCO continued, John replied, "I already have my assignment orders. I have been ordered by Captain Whitaker to report directly to him."

"And who might Captain Whitaker be?"

"He commands D Company, Fourth Regiment of the North Carolina Volunteers."

"Well, your captain has been through some hell. For your sake I hope he is still alive. Yorktown has been under siege for the last month. I understand our men are short of both supplies and ammunition. The scuttlebutt is our guys withdrew to Williamsburg last Friday, the second. As of yesterday McClellan was still pounding Yorktown, which may indicate he does not know our guys have abandoned the town."

"Williamsburg, you say?"

"That's right."

"I best get going so I can link up with them."

"Sergeant Daniel, I'm not sure you can get past McClellan's army to get to Williamsburg."

"I got to try!" said John as he quickly exited headquarters.

After a gallop to the eastern outskirts of Richmond, John put Bolt into a run. After a mile or so of running, John reined Bolt into a canter and then slowly into a walk. Alternating between a run and a walk gave Bolt opportunities to rest. The distance from Richmond to Williamsburg was approximately fifty miles, and in spite of deep wagon-and cannon-wheel tracks, the center of the road was in good condition. And the closer he got to Williamsburg, the more careful he would have to be. He did not want to encounter any Union soldiers. He figured that close to Charles City, which was approximately twenty miles from Williamsburg, he would take to the woods. Hopefully, he could reach Williamsburg undetected.

Never entering Charles City, John steered Bolt into a wooded thicket. Once in the woods, he let Bolt pick each of his steps; he just kept him pointed in the right direction.

After another slow ten miles, Bolt suddenly stopped. His ears were up, and he was looking toward his right. John quietly slid out of the saddle and tied Bolt to the nearest tree. Armed with both his rifle and revolver, John started making his way in the direction Bolt had been looking. It could be man or animal, but this close to Williamsburg, John was not going to take any chances.

Careful not to step on any dry limbs or anything that might suggest his presence, he made his way slowly, ducking under low branches and using each tree as cover. It wasn't long before he caught the smell of burning wood. "Someone has built a fire," thought John.

About twenty yards to his front, he thought he spotted movement through some low-hanging branches. He stopped, squatted down, and checked his rifle. He kept a round chambered but always released the hammer so as to avoid a misfire should he fall or the rifle got caught in a vine. Now he pulled the hammer back and carefully moved forward for a better view. Sure enough, squatting around the fire were two Yankee soldiers. Their rifles were propped against a nearby tree. To reach them, they would have to move several steps. For them to do so would be an indication John had been heard. He didn't want to shoot the boys because the sound of a rifle shot might bring some more. John speculated the boys were Union scouts positioned to spot any flanking movement designed to mount an attack on McClellan's army and relieve the forces under siege in Yorktown. John's intent was to get as close to the boys as possible before they knew he was there. He wanted to make it clear that should anyone try for his rifle, the Southerner had the advantage, and they would be shot.

When John stepped from the cover of the thicket, he was only about twenty feet from the boys. One was busy skinning a rabbit that had been killed earlier, and the other was stoking the fire. John calmly, in his command voice, said, "Boys, unless you want to die before you have the opportunity to enjoy a rabbit dinner, I suggest you raise your hands. Should either one of you think you can make it to your rifle, you best be faster than a bullet."

Initially, neither raised his hands, but they continued to stare at the fire as if considering their options. The one on the left began to slowly raise his hands; the other must have been determined not to be taken by a rebel, because he dove for his rifle. Too far and too slow. John fired one shot, striking the boy in his right leg. Simultaneously, he chambered another round and pointed his rifle at the chest of the other one, who had turned to face him.

"If you have any thoughts other than getting on your knees with your hands in the air, you gonna be in worse shape than your friend."

The boy who had been shot was in a fetal position holding his right leg at the calf. He could not have been older than seventeen. He had tears sliding down his cheeks.

Glancing in the shot boy's direction, John said, "I know it hurts, but be thankful I'm a lousy shot. I was aiming a little higher." Looking back at the kneeling boy, he said, "Now I want you to lie flat on your stomach and stretch your arms out. Most importantly, once you do that, don't move anymore. I may misinterpret your move and shoot you."

John then pulled his hunting knife from his boot, walked over to one of the saddles lying on the ground, and cut the rope around the bedroll on the back of the saddle.

With that piece of rope, he tied the hands behind the back of the boy lying on the ground. He then pulled the bandanna from around his neck and tied it around his mouth as he quietly whispered in the soldier's ear, "I don't like the sound of a Yankee voice."

He then walked over to the one he had shot, who by now had raised himself to a sitting position. With his hunting knife, John cut the strings of the boot on the boy's wounded leg and said, "Before I tie this around your leg to keep you from bleeding to death, why don't you tell me how many more of you are out there?"

The boy looked down at his bleeding leg. His pant leg was already saturated in blood. The boy then looked at John with pleading eyes and said, "We're the only two. We were sent to what was believed to be the most likely avenue of enemy approach. We were ordered not to engage but to return and report."

Considering there were only two of them, the explanation made sense to John. He tied the shoestring around the boy's upper leg. With another piece of bedroll rope, he tied the boy's hands behind his back.

After taking the reins from one of the boys' horses' bridles, he dragged the uninjured boy next to the injured boy. With them back to back, he tied them together. He then placed the injured boy's bandanna around his mouth and said, "Don't want you boys talking to each other. You just might come up with an escape plan. Now, I know you're concerned about being left out here tied up by yourselves, but at least you're alive. I'm gonna turn your horses loose, and they'll make their way back to your camp. When they arrive without you, I suspect someone will come looking for you. And be thankful I let you live. Good luck, you hear?"

John returned to Bolt, and within a matter of minutes rode past the two boys tied together. As he did, he tipped his hat to them and never looked back.

CHAPTER 11

WITHDRAWAL TO RICHMOND

Sergeant John Robert Daniel knew he had to get through the Williamsburg defense perimeter before darkness; otherwise, his chances would be slim to none. He cautiously approached the outer limits of the town, scanning for any sign of life. He had a feeling of pride when he saw the hasty but effective fortification that had been accomplished using whatever was available within the town. Maybe he had taught the boys something after all.

There were wagons, furniture, and hay bales blocking roads entering the town. He knew soon he would encounter a sentry who would challenge him for a password. He didn't know how to respond, which made him a likely target for a nervous sentry. To preclude being shot, he needed to respond in an appropriate manner.

As he approached a barricade, the sun was hanging low in the sky, but certainly there was enough daylight remaining that he could be identified. Even the dumbest sentry would know the enemy was not going to try to infiltrate during daylight hours. But after days of continuous bombardment in Yorktown, the brightest of sentries might not be willing to take a chance with anyone outside the perimeter approaching.

When he was twenty feet from the barricade, a voice from within called out, "Halt! Who goes there?"

"Sergeant John Robert Daniel, D Company, North Carolina Volunteers."

"What is the password?"

"Orders from Captain Junius B. Whitaker."

Then a familiar voice replied, "Well, you're late. Get your sorry ass in here, Sergeant Papa John."

No sooner than the words were said, Luke appeared from around the barricade. John jumped from his saddle and ran to embrace Luke like his long-lost brother.

Two other men removed some of the barricades so John and Bolt could enter. Once all were safely behind the barricade, Luke was the first to speak, and the words came flowing like a horrific waterfall. "You have missed all the action. We just got the crap kicked out of us in Yorktown, and unless a decision is made soon, it's gonna happen again."

"Any of our guys been hurt?" asked John.

"Yeah. Two were killed from the third platoon, and Paul got some shrapnel from one of the cannonball explosions. Nothing serious, but you know Paul. He's proud of being wounded. Says it makes him feel like he has been in combat."

"Can you take me to the captain?"

"Sure, Sarge, just follow me. Tell me how you've been. The last time I saw you was when Paul and I put you in the hospital."

On the way to the building where the captain had established his command post, John brought Luke current on all he had been through, including being detailed to the fortification work being done around Richmond.

Luke's only response was "General Johnston must be expecting one hell of a battle. I never thought of us as ever having to be on the run, and here we are in our first battle, retreating toward Richmond. The damn Yankees have outnumbered us more than anyone here ever expected."

"Luke, I need you to take me to Captain Whitaker," said John.

"Follow me," said Luke.

Captain Whitaker had made his command post in the back office of a mercantile store in the heart of Williamsburg. Luke led John through the store to a closed door in the rear of the store and said, "He's in there."

John gave three solid raps on the door. Inside, a tired voice said, "Enter."

John stepped in, saluted, and said, "Sir, Sergeant John Robert Daniel reporting as ordered."

A haggard-looking face looked up at John. John had never seen the captain look so tired. He looked as if he had aged twenty years. A smile appeared on his tired face. Probably his first smile since before the battle at Yorktown. The captain asked, "How in the hell did you get through McClellan's army? I thought he had us surrounded after the pounding we took at Yorktown."

John smiled and said, "It's good to see you also, sir. I thought orders were meant to be obeyed."

Captain Whitaker jumped up from his desk and rounded it to give John a bear hug. He said, "It's good to see you again, my ole friend, but I just can't believe you made it here without some difficulty."

John said, "Sir, if we can sit down, I'll take you through what I encountered." He then told of the two scouts who were positioned to provide notice of any flanking movement by the Southern army and how he had subdued them. But more importantly, as far as he could tell, there was open passage all the way to Richmond.

Whitaker said, "That's great news. Come with me. I want you to share that with General Johnston's executive officer." As Whitaker, John, and Luke exited the mercantile store, they could hear cannon fire in the direction of Yorktown and explosions hitting the eastern edge of Williamsburg.

As they hurried toward the general's command post, Whitaker said, "I believe McClellan has discovered we are no longer in Yorktown, and he is planning to pursue us until we are completely destroyed."

General Johnston's exec found Sergeant Daniel's report to be welcome news. He wanted John to immediately share it with General Johnston, which John did. Johnston's first decision was to withdraw his main body of soldiers back to the city of Richmond to regroup and decide their future actions. He would leave behind a battery of artillery to fire upon McClellan's advance so as to give the impression of a plan to hold Williamsburg at all costs. Once the main body had cleared Williamsburg, the artillery would withdraw to join up with the main body. If all went as planned, he should have the protection of Richmond within a couple of days. He was confident McClellan did not have the forces to lay siege to Richmond. He then thanked John by saying, "Sergeant, your information may have saved us to fight another day."

As Whitaker, John, and Luke were departing the general's office, they could hear him yelling for his staff.

By nightfall, Johnston's forces were on the move toward Richmond. Since Sergeant Daniel had already traveled the planned withdrawal route, Captain Whitaker was told to provide the point scouts for the advance party. For Captain Whitaker, that was the easiest task he had been given since they had left Richmond almost two months ago. He said, "Sergeant Daniel, find you a third scout, and you and Luke cut us a route to Richmond."

John turned to Luke and, said, "Is Paul fit to ride?"

Luke's reply was "He will be when he learns you have the lead."

CHAPTER 12

SEVEN PINES

By May 12, 1862, General Johnston had his forces safely within the confines of Richmond. But he soon found another immediate command decision was required. General McClellan, upon discovering Johnston had successfully withdrawn from Williamsburg and was secure in Richmond, altered his plans and moved northwesterly to link back up with other elements of the Union Army of the Potomac.

General Johnston's scouts had no problem detecting that McClellan's forces were going to bypass Richmond. However, Johnston interpreted this action by McClellan as a plan to strengthen his army and then launch a major attack upon Richmond from the north.

Johnston was now in a stronger position to counter McClellan because by early May, the Fourth North Carolina Regiment was fully constituted and under the command of Lieutenant Colonel Bryan Grimes. Grimes had been promoted and assumed command of the Fourth Regiment when Colonel George B. Anderson was elevated to brigade commander.

Fully formed, the Fourth Regiment consisted of ten companies totaling 520 men and twenty-five officers. At that time, North Carolina had formed approximately sixty infantry regiments with four to six regiments per brigade. North Carolina also had cavalry regiments and artillery regiments they provided to the war effort.

General Johnston decided to move the main body of his forces from Richmond through Manassas, where he could acquire additional forces, and then make his stand at the village of Seven Pines, Virginia. Seven Pines was approximately twelve miles northeast of Manassas.

A second decision Johnston made was received with mixed feelings by the men of the North Carolina Fourth Regiment. Johnston decided, based upon the Fourth Regiment's outstanding performance both at Yorktown and Williamsburg, that the Fourth would spearhead the assault into McClellan's forces. In Johnston's explanation to Lieutenant Colonel Grimes, he said, "Your boys proved themselves to be well trained and disciplined fighters at both Yorktown and Williamsburg. I believe the Fourth is the regiment to lead the way against McClellan at Seven Pines. Considering your boys were outnumbered and under siege, they still gave much better accounting for themselves than what they received."

Although Grimes acknowledged his men had done extremely well in their first encounter with the enemy, he viewed Johnston's words as a way of putting a positive spin on what Grimes saw to be a retreat. Now, it was left to him to advise the Fourth of the honor Johnston had bestowed upon his men.

The news that the Fourth Regiment was going to be at the forefront of the next battle was met with much exuberance and excitement by many of the men. They felt they had, in their first test, proven themselves to be worthy of the honor bestowed upon them by General Johnston.

While some of the men cheered about what they were going to do to the Yankees the next time the two forces met, others, like Captain Whitaker and Sergeant Daniel, were not jubilant. Captain Whitaker, having been trained at West Point in military strategy and tactics, could visualize the horror of men standing face-to-face and firing at one another until one side had killed more than the other to win the day.

Although Sergeant Daniel had never studied military strategy and tactics, he was well educated in forty-four years of experience. He knew that with the Fourth as the spearhead and the high probability that D Company would be the tip of the spear, only God knew what casualties the regiment would take. And he seriously doubted that many from D Company would survive. And those who did would most likely have life-threatening wounds. Logic to Daniel seemed to be to establish a perimeter of defense and invite the Northern army to try to penetrate. Cover and concealment would provide some protection. But for all these good young men to charge headfirst into a wall of lead defied all logic to Sergeant Daniel.

As is the case in battles fought in any war, logic and reason are seldom conveyed to the foot soldier. The siege at Yorktown and Williamsburg was Johnston's strategy to slow and repulse the Army of the Potomac from any advancement toward Richmond. With the Army of the Potomac only miles from Richmond, Confederate President Jefferson Davis, upon the advice of his military adviser, General Robert E. Lee, demanded action by Johnston to prevent any further advancement toward Richmond. All indications were that the Fourth Corps of the Union army was already on the move toward Seven Pines.

Johnston accomplished his movement back to Manassas by foot, train, horseback, and wagons. No attempt was made to cover their movement by traveling only at night. Johnston knew the massive movement of his forces would easily be detected by McClellan spies and scouts.

From Manassas, Johnston's forces traveled either by foot, horseback, or wagon. The mission was to get to Seven Pines as quickly as possible, establish a perimeter of defense with some hasty fortifications, get his men and artillery in place, and be prepared to launch an attack on General Erasmus D. Keyes's Fourth Corps no later than May 29. The Fourth Corps was alone south of the Chickahominy River. If all went according to Johnston's plan, he would shatter the Fourth Corps and then launch an attack on Third Corps.

On the evening of May 29, Sergeant Daniel was alone in his tent cleaning his weapons for the third time. The planned attack was scheduled for daybreak, with the Fourth leading the charge. D Company would be in the center sector of the regiment. Daniel knew this might well be his last night on this earth. He had written a long letter to Becky and the family and placed it with his personal effects. Should he die, she would find the letter in his personal effects when they were sent to her.

As Sergeant Daniel sat on his cot, deep in his thoughts and cleaning his revolver, the flap to his tent snapped open, and in walked Paul. He immediately blurted out, "Have you heard the latest news?"

Daniel looked up saw Paul and others following him. He said, "Tell me McClellan has surrendered!"

"Naw. The news is not that good, but we'll not be attacking tomorrow."

"Why not?" asked Daniel.

"What I heard was that General G. W. Smith, Commander of the Army of Northern Virginia, has failed to get in his position, which has caused a twenty-four-hour delay. Word is General Johnston is raging mad."

"Well, from my view, that is not exactly good news. I am for getting on with what has to be done. Delaying only gives the Fourth Corps more time to prepare for us, and it gives us another day to roll this battle around in our minds," said Daniel.

By now there were at least a dozen soldiers crowded into Sergeant Daniel's tent. A little puzzled, Daniel asked, "Now, to what do I owe this gathering? Certainly it was not just to bring me that news."

Luke, more the thinker in the group, spoke up. "Sergeant Papa John, we're worried about what to expect—and how we'll respond. You know, in both Yorktown and Williamsburg, we were holding ground and defending our position. We have never been in a major battle where we were the attacking force."

John studied the group before him. He could see anxiety and fear in every eye. He also knew exactly what they were feeling because he had never been in any battle, either on the defense or in the attack. But he had also come to accept the fact that he had become the father figure for many of the boys. He could see they were anxiously awaiting some fatherly advice.

John laid his rifle aside, leaned forward on his cot, and, after making eye contact with every member of the group, said, "Men, I share your concerns. I have never experienced any battle. Not even Yorktown or Williamsburg, like you did. But in those engagements, you demonstrated the heart of a soldier beats in your chest. You fought with courage and all your energy, and you came to know the brotherhood you share with one another.

"Yes, this battle will be much different. You are being depended upon to lead a charge that will culminate in a major victory for the South. During that charge, as you see your enemy soldier falling before you,

you will see and know your fellow soldiers are falling beside you. And although you will want to stop to help your brother, he understands and wants you to continue your advance until you achieve victory. You must believe that if either you or your brother is wounded, the stretcher-bearers of the medical corps will be there to recover you and get you to an aid station. We all must remember to keep putting one foot forward until we receive a different command or hear the bugle that signals our withdrawal. You have been trained to make every bullet count, and I believe you will do so."

There was a moment of silence. John could see the young boys were pondering his words while at the same time appearing to have accepted their fate.

It was Paul who broke the silence. "Sergeant, will we be seen as cowards if during the advance we seek refuge behind trees or fallen debris?"

"Paul, you have been taught how to seek cover and concealment. To seek the advantage of a firing position is not being a coward. You are still standing your ground and firing. A coward is one who quits firing, turns, and runs toward the rear for safety. I am certain there is not one of you who will not conduct himself in an honorable and brave manner when the time comes. Do any others have any questions?"

All nodded a negative response.

Sergeant John Robert Daniel, with a reassuring smile on his face, said, "Fellows, know that I will be with you when the time comes. Fight for your family, for the brother next to you, and for self-determination of the South. It is my prayer that after the battle, we can regroup here to celebrate and discuss a great victory for D Company, the Fourth Regiment, and our Confederate army. Good luck, and may God watch over and protect you."

"Ma, you gotta read this!" exclaimed William as he burst through the front door of their house. He was clutching in his hand a newspaper. He had returned from Adamsville, where he had taken some sugar cane to be made into syrup. He said, "While in Adamsville, I picked up a copy of *A Daily Bulletin.*" That was Goldsboro's daily newspaper.

"Well, you see I'm up to my elbows in flour, so why don't you read to me what you want me to know?" said Becky.

William began. "The headline reads, 'Wayne County Men Defend Yorktown and Williamsburg, Virginia.' Here is the article: 'The Fourth Regiment of the North Carolina Volunteers demonstrated tremendous courage and valor as they defended both Yorktown and Williamsburg from horrific bombardment by General McClellan's Army of the Potomac. Although outnumbered and lacking sufficient artillery support, the Fourth endured constant bombardment from April 5 to May 4, 1862. They successfully repulsed every attempt to break through their lines while suffering light casualties. On May 5, the regiment withdrew to defend Williamsburg. It is suspected that General Johnston, commander of the Confederate forces, believed McClellan was going to feint a siege on Williamsburg and then attack Richmond. Accordingly, General Johnston surprised McClellan by withdrawing his forces to defend Richmond.' Now, Ma, here is the good part. 'It was reported that Sergeant John Robert Daniel of Saulston, North Carolina, guided General Johnston's Army on a route around McClellan's scouts back to Richmond without incident.' Ma, they're talking about Pa! He is a hero!"

A large smile came upon Becky's face. She said, "I believe you are right, William. And more importantly, it tells us your father is safe and sound. That is probably the reason we haven't received a letter lately. He's been just too busy."

"But Ma, doesn't that make you proud of Pa?"

"It does, William, but I have always been proud of your Pa. He is a man who I hope you will grow up to be like. After you read the article to the others tonight at the dinner table, I want to cut it out of the paper and place it in our family Bible. When he gets back home, he can read what has made the people in Wayne County so proud of him."

William laid the paper on the top of the bread box near the back door, and with a spring in his step and a heart about to jump out of his chest, he went out the back door to check on the chores he had left the others to do while he was in Adamsville.

At four in the morning of May 31, the early morning quiet was filled with the sounds of cannon fire and explosions in the distance. This was the signal that Johnston was just about to launch a full attack.

It was not long before one could hear cannon fire in the distance and explosions just outside the Southern army's perimeter of defense. For the veterans of Yorktown and Williamsburg, the incoming cannon fire was a familiar sound.

All were dressed and equipped to do battle. Some moved closer to the defense perimeter to view the fireworks. All could feel the ground shake as the cannonballs hit the earth and exploded. Some of the cannonballs were aimed high to cut the tops off trees.

As the thunderous noise continued to hammer the air waves, the men of the Fourth began to move to their predesignated positions to await the order to fall into formation and prepare to engage the enemy.

The waiting was the hard part. Some began to question if they should not slip out of the battle behind the main force while so much attention was focused toward the enemy. Sergeant Daniel knew there was always the possibility a man would decide he couldn't charge into the jaws of death. So he walked continuously among the soldiers, offering reassurance, vigilant for the one who might decide to leave, and mentally taking a count to ensure all of the ones he was responsible for were present.

Approximately an hour before the sun appeared above the horizon, the men were ordered into formation and to check their weapons to ensure they were fully charged and ready to fire. The first echelon was ordered to fix bayonets. To avoid an accidental stabbing of a soldier in the back, the other echelons would only be ordered to fix bayonets prior to the order to charge.

As streaks of light from the still-hidden sun began to appear upon the horizon, Lieutenant Colonel Grimes was seen trotting his colorful Appaloosa horse the length of the first echelon of the Fourth Regiment. He was leading 25 officers and 520 enlisted men to the field. He had nothing more to say to the men; his focus appeared to be on the battle that lay before him.

Captain Whitaker, likewise, was riding his horse the length of the first echelon of D Company. Unlike Grimes, Whitaker was continuously shouting words of encouragement. His frequently repeated words were "Men! Give the Yanks a reason to remember D Company!"

Sergeant John Robert Daniel looked across an open field of two to three hundred yards into an ocean of blue coats. As far as the eye could see, from left to right was a line of soldiers, shoulder to shoulder.

The length of the echelon of gray coats was also as far as Sergeant Daniel could see in either direction. However, one glance was all he needed because his focus was to his front. To his left was the hard-charging, do-or-die Paul, and to his right the constantly thinking and maneuvering Luke. John knew he could not be in better company on this day. He prayed that at the end of the day all three would be able to reassemble and once again enjoy one another's fellowship.

Then John heard the order from Captain Whitaker: "Port arms!" That was the command for all to bring their weapons up to chest level. Whitaker then wheeled his horse in the direction of the enemy and commanded, "Forward march!" There was no turning back now.

As the gray line advanced, so did the blue line. The distance between the two armies was closing. From the corner of John's eye, it appeared the left flank of the gray line was ahead of the remainder of the gray line. In his mind, if there was not either a coordination or communication problem, the staggered alignment must be a strategy to try to roll up the right flank of the Army of the Potomac. Rolling up the right flank would cause the outer perimeter of the Northern army to maneuver more toward the center of the killing zone. But that was not John's immediate problem. His attention was to focus upon when the first shot was fired.

He did not have to wait long, because when the two armies were separated by approximately one hundred yards, the blue coats opened fire. Simultaneously, their cannons began to bellow, and the swish of cannonballs could be heard passing overhead, followed by explosions in the rear echelons.

Cannon fire from Johnston's artillery responded. Again, John could hear the sound of cannonballs passing over his head and exploding to his front. In between rifle fire and cannon fire, he heard Whitaker order "Charge! Fire at will!"

As he ran forward, firing and trying to make every round hit an enemy soldier, he lost sight of Paul and Luke. His conscious mind stayed focused on what was in front of him. To his right he saw Captain Whitaker and his horse go down. Although he had told the others to avoid rendering aid to a fallen comrade because that was what they would have wanted, he could not help but rush to the aid of Captain Whitaker.

When he reached Captain Whitaker, he found him lying between the front and rear hooves of his horse. The horse was dead. Whitaker was still conscious but with a severe wound in his side.

Whitaker mumbled, "Sergeant, leave me! Stay with the men!"

John, with his revolver in his right hand, used his left to push Whitaker as close to the horse's belly as possible. He then said, "Yes, sir! Don't move. I'll be back for you."

Seeing the horse's belly give in slightly, John looked up to see a blue coat standing on the horse and pointing his bayonet in John's direction. Instantly, John fired his revolver into the face of the Yankee soldier. The soldier dropped his rifle and fell upon the horse's neck. John grabbed the dead soldier and pulled him across the horse's neck so that half of the soldier's body was covering Whitaker's upper body. Hopefully, the two bodies intertwined would convey the impression the two had killed each other.

No sooner than he had cleared the dead horse, he picked up his rifle and, using its stock, parried a bayonet lunge toward him and fired his revolver, killing the Yankee.

By now there was no integrity in the forces. Soldiers from various companies and brigades were mingled together. John could hear no one communicating commands, and there appeared to be no orchestrated coordination of the forces. It was as if every man was for himself. By midday, John had used up all his ammunition and was using his rifle as a club and his hunting knife as an instrument of death. At the point of total exhaustion and no longer seeing any members of D Company, he heard the bugle sound for the lead forces to withdraw to regroup and resupply ammunition.

Disengagement from the enemy was difficult because reinforcements seemed to be slow in arriving. However, within twenty minutes John had fought his way into a more secure rear element. There, mostly what he saw were aid stations packed with wounded soldiers. Some men were grabbing a quick bite to eat, and others were drawing more ammunition from the arms wagon. He grabbed a slab of beef jerky, reloaded his rifle and his ammunition pouch, and grabbed bandages to put over the cut place in his left thigh and left side. Apparently the soldier who cut him in the side had gotten lucky and also stabbed him in the thigh. John did not recall receiving either of the wounds. The battle was so intense and his adrenaline was pumping so fast he did not realize he was wounded until returning to the rear and seeing the blood.

In the short time John was in the rear, he observed what appeared to be a confused command structure. He heard rumors that reinforcements were delayed because of the three main thoroughfares being jammed. Apparently, General D. H. Hill's assault had been delayed by General James Longstreet changing the plan of attack he had agreed to with General Johnston. Further evidence of a confused army was when Hill, around 1:00 p.m., launched an attack without knowing whether other elements of the Confederate army had reached their designated positions.

John, after his short pause, reentered the battle, stepping over dead bodies and wounded soldiers crying for help. This time he took his own advice he had given the men in his tent two nights before: "It's not cowardly to seek a protective firing position." And this he did.

From a depression in the ground made by an exploding cannonball that also brought down a pine tree across the leading edge of the sunken depression, John made his stand. He was determined no Yankee soldier would either make it to his position or bypass his position. He also resolved every shot would take down an enemy soldier.

Around 3:00 p.m. the firing began to subside. It was later learned this had resulted from General Hill's successful assault upon Union division commander Silas Casey's division. This caused the Union army to pull back to its firing pits, giving the Confederate army the relief it needed to regroup and prepare to resume the battle tomorrow. Besides, General Hill's men had run out of steam.

As the Confederate army disengaged from the battle, John began to seek out Captain Whitaker. After an hour of bending low and moving quickly across a battlefield scattered with dead and wounded soldiers and litter bearers attempting to recover the wounded, John spotted Whitaker's dead horse.

He rushed to the horse, where he found Captain Whitaker just as he had left him earlier, with the dead Union soldier draped over him. John rolled the dead soldier off the captain and, to his surprise, found Whitaker still alive but critically wounded. Without waiting for a litter bearer, John gathered up the captain, placed him on his shoulders, and started walking as fast as he could toward the nearest aid station. He was instructed to place the captain on the ground, and a doctor would see him as soon as possible. The captain was not conscious, but, John still told him that he would return to check on him. For now he wanted to find what remained of D Company.

John, while needing some medical attention himself, knew he must find the boys who had sought his advice two nights before the battle. After two hours of searching among the living, he found only ten men who were assigned to the Fourth. He found only one assigned to D Company and none that he had talked with two evenings ago. The one he found from D Company said he thought he had seen Luke in the aid station, but he wasn't sure because of the extent of the soldier's injuries. John returned to the aid station to walk among the wounded.

Back at the aid station, the ground was littered with soldiers moaning and crying for help. The litter bearers, exhausted and covered in blood, continued to come in from the battlefield with the bodies of wounded soldiers. John walked slowly among the wounded. Periodically, when he recognized a soldier from the Fourth, he would stop to try to offer some words of comfort and encouragement. And if the soldier was able to speak, John would ask about Paul or Luke. None could remember seeing either during the battle.

As John was just about to give up his hunt, he spoke to one more soldier. The soldier responded, "I haven't seen either of the two."

It was then that John heard a low voice, behind him, straining to speak. "Is that Papa John?"

Turning toward the weak but familiar voice, and with tears of joy in his eyes, John looked down upon what was left of Luke. Luke's head was bandaged, with only his right eye visible. His body was also bandaged, but his left arm was missing above the elbow. John could not see below Luke's waist, as he was partially covered with a blanket.

John dropped to his knees and said, "I'm here, Luke."

A comforting smile appeared on Luke's face. He asked with sincere emotional concern, "Papa John, are you all right?"

"Yes, Luke, I am fine."

"I knew you would be. I wish I could have stayed closer to you. It was like one minute you were there, and then you were gone. I thought you must have been hit."

"No, I am just fine. Do you know what happened to Paul?"

"No. He was like you—one minute he was next to me, and then gone."

"Don't worry, Luke. I'll find him. With all the turmoil and confusion, he may well be with another company right now."

"Have you seen any of our other guys?"

Not wanting to burden Luke with worry about the others, John lied. "Yeah, there are a few of us still walking around. I suspect there are a few more somewhere here at the aid station. I have not been completely around the compound."

"If you see any, give them my best wishes."

"I will, Luke. Now, you just concentrate on getting better, and I'll be back to see you. I'm going to see if I can find Paul."

"Okay. Tell him to come see me, if he can."

"I will!" John brushed his hand across Luke's forehead, much like he had done many times before with William. John knew now the only place he had not looked was among the dead on the battlefield. It was now dark, and to be out there with any light was to be asking for a bullet.

❧

The morning of June 1, 1862, began with bad news for the Confederate army. The men learned that the previous evening around nightfall, General Johnston had been gravely injured by a Union shell. It was reported that General Johnston was riding behind Confederate lines making a personal inspection when he was warned he was riding dangerously close to the front lines. He is alleged to have replied, "Colonel, there is no use dodging; when you hear them they have passed." Almost immediately thereafter, an artillery shell burst in the air, throwing fragments into Johnston's chest and thigh. With Johnston gravely wounded, General G. W. Smith temporarily assumed command of the Confederate army.

The remnants of the North Carolina Fourth Regiment were assigned under the command of General D. H. Hill. At 6:45 a.m. General Hill renewed his attack against the Army of the Potomac. The battle went much the same as the previous day.

Likewise, Sergeant Daniel resumed his role in the battle much like he left it the previous day. He took every advantage of the natural cover and tried to ensure each of his firing positions offered cover and concealment. He ensured no enemy soldier was close enough to require hand-to-hand combat.

At 1:30 p.m. President Jefferson Davis arrived at Confederate headquarters and informed Smith that General Robert E. Lee would take command of the army. It was later reported that Smith resigned due to illness.

By 2:00 p.m. neither army had made any headway. Both armies withdrew, and the battle was deemed to be a stalemate. The Union army had 5,031 casualties (790 killed, 3,594 wounded and 647 captured or missing). The Confederate army had 6,134 casualties (980 killed, 4,749 wounded, and 405 captured or missing). The Battle of Seven Pines was over.

For the North Carolina Fourth Regiment, the battle was a disaster. The regiment went into battle with 520 men and 25 officers, who became known as "the noble 545." When the battle ended, 24 officers had been either killed or wounded. Lieutenant Colonel Grimes was the only officer not injured. With respect to the enlisted men, 462 men were either killed or wounded. This battle was considered to be the bloodiest charge of the war for the North Carolina Fourth Regiment.

Captain Whitaker survived, as did Luke. Both were medically discharged and returned home. Paul's body was never known to be recovered.

John continued to serve as a member of Anderson's Brigade, which was assigned to Hill's Division of the Army of Northern Virginia.

CHAPTER 13

SEVEN DAYS BATTLES

The Seven Days Battles were a series of seven battles over seven days, with the first battle being the beginning of the end of the Peninsula Campaign. They also presented some much-needed decisive victories for the new commanding general of the Confederate army, General Robert E. Lee.

From June 3 to June 24, John had the opportunity to get some rest and renew his energy. He very much missed his friendships with Paul, Luke, and Captain Whitaker. He knew that both Luke and Whitaker were safe and secure in Richmond hospitals recovering from their wounds. Hopefully, before too much longer, they would be returning to their homes in North Carolina.

Of course, he still had worries about Paul. Knowing how tough Paul was, he could not reconcile himself to the possibility that Paul was dead. He wanted to believe Paul had survived and was now a prisoner of war. And, maybe, just maybe, all could be reunited after this war.

John also took the opportunity to write another letter to Becky. He had been away from his family near on a year now and still had not heard anything from them. But he could only blame himself for that because he had adamantly discouraged attempts to write him since he never knew where he was going to be or how long he would be there.

So on a mid-June day, while in Richmond, John took pen in hand and wrote,

> My dearest Becky and family,
>
> Sorry I haven't written you in a while, but I suppose if the news is making its way to Saulston, you know I have been very busy. While I am safe and without injuries, I can tell you the battle at Seven Pines was worse than anything that you may have read in the newspapers. I lost some dear friends, but fortunately, two of my best friends, while seriously wounded, will recover and be returning to North Carolina. Now, don't yawl go worrying about me because I have found my age has given me the experience to remain safe. I pray for all of you each night and for there to be a good harvest this year. I know William will do everything he can to make sure that happens. Hope this war ends quickly and I will be home soon.
>
> Your loving husband and father,
> John.

After asking lots of questions and aggravating the brigade surgeon, he finally learned that both Whitaker and Luke were in Chimboraza Hospital Number 1 in Richmond. John found Bolt walking around in circles in the corral. He put a saddle on him and said, "Big fellow, you ready to take me to visit some friends?"

When John arrived at the hospital, he discovered his friends were in separate wards. Whitaker was in a recovery ward, and Luke was in a rehabilitation ward for those who had lost limbs. He decided to visit Luke first.

When he entered Luke's ward, a nurse was kind enough to escort him to where Luke was walking with a limp around his bed. John approached from Luke's left side. Luke did not see John until John spoke. "Private, don't you go strain yourself!"

John's voice startled Luke, causing him to turn around so quickly he lost his balance and would have fallen had John not grabbed him. When Luke looked into John's face, tears started to roll down his left cheek, and the two brothers of war embraced each other.

After stifling a sniffle, Luke said, "I prayed you made it out of that hellhole alive. I was beginning to feel guilty that I might have been the only one to survive." Luke continued, bubbling over with questions. "Did you find Paul? What happened to the captain? I saw him when he went down. Did anyone else…"

"Hold on a second, Luke. I'll try to answer your questions. But first, you need to sit down on your bed, and I'll get a chair," replied John.

Before John could finish his sentence, the nurse had a chair for him. She then commented, "Please stay awhile, Sergeant. He's already said more to you than any of us here."

After backing Luke up to the bed and ensuring he was seated, John sat down. "Now you just sit there and listen, and I'll tell you what I know."

It was quite apparent to John that he had Luke's undivided attention. "First, others did survive. As a matter of fact, I don't think Lieutenant Colonel Grimes got a scratch, and he was in the center of the whole mess. With respect to Paul, I have not been able to locate him, but you know Paul. He may well have been captured and will serve out the war comfortably in a prisoner-of-war camp. With respect to Captain Whitaker, he is here in this hospital, just a few wards from you. I don't know the extent of his injuries. He was unconscious when I left him at the aid station, but he had a wound in the right side of his chest. I plan to see him after my visit with you. I'll let him know where you are."

After an hour of talking, the nurse reappeared and tapped John on the shoulder and said, "Sergeant, he needs to get some rest now."

Luke said, "Please don't let him go yet!"

John said, "The nurse knows best. I'll try to see you again before too much longer. Should I not get back, know it is because orders have moved me to another location."

John then gave Luke a bear hug and departed to visit with the captain.

The captain was sitting up in bed when John entered his ward. He must have been watching the doorway because as soon as John entered, he heard the captain say, "Sergeant Daniel, get over here right now!"

John hurried over to the captain, who had his right arm in a sling; rendered a salute; and said, "Reporting as ordered, sir!"

"The hell with that saluting and that 'sir' bull crap. You give me a hug. I owe you my life."

John had never seen this side of Captain Whitaker, and he wasn't sure about how friendly he should be with him. But orders were orders, so he gave the captain a bear hug.

The captain continued. "Pull up a chair, and tell me what is going on, John...you don't mind if I call you John, do you?"

"No sir...Captain."

"By the way, my name is Junius...all my friends back home call me JB, but for the man who saved my life, you can call me anything you like."

"Okay...JB."

"Now tell me what happened after fragments from that cannonball killed my horse and almost killed me."

John told him the whole story, including leaving him on the battlefield all day covered by a Yankee soldier.

The captain laughed and said, "Hell, if I knew the name of that Yankee soldier, I'd write his mama a letter thanking her for her son's protection."

Finally, John got to ask, "JB...it appears you're doing well, but what was the extent of your injuries?"

Again Whitaker laughed. "Enough to keep me out of the rest of this war. Fragments from the cannonball broke my right arm just below my shoulder, broke several ribs, punctured my right lung, and ripped a hole in my belly. Other than that, I am doing well. Now you tell me about our company."

"Wasn't much left of our company, JB. All the officers in our regiment, except for Lieutenant Colonel Grimes, were either killed or injured. I have only been able to find five members of our company that survived. You remember Private Luke Brown, one of your Biblical Three? He's over in ward four. He lost his left eye and left arm. I told him you were here, and he is hoping you will visit with him. Paul, the other member of the Biblical Three, has not been located. I'm hoping he was captured and is being held as a prisoner of war."

"I hope you're right, John. And yes, I will make a point to visit with Private Brown tomorrow."

After another thirty minutes of chatting, John could see the captain was tiring. He left the captain with the same words he had left with Luke. "If I don't come back in a week or so, know that I have been ordered to a new location."

John could not leave without rendering a salute.

The captain smiled weakly and returned the salute and said, "Hope to see you again soon, John."

ⅆ

On Wednesday, June 25, 1862, the first day of the Seven Days Battle began. It commenced with a minor battle in Oak Grove, Virginia, which is approximately fifty miles northeast of Richmond. Lee's army hit McClellan hard and seized the initiative, forcing McClellan to retreat to Beaver Creek Damn, near Mechanicsville, Virginia, on June 26.

With Lee still applying pressure, McClellan was forced to retreat seven miles farther south to Cold Harbor, where, on June 27, the Battle of Gaines Mill took place.

As McClellan focused upon defending his positions at Garnett's and Golding's Farms, Lee outmaneuvered McClellan and attacked his rear guard at Savage's Station on June 29. Still unable to establish a stand against Lee, by June 30, McClellan had withdrawn his forces to Glendale, Virginia, where Lee pounded him at Nelson's Farm.

On July 1, McClellan had finally retreated to what became his safe haven, Malvern Hill. Malvern Hill was about twelve miles southeast of Richmond and about two and a half miles north of the James River, with modest elevation. This position gave McClellan a clear advantage for a defensive position. Not only did he have elevation to his advantage, but sloping open fields lay to his front, providing excellent fields of fire. Just as importantly, to his rear was the James River and the United States Navy. With his artillery on the crest of the hill and seventy thousand infantry in reserve on the back side of the hill, McClellan welcomed any attempt by the Confederate army to push him any farther.

Lee quickly recognized McClellan's advantage, and in coordination with General James Longstreet, there was an attempt to suppress the Union artillery batteries.

When the Confederate bombardment failed, Lee's infantry attacked in a series of charges. Every attempt failed as the Union artillery proved to be dominant over the Confederate infantry. After six days without success, frustration set in among both the officers and the enlisted soldiers.

Sergeant Daniel, now appointed as a platoon sergeant, felt, in addition to frustration, anger at what he viewed to be a lack of recognition of the advantage held by the Union forces. He was being directed to order his men to charge up a hill and across open ground into artillery fire. It might have been different if they were charging against other infantrymen, but it seemed only those making the charge understood that only effective artillery could kill artillery, and on this day, Lee's army did not have effective artillery.

The primary reason for the Confederate lack of effective artillery was their location at the base of a hill that had a gradual upward slope for at least a quarter of a mile. This meant the infantry, attacking uphill, had virtually no artillery support, whereas Union artillery was its primary defense. In the final analysis, one-third of the Union army defeated a large part of the Confederate army.

By the end of the second day, Lee realized that while he could not claim a victory, neither could McClellan. However, the casualty count told a different story. The Union casualty count was three thousand killed or wounded, whereas the Confederate count was five thousand killed or wounded.

The Seven Days Battles had covered an area from the north of Richmond around its eastern side to the southeast of Richmond.

Disappointed with the outcome, Lee withdrew his troops to Richmond. Likewise, Sergeant Daniel, after seeing the Yankees on the run for six days, was now returning to Richmond with his fellow soldiers, like dogs with their tails between their legs. The only bright spot for him was in the seven days of fighting. His platoon had only three men injured, and none of their wounds were life threatening.

Still under the command of now Colonel Grimes, Sergeant Daniel's platoon, in the reconstructed D Company, participated in a number of skirmishes but no significant battles from the end of July until early September. When it appeared Richmond had become his primary location when not in battle, John wrote and told Becky she could write to him there.

In mid-August, 1862, John received his first letter from Becky and one from William. Becky's letter read.

> My Dearest John,
>
> I hope this finds you well and safe. Periodically, there are articles in Goldsboro's *Daily Bulletin* about the 4th Regiment. There was an article about you leading the army from Williamsburg to Richmond. Everyone in Saulston and, I believe, Wayne County, is proud of you. We also read of the serious battle at Seven Pines and of the tremendous loss of men. We were relieved to read you were one of the survivors and were very sorry your captain was seriously injured. Please promise me you will continue to be safe. We pray every night the war will be over soon and you will be coming back home to us. Remember our love and prayers are with you and that we are all doing well.
>
> Forever,
> Your loving Becky and family.
>
> P.S. William is also viewed as a hero in Saulston. He captured a wanted man and earned himself a handsome reward. I'll let him tell you about that.

John's heart was warmed to hear from his family and was curious as to how William had captured a wanted man. He quickly tore into William's letter. It read,

Dear Pa,

Pleased to tell you our crops look great this year. I did hire a couple of boys to help me with last year's harvest. However, the two of them could not do the work you would have done. Pay no attention to what Ma said about me being a hero. I just did what you taught me to do. We had a drifter stop by the farm, and he tried to get too friendly with Nancy Ann. And when he started to pull his gun on me, I shot him in the arm. Sorry, Pa, I was aiming for his chest, and he turned at the wrong time and my bullet hit him above the elbow in his right arm. After I turned him in to the constable in Saulston, I learned there was a reward for his capture. I won't say in this letter how much it was, but I think it is enough to get me through law school. Now, don't you go worrying bout the family. I promise you I will keep them protected and keep the farm going like you would want me to. Stay safe, and don't go and try to be no more hero.

Your loving son,
William

As John laid William's letter down on his cot, he thought, "At fifteen, my William ain't no boy any longer…he's a man. Probably the best decision I ever made was to ensure he stayed at home to look after the family and the farm. I am so proud of him and hope he never has to see what this war is like. I know this experience will change the lives of all those who live through this experience. There will always be the memory of friends lost and the questions of whether or not I did the right thing at the right time. If I had done something differently, would some of the boys still be alive? Lord, I hope this ends soon. I don't know how much more I can take of the constant shelling, explosions, and seeing young boys never having the opportunity to fulfill their dreams. Surly there is someone who can see all this killing needs to end."

John picked up the two letters and read them one more time before he stuffed them into a box he kept under his bed. In a day or so, he would pull them out and read them again.

In late August Sergeant Daniel received word that Colonel Grimes, the regimental commander, wanted to see him immediately. He wasted no time in getting to Colonel Grimes's tent.

Upon entering, Daniel saw the colonel was not wasting time for the traditional changes of salute by directing, "Sergeant Daniel, take a seat. I'll get right down to business. I understand you have proven yourself as a plotter of routes of maneuver for army elements. Sources tell me you were able to find a route for General Johnston from Williamsburg without encountering enemy forces. That is my desire of you now. I need you, within the next three days, to find me a passage across the Potomac River somewhere near White's Point. I want to be able to move to and cross the river undetected. Think you can accomplish that in three days?"

"I can try, sir!"

"You have to do more than try. This is important for our next engagement. Take whoever and whatever you need to accomplish your task. Any questions?"

"Only one, sir. You're talking about a crossing that can be accomplished with a regiment-size movement?"

"That is correct. The next engagement will only involve the Fourth."

Daniel had already figured out that the urgency of the task eliminated the time it would take to employ inexperienced scouts whom he would have to train during the course of the mission. Accordingly, he replied, "Sir in light of the urgency, I will be traveling alone with only what I need for no more than three days."

"Fine. I anxiously await your report. You are dismissed."

Sergeant Daniel rendered a parting salute, but the general had too much on his mind to respond. On his way to the corral to get Bolt, John went by way of the mapping tent to get a sketch of the location of White's Point. He found it to be fifty miles northeast of Richmond.

Within the hour, Daniel, astride Bolt, was dressed in civilian clothes with his Confederate gray uniform in a waterproof bag inside one of his saddlebags. In the area he would be going, it would not be good to be seen in a Confederate uniform. In the other saddlebag, he had three days of rations. His bedroll was tied behind his saddle.

He rode hard that afternoon and into the night. He encountered no blue coats, arriving at 3:00 a.m. approximately two miles north of White Point. He decided to catch a quick nap before he approached White Point. From the map sketch he had acquired, he saw, although the crossing varied from a half to four miles in width, that it was the narrowest point along the Potomac River.

By 6:00 a.m. the sun was beginning to make an appearance, and he had already had a cup of coffee and hardtack for breakfast. Bolt was saddled and ready to travel.

John spent most of the day scouting out White Point. There he saw a ferry attached to a cable. Because of the swiftness of the current, the ferry required four men to control its movement across the river. To cross at this point would require Grimes to seize the ferry. The other problem was the ferry had significant traffic, which would require the regiment to capture those wanting to cross and retain them until all the regiment was across. The last thing they needed was for someone to spread the word to the Yankees, causing them to be trapped in a cross fire before reaching their objective, whatever that might be. Colonel Grimes had not shared that information with him.

After observing the activity around White's Point for half a day, John thought, "Farther up the river, there may be a crossing point with less traffic and less observation. It would be more to our advantage the less attention we can bring to our movement."

He then mounted Bolt and started moving west along the riverbank. After two miles he came to a place where the bank of the river jutted out into the river about fifty yards. Beyond that point, the river formed a small cove where the ground had a gentle slope down to the river. About a mile out into the river was a small island.

John could not determine from his current the width of the island, but he was thinking, "If the island slopes into the river from both sides, it may be that we can ford the river from the area of the cove to the island. Then from the island to the far side of the river. I guess there is only one way to find out."

He nudged Bolt to enter the cove and then into the water. John noticed the current was swifter than it appeared from the bank. Then it suddenly happened! As Bolt eased into the water and the water began to rise to his chest, he dropped instantly to where the water was up to his neck. The water was now to John's waist.

John immediately came out of the saddle so as not to add weight to Bolt, as both were trying to swim in the fast-moving current. The current was moving them toward the point that jutted out into the river. John experienced that anxious moment of knowing that if they bypassed the point, they would be taken into the middle of the river, where both would drown.

John placed the reins into his mouth and swam as hard as he could with Bolt right behind him. He aimed straight for the shore, knowing the current would continue to pull him into deeper water.

Apparently Bolt also sensed the urgency of their situation because he was also swimming toward the shore. John knew escaping the current and making it to the point was going to be close, but there was nothing else to do.

When the two were twenty feet from going around the point, Bolt's hooves struck the bottom leading up to the point. John, totally exhausted, reached out and grabbed onto his saddle horn. As Bolt continued to rise from the water, he dragged John with him.

Finally, they both were again on solid ground. John lay on the small beach the cove had formed, too tired to get up. Bolt shook his body, sending a shower of more water onto John. John couldn't have cared less. He thought, "We're safe. Shake all you want."

Bolt wasn't the only one shaking. Whereas he was shaking to rid himself of the water, John was shaking from the coldness of the river water. He finally lifted himself up, only to feel like every joint in his body was frozen.

After scrounging up some dry wood and stacking it for a fire, he pulled the saddle off Bolt. Then digging into his saddlebag with the gray uniform inside the waterproof bag, he found in one of his trouser pockets some dry matches. As soon as he had a fire going, he started to peel off his wet clothes. Naked and hovering over the fire, John put on his dry gray uniform. For now it felt good, but he knew it also made him a target for any Union soldier who might see him. He thought, "Getting shot might not be so bad if it will end this cold feeling."

By dark John had stopped shaking. The warmth from the fire gave him some renewed energy. Since he was tired from the lack of rest the previous day and night and from fighting the river current, he decided to spend the night in the cove, and tomorrow, during the daylight hours, he would scout a route back to Richmond—a route the regiment could travel to White's Point. Back in Richmond he would lay out some options for Colonel Grimes to consider.

The following day John set out thinking about the requirements of the route he needed to plot for Colonel Grimes. He was thinking, "I must find the shortest route having terrain for easy movement of soldiers and equipment. The route has to be sufficiently wide to permit the movement of a regiment as much as possible in a unit formation. And I need a route that allows for plenty of cover and concealment." He already knew from his ride to White's Point that there was plenty of cover and concealment the regiment could take advantage of.

When he was ten miles from the river, he spotted a small farmhouse. Since he was in his gray uniform, he knew he needed to skirt the house without being seen. Although Virginia was a Southern state, its border was with Maryland, a slave-holding state that did not secede from the Union but did have a number of sympathizers in the southern and eastern part of the state. From Maryland, a number of spies had infiltrated its neighboring state, Virginia.

Remaining in the shadows of the wood line, John skirted the house. He was almost around the house when he heard a woman's voice screaming for help.

Reining in Bolt, he looked toward the house and asked himself, "Do I get involved or keep riding?" He knew that getting involved was counter to his mission, but the screams sounded so desperate. But he was also reminded of William's letter in which a drifter had tried to get too friendly with Nancy Ann. He believed he had no choice but to investigate the scream for help.

Approaching the house from the front, he saw no one, but the screams were desperate with the repetition of, "Please don't do this. My husband is a soldier like you. Please, not in front of my children."

John quietly walked along the side of the house, and, after taking off his hat, peered around the corner. What he saw brought his blood to a boil.

The woman was lying on her back on the ground. One soldier was holding her wrists above her head. Another soldier was standing between her feet with his pants down to his knees. He was not wearing under-pants, so his naked butt was there for the world to see.

Nearby was a tree where two children, who appeared to be between the ages of five and eight years old, were holding each other and crying.

With all the commotion, John was not seen until he spoke. And he didn't speak until he was within twenty feet of the two men. Both were concentrating their attention on the woman lying on the ground with the top of her dress torn open, exposing her breasts.

John, with his revolver pointed at the man with his bare butt show-ing, said, in a calm and deliberate manner, "Let her go!"

The bare-butt man turned to see where the voice had come from. His pistol, still in its holster, was lying ten feet from him, where he had thrown it. He saw there was no way he could get to it without getting shot.

The man holding her wrists stared at John but didn't release his hold.

The bare-butt man said, "Hey, don't get all bent out of shape. There's enough here for all of us." A big grin came upon his face.

John pointed his revolver at the one holding the woman's wrists, and this time, in a tone that registered what he had meant the first time, said, "If you don't turn her loose now, I will put a bullet between your eyes!"

Glancing in the direction of the other man, John said, "And if you think for one minute you can make it to your pistol without tripping over your pants, go for it!"

The woman's wrists were released, but the man did not attempt to stand up. He was uncertain as to how any of his movements might be interpreted by the man with the gun.

The woman scrambled up from the ground, attempting to cover her breasts as she did so.

Never looking in her direction, but with his attention on the two attackers, John said, "Ma'am, take your children inside and lock the door. These two are just about to leave your farm. And please, once inside, don't look outside."

The woman gathered her children and raced for the house. When she was on the porch and had the children safely inside, she called out to John, "Thank you, kind sir! I will always remember what you have done."

John, looking at the disgusting sight before him, said, "And fellows, she is not the one that is going to be remembered. You, on the ground, get up, and with your left hand, unbuckle and drop your gun belt." John knew the man was right handed because he wore his pistol on his right side.

"Now, I want the both of you to walk a little closer to me."

The one with his pants around his knees started to reach down to pull up his pants.

"That won't be necessary," declared John. "Just waddle a little closer."

When the men were standing in front of John, John said, "Now strip!"

"What?" both men yelled simultaneously.

"You heard me. I want you to know how it feels to be buck naked for all the world to see."

"I'm not doing that!" exclaimed the man with his trousers already to his knees with his privates showing.

"You're halfway there; you might as well finish the job. You can do it with either one hand or two, because if you don't, I'm putting a bullet in one of your hands."

Obviously, from John's tone, both knew he was not kidding. As they stood there, in the nude, looking at John, John pointed to the one who had been holding the woman and said, "You see that fire over there where there is a boiling pot? Go throw all the clothes into the fire."

Both men had blank stares on their faces, but the one who got the instructions complied.

By now, John had gathered up the men's gun belts. He said, "Now let's take a little walk around to the front of the house where I have my horse."

As they passed the back porch, John called out, "Ma'am, I'm leaving you two guns on your porch. If you get any more stragglers, don't hesitate to use them."

When they reached the front yard, John swung up into his saddle.

One of the men said, "What about our horses?"

John said, "They're your payment for what you did to that lady. Now, move out in front of me while I think about what I'm going to do with the two of you."

Five miles down the road was the town of Loretto, Virginia. John had heard this town was Confederate proud, so he marched the men into the town and down Main Street with them trying to cover their privates with their hands. This first person John saw, he asked the location of the town constable. When John finally reached the constable's office, most of the townsfolk were standing outside laughing and pointing.

John explained to the constable what had happened and that he believe the men to be Union deserters. The constable welcomed them into his jail, gave them a blanket to wrap around themselves, and said he would turn them over to the Confederate company camped five miles away. The constable speculated that once the men in the Confederate company heard what the men had done, they probably would not make it to a POW camp. Around Loretto, an assault upon a Southern lady normally resulted in a hanging.

When John was asked why he hadn't killed them, he replied, "The only killing I do is what I have to do in a battle." With those words, John gave Bolt a gentle kick and galloped out of Loretto.

CHAPTER 14

GENERAL HOSPITAL AT CAMP WINDER AND GENERAL HOSPITAL NUMBER 4

When John went to brief Colonel Grimes on what he considered to be the best route to White's Point, he had already sketched the route on the sketch map he had been provided before his departure. It was then he learned the actual target of the regiment was White's Point. The colonel explained he had not told that to John in advance of his scouting mission in the event he was captured. If captured, he would not know the regiment's target and therefore could not divulge it to the enemy.

Grimes explained the regiment's mission was to capture White's Point to facilitate, without delay, the advancement of corps-size units to Fox's Gap. After successfully overrunning Fox's Gap, the army would advance to Sharpsburg to engage the enemy in a battle that later would be referred to as Antietam.

Colonel Grimes, detecting that John's body was having sporadic shakes, asked, "Sergeant Daniel, did you encounter any problems during your mission?"

Daniel replied, "Not really." He then explained the episode of his capture of two Yankee deserters and his turning them over to the constable in the town of Loretto.

"Well, how do you explain these nervous shakes you seem to be having?"

Daniel then revealed his miscalculation of the place to ford the river and how he and Bolt had to swim back to the shore.

Colonel Grimes suggested, "Sergeant, I think you best go by the aid station to see if you might have a touch of pneumonia."

Sergeant Daniel replied, "Yes, sir."

The colonel then said, "On second thought, so there is no confusion or misinterpretation of a suggestion or a request, that is an order. And do it now."

John replied, "Yes sir," and departed for the aid station.

The doctor's preliminary diagnosis was a possibility of pneumonia and confined John to his cot for the next week.

On September 4, Sergeant Daniel was no better. He was beginning to experience more aches and pains in his joints. Accordingly, he missed the departure of the regiment for White's Point.

A few days later, with no improvement, John received word of Grimes's accident at White's Point. According to the word John received, in the course of loading the horses onto the ferry, Colonel Grimes passed behind a horse that gave him a severe kick in his leg. Grimes continued the march but did so in an ambulance.

By September 16, 1862, John's condition had worsened, and the diagnosis changed from pneumonia to rheumatism. He was admitted to a large hospital complex in Richmond known as Camp Winder.

Camp Winder became the largest hospital of the Confederacy. At the time it opened, it could handle 3,000 patients, but later the capacity increased to 4,300 with a complex of ninety-eight buildings situated on 125 acres of what previously had been farmland.

On September 18, John was released from the hospital and ordered to report to Sharpsburg to join a contingent of reinforcements in the battle of Antietam.

After riding a short distance, on the outskirts of Richmond, Sergeant John Robert Daniel's luck ran out. From every jolt caused by the galloping of Bolt, sharp pains ran through John's joints. Just as he was beginning to think that he might not be able to make the journey, his thoughts were confirmed.

As the lead element of the reinforcement contingency rounded a bend in the road, it ran into a well-planned ambush. As John spun Bolt to look for some cover, he saw other soldiers falling from their horses.

Seeing a thicket of brush and pine trees near the edge of the road, he gave Bolt a kick as he directed him toward the thicket. It was then he felt a solid impact in the back of his right shoulder blade, and then there was a searing, burning sensation ripping through his body into his chest.

With the sensation of falling face forward toward the ground, John never saw nor felt himself hit the ground. He vaguely recalled being placed in the ambulance wagon, but now he was in a hospital bed. Soon a nurse appeared and commented she was glad to now see him awake.

He first asked, "Where am I?"

The nurse replied, "You're in General Hospital Number Four in Richmond."

"What happened to me?"

"You were shot, but the doctor will discuss those details with you later. For now you are to rest and recover."

"What day is it?"

"It's Sunday, September twenty-first. You were admitted on Friday the nineteenth. Just be patient. The doctor will see you soon after I report you are now awake." She then turned and walked over to another patient.

John lay in bed trying to reconstruct what had brought him here. He remembered he and about twenty other soldiers had been on their way to Antietam when all hell broke loose. He thought they might have been ambushed but couldn't recall any of the events. He was well aware that any time he tried to shift his position, the back of his right shoulder let him know it was less painful to lie still.

A couple of hours later, a doctor appeared with some papers in his hand. Looking down at John, he said, "You look much better today. And for the record, you are one lucky soldier."

With an inquiring look, John said, "I guess you're right. I'm still alive, and it appears all of me is still here."

"You're here today, but within the week, you will be gone."

"Has the battle at Antietam been waiting for me?"

"Sergeant, you will be going home. Your army days are over. Appears you turned forty-four in August, and your body is no longer able to endure the hardships of war. In addition to your gunshot wound, there is evidence you have rheumatism in practically every joint in your body. I don't know how you've managed to hang on this long."

John didn't venture to tell him that his hanging on was to keep his son out of war.

The doctor continued. "In a few days, I will make a decision about your medical discharge. So for now, focus on getting better so you can go home. I'll see you later."

A short time after the doctor had left, John realized the doctor had not said anything about his injury, nor had he remembered to ask. Anyways, he was tired for now, and discussing it later might be better when he wouldn't be so confused.

The following day when the doctor was making his rounds, John was sitting up in bed, ready and waiting to ask for more details regarding his injury.

It was early afternoon when the doctor made it to John's bedside. Before the doctor could say "Good afternoon," John started with his questions. "Doctor, tell me about my injury. How long will it take for me to recover? When will I be discharged? How will my discharge affect my teenage son being conscripted?"

"Whoa, just a minute. Let's take things a little slower. First, as I told you yesterday, you are a very lucky man. The bullet struck something metal before it went into you. Only about half a bullet entered the back of your right shoulder. It penetrated about six inches. Most of the tearing in your shoulder and the crack to your shoulder blade was caused by some other shiny piece of metal. Do you recall wearing something over your shoulder that could have partially deflected the bullet?"

"Yes, sir. My rifle. The barrel would have been up about three inches higher than my shoulder."

"I suspect that is what the bullet hit first. It probably split, sending one-half into your shoulder, and the other half took some of your rifle barrel into your shoulder. The barrel fragmented, causing multiple punctures into your back. Fortunately, nothing struck a vital organ. The main things now are keeping the wound clean to avoid infection and giving it the opportunity to heal. To stabilize the healing, I'll want your right arm in a sling for at least six weeks. Now, what were the other questions?"

"When will I be medically discharged?"

"Probably within the next three to four days. We need to see the beginning of some mending without any infection."

"Will my medical discharge result in my son being conscripted?"

"I can't answer that question. But if you're concerned about your oldest son being conscripted to take your place, I will annotate on your medical records that he should remain at home, at least until you are fully recovered. If you don't have any more questions, turn around and let me have a look at your wound."

CHAPTER 15

HOMEWARD BOUND

On September 26, 1862, Sergeant John Robert Daniel reported, as directed, to the office of the hospital administrator for General Hospital Number 4. The administrator provided him with his medical discharge papers and a letter stating that in the interest of his family, his eldest son should not be conscripted into the army until after Sergeant Daniel was fully recovered from the injuries he sustained in combat.

Sergeant Daniel was then instructed to report to the paymaster to collect all the back pay he had not received and his mustering-out pay. There he would also be given a train ticket for Goldsboro, North Carolina.

When John reported to the paymaster, he was informed that he was entitled to fifteen months of back pay. He had not been paid since he left Wayne County. At $17 per month, the paymaster counted out the $255 that John was owed. In addition he was given $50 mustering-out pay. John stuffed the money into his pants pocket. He was then handed a train ticket that would take him from Richmond to Goldsboro, North Carolina.

As he walked to the train station, the only personal effect John now had was his revolver, which he wore around his waist. Within the hour he had boarded the train that ran from Richmond to Wilmington, North

Carolina. When the train passed through Goldsboro, he would get off, and with his $305, he would purchase another horse to ride to Saulston to surprise his family.

As he settled into his seat, he thought, "For me, I'm glad it's over. I've lost many good friends, and I don't want to be around to see others die. Hopefully, I will be able to locate Captain Whitaker and maybe Luke. But my first priority is to spend a few months making up for my lost time with my family. It is so unreal that I am now going home. I just might take my time healing because I don't want William to see what I've seen or experienced." With happy thoughts of going home dancing in his head combined with the movement of the train, John fell asleep. Periodically, when the train stopped, John would look out the window to read the depot sign and think, "I'm getting closer to home with each stop."

Several hours into the trip, John was awakened when he heard the conductor say, "Next stop, Weldon, North Carolina. A good place to get yourself something to eat or drink and visit the privy. The train will be there around thirty minutes."

John could feel the train starting to slow, and he was thinking, "I'm not hungry or thirsty; but it might feel good to stretch my legs and to locate the privy."

When the train had stopped and people, probably with the same idea as John, started moving toward an exit door, so did John. As he walked down the aisle, peering out the windows, he could see the depot was a busy place. It was somewhat congested with some people trying to board and others trying to get off.

Finally, John made it through the door and down the steps. He thought, "That's the last time I get off. No one seems to have any regard for the fact my arm is in a sling." The pushing and shoving had caused him some pain.

On the platform he didn't see any sign providing directions to the privy, so he decided to ask a couple of soldiers leaning against the wall by the telegraph office. He knew both were soldiers because they were dressed in well-worn gray uniforms. He suspected they were waiting to catch a train.

As he started to walk toward them, it became apparent that with the exception of a nasty scar on the side of one's head, they were identical twins. Trying for a little humor, John said, "Appears you boys might be slightly related?"

"Didn't figure you would notice considering this scar a damn Yankee gave me," said the one with the scar on his face.

The other said, "I don't know why you complain about a scar when I killed the bastard that gave it to you. Just think how better off you are than he is."

John said, "Well spoken. Would either of you know where the privy might be?"

Before answering John's question, the one without the scar said, "Looks like you might have had a little bad luck yourself?"

"Yeah. I took a round just north of Richmond," replied John.

"You must be on furlough," said the scar-faced soldier.

"No, I was medically discharged," replied John.

"Oh!" said the other soldier. He then held out his hand and said, "My name is Herman; my brother who can't seem to get over his war wound is Thurman."

John shook both men's hands and said, "Glad to meet you."

Thurman then said, "Guess you got a sizable chunk of change with your back pay and mustering-out pay?"

"Not really," replied John. "Should be enough to buy a horse to get me home."

Herman said, "I'm sorry. I believe you were looking for the privy?"

"That's correct," said John.

"Follow me and I'll show you. It's right behind the depot."

Herman led the way, and John followed. Behind John, Thurman seemed to linger, but not in a way that caused any concern for John.

Once behind the depot, Herman gave the impression he was looking for the privy and then pointed out a long building with multiple private entrances. "There they are," said Herman.

Suddenly, John was on the ground. His head hurt as if he had been hit with something. As he was trying to push himself up from the ground with one hand, he saw the toe of a boot coming toward this forehead. Before he blacked out, he felt multiple and simultaneous impacts into his belly, back, and head.

William was exiting the cornfield, having taken inventory of what corn remained to be harvested. This corn had remained in the field to dry out so it could be used for winter sweet feed for the animals. As he cleared the cornfield, he thought he heard the pounding of horse hooves coming toward the house.

The sun was already beginning to drop in the sky, so for there to be rider coming at this hour, and at the pace he was traveling, he was coming to bring either news or trouble. William no longer carried his revolver in his waistband. He now wore it in a holster on his side. After his apprehension of big, bad Buck, he thought it was important for anyone coming toward their house to see that he was armed.

The rider, upon seeing William, held up a paper and waved it at him. William recognized the young rider, who was about his age, to be one of the messengers from the telegraph office in Saulston.

William ran onto the path to meet him. When the rider had reined his horse in to a stop, he yelled, "Got an important message for your Ma!"

William immediately feared the worst. "Pa's been killed," he said. "Give it to me. I'll take it to her."

The rider relinquished the telegram to William. After having read the telegram when it arrived at the telegram office, he was thinking, "Sorry, William!" He then spun his horse around and started back down the path as fast as he had come.

William ran to the house, leaped onto the front porch with one bound, and was through the front door, hollering, "Ma, you got a telegram! It's got to be important to be delivered this late."

Becky came from the kitchen with her apron tied tightly around her waist and said, "Let me see it!"

William thrust it in her hand. Her hands were shaking as she opened the telegram.

"Read it out loud!" exclaimed William.

As the other children gathered around, Becky read, "Date September 30, 1862, STOP. To Rebecca Daniel, Saulston, North Carolina, STOP. From Dr. Simon Tidwell, Weldon, North Carolina, STOP. Sgt. John

Robert Daniel seriously injured in Weldon, STOP. Under doctor's care in Weldon, STOP. Requires continuous medical attention and escort to Saulston, STOP. Advise immediately, STOP."

All the children looked at Ma in bewilderment. William was the first to speak. "This can't be right. The last we heard, Pa was in Richmond."

Becky thought for a minute or so and said, "This is right. All identifying information is correct. I must leave at first light tomorrow morning to go fetch him."

"Ma, you know Pa would not want you to leave the children and go for him. I'll go and take Nancy Ann with me."

"What does Nancy Ann know about caring for your Pa? I'm the one who takes care of him."

"Ma, until we can get Pa home, the only care he needs is to be made comfortable. Nancy Ann can do that. And if he needs to be carried, I'm strong enough to do that."

"I'm not sure, William."

"Ma, Nancy Ann and I can leave before daybreak with the wagon. In Goldsboro, I'll stable the horses, then she and I will take the train to Weldon. We'll get Pa on the train, Nancy can make him comfortable, and I'll watch over him. When we get back to Goldsboro, I'll put him in the wagon and bring him home. Pa would want you to stay home with the other children to reassure them that he will be all right and they are safe."

Becky knew William was speaking the truth. Besides, Nancy Ann was now stronger than she was, and if William needed help in carrying Pa, Nancy Ann would be of more help. Furthermore, her staying at home would be of more comfort to the children. The telegram had upset the little ones so much they were questioning if their Pa was going to die.

Becky said, "I agree. You and Nancy Ann go for Pa tomorrow."

William started out the door to get the wagon so that all he would have to do tomorrow morning was hook up the horses. He said, "Nancy Ann, you get some quilts and pillows so Pa will be comfortable."

Becky watched William, thinking, "That William is so much like his Pa. He knows how to take charge of any situation, and I know he will have his pa back here in no time."

The following day as the sun rose in the sky over Goldsboro, William gave Nancy Ann sufficient money to purchase their round-trip tickets to and from Weldon. He assumed his pa already had a ticket to Goldsboro. While she made the purchases, he stabled the horses at a local livery stable.

When William returned to the depot, he found Nancy Ann loaded down with blankets and pillows and clutching their two round-trip tickets. When he sat down beside her, she said, "The next train for Weldon will be arriving here around eight fifty." It was currently eight o'clock.

A teenage girl came running from behind the depot screaming, "Someone come quickly. A soldier has been hurt really bad!"

Several men started to run to the back side of the depot. The telegraph operator told one of his messengers to run and bring Doc Tidwell. Turning to the other messenger, he said, "You go get Constable Joyner and tell him he might want to send someone to get the sheriff."

Both boys left running as if they were delivering the most important message of the day.

A circle quickly formed around the body lying in a fetal position on the ground. There were some papers scattered about. One man checked the prone man for a heartbeat and then announced to the crowd that had gathered, "He's still alive, but he needs a doctor now!"

Doctor Tidwell and Constable Joyner arrived about the same time. Tidwell immediately checked the man's vital signs and instructed the four men standing the nearest to him to get the man up and take him to his office, which was across the street from the depot.

Constable Joyner, while collecting the papers scattered on the ground, which included a train ticket to Goldsboro, asked if anyone had seen what had happened. One citizen said he had seen two other soldiers walking with the soldier who was lying on the ground toward the rear of the depot. In a short time, the two soldiers came back around the corner of the building, got on their horses tied in front of the telegraph office, and rode west, in the direction of the town of Roanoke Rapids. Joyner asked if anyone recognized the men or if there was anything unusual about them.

One lady said, "I also saw two soldiers standing in front of the telegraph office before the train arrived. They looked almost identical, except one had an ugly scar on the side of his head from the top of his ear to his chin."

Joyner then asked if anyone had seen the color of the horses they were riding.

By now the telegraph operator had closed the telegraph office and joined the gathered crowd. He spoke up. "I did, Constable Joyner. Their horses were tied just outside my office. One horse was white with brown spots, and the other was brown. Both had what looked like cavalry saddles."

As Joyner sorted through the papers, he asked, "Did anyone know any of the men, including the one that was injured?"

One citizen said, "The man on the ground had just gotten off the train. I saw him holding his right arm, which was in a sling. He looked like he was trying to prevent anyone from bumping into him."

All the others shook their heads.

"If any of you think of something that might be helpful, contact me. For now, I'm going over to Doc Tidwell's office to see if the man can tell me anything."

Just as the telegraph operator, whose name was Hand, turned to leave, Joyner said, "Hand, I want you to send out a message providing a general description of the two men and their horses. For now, send your messages to the north and to the west."

"I sure will, Constable Joyner. We can't have things like this happening in Weldon."

When Joyner arrived at Tidwell's office, Tidwell said the man was still unconscious. He believed the man had suffered a concussion and some cracked ribs, and some stitches that had been holding together a wound, which he had apparently received about ten days ago, had been torn out. He then asked the constable if he had any suspects or a motive for the attack.

Joyner asked, "Did you find any money on him?"

"Not any," replied the doctor.

"Then I think we have our motive. In the papers I picked up from the ground was a medical discharge and two pay vouchers. One was for two hundred and fifty-five dollars in back pay, and the other was fifty dollars for mustering-out pay. I think the two soldiers who attacked this man were deserters with the motive of robbery

"Do the papers identify this man and his next of kin?" said the doctor.

The constable looked over the papers again and said, "It appears he is Sergeant John Robert Daniel of Saulston, North Carolina. He listed his wife, Rebecca Daniel, as his next of kin."

"Well," said Tidwell, "once I can get him stabilized and he is fit to travel, I will contact her to see if someone can come for him. I want to keep him at least a couple of days once he regains consciousness."

"Be sure to let me know when he comes around because I will have a few questions for him. Hopefully, he will be able to tell us what happened and who did this to him."

🙾

William and Nancy Ann arrived in Weldon at 1:30 p.m. After getting off the train, William inquired of the conductor if he knew the location of Doctor Tidwell's office. The conductor pointed out through one of the windows on the east side of the train and said, "It's in that building right over there. Hope the train ride didn't make you sick."

"No. Thank you."

As William and Nancy Ann stood in line to get off the train, William leaned forward and said in her ear, "Get off on the right side. The doctor's office is just across the street."

After entering the door with the shingle on the door that read "N. Simon Tidwell, Doctor of Medicine," William and Nancy Ann were greeted by an elderly receptionist, possibly the doctor's wife, with "This is Doctor Tidwell's office, and how may I help you?"

"My name is William Daniel. Our family received a telegram from Doctor Tidwell saying our Pa was his patient…I'm sorry; this here is my sister, Nancy Ann."

"Your father is a patient. If you will have a seat, I will tell him you are here."

William, holding the blankets, and Nancy, holding the pillows, took a seat in two of the wooden chairs that lined the back wall. There were no others in the waiting room.

Within a matter of moments, a door opened, and a man in a white coat stood in the entrance way and said, "I'm Doctor Tidwell. Please come in, and thank you for responding so quickly."

The two young folks gathered up the items they were carrying and entered the doctor's office.

Nancy Ann said, "Can we see our Pa now?"

Doctor Tidwell very calmly and politely said, "Before you see him, I think you should first know the condition he is in so you won't be surprised. He's resting comfortably, but unfortunately, he's not talking, nor is he maintaining any eye contact. When awake he is constantly looking around as if he is looking for something familiar."

"What happened to him?" William asked.

"He was severely beaten and left for dead. I believe he's suffering from a near-death concussion. Evidence suggests he was hit in the back of the head with a blunt object and then, while on the ground, stomped and kicked. He was then robbed. Your dad is one tough man to have survived what he went through. He also received some broken ribs, possibly a bruised kidney, and reinjures to a war wound."

"A war wound? We didn't know Pa had a war wound."

"The best I can determine, he was shot about two weeks before he was beaten up. His medical discharge papers state a combat wound to be the reason he was discharged."

"Discharged? This is all news to us," said William.

"Well, I'm sorry to have to be the one to share all this information with you at one time."

"Will he recover…be normal again?" asked Nancy.

"I can't readily answer that question, young lady. But if anyone can, I believe it to be your pa. That is why I wanted to get him back in his familiar surroundings as soon as possible. You need to know his recovery will be slow and take lots more time than you now are thinking. His physical recovery should be quick. My concern is his mental recovery. He may never recall exactly what happen or remember who did this to him."

"Do you know when the next train will be going back to Goldsboro?" asked William.

"Just one moment." The doctor then yelled out, "Lizbeth, please come in here." When she entered, he said, "Do you know the next train to Goldsboro?"

Lizbeth said, "Give me a minute." She departed, leaving the door open. She quickly re-entered, holding a piece of paper in her hand, and said, "According to the schedule, it will be around six p.m."

"Can we now see Pa?" asked Nancy.

"Yes, but don't be surprised that he doesn't look like the Pa you remember," replied the doctor.

Upon entering the room where John was lying in the bed with his eyes closed, both William and Nancy were shocked. John's head was bandaged, his face was swollen, his right arm was in a sling, and there were bruises all over his exposed skin.

Nancy walked cautiously to the side of her father's bed and said, "Pa, it's Nancy Ann. William and I have come to take you home."

John did not move or open his eyes. The doctor hastened to say, "His nonresponse is not unusual. When he is in a deep sleep, it is difficult to wake him. Just keep talking to him very softly, and he should open his eyes. You have to be patient. It may take a while."

William, in a very low voice, said, "Pa, it's me, William. I want you to know I'm here when you need me."

Again, there was no reaction from John.

Turning to Nancy, William said, "You stay here with Pa. I going to talk to the constable to see what has been learned about Pa's attackers." Then, looking in the doctor's direction, he asked, "Can you tell me the location of the constable's office:"

"Yes," replied the doctor. "Just go one block to the east and two blocks south. There will be a sign on the window that reads, 'Joyner's General Mercantile and Town Constable.' You can't miss it."

"Thanks!" said William. To Nancy he said, "I'll be back shortly." He then hurried out of the room and out of the doctor's office.

"A man on a mission" is the only way to describe William's entry to Joyner's Mercantile. He immediately and in somewhat of a demanding voice said, "Where can I find the constable?"

An elderly man standing behind the counter and wearing an apron and sleeve garters observed that young William had a revolver strapped around his waist. The man slowly reached under the counter, pulled out a pistol, and laid it on the counter. He then said, "You might want to re-ask that question, making it more polite while identifying yourself, and see if you don't get a better response."

William, realizing that he was letting his emotions get in the way of being respectful, said, "Sir, I'm sorry. I am William Daniel, and I just visited my father in Doctor Tidwell's office."

"And your father's name is…" asked the storekeeper.

"John Robert Daniel. He was recently beaten up, pretty bad, behind the train depot."

The storekeeper called out, "Mary, will you please come tend the counter? I need to talk to a young man." The man placed his pistol back beneath the counter. He then said, "I'm Constable Joyner. Why don't you step into my office?" He pointed to a desk in the back corner of the store.

William joined the constable, who took a seat in a chair behind the desk. He then pointed to an empty crate and said, "Pull up a chair so we are both more comfortable."

William grabbed the crate and took a seat on one of its ends.

The constable took his time sizing up William before he spoke. "Let me tell you what I know to be facts, and then I may speculate some. First, your father got off the train to use the privy. Before he got to the privy, he made an acquaintance with two other soldiers. Somehow they learned he had some money, and they beat him up and took it. I was surprised your father lived through the beating he was given.

"My investigation has led me to believe the two who attacked him were twin brothers, Herman and Thurman Rouse from Tennessee. After sending out a vague description, I received this poster in the mail."

The constable withdrew a poster of a hand drawing of two identical men, one with a scar on the left side of his face. The poster read,

"WANTED DEAD OR ALIVE—The Rouse Brothers, $500 reward each, Herman and Thurman Rouse, identical twins. Thurman scarred on left side of face. Both Wanted For: Desertion, Assault, Murder, and Robbery. Considered armed and dangerous."

The constable continued. "I believe these are the two who assaulted your father, but as of yet, I have not been able to confirm my belief. I also believe them to be heading back to Tennessee because they left here heading west. I did get a report they passed through the town of Littleton two days after leaving Weldon. But I have not received any more reports."

"May I have one of the posters? Once my father gets better, I can ask him if these are the men."

"Certainly! And should he be able to confirm them as his attackers, please let me know."

"Sir, I will. And please accept my apology for being so rude when I entered your store. I should not have let the stress of seeing my father, even in his current condition, affect me the way it did."

"I understand, and your apology is accepted. Just remember when you want information, use sugar rather than salt for your introduction."

John picked up a copy of the wanted poster, bid the constable good-bye, thanked him again, and returned to the doctor's office.

CHAPTER 16

HOME AGAIN

When William returned to the doctor's office, he went directly to his father's room. Nancy Ann was sitting beside the bed, and Pa was awake and sitting up. However, he seemed to show no recognition of the two.

Nancy quietly commented, "He has been this way for the last hour. He looks at me when I talk to him, but he will not respond."

"I'll see if he will communicate with me," said William. "Pa, are you ready to go home?"

John turned his eyes toward John but still did not say anything. Hoping for some reaction, William said, "Pa, I'm your son, William. If you understand, please nod your head up and down."

John just stared at William without any movement of his head.

Unexpectantly, the doctor entered the room. After observing the lack of interaction, he said, "Both of you need to understand, for now, this is normal for him. I'm hoping the more he is around the family, the quicker he will recover. But I must prepare you, this could be permanent. Without knowing the extent of the injury to his brain, there is no way of knowing how much he may recover. Keep in mind there are two types of recovery he will go through, and we do not know the priority or the extent.

"There needs to be both mental and physical recovery. It is possible for him to regain his mental abilities but not his physical. Or he could regain his motor skills but not his ability to perform mental exercises or remaster his communication skills. Professionally, we know very little about how the brain recovers from a serious injury. We will have to take each day slowly and consider any improvement as a reward from God."

Nancy asked, "Is there any other place we can take him for more tests and examinations?"

"The more skilled places are up north. I don't know that your father could survive the journey, nor do I know a hospital up north that would see a Southern soldier," replied Tidwell.

William said, "Nancy, you stay with Pa while I go to the depot to arrange Pa's travel back to Goldsboro."

The depot was most accommodating in assuring William they would try to provide the best accommodations they could for John. Some even apologized for his father being injured at the depot in Weldon. He was told to have his father at the train depot no later than 5:30 p.m.

The doctor had arranged for his buggy to be at the front door of his office at 5:00 p.m. There, the doctor, the janitor, Nancy, and William lifted John from his bed and carried him to the doctor's buggy for the short ride to the depot. Nancy had made John a bed in the back of the buggy.

The depot manager advised that he had made arrangements for John and his family to ride in the caboose of the train. In the caboose was the conductor's bed, where John could rest during his ride to Goldsboro. All seemed to be falling into place for the Daniel family to get John home.

The train arrived in Goldsboro around 1:00 a.m. The conductor had arranged for four big men to help get John off the train. While the men were helping Nancy get John off the train, William ran to the livery stable and hooked up his two horses to their wagon. Within a short time, he was back at the train depot. William then helped Nancy make a bed in the back of the wagon. With the help of the four men, John was lifted over the side of the wagon onto the bed Nancy had made for him.

William had already told Nancy that if need be, they would ride through the night to get Pa home as soon as possible. He knew Ma was anxiously waiting. Pa had slept from Weldon to Goldsboro, and he suspected that although the wagon ride would be bumpier, Pa would sleep until they arrived home. Without any incidents, they should arrive home close to 4:00 a.m. Nancy rode in the back watching over Pa.

At 3:30 a.m. William reined the horse onto the path leading up to the house. Knowing where they were, the horses picked up their speed into a faster walk. If William had not been holding them back, they would have easily moved to a fast trot.

Ma must have been watching for them because as soon as the wagon stopped, she was on the front porch in her nightgown. She rushed to the wagon and peered into the back. With only the moonlight, she could see her John sleeping like a baby. She was afraid to speak because it might awaken him.

Nancy Ann appeared to have matured during her trip to Weldon. She quickly said, "Ma, Pa is not in good health. We need to get him inside and into bed, and then I will give you all the details the doctor gave us."

Much like her Ma, and somewhat surprising to William, Nancy Ann said, "William, we are going to slide Pa out the back of the wagon. Ma and I will take the foot end of the bed, and you take the head." Then she called out to her sister, "Fannie, you get out here and hold the door open for us."

Without any questions, all complied with Nancy's instructions. Without the slightest jar, Pa was carried up the front steps, through the door held open by Fannie, and to the side of Ma and Pa's bed. There she instructed William to go to the foot of the bed and lay Pa's head and shoulders on the bed first. She then told Fannie to come help Ma hold Pa's feet and for William to go to the other side of the bed. Then William was to grasp one corner of the blanket Pa was lying on, and she would get the other side. The two of them would pull the top of Pa's body onto the bed. Ma and Fannie were to guide his feet until he was completely on the bed.

Once that was done, Nancy looked at all with one of those looks Ma could use when all was going according to her plan and said, "Fannie, you need to go back to bed. William, go unhitch the team and bed them down for the remainder of the night. Ma, you sit here on the edge of the bed and hold Pa's hand while I tell you everything the doctor told us."

All now knew that a new domestic leader in the family was emerging. For William it was amazing how he had taken an eleven-year-old girl to Weldon and brought back a young woman who acted his age. But in William's mind, he knew she was going to have to learn that she didn't tell him what to do.

In the view of the Daniel family, Pa's recovery progress seemed awfully slow. However, to all those who visited to offer their help and prayers for God's speed in Pa's recovery, they always departed commenting on how well they thought he was doing.

Just before Thanksgiving, 1862, Pa was mentally where he recognized all the family members but not the names of the smaller children. He did call Ma Becky when he needed her, and he had returned to calling William Billy Boy. That was the name Pa had given William until William turned ten. At that time, Pa started to call his eldest son William.

He also remained confused as to which girl was Nancy and which was Fannie. He seemed to love to sit and listen to what William would tell him about what was being done on the farm. There were times when he would shake his head in a positive way as though he approved of what William was telling him. He still carried on no real conversations, but that might have been caused by the difficulty he seemed to have recalling the words to use.

Physically, he could now stand with Becky or William's help and sit upright in chairs, but he could not take any steps. This seemed to be his greatest frustration. It was as though he could recall being able to do whatever he wanted, but now, without the help of others, he was for the most part disabled. Probably his feeling of real accomplishment came when he relearned how to feed himself.

In early December, around midmorning, John had a visitor, which created a bold step forward in the progress of his recovery. Unexpectedly, Captain Whitaker appeared at their house. He had learned through a friend that John had returned home seriously injured. At the time, he did not know how John had sustained the injury.

When Whitaker entered the sitting room, John was sitting in his rocker by the fireplace. The fire had a healthy blaze because one of John's favorite pastimes during the winter was pitching more pieces of dry wood upon the fire so that he could observe a constant and brilliant blaze. Whitaker said, "Sergeant Daniel, how is my old friend doing?"

At the sound of the captain's voice, John looked up. Tears started to slide down his cheeks as he said, to everyone's surprise, "Ca…Ca… Cap…Captain!"

"Yes, it's me, John. I wanted to come to see how my best sergeant was doing."

For the first time, a smile of recognition was seen on John's face as he once again said, "Captain."

The remainder of the morning, until lunchtime, the captain talked constantly about his and John's war experiences. In particular, he wanted the family to know how John had saved his life. Periodically, John would nod his head in remembrance of the story the captain was telling.

After a sumptuous lunch of pork, corn on the cob, butter beans, and greens accompanied by fresh-baked biscuits and homemade butter, the captain pushed back and said, "Mrs. Daniel, that is, without a doubt, the best meal I have had since I have been back in Wayne County."

Becky quickly replied, "I hope you left room for my apple pie. I made it from the apples that came from trees John planted when he first built this house."

During the meal, John had proudly displayed his ability to use his fork and spoon. Becky had cut his pork for him before he came to the table.

At the sound of the apple pie, John looked at the captain and said, "Pie, good."

Whitaker replied, "I know it is, because everything has been just wonderful."

Again, when Becky served the pie, she cut John's serving into bite-size pieces so that all he had to do was pick up each with his fork.

After the meal, Becky suggested the two men have some time alone, and she and all the children returned to their daily chores.

William again thanked Captain Whitaker for the agreement he had with his father, explaining how the care of the farm had been a full-time job for him, and it would have been impossible for his mother to do it alone while caring for the other children.

When the two men were alone, Whitaker reassured John of his confidence that John had the fortitude and grit to overcome his temporary disabilities. He encourage John not to be discouraged by periodic setbacks and not to rush his recovery. While he did not know the internal struggle John was dealing with, he could identify with the trials of physical recovery. For him, he would have to live with the fact that his left leg would always be shorter than his right, giving him a permanent limp. Furthermore, he also endured daily pain in his back from his horse falling on him when they were shot. And, while his daily progress had discouraged him, he came to realize he should be happy with the abilities he had reacquired.

John listened quietly, occasionally nodding his head that he understood and agreed with the wisdom the captain, his younger, offered. As the captain was bidding John goodbye and reassuring him he would return to see him, John smiled and nodded. And then, for the first time, John made his first complete sentence. "Thank you, Captain, for coming to see me."

The captain replied, "Thank you, John, for saving my life."

From that day forward, John seemed to turn on a burst of energy from within. He insisted that when William got up, he was to come get his father and help him walk up and down their long hallway. He refused to let Becky cut his food for him, even if it did take a lot longer for him to eat. And for the children, he came up with clues to help him remember their names. For example, Fannie had lots of freckles on her face. Her freckles helped him to remember freckles equaled to Fannie.

By the beginning of 1863, John was walking around the house with one hand against a wall and the other carrying a cane. He soon discovered the more he was standing, the harder he worked to regain his balance. He had made up his mind that the next time the captain came calling, he would meet him on the front porch without the assistance of anyone. Furthermore, he told William that he would be helping him with the planting for the next year.

While William was not too sure his father wasn't being overly optimistic, he did not discourage his positive attitude. It was during this time William decided to see how much his father remembered about his attack.

John now seemed to recall his arrival in Weldon and getting off the train but little else. Then William brought out the wanted poster for the Rouse brothers. At first his father looked at the poster picture with puzzlement. He then said, "I don't think I know these two."

But he continued to study the picture. Then it was like a lightning bolt struck him. John proclaimed, as he pointed to the one without the scar on his face, "This is the one who told me the privy was behind the depot."

William asked, "Did he tell you, or did he show you?"

John thought for a few seconds and said, "The best I remember, he showed me."

"Do you remember where the other man was?"

"I think he followed us."

"Do you remember anything after that?"

"No. The next thing I remember is being here."

"Do remember having any money with you?"

"I think I may have had about three hundred dollars. I remember I had enough to buy another horse to ride home to surprise your Ma."

"Do you remember telling anyone about the money?"

"Not really. I may have since the other two were soldiers, like me."

For William the pieces of the puzzle were coming together. Now he remembered the other two were soldiers, which coincided with what Constable Joyner had told him. His Pa had probably mentioned getting paid when he was discharged. Pa had asked Herman where the privy was, and Herman probably volunteered to show him. Thurman, following along behind, was probably the one who hit his Pa in the head with some blunt object. Knowing his father, he surmised that he probably was not knocked completely out, so the two then tried to beat him to death.

The more William thought about the incident, the angrier he became. He thought, "If the two have not paid for their crimes, they need to do so. There has to be justice. There has to be some sort of settlement." For now, he was going to send a telegram to Constable Joyner confirming his father's attackers were the Rouse brothers and question if they had been apprehended. If they had not been, they had to be.

A plan started to hatch in William's mind. If Constable Joyner advised that the Rouses had not been apprehended, he would track them down until they paid for their crimes, even if it was with their lives. After the crops were planted and Pa was in a position to oversee the boys he hired to harvest the crops, he would set forth to bring the men to justice.

PART II

WILLIAM HENRY DANIEL

CHAPTER 17

THE TRACKING BEGINS

In late January 1863, William Henry Daniel sent a telegram to Constable Joyner in Weldon, North Carolina. The message read, "Father, John Robert Daniel confirmed to me, William Henry Daniel, his son, that Herman and Thurman Rouse attempted to murder him on September 27, 1862. They robbed him of over three hundred dollars and left him for dead. What is the status of the Rouse brothers?"

In early February 1863, Constable Joyner replied, "Rouse brothers still at large. Believed to have returned to home state of Tennessee. Armed and dangerous. Do not, repeat, do not attempt to apprehend."

William's father was never informed of the messages between his son and Constable Joyner. William continued to work the land for planting season and secured two boys to help him. He did so with some of the reward money he received for his capture of Buck Larson. Also, unknown to his family, he purchased a new Colt revolver, gun belt, and holster. He also purchased a new repeating rifle, which he kept hidden in the horse barn. When the time came, he would leave a letter and depart at night. He knew his Ma and Pa would not understand or approve of what he felt needed to be done. But someone must bring these men to justice, dead or alive.

William had watched his father battle both the mental and physical disability that had been inflicted upon him by those whom he thought to be his fellow soldiers. It hurt to see his robust yet kind and gentle father go through such agonizing torture while his assailants went free. He also felt guilt that his father had volunteered to go to war in order for him not to have to go. He knew he could not live with himself until this matter was settled. The Rouses needed to learn one doesn't harm a member of the Daniel family without experiencing the consequences.

At the same time, William was dealing with the guilt and pain of watching his father go through difficult challenges, he had to acknowledge that his father's communication skills had almost returned to normal. He still had difficulty pronouncing some words, but other than having no memory of what actually happened, his mind was sharp enough to manage the farm.

Physically, his father walked with a cane, but he could mount Lucky Boy by standing on a block of wood or a tree stump. Pa came up with the idea of tying a rope to a block of wood, which, after getting into his saddle, he could pull up with the rope and tie in behind his saddle. He could dismount without the use of the block. Once in the saddle, he sat as straight as he always had. Ma did not like to see him put Lucky Boy into a gallop because she was afraid he would fall. But Pa was stubborn and confident that Lucky Boy would go no faster than Pa could ride.

With all the work William was doing, the winter months slipped by quickly, and in short order, the land was prepared for planting. By the end of May, all seeds were in the ground, including some of Ma's vegetable garden. The boys William had hired to help Pa were ready to go to work by the first of June. Also unknown to the family were the long hours of practice William had put in quickening the draw of his new army Colt revolver and firing with a high degree of accuracy from the draw. When he shot Buck Larson, his weapon was already drawn. Now he needed the same degree of accuracy when his revolver was leaving the holster. In his opinion, he had now mastered that requirement, and all was ready for his departure, except for the letter he needed to write explaining his decision.

On May 30, William wrote:

Dearest Ma, Pa, and Family,

I beg you forgive me for slipping away during the night, but to do otherwise would have been too difficult for all of us.

I am sure you will question my abilities for the actions I am undertaking. Please be assured my abilities are far more advanced than my age. The following is why I feel I must undertake this endeavor.

Pa sacrificed himself for almost two years to preclude my having to serve in this ongoing war. And while we all knew of the possibility of him not returning to us, we never suspected his worst injuries would come from his fellow soldiers who turned scalawags. They completely disregarded Pa's war injury for money they did not earn. Their intent was to kill Pa for his military pay. Furthermore, I am sure they believed, with confidence, that at the height of this war, no one was going to be looking for them. I cannot permit that to happen.

After what Pa has done for me, I could not live with myself knowing those who inflicted so much harm on Pa got away without anyone, in particular me, doing anything to bring them to justice. They must pay for what they have done to our family.

Pa taught me where there is an injustice, there must be a settlement. The injustice Pa experienced must be settled. Once that has been done, either by someone else or me, I promise I will return home. Do not worry about me. Only pray for me and know I love all of you.

Forever, your loving son and brother,
William

Before William exited the rear door of the house, he was careful to place his letter in the center of the dining table, leaning against Ma's sugar bowl. He walked in his sock feet, carrying his boots in his hands. Once outside William pulled on his boots and headed for the horse barn.

Preparations for his trip had been occurring over the last month. One saddlebag was stuffed with beef jerky, flour, and other food items. The other saddlebag contained a change of clothes, a hatchet, his new Colt revolver, ammunition, and a small cooking pan. His duster was wrapped around his bedroll and tied on the back of his saddle, and his new rifle was in its sleeve case that rode inside his right leg.

When William entered Taz's stall, he received a look from Taz that seemed to convey the question, what are we doing rising so early? The time was two a.m. By two-thirty, William and Taz were on the main road to Weldon, North Carolina. William wanted to consult one more time with Constable Joyner before he began his hunt for the Rouse brothers.

Ma arose at five a.m. and went into the kitchen to start breakfast. She was expecting the fire in the cooking stove to have already been started. Normally, William arose before she did, and on his way to do his morning feeding of the animals, he lit the stove. But he had not done so this morning.

Somewhat concerned, Ma made her way to where William slept to see if by chance he had overslept, but his bed appeared as if he had never slept in it. She knew that wasn't the case because he had kissed her and told both her and Pa good night before he went to bed.

She then returned to the back door to see if there was any lantern light coming from the horse barn. There was none. Ma then rushed back to her bedroom and gently nudged Pa.

Pa, opening his eyes, said, "Is it time to get up already?"

"I can't find William!" exclaimed Ma. "He's not in his bed, he didn't start a fire in the cook stove, and I don't see any light in the horse barn."

"Calm down, calm down, Becky. I'm sure there's a good explanation. Let me get on my trousers, and I'll walk down to the barn to make sure everything is okay. He probably had something on his mind and just forgot to start the fire."

"He has never forgotten in the past!"

"Becky, my dear, there can always be a first time. I'll start the fire and then check the barn."

"You check the barn. I'll start the fire," said Becky.

Within a matter of minutes, John had on his bib overalls, had his cane, and was out the back door, limping toward the horse barn.

Within ten minutes John had returned to the house. Upon entering the back door, he could see a lantern was burning in the dining room. He entered the dining room saying, "Taz is not in his stall?" There he saw Becky holding a paper and shaking as she read it. He could see she was becoming upset.

Finally, with tears streaming down her face, she handed the paper to John and said, "Read this."

As John read he shook his head in disbelief. He knew William had matured a lot since he had been gone, but he never would have suspected, nor would he have ever believed, that William would attempt such a venture without first talking with him.

John dropped down onto the dining table bench that ran the length of the table. He then said, out loud but more to himself, "How could have I missed the signs of what he was thinking? He was always in such a hurry and so deep in thought. I thought it was all his involvement in the work that had to be done and his worry about me. Becky, what did I miss? Do you think I should go after him?"

Wiping her tears, Beck replied, "No, John! First, you would never catch him. And second, even if you did, you could not bring him home. He is a man now, and he must do what he believes a man should do. He views what happened to you as not just a violation of you but as a violation of our family. He's headstrong, like you. We must pray for him and wait for his return. Like you, he promised to come back home, and he will."

John shook his head in acknowledgment of the truth Becky had spoken. He said, "We'll share this with the others over breakfast."

Throughout the day, as William worried about the reaction of his parents, he pushed Taz hard. He wanted as much distance as possible between him and Pa when Pa realized he was gone. After a few hours, logic finally entered William's mind. "Pa couldn't sit in the saddle as far as Adamsville, much less to Goldsboro to catch a train. Pa is smart enough to know that I would start my journey where he was injured. He also knows the need to have a man around the house during these troubled times." With those more practical thoughts in mind, he reined Taz into a steady but comfortable walk. He had decided to skirt the east side of the village of Halifax and camp on the south side of the Roanoke River. He would ride into Weldon early the next morning.

He found a nice grassy spot for Taz to graze near a pool of river water. After he took the saddle off Taz and threw his bedroll on the ground next to his saddle, it was time to think about something to eat. From his saddlebag he retrieved a long string of twine with a pin tied on the end. Under a rock he found some live bait. He placed the bait on the hook and pitched it into the river. The other end he tied to a small pine tree that would wave or bend when he snagged a fish.

He then went about gathering dry twigs and branches for his fire. While the fishing line bobbed in the river, William used his flint and hunting knife to start a fire. It was then he realized how relaxed he felt.

For the first time in two years, he felt relief from his constant worry of providing for and protecting the family. It was as if he were on a camping trip like he and Pa would take when he was six and seven years old. For a brief moment, a sense of guilt swept over him for having a feeling of freedom. But he snapped back to reality when he saw the little pine tree take a serious bend toward the ground. Supper was on the line.

At seven o'clock the following morning, William was sitting on the porch of Joyner's Mercantile awaiting the arrival of Constable Joyner. Taz was tied to the hitching rail. The fullness of his stomach caused him to reflect upon the previous evening. He had dined on at least a pound of rockfish and a couple of Ma's biscuits he had stowed away for travel purposes.

The gentle breeze from the river kept the mosquitoes away, and the sound of the river current swirling around the rocks made a melody for a good night's sleep. At one point he awoke to see, in the moonlight, Taz stretched out in a field of clover. Both could not have had a better night on the trail.

Now as he waited for Constable Joyner's arrival, he mulled over the questions he had for him. He also tried to prepare himself for any discouraging suggestions Constable Joyner might present. He had made up his mind that justice for his father was now his mission.

He sat there waiting with his eyes closed, as he was facing into a bright sun. Hearing the sound of boots striking the wooden walkway at a somewhat fast pace, William opened his eyes to see Joyner approaching.

Joyner's first words were "Sorry I'm running a little late this morning. Normally, I'm open by seven, but I couldn't locate the dang key to the store. Left it in the pocket of the trousers I wore yesterday."

William found it a little amusing that Constable Joyner found it necessary to explain his tardiness. William responded, "Not a problem for me, sir. I'm an early riser and had no other place to be."

Joyner stopped and stared at William for a moment and then asked, "Why is it not a surprise to me to find you here? When I first met you, I sized you up to be a young man who would not permit an unjust act to go unpunished. I hope you're not here hoping to seek revenge upon those who hurt your father."

"Not revenge, Constable. I only want justice, and I hope you can help me with some answers to a few questions. I promise to be more respectful than I was at the beginning of our last meeting."

As Joyner placed his key in the door lock and gave it a decisive twist, he said, "Come on in. All is forgotten. I know you were just upset over your father. Reminded me much of the way I use to approach issues when I was your age. And speaking of age, how old are you?"

Entering the store, William said, "Fifteen."

Opening the window shades, Joyner said, "Your size caused me to guess around seventeen, and even that is mighty young to be thinking about bringing two killers to justice. Why don't you have a seat over there in my office, and we'll talk until I start getting customers."

The two walked over to Joyner's desk in the far back corner of the store. During William's previous visit, he gathered this was where Joyner conducted his constable business.

When both were seated, Joyner said, "Now, young fellow, before you ask your questions, tell me how your father is doing."

William began. "Much better, sir. He needs a cane to get around, and he has some communication and memory issues. But when I showed him the wanted poster for the Rouse brothers, he recognized them. He said Herman was guiding him to the privy, and Thurman followed him. He remembers being hit from behind and recalls being kicked, but nothing else. He also remembers that he had slightly over three hundred dollars in his pocket from his military and mustering-out pay."

Joyner leaned back in his chair and said, "That tracks with the investigation we did here. Witnesses here remember seeing the three go behind the depot with Herman leading and Thurman following. Shortly thereafter, the brothers returned and quickly got on their horses and rode out of town. After they became suspects, I sent a message to all the surrounding towns to be on the lookout for them."

Before Joyner could continue, William impatiently asked, "Were there any responses?"

A slight smile came on Joyner's face at William's impatience. "Yes, but keep in mind it took a couple of days to figure out what exactly had happened. I received a message from the Town of Warrenton, which is about thirty-five miles west of here, saying it believed the two had passed through there a day or so after the incident here. They believe so because a store had been broken into. Two suits of clothing and ammunition had been stolen. Two miles west of the town, a farmer found two discarded Confederate uniforms in the woods that bordered his farm.

"From the Town of Emporia, Virginia, I received notice the Rouse brothers were wanted in Virginia for desertion, murder, assault, and armed robbery. Likewise, our sheriff published a poster wanting them for assault, robbery, and breaking and entry. The Virginia poster is offering a five-hundred-dollar reward for each of them, dead or alive. The North Carolina reward is three hundred dollars each."

"Is the North Carolina reward also for dead or alive?"

"It doesn't specify."

"Constable Joyner, is there any speculation as to where the two may be going?"

"I was able to learn the boys are from Powder Springs, Tennessee. They may be heading back home. I am not aware of any crimes they may have committed in Tennessee."

"I guess I'll head in that direction," said William.

"Son, let me give you some advice," said Joyner. "First, just because they are wanted in North Carolina and Virginia does not make them wanted in Tennessee. To my knowledge, they have not been declared criminals of the Confederate states, even though they are deserters,; nor have they been declared criminals of the Union states. Hell! They may be considered heroes of the Union states.

"Second, these are proven dangerous men, prone to killing for no reason other than money. I look at you and see a young man who doesn't even carry a weapon."

"Sir, if it's any comfort to you, I have a weapon and know how to use it effectively. I choose not to wear it unless I expect I will need it."

"William, my final advice to you is that in these times, you will never know in advance when you will need it. And there are others, like the Rouses, who are not going to give you the time to go strap your weapon on. If you're looking for trouble, it will find you before you know it's there."

William stood up and said, "Thank you, Constable Joyner. I will keep that advice in mind."

Joyner, with great concern registering on his face, said, "Son, what are you going to do?"

"Get justice for my father...dead or alive. Thank you, Constable Joyner." And with those words, William departed Joyner's Mercantile.

CHAPTER 18

THE BLUE RIDGE MOUNTAINS

William departed Constable Joyner's office with good advice but with no deterrence to his mission. He was still reluctant to strap on his weapon, as he viewed that as an invitation for someone to challenge him. Furthermore, being armed caused others to be more on the defensive when one was seeking information. The appearance of an unarmed boy would not raise a warning sign that he might be a threat. For now he would leave his weapon in his saddlebag.

From his discussion with Joyner, William concluded the probability was high that the Rouses had returned to Tennessee. Accordingly, his plan was to parallel the North Carolina–Virginia state border to Tennessee and from there make his way to Powder Springs. Should he have little difficulty in finding places where he could cross rivers and navigate through the Blue Ridge Mountains, he hoped to make the Tennessee border within ten days.

On his third day of travel, William accepted the fact that his ten-day target was too optimistic considering the leisurely pace he was taking. For the first time in his life, he did not feel the necessity to rush to complete the task that lay before him. With a slight twinge of guilt, he felt the freedom to travel at a pace he could enjoy seeing new parts of the state. He made a point to skirt all towns and villages, leaving him void of any communication with people, and he could fully embrace the beauty and sounds of nature.

For the first time, he was completely dependent upon nature for his food, water, and shelter. Normally, around midafternoon he would start looking for his evening meal. He made a point not to kill anything more than he could eat. His diet, for the most part, consisted of rabbit, squirrel, raccoon, wild turkey, and fish.

In the late afternoon or early evening, he would start looking for a place for him and Taz to bed down for the night. Weather determined whether he needed to find a cave or build a shelter using his water-repellant duster. Regardless of the conditions, he was, for once, enjoying having only to concern himself with his personal needs. And in accordance with Ma's directive, he always managed to find a creek, pond, or river to take his weekly bath. Shaving was still not an issue for him because to some extent, in spite of his height of five feet, ten inches and weight of 165 pounds of solid muscle, his face still conveyed a boyish appearance. Nevertheless, he had long ago proved he could do the physical work of any man and that his boyish look made him no less a man.

To William, the wilderness of forest and wild animals was more than any person could want. On his eighth day, he emerged from the woods to peer down upon the most beautiful valley he had ever seen. There was beautiful grassy land with a backdrop to the west of a ridge of the first mountains he had ever seen. A stream, as far as he could see, ran from the mountains behind a small white house and disappeared into the hills to the east. He believed he was about twenty miles east of Boone, North Carolina.

The grassland appeared to be dotted with images of cows grazing. A field of what he believed to be corn was growing between the house and the mountain stream. The view caused him to think, "This is a place I could settle down. I don't think there is any place between here and Wayne County that I have seen more beautiful. I think I'll ride down for Taz and me to have a drink of water from that stream. I might be able to get some news on what is happening with the war. Maybe in the last few days, it has ended. I sure hope so!"

William turned Taz in the direction of the small white house, which appeared to be about two miles away. Taz picked up his pace, as though he was anxious to taste some of that grass that was bending in the gentle breeze that was blowing through the valley.

As William moved Taz through the tall green grass, he could not help but become amused at Taz grabbing a mouthful of grass every three to four steps. When Taz held his head up to chew, the grass protruded from each side of his mouth to give the appearance of a green mustache. He was eating as though he would never again see such a plush field. Watching Taz eat caused William to display no hurry to get to the little white house.

Approximately twenty minutes later, William approached the entrance to the farmhouse. The house was surrounded by a white picket fence. Flowers were planted along the walkway to the house, and shrubs bordered the front porch. Two men were standing in the walkway, one with his back to the entrance and holding the reins to his horse, the other in bib overalls. William could see the man with his back to him had his revolver tied to his leg. The other man, unarmed, William surmised to be a farmer.

Walking Taz, slowly through the gate entrance, William heard the man with his back to him say, "You can leave voluntarily or be torched out."

Until then, although William was certain the farmer had seen him approaching, the farmer had never given any indication that William was near.

William, when he saw the farmer looking past the man in front of him and in his direction, said, "Sir, I'm sorry to interrupt your conversation. I just would like to fill my canteen and give my horse a drink of water, if that's all right with you."

The man with his back turned suddenly spun around with his hand going for his gun. Seeing William was unarmed, he said in a snarly manner, "Boy! Around here you don't come up behind a man without announcing yourself!"

William quickly replied, "I'm sorry, sir, but I'm not from around here. I'm just passing through and hoped to get some water for my horse and me."

The farmer motioned toward the water trough and the water well and said, "Help yourself, son."

William continued toward the water trough but kept listening. He could hear the man's hand slap on his saddle horn, and the man said to his horse, "Whoa!" Still not looking back, he heard the man say, "I'll be back tomorrow, and you best be out of here!"

As William lifted himself out of his saddle, he could hear the man's horse galloping off into the distance. He led Taz to the water trough, where Taz dropped his head and started drinking.

William lifted his canteen off his saddle horn and walked over to the well. As he lowered the bucket to get some water, he could hear the farmer coming up behind him.

"Son, I hope you overheard some of that conversation," said the farmer.

"I did, sir, but I wasn't eavesdropping. The fellow spoke loud enough for anyone to hear. What was all that about…torching you out?"

"After you take care of your horse, come on up to the front porch and join me. I'll tell you all about it. Do you have a place to stay tonight?"

"Yes sir. Under that big beautiful sky."

"Nonsense! You bed your horse down in my corral, and you can sleep in my hay barn tonight. While you take care of your horse, I'll tell my wife to set another plate at the table for tonight. Bet you haven't had a good home-cooked meal in a while."

"You're right about that. Been on the road now going on two weeks."

"Well, you plan to spend the night here. Besides, I need someone besides Lilly, my wife, to talk to. By the way, I'm Alfred Jones."

William reached his hand out to shake hands and said, "Good to meet you, Mr. Jones. My name is William…William Daniel. I'm from Wayne County."

"Heard of it but never been there." Mr. Jones then turned and started walking toward the house.

John sat at one end of the dining table with his back against the wall, and Becky sat at the other end with her back to the kitchen door. The children all sat on the long benches on each side of the table. All had finished dinner, and the children had been excused to complete their daily chores.

"How did your trip into Saulston go today?" asked Becky. This was the first time John had made a trip by himself. And while Becky thought it was too soon, she knew John was yearning for the experience of being independent again. It had now been almost ten months since John's injury, and while she would not admit it to John, William's departure had pushed John into taking on the responsibility of managing the farm and motivating him to accept more physical challenges.

John replied, "Went well. Picked up a few things the boys needed to work the farm. A file was needed for sharpening the shears and the hoes for chopping the weeds from around the tobacco plants. Also, another halter was needed for Jake." Jake was one of the mules.

"Any news about the war?"

"Yeah. Seems the Carolina boys got hit rather hard in the Wilderness Campaign. No one had any specifics. Went by the telegram office to see if there had been any news from William. Found we had a message from Constable Joyner in Weldon. Said William had stopped in to see him. Had questions about the Rouse brothers. Told him they were wanted in both North Carolina and Virginia. Said he was going to find them and get justice for me. Ended his telegram by saying I could be proud of him and that he was confident William will be able to take care of himself."

"That was certainly nice of Constable Joyner to tell us about William's visit. He's grown up awfully fast, but I still worry about him."

"I know what you mean, Becky. All we can do is to continue to pray for his safety and that he'll be back home soon."

Becky stood up and said, "I know. Let me see if I can clean the kitchen, and maybe we'll have some time for you to read us a few verses from the Good Book before we all have to go to bed."

"Okay. I'm going out to make sure the boys got everything ready for tomorrow before they left this afternoon. William certainly picked some good help for me. I didn't know there were any other boys around Saulston that could work as hard as William. And while they're good workers, they're not much in the way of independent thinkers."

Beck laughed and said, "That's because they weren't trained by you."

ঽ

After William had placed Taz in Mr. Jones's corral and his saddle, sad-dlebags, and bedroll in the hay barn, William returned to the front porch, where Mr. Jones was seated puffing on his pipe.

"Thank you, Mr. Jones, for permitting me to spend the night here and offering me a home-cooked meal," said William as he took a seat on the porch, leaning his back against one of the porch columns.

Jones smiled and replied, "Got to tell you, there is motive behind my offer."

"Fair enough. What can I do for you?"

"It's not normal for me to seek counsel from someone so much younger than me, but those older, and whom I regarded to be wiser, have disappointed me. My initial impression of you is that you are much wiser than your age might suggest. Furthermore, you don't know what has been happening around here and might be a little more objective. I would like for you to hear me out and tell me your honest opinion."

"Yes sir, I can do that," said William. "But what I will tell you is what my Pa would have told me."

Mr. Jones began. "About five years ago, a man from Raleigh, named Hamstrome, moved here with some mighty deep pockets. Rumor is he made his fortune with the railroad. Anyways, he started buying up land between here and Boone. He now owns most of this valley. And he's been offering a fair price for the land. Most folks took his offer as soon as he made it.

"But a few, like me, were not interested in selling. He suggested to them they might want to reconsider his offer, since folks who live in isolated areas are subject to unpleasant accidents. Some who declined his offer found their cattle dead from an unknown cause. Poison was sus-pected but couldn't be proven. Others had mysterious fires in their barns. Barns that had weathered all kinds of storms for years. These accidents of unknown nature resulted in those folks selling out to Hamstrome at about half of his original offer.

"He now owns the land on both sides of me. He continues to push me to sell. A month ago he personally came to see me and reminded me of all the accidents my neighbors had. He then went on to say that if I didn't sell, Mother Nature could make things a lot worse than anything my neighbors experienced.

"I interpreted that to be a threat, so, I told the sheriff. The sheriff said he did not think I should interpret a simple fact stated by Hamstrome to be a threat. Hamstrome only stated what Mother Nature could do to any of us, and he did not consider that to be a threat.

"Since then I have had periodic reminders from Hamstrome's men that either I accept the offer being made to me, or I could end up with nothing. You heard part of the latest conversation this afternoon. The man that was here is a hired gun. The latest strategy by Hamstrome is to make his final offer tomorrow. If I decline, a torch will be set to my house. I will then have to leave with nothing more than a token offer of what Hamstrome originally offered for my farm. A token that will not replace my losses, much less obtain another place to live.

"I'm forty years old. This farm has been in our family since North Carolina became a state. I have two boys who are ten and eight. I had plans to leave this farm to them. So I either take the offer or lose everything I have."

William could see Jones was torn between raw emotions and bitter anger. Jones wanted to fight back, but the future of his family was at stake.

After several minutes William said, "Mr. Jones, you and only you can make your decision. And the decision you make, you will have to live with it. If you walk away, you will always wonder if you did the right thing. And you should expect members of your family, one day, to question your decision.

"Should you stand your ground, I believe your chances to be at least fifty-fifty. Hamstrome has sent one man to take care of his business. And, while he may have more, there are only two of us."

"Are you saying that you will stand with me?"

"Yes sir."

"Why?"

"Because you took me in without knowing anything about me. And it's exactly what my father would do."

"Son, you don't even have a weapon, and all I have is a shotgun."

"If you have that shotgun trained on the man that is doing all the talking, all the time that he is here; and, he knows you will use it, he is not going to be too quick to go for his pistol. If his hand touches the handle of his pistol, you empty both barrels on him."

"And, what will you be doing, William?"

"I'll be backing you up."

Jones thought for a few minutes and then said, "I'm gonna take your fifty-fifty odds. But don't say anything to my wife, Lilly."

That evening William had the best meal he had since he left home. He thoroughly enjoyed meeting Lilly and the two boys, Todd and Robert. He and the boys talked about fishing, and the boys had a funny story about their first encounter with a skunk. However, Lilly didn't find it all that amusing, considering she had to clean the boys afterward. The only thing said about the next day was that if a man came to the house tomorrow, everyone was to stay inside the kitchen area. They were not to come outside until Jones told them they could. Of course, the boys wanted a reason, and the reason was "Because your dad said so!"

CHAPTER 19

IN THE VALLEY

The next day began with two significant preparations for the expected gun-slinging visitor. First, William found a can of black paint in the barn. He then took the top half of one of the stalls' hutch doors off its hinges. Using the paint and one end of a horse brush, he painted in bold capital letters the words "NO TRESPASSING." He placed the sign against the fence at the entrance to the yard.

Second, Jones, with shotgun in hand, took a seat in his rocking chair on the front porch to await the arrival of the unwelcome guest. As the clock inside the house struck 8:00 a.m., Jones detected a cloud of dust in the distance. In front of the cloud was a speck that became larger the closer the cloud moved toward the house. There were no other riders.

Jones hollered to William, who was standing near the well, "We've got company coming, one rider, and he's moving fast."

"Okay! Remember what I said. If he takes his right hand off the reins, you let him hold both barrels because he'll be reaching for his gun. We'll have him for trespassing, and you'll have been acting in self-defense," replied William.

"Where will you be?" asked Jones.

"I have to go to the barn, but I'll have you covered."

The rider, the man from the previous day, rushed through the entrance and then reined in his horse so hard that the horse's rear almost touched the ground.

Jones was already on his walkway with his shotgun pointing at the man. The man glared at how brazen Jones had become from the previous day and the man thought, "Doesn't he know who he is dealing with?"

Jones, being as calm as he could be, said, "Before you say anything, know that you are trespassing, and should you remove your right hand from your reins, I will interpret that as going for your gun, at which time I will, in an act of self-defense, blow you out of your saddle with both barrels of this gun."

The rider, not letting go of the reins, looked around to see if anyone else was watching. Seeing no one, he said, "Either you are a very brave old man, or you're very stupid. I'm not sure you have what it takes to pull the trigger, and one moment of hesitation on your part will be all I need to put a bullet between your eyes."

Then he heard another voice from his right side say, "I won't hesitate!"

The man turned slowly and looked to his right. There stood William, his Colt on his side with the holster strapped to his right leg. His right hand was just above the grip of his Colt. When the hired gun turned back to look at Jones, he found he was staring directly into a double-barreled shotgun.

The man's composure was obviously shaken when he said, "This is not the end of this."

"The end of what?" asked William.

The man was lost for words and outgunned.

William continued. "Take this message to Mr. Hamstrome. This farm is not for sale. If you or any of his men are seen on this farm, they will be considered to be trespassers and will be shot on sight. Should Mother Nature have an accident on this farm, Father Devil will have one on Hamstrome's place. Now, that is just a fact, not a threat. The sheriff might want to be so advised."

"Why should I believe a wet-behind-the-ears brass-talking kid?" asked the gunslinger.

William had already seen a folded paper sticking halfway out of the man's front shirt pocket. He assumed it was the sales contract that Hamstrome expected Jones to sign. With a swiftness of hand the hired gun had never expected nor seen before, William drew and fired. The round from William's Colt shredded the paper in the man's pocket and gave a burning sensation to the man's chest where his pocket had been.

With the steely eyes of a rattlesnake that had just struck, William said, "Now you see it; now you don't." Bits of paper blew to the ground as William holstered his Colt.

Both the hired gun and Jones were stunned at what they had just witnessed. The hired gun started to rub the burn in his chest where his pocket had been.

William, in a calm but stern manner, said, "You deliver this message: for the safety of all concerned, there are to be no more visitors to the Joneses' property, and any unusual events that might occur here will be viewed as man-made complications to what otherwise is a peaceful valley. Now get, before I try to lift your wallet with my next shot."

The rider whirled his horse around and left as fast as he had arrived.

"I still can't believe what I just saw with my own two eyes," said Jones.

William unbuckled his gun belt, threw it across his shoulder, and turn for the barn. "I hope that will end your troubles, Mr. Jones," said William.

William spent one more day at the Joneses' farm to see if there was any response from Hamstrome. There was not. He decided it was time for him to move on. Before departing, he told Mr. Jones if there was any backlash from Hamstrome, it would be when Hamstrome learned that William was no longer there. William said, "In a week, send a telegram to me in Asheville to let me know iffen you have had any more problems. If you need me, I'll return. Otherwise, the next time I'm by this way, when I'm on my way back home, I'll pay you a visit." He then said his goodbyes to the Jones family and pointed Taz in the direction of Boone. William was thinking, "For now there is peace in the valley."

CHAPTER 20

THE BRIAR PATCH

After departing the Joneses' farm, William and Taz took their time traveling as they started their climb toward Boone. Boone was a relatively new village. It had been incorporated less than twenty years earlier and was named in honor of the frontiersman, Daniel Boone. The three-thousand-foot climb was rigorously winding and twisting up and across mountains.

William arrived at the outskirts of the village in the late afternoon. Here in the shade of some tall trees near a bubbling stream, William decided he would spend the night. Food was not an issue this evening because Mrs. Jones had packed him a meal of fried chicken, a baked sweet potato, corn on the cob, and a couple of biscuits about the same size as the apple she placed in a cloth bag. He had been thinking of that bag most of the day.

The following morning the glow of the sun radiated above the mountains from the east. By the time it was fully above the mountains, William's plan was to be in the saddle and drawing near to Boone. As he rode he munched on a biscuit he had not eaten the previous evening.

William found Boone to be an interesting mountain village with a view of a rugged mountain range to its west. The range had a blueish haze that engulfed the ridge lines and obscured much of the forest that rose toward some of the mountain crests. William had never seen clouds that wrapped themselves around mountains where one could see the foot of the mountain and the peak with its middle being a white belt of clouds.

There were two places he was looking to visit. The first was the sheriff's office, and the second was the newspaper office. His revolver was safely inside his saddlebag.

Before entering the sheriff's office, he saw a sign that read Sheriff Todd McCaine—The Law. Upon entering, William immediately concluded that one's appearance was not a prerequisite for the sheriff of Watauga County. The sheriff had a long, unkempt beard; his clothes had not been cleaned in the last month; and his body odor filled the small room. He appeared to be chewing tobacco or dipping snuff, as his beard around the right corner of his mouth had a brownish stain.

Before inquiring as to William's business with him, he leaned to his left side, raising the right cheek of his butt, and let out a loud fart. With a sheepish smile on his face, he said, "More room on the outside than on the inside." He then laughed.

William was thinking, "Is this some kind of joke? I've never met a public official with such a disgusting and impolite attitude."

"What can I do for you, boy?" asked the sheriff.

"Sheriff McCaine, my name is William Daniel, and I'm just passing through town. I want to ask you one question and provide you some information," said William.

"Go ahead and ask. I got no place to be right now."

William reached inside his shirt and pulled out the wanted poster on the Rouse brothers and handed it to the sheriff. "Sir, I was wondering if you might have seen these two pass through your town."

McCaine studied the poster for a few minutes and said, "And what's it to you?"

"The two tried to kill my pa. They robbed him of all his military pay and left him for dead. I'm trying to locate them so I can tell the law and the law can arrest them."

"You're not out here seeking revenge, are you, boy?"

"No, sir. You can see I don't carry a weapon. I'm just looking for justice for my pa."

The sheriff seemed to turn a little sympathetic to William. "No son, I haven't seen them. But iffen I do, I'll sure put the cuffs on them. Those two no-gooders are needin' a necktie party." Handing the poster back to William, he said, "Son, don't you go get yourself killed messing with the likes of them. Now, what is it you want to tell me?"

William then shared with the sheriff the incident at the Joneses' farm. He made no mention of his involvement, only that he had overheard the threat to torch Mr. Jones's house if he did not sell to Hamstrome. Believing the sheriff and Hamstrome might have some personal relationship, he hastened to add that Hamstrome might be unaware of the intimidation being extended by his men. And how he hoped the sheriff would take a personal interest in the welfare of Mr. Jones and his family.

The sheriff seemed to be thinking about what William had said. Now an outsider was telling him what Jones had also told him. It might not be a good idea to continue to turn a blind eye to Hamstrome's activities. He then said, "I thank you for sharing that information with me. I'll ride out to the Joneses' farm in a day or so to make sure everything is all right. I'll also let Hamstrome know his men can't be misinterpreting his instructions and threatening harm to the farmers who don't sell to him."

William stood up and said, "Thank you, Sheriff. I'm sure Mr. Jones will be happy to learn you have his and his family's welfare in your best interests. Have a good day." William departed the sheriff's office in search of the local newspaper.

Across the street and three doors down from the sheriff's office was a shingle hanging above a door that read, Watauga Enterprise—Publisher & Editor, Thomas E. Bingham.

Upon entering the newspaper office, William saw a short, stout man standing at a printing press who appeared to be rearranging letters on a large printing plate. When he entered, a bell above the door gave a short ring to announce his presence.

The man looked up from what he was doing, adjusted the glasses from the bridge of his nose to his eyes, and said, "Name is Bingham. How may I help you?"

"My name is William Daniel. I've been on the road for about a month without any news and was wondering how the war was going."

"I wish I could tell you to buy a paper, but I've sold out of last Thursday's edition, and next edition will not be out until next Monday. I suspect you'll be riding out before then, so you just may be the benefactor of some free news."

William laughed and said, "I sure would appreciate anything you can tell me."

Bingham walked away from the press and said, "Well, have a seat, and I'll give you the short and dirty what's been going on."

William took a seat in one of the two chairs in the newspaper office.

Bingham began. "The fighting I know the most about is taking place in the Shenandoah Valley. From the bits and pieces I've gotten, there seems to be a lot of pushing and shoving from both sides with no clear victor. Course, if you talk to anyone around here, they'll tell you the rebels are kicking butt. Trying to be more objective, I'd say the Yankees are holding their own. Don't think it will last much longer. What's your interest? Worried about being called up?"

"No sir, not worried about that. I'd gladly serve iffen it weren't for my Pa. He got badly hurt north of Richmond and was medically discharged. I've been trying to take care of things around the farm."

Bingham must have assumed the farm was close by because he didn't inquire as to where William was from. And before he did, William hastened to inquire, "Mr. Bingham, I have to go to Asheville. Can you tell me the best route through the mountains to get there?"

Bingham put his thumb and forefinger up between his eyes and pinched his glasses a little tighter and said, "Young man, there is not an easy way from here to Asheville. 'Pending on who you talk to, you will probably get differing answers. But if you're not familiar with this area, my suggestion would be to take the road in front of my office west. When you get out of town, you'll see to the southwest a large mountain range that when you look closely you will see what appears to be the profile of a man's forehead, nose, and beard. That is Grandfather Mountain. Follow that ridge, remaining on the north side. Crossing there might be shorter, but it will also take you longer.

"Once that view is behind you, start looking to the south for a big rock that is round with a flat top. That is Table Rock. Ride toward it. The terrain will be rugged, and you will probably walk more than you ride because the going can be tough on the best of horses. Couple hours later, you should come to a wagon road. Follow that road west, and eventually you will see a sign pointing you in the direction of Asheville."

"I certainly appreciate that information, Mr. Bingham. How long would you estimate it will take me to get to Asheville?"

"Well, iffen you could fly like a bird, maybe two to three hours. But on your horse and your feet, you need to allow a couple of days. It's not an easy trip."

"Again, I thank you, and I will now be on my way." William departed the *Watauga Enterprise*, and the little bell bid him goodbye as he opened the door.

Back in the saddle, William said to Taz, "Big fellow, sounds to me like what we have experienced so far has been a cakewalk compared to what lies in front of us. Hope you got rested up during our short stay at the Joneses' farm." He then gave Taz a little nudge with his knees, and Taz started to trot out of the village of Boone.

Two miles outside Boone, the Grandfather Mountain Range was in prominent view, and what had been a wagon-wheel road narrowed to about half its previous width. While the terrain was winding and twisting combined with steep inclines and sharp drop-offs, it wasn't as difficult as William had anticipated. But that was about to change.

It was near midafternoon before William identified Table Rock. According to Bingham's instructions, he was now to turn in the direction of the rock. At that point the vegetation became denser, and the incline became steeper. The reason was that now he was going to have to cross the ridge line that connected with Grandfather Mountain. This required him to get off Taz and start to maneuver his way through the thick undergrowth, avoiding hidden and dangerous crevices.

After two more hours of struggling uphill and through the thick vegetation, he decided he and Taz had traveled far enough for the day. It took him a while, but eventually he located a fairly level place where he could camp for the night. At this time he had not spotted anything he could shoot for dinner, and there was no sound of a mountain stream nearby. For him, dinner was going to consist of beef jerky and water. Taz was already nibbling at the grass between the rocks and closest trees. If all went well, tomorrow they should make Asheville. There he would find the telegraph office to see if he had a message from Mr. Jones.

By midmorning the next day, William had crossed the ridge line and was on the downward slope of the mountain. At lunchtime he came upon an east–west trail. While not exactly what William considered to be a road, he believed it to be the route that Bingham had referred to. He turned Taz west and said goodbye to his navigation point, Table Rock.

After five miles of lower inclines and less rugged terrain, he saw where another trail merged with the trail he was riding. At the merger was the sign Bingham had told him about. The word Asheville was printed above a black arrow pointing in a southwest direction. It was his hope to make Asheville before the sun set. Knowing that Taz would stay on the trail, he could look for whatever wild game he could find for his evening meal.

By nightfall, William had bedded down Taz and had a rather good rabbit stew. He cut the rabbit up into small bites, which he put in a pan with water, flour, wild artichokes, and corn from a stalk he had gotten at the Joneses' farm. As the stew simmered, he added a pinch of salt he had brought with him from home. Tomorrow he would fulfill his commitment to Mr. Jones. He prayed all was well because he did not want to cross that mountain range again to return to the Joneses' farm.

Arriving the following morning in the town of Asheville, William was surprised to see how much the town reminded him of Goldsboro. The town seemed to be very much alive as people hurried to and fro, either going to work or conducting early-morning shopping. Were it not for the absence of young men, one's initial impression might be the war was bypassing Asheville. That aside, his main mission today was to locate the telegraph office to see if he had received a message from Mr. Jones.

William suspected the telegraph office to be located either in the train depot or nearby. Fortunately, that was not hard to locate because he could hear a train whistle a short distance west of the main street. Steering Taz in the direction of the sound, he had ridden two blocks when he saw the train tracks.

Once he was closer to the tracks, he could see a locomotive engine beginning slowly to leave the station. He could see people leaning out train windows waving goodbye to loved ones or friends, and from the station, he saw similar responses.

Near the station was a hitching rail, where he tied Taz. He then started to walk along the platform looking for a sign that would identify the telegraph office. Upon seeing the sign, he strolled to the window and peered inside.

A man wearing glasses and a visor hat was busily organizing some papers while keeping an ear in the direction of the telegraph machine. William tapped the top of a bell, much like one seen on hotel counters, to signal a need for service.

The man turned with an agitated expression on his face, as if he was busy doing a very important job.

William stared back and said, "Sorry to interrupt, but I need to know if you have a message for me."

"And who are you?" asked the man as he pushed up his sleeves and walked toward the window.

"William Daniel."

"Name sounds familiar. Let me check." The man walked over to a long wooden file box and began to sort through messages contained in the box. Obviously, he was highly organized, because within a matter of seconds, he withdrew a paper. He walked over to the window and, before handing William the message, said, "That will be five cents."

William dug down into his trouser pocket and extracted some coins. He counted out five one-cent pieces, and the man handed William the message. William stepped to one side and began to read: "All is well, stop. H. paid visit with Sheriff, stop. Agreed if I should ever decide to sell, he had first option, stop. Thanks and be safe, stop. Jones."

"Whew!" thought William. "Now I can continue to Powder Springs without any further delay."

On the spur of the moment, William stuck his head back in the window and said, "How much will it cost for me to send a message to Saulston, North Carolina?"

The telegraph operator seemed more interested in sending than retrieving an already-sent message. "A penny for every five words," came the reply.

"Got a pencil and a piece of paper I can write on?" asked William.

The man handed William a pencil and paper and said, "Don't forget to return the pencil."

William filled in the blank that read: "Send To:" with "John Robert Daniel, Saulston, North Carolina." Then he scratched out the following message: "Family, all is well. In Asheville. Destination is Powder Springs, Tenn. Don't worry. Will advise on my return. William." He then handed the paper and pencil back to the operator.

After looking over the message, the operator said, "That will be four cents."

William counted out four pennies and asked, "When will the message be sent?"

Now that the man had the money, he quipped back, "As soon as you leave me to do my job."

William chuckled to himself as he made his way back to Taz. The thought running through his mind was "No more delays. Now I can do what I started out to do." Little did he realize, even the best of plans have unexpected risks.

Two days from Asheville, William was traversing some of the most rugged terrain he had experienced to date. He was heading in a northeasterly direction, and most of this travel was on foot with Taz following. Even when he had cleared a path for himself, he found he had to return to untangle some of the vines that appeared to reach out and grab his saddle horn or saddlebags. Taz would stand patiently for William to free him, and they would then proceed. Several times, had William not been on foot, they would have probably ventured into a ravine that was unseen for its vegetation coverage. William was beginning to think he must have made a wrong turn somewhere for there not to be a clearer passage. What he had failed to foresee, not being familiar with traversing mountain ranges, was that there were better routes, but they tended to skirt around the mountains until there were clearer trails. Of course, the trails might add significantly more mileage to the trip, but in the long run, the farther distance might be faster.

It was during one of his rest breaks from breaking a new path through a web of mountainous terrain that he thought he heard a sound that was not one made by any wild animal he knew. He quickly looked in the direction of Taz. He knew if he heard something, so did Taz.

Taz had his head turned to his left, and both ears were up and pointing in that direction. "He heard something also!" thought William.

William remained next to Taz to ensure he remained perfectly quiet. He strained to hear the sound again. Again, after several minutes he thought he detected a faint whimpering sound. It was as if someone was trying to stifle pain and in fear of being heard.

Taking no chances, William retrieved his rifle and began to move as silently as possible in the direction from where he believed the sound had come. He picked each step carefully and gently removed vines that tried to entrap him. He would move a few feet and listen, move another few feet and listen again.

The sound seemed to be coming from a short distance to his front but below him. From his current stand, the ground appeared to be flat but obscured by thick vegetation consisting primarily of briars.

He moved a few steps farther and saw a slight movement in a thicket of briars. His next footstep did not make contact with solid ground, and to avoid falling forward into the thicket, he twisted his body, pushed off with the foot that was on firm ground, and dove backward. His immediate thought was "If had fallen into that ravine, and if it's over six feet deep, I probably would never get out." And then he was hit with the thought that possibility someone could be entangled in that briar patch.

Lying on his belly, he inched himself back to where the ground made a sharp descent. The thick vegetation kept him from getting any perspective of the size of the briar-infested ravine. With the barrel of his rifle, he tried to push some of the vegetation to one side to get a better view of what might lie deeper in the briars.

When he was just about to give up, he thought he saw the movement of a color that contrasted with the foliage. He hollered, "Anyone in there?"

There was no response. Again, he hollered, "If there is someone in there, say something, and I will try to help you."

This time he heard a low moan in what he believed to be a woman's voice. He looked around and found a limb that was longer than his rifle and began trying to move the briars where he could get a better look. The shadows cast by the overhanging trees were not helping. After pushing more vines around, he saw what appeared to be a small bloody leg. The upper body appeared to be lower and hidden by the briars.

William hollered again, "Don't move. I'm going to get you out. I must first get my horse and some rope. I'll be right back." He then laid his rifle on the ground with the barrel pointing in the direction of the leg.

William retrieved Taz and brought him to a tree near the hidden ravine and positioned him where Taz could move backward if need be. He then took his lariat from his saddle and tied one end to his saddle horn, and he tied the middle of the lariat around his waist in a way that he could lower himself as he cleared a way through the briars. Also, should he start to fall, he wanted to be in a position where he could command Taz to back up. When Taz obeyed his command, he would be pulled back to a safe position.

With his hunting knife, William began to vigorously cut away briars and cast them aside. As he cleared the briars from around himself, he would then lower himself deeper into the ravine. His real concern was that if the person he was trying to reach moved any, she might cause herself to fall deeper into the briars.

At last he reached the exposed leg. From that position he could see the body was lying at a forty-five-degree angle, head first into the briars. Getting her out without hurting her more was going to be difficult. Since briars overlapped her body, there was no way of knowing her condition or how long she might have been there.

He could now hear a low moan, indicating that she was alive but in great pain. When he had the briars cut away from around her waist, he tied the other end of his rope around her waist so she would not descend farther into the ravine as he cut other briars from around her.

When he cut the briars from around her shoulders, he could see her long black hair was matted into the briars. She was wearing a dress made from deer hide. Had she been wearing anything else, she would have had more cuts and scratches.

Although she had not tried to say anything, he knew she would probably be upset that he was having to cut her hair from the briars. However, cutting her hair was much easier and faster.

Once she was free of the briars, she was still motionless. If he tried to pull her directly out of the briars in her position, she would be cut even more on her face and arms. He needed a better approach. His only immediate solution was to let his body be her stretcher.

He moved his body as close to hers as possible. His weight combined with her weight caused the vines that were holding her up to start giving way. He knew he now had to act fast. While the lariat would hold her from falling more than a foot or so, that would mean her already cut face and shoulders would experience more damage and pain.

William quickly rolled her body over on his body so that her back was against his chest. With his arms under her armpits, he yelled to Taz, "Back, Taz! Back, Taz! Back, big fellow!"

William felt his back begin inching up out of the ravine as Taz dutifully obeyed his command. The briars cut deep into his back, shoulders, and hips. He thought, "If this woman could bear the pain as long as she has, I know I can endure the few minutes that it will take for Taz to pull us out."

As William's shoulders breached the rim of the ravine, Taz stopped pulling. William knew that as soon as Taz saw his head, Taz would think his job was over. William yelled again, "Back, Taz! Back now, big fellow!"

This time Taz pulled until William and the woman were out of the ravine. William gave the command "Whoa! Whoa, Taz!" and Taz immediately halted the pull.

William squeezed his body from under the woman as carefully as he could. He got to his knees quickly to see if the woman had opened her eyes. She had not.

What William did see, with cuts, scratches, a swollen face, and lots of dried blood, was that she was about his age and the most beautiful girl he had ever seen. As a matter of fact, she was the first Indian girl he had ever seen.

He wished Ma were there to tell him what he needed to do first. But instinct kicked in, and he knew the first things were to make her comfortable and to get some nutrition in her. Her cuts and scratches could be tended to later.

He made her a bed with his bedroll under a nearby tree. Tomorrow he would find them better shelter. He then built a fire, and from the rabbit he had killed earlier in the day, he started cooking her rabbit soup. While the soup was cooking, he bathed her face.

The cool water caused her to open her eyes. A frightened look came on her face. William understood her first instinct would be to flee. So he started to talk to her in a calm and comforting voice while offering her a sip of water from his canteen. And although she accepted the water, he knew she remained extremely frightened of him, and it was obvious she did not understand what he was saying. He tried his best to keep his voice in a soothing tone and convey the attitude that he did not represent any harm to her.

He purposely had hidden his weapons and placed his blanket over her. He motioned with his hand to his mouth to ask if she wanted something to eat. She gave no reaction.

William smiled at her, stood up slowly, walked to the fire, and from the pot dipped out a small pan of soup. He then returned slowly to her side, knelt down, spooned out a small portion of the soup, blew on it to make sure it was not too hot, and extended it to her mouth.

Her eyes never left his every action. She first smelled of the soup. William touched the spoon to her lips. She first hesitated, then quickly took in the spoonful. Thereafter, each time William placed the spoon near her lips, she readily accepted the food. William thought this was a good indication she knew that to get stronger, she needed to eat, and she might be showing him a little trust.

CHAPTER 21

TRUST AND RECOVERY

The Indian girl slept soundly all night. Periodically, William checked to ensure she was still alive. Her motionless body kept him anxious, precluding him from getting some much-needed rest.

He arose before daybreak, stoked the fire and placed more wood on it, and prepared some flapjacks with the flour he had. He also warmed some beef jerky. She slept until the sun started to warm the ground.

When she awoke, she squirmed around some as though she was trying to sit up. William walked over and put his arms under her armpits and lifted her to where her back was resting against the tree that had been near the top of her head. He then placed a pan of the warm beef jerky and flapjacks in her lap. She gave the impression she was independent and did not need him to feed her.

Without being obvious that he was watching her, he saw from the corner of his eye that she smelled the food before she put it near her mouth. At the time, he was heating some water. Earlier he had secured from his saddlebag a bar of lye soap his ma made and a small tin of salve she had insisted he have with him at all times in the event he incurred a wound. When the girl finished eating, he hoped to try to remove some of the dried blood and cover her wounds with the salve.

When she had finished, she sat the pan to one side. William walked over, secured the pan, pointed to her, and with his hand indicated eating from the plate. He was trying to ask her if she wanted more. She shook her head that she did not.

He then secured the heated water from the fire and got his bandanna and soap. She withdrew some when he knelt beside her. He first put some soap on the wet bandanna and rubbed it on one of the scratches on his arm. She watched carefully as the dried blood on him was erased.

He then motioned to her to extend her arm, and he would wash away her dried blood. She cautiously extended her arm. He took extra care to wash gently. Her eyes never left his movements.

When he finished her right arm, she voluntarily extended her left. After he finished her left arm, he wiped his face and then extended his hand to wipe her face. This time she pushed her head back against the tree trunk.

William did not withdraw but gently washed her forehead and worked his way to the bridge of her nose, cheeks, and chin. She reminded him of when his sisters were young and Ma tried to give them an unwanted bath.

Finally, he worked his way to her knees, around her calves, and to her feet. When he washed the bottom of her feet, a slight smile came upon her face as she felt a tickle.

Once all the visible dried blood had been removed, William demonstrated the application of the salve by putting some on himself first. Then he made a motion that she needed some. She showed no resistance. William made sure every cut and scratch he saw had some salve placed on it.

Then she did something that William, at first, did not comprehend. She pointed toward some vegetation near a rock, made a fist, and simulated a pulling motion.

William interpreted that to mean she wanted him to pull up some of the vegetation near the rock. When he started to, she grunted, shook her head, and pointed again. Obviously, he was not pulling up what she wanted. So he continued by pointing at each plant until she shook her head in approval. She then pointed toward where she heard the rushing stream of water going down the mountain. With an up-and-down movement of her hand, William understood that she wanted him to bring her a fish.

Fifteen minutes later, William returned with a fish. She pointed toward the pan of water and then to the fire. William thought, "I guess she wants me to reheat the water," which he did.

When the water was boiling, she first pointed for William to put the fish in the water and then to William's hunting knife. She held out her hand, indicating she wanted the knife. William, with some hesitation, handed it to her.

Looking in the vicinity of the tree, she picked up a flat rock. With the knife and using the rock as a cutting block, she cut up the roots off the vegetation William had pulled up. She then cut some of the moss off the tree and from the ground around the bottom of the tree.

William watched intently at what she was doing. She then pointed to the water with the fish, which was now boiling. She took the fish out of the water and laid it on the rock. She poured some of the water out of the pan and placed into the pan the roots and moss she had cut up. She stirred the pan with the hunting knife. As the water cooled, she added a little dirt, causing a paste to form in the pan.

She then began to apply the paste to some of the more severe cuts she had received. By now the sun was high, and heat was beating down on William. The heat caused the cut places on his back to begin burning. He decided to remove his shirt and wet it in the stream to cool his back.

As he started toward the stream, she said something that William did not understand, but it got his attention. She then motioned for him to come sit beside her. He did as he was told.

She placed her warm hands on his shoulders and turned him so his back was toward her. She then began to apply the paste she had made to his back. While it felt a little yucky, he didn't resist because now they were communicating.

When she had finished applying the paste, William said, "Thank you." He then added, pointing to himself, "Will...yum!"

She repeated, "Will...um." She pointed to herself and said, "Al... ylana."

William repeated back to her, "Al…ylana." William added, although he knew she would not understand, "Aylana, stay here!" Using hand language, with both hands open and turned toward the ground, he pushed downward. He then said, "William hunt!" He pointed toward his mouth and then got his weapon. Alyana nodded her head as if to say she understood.

In addition to hunting, William was also going to look for a better place for her to recover. It was now October, and the weather was getting colder at night. He did not know how soon it would be before it started snowing in the mountains, but he knew they needed a dryer and more secure shelter. He took only his rifle so that she would know that he was returning. Taz showed no interest in following William.

For the next week, the daily routine was much the same. Aylana continued to get her strength back. She was now walking and helping to prepare their meals. One afternoon while William was hunting, she went down to the mountain stream with William's bandanna and soap, took off her clothes, and took a bath. She discovered some places that needed some of her healing paste, which she applied before putting her clothes back on.

William continued to hunt and fish. Feeling confident that she was not going to venture too far from camp, he felt at liberty to expand his search area for their relocation. Farther up the mountain, he found a small entrance to what appeared to be a cave, but inside, it opened into what was more of a cavern. However, his visibility was very limited, which precluded his assessment of whether this would make for a suitable dwelling.

Back outside he found a stick, which he fashioned with some dry vines to make a torch. When he reentered, he found there was lots of space with a high ceiling. The smoke from the torch drifted toward the back of the cavern. There he found where the smoke was being dispersed between the rocks before it left the cave. This meant the cavern would be ventilated in a manner so as not to disperse a lot of smoke from one outlet. This would make it harder for anyone to detect visually where the smoke was coming from, which added to their security.

Because of the small entrance, he would have to build Taz an outdoor shelter. He was confident that with Taz's winter coat and a shelter to keep the snow, wind, and rain off him, he would do just fine. William was excited to be able to return and tell Aylana what he had found.

In the evening the two would practice their communication skills. He soon came to believe she was Cherokee. Each would point to something and say it in their native tongue, and the other would repeat it.

It was during their broken discourse sessions that he learned how she came to be in the briar patch. Her family was relocating with her tribe to a place farther south. Her mother asked her to go find some berries for their evening meal. She came upon a mother bear with a cub. The mother bear started to chase her, and before she knew it, she misstepped and went headfirst into the briar patch. She vaguely recalled her father calling for her but could not remember if she responded. Apparently, when they could not find her, the family continued their movement with the tribe. She did not know how long she had been in the ravine.

William did not tell her his real reason for his being there. He only said he was traveling through the area on the way to Tennessee when he happened upon her.

He told her that once they made it through the winter, he would take her to wherever she believed her tribe might have relocated.

On this particular day, he told her he had found a place where they could shelter for the winter months. Once they had relocated, he would travel down the mountain to try to find a few more winter provisions for them and Taz. If there was a village nearby, he might be able to obtain some dry goods and some corn for Taz.

The next week William and Aylana packed up their camp and moved a mile farther up the mountain into their cavern. Their wounds were healed to the point where there were now only some scars. More importantly, the two gained trust in each other and had come to understand their very survival depended upon their reliance on each other.

CHAPTER 22

A WINTERTIME HOME

As William and Aylana began to settle into their winter dwelling, William was surprised how much one could accumulate by just staying in one location. As he roamed through the woods to retrieve the snare traps he had set to catch rabbits, beavers, and raccoons, Aylana packed up their provisions, bedding, and pelts. From beaver pelts she had made herself a new pair of moccasins. The others had disappeared in the briar patch.

When William returned from gathering his traps, he, with his hatchet, cut two long poles. After placing the saddle on Taz, he tied the end of each pole into each stirrup. He then opened his bedroll and tied it across the two posts to make a drag upon which Aylana could attach all their belongings. As she went about that chore, she reminded William not to forget his fish traps.

She had shown William how to configure fish traps that allowed the mountain trout to swim into the trap but not out. This had precluded William from having to set fish lines each day with the hopes of catching something on a hook.

And while their journey was not much more than a mile, it was a gradual uphill climb. He tried to convince Aylana that he would take her up first on the drag and then return for their supplies and provisions. She would not agree. In that regard, she reminded William of Ma when she made up her mind she was going to do something her way. Pa never had a chance, once her mind was set.

After reassuring himself they had everything, William led out with Taz following on a lead line. Behind Taz was the drag, and behind the drag walked Aylana.

Periodically, William would look back to see how Aylana was doing. Frequently, she adjusted an item on the drag, but she never slowed. William was thinking, "With all she has been through, she is one tough woman." If she missed her family, which William was certain she did, she did not mention them. It was as if she knew how to accept the present without dwelling on the past. She gave the impression that if it was her fate to see her family again, that would happen, but for now she accepted her circumstances. Personally, William could not have been happier. It was just two young people exploring what the world had in store for them.

Upon arrival at the entrance to the cavern, William pulled from the drag two torches he had made. He lit one, which he gave to Aylana, and the other for himself. Then he motioned for her to follow him.

The light from the torches cast their shadows on the walls. Aylana walked around the walls, taking in what would be their shelter for the winter months.

William stood in one place, just to watch her reaction. She soon returned to where William was standing with a smile on her face and nodding her head in the affirmative. In rapid fire she began to talk in Cherokee while pointing to various points. William gathered she was telling him where everything was to be placed. William nodded he understood, and after fixing his torch into a crevice in the wall, he went back outside to unload the drag.

As she pointed out where she wanted him to place things, William suddenly realized the glow he felt inside and the peace she could cause him to feel. From that moment, he realized he had a very special feeling about this one he had found by accident…or was it fate?

That evening as the two sat around the fire inside the cavern, Aylana brought up the subject of larger pelts. Between her hand motions, broken

English, and Cherokee words, she made it clear to William that in order for her to prepare for the winter months, she needed William to bring in larger game, as larger pelts were needed to make warmer coverings.

In the past, William looked for the game he hunted strictly as food. He had never given thought to them as potential clothing or bedding. He agreed he would do a better job starting tomorrow morning.

For the next week, William hunted in the mornings and worked to build Taz a winter shelter. Fortunately, the previous lack of hunting of big game in the forest meant deer were plentiful. Each morning he would bring back to the cavern a killed deer, and Aylana immediately went to work dressing it out. William was amazed at how quickly she could skin a deer, and she was careful to extract the meat she could preserve by drying out.

As she worked with the animals he had either killed or trapped, he cut branches and limbs for the construction of a shelter for Taz. He could really use a tarp to provide a roof to the shelter. He added that to a list he had started to develop in his head for winter provisions they did not have. As he was mentally plotting his most direct course to Powder Springs, he recalled from a map at the train depot in Asheville that about midway, there was a village named Sugar Creek. He figured from their current location, Sugar Creek should be about a day's ride.

In the evenings they continued to practice each other's language. He told her of his family, and she told him of hers. When bedtime came she slept on one side of the fire, and he slept on the other. Throughout the night when one would wake up, they would place more wood upon the fire. Surprisingly, the ventilation system worked well, and there was seldom any smoke lingering inside the cavern.

One evening William told her of his need to locate Sugar Creek for some additional winter supplies. He needed more ammunition, salt, flour, matches, trousers, rope, and a tarp. But before he left, she needed to learn to use his rifle. He did not want to leave her without a means of protecting herself. He told her he thought the trip would take him about two days. He asked, "Is there something I can get for you?"

Aylana showed him the sharp splinter of a bone she had been using to sew with and the narrow strip of leather she was using for thread. She asked, "Store have this?"

William replied, "Yes, I think so."

Aylana smiled and said, "Good!"

The following morning, it now being late October, when William went outside, he found a dusting of snow. This meant winter, in the mountains, was not far off. That day he started teaching Aylana how to load his rifle, how to chamber the rounds, and how to fire the rifle. She proved to be a quick learner, and by the second day, she was hitting rocks about a foot in size from a distance of ten yards. He instructed her, "Aylana, I want you to stay inside the cavern at all times. However, if you have to go outside, you are to take the rifle with you, and be sure the rifle is ready to fire when you do go outside. Should someone try to come inside, first fire one warning shot into the entrance wall. If the person or animal continues to come in, you fire to kill. Do you understand?"

Aylana nodded her head that she understood.

After his instructions, he went outside to check his traps. At one trap a large bear was trying to get to a rabbit that had been caught. The thought that immediately ran through William's mind was "Aylana has been wanting some larger game. I wonder how she will react to a bear." With that thought, he fired two shots into the bear.

The bear's reaction was one of anger as it lunged at William. William jumped to one side and fire another shot into the bear's head.

The bear shook its head and looked at William. By now, William was wondering if he had made a mistake, because with two shots in its chest and one in its head, the bear still appeared to want to take a bite at William.

William started backing up and chambering another round. The bear made one lumbering step toward William and dropped to the ground.

"Is he dead?" William asked himself.

The bear made no more movements. William approached him cautiously and poked him with the barrel of his rifle. There was no movement. Its tongue was hanging out of its mouth, and its eyes were rolled back in its head. The bear was dead.

With his hunting knife, William marked several trees on his way back to the cavern. These marks would serve as to the location of the bear on his return trip.

Once back at the cavern, William got Taz and some rope. Before dark and with the strength of Taz, William managed to pull the bear back to the cavern. He then went in and announced. "Aylana, I have a surprise for you. Come outside."

When Aylana saw the bear, in particular its size, she was excited. She said, "You give me much work to do while you are gone. Before you go, you must hang him up so I can cut him."

William surmised that what Aylana was seeing was either a winter coat or a winter blanket. He said, "I will do it before leaving tomorrow morning."

The following morning after the bear was hung onto a tree limb, Taz was saddled and the drag attached to him. The drag was loaded with extra pelts William and Aylana had accumulated. Although he had some cash left from what he had drawn from his bank account before leaving Saulston, William wanted to be in a position to barter if the shopkeeper was of a mind to. William was now prepared to leave for Sugar Creek.

Aylana came outside to bid him farewell and to remind him to hurry back. William was wearing his duster for warmth and in the event he experienced any snow. With the raccoon hat that Aylana had made for him perched upon his head, he was beginning to look like a mountain man. Before climbing into the saddle, William surprised himself with what he did next. Without hesitation and in an act that seemed perfectly normal, he leaned over and gave Aylana a kiss on the cheek. Her immediate reaction was to place her hand on the spot where he had kissed her.

He smiled, turned Taz, and started for Sugar Creek.

Aylana watched him until he disappeared into the forest. He sat straight in the saddle like an Indian brave going off to battle.

CHAPTER 23

SUGAR CREEK

Near the end of the day, William came in sight of what he believed to be the village of Sugar Creek. From this distance the village appeared to consist of three or four buildings and several houses. He decided for tonight he would sleep under the trees at the edge of the forest. Tomorrow morning he would approach the village.

Before riding into the village the following morning, William strapped on his Colt revolver. A stranger approaching a peaceful village needed to be careful that his entrance would not be misinterpreted. An armed person seemed to draw more respect and caution from these mountain folks. William wanted no problems. He just wanted to get his supplies and return to Aylana as soon as possible.

The general store was located in the center of the village. He saw a shingle identifying a doctor's office farther down the street and across from what appeared to be a drinking establishment. Upon entering the village, he had noted a livery stable on the right side of the street. And just beyond the doctor's office was a small church. A few houses were mixed between some of the buildings. The general store had a porch, but there were no wooden sidewalks connecting the buildings.

On the porch of the general store sat a grizzly looking man with a beard, wearing a bearskin coat a beaver-skin hat. He had a shotgun across his lap. William had now learned that appearance could be deceiving among mountain folks. The man could either be the law, a trapper, or just a down-and-out villager.

As he entered the store, he tipped his hat to the grizzly looking man but received no indication he had even been noticed. Approaching the shopkeeper who was behind the counter, William said, "Sir, I have a list of supplies I need and also some pelts that I am hoping you might have an interest in bartering for some supplies."

"What kind of pelts do you have, young fellow?"

"The name is William, sir. I have mostly beaver and raccoon."

"Well, I'll take a look at them after I fill your list, if that is fair with you."

"Yes sir, that is fair with me."

As the shopkeeper was checking off the items on William's list, William browsed through the store to see if there was something else he might need he had forgotten. He couldn't help but notice the grizzly man who had been sitting outside was now inside watching the shopkeeper assemble William's list of goods.

At one point the shopkeeper handed William a pair of trousers and told him that he could go behind the curtain at the back of the store to try them on.

In a matter of minutes, William returned and said, "Yes sir, they will do just fine."

"You probably noticed I tried to get a pair I thought might be a little large for you. I know during the winter we have a tendency to put on a little weight. I know that I do." The shopkeeper patted his stomach and laughed.

William returned the laughter, but he was starting to get a little suspicious of the grizzly man, who seemed to take an interest in the purchases William was making. Finally, the shopkeeper said, "I believe I've gotten everything on your list. I had some leather boot strings that will fit through the eye of the needle I got for you. That's what most use around here when they're sewing hides together."

"Yes sir, that will be perfect. Also, please include these two sticks of peppermint candy I pulled from your jar over there," replied William.

The shopkeeper continued. "I only had one size of tarp, which is about the largest made. If you need smaller, you can always cut it down."

"Thank you," said, William. "Also, would you add four cans of those beans you have up on that shelf?" William pointed to the shelf behind the shopkeeper's head.

"Now, how much I owe you?" asked William.

"Your bill is now twenty-one dollars and eighteen cents. But before you pay, let's take a look at the pelts you have."

William and the shopkeeper went back outside. William saw the grizzly man had returned to his seat outside the store. The shopkeeper ignored the man and went directly to the drag behind Taz.

William uncovered the pelts, and the shopkeeper went through them, feeling each one. He then said, "These have certainly been quality treated and dried. Reminds me of some I traded for one time with some Indians that were passing through. They really knew how to treat hides to make them soft and pliable. Tell you what—I'll give you six dollars and eighty cents for the lot."

"It's a deal!" said William.

Back inside the store, the shopkeeper picked up his pencil and began to refigure William's bill. He then said, "That's a pretty good lot you have there, and because you're a very respectful young man, I'm going to give you seven dollars, making you owe me fourteen dollars and eighteen cents."

After paying the shopkeeper, William asked, "Is there a post office in the village?"

The storekeeper smiled at William and said, "You're looking at the postmaster."

"Well, sir, I would like to buy a sheet of paper and an envelope from you to write my folks a letter."

The shopkeeper handed William a sheet of paper, an envelope, and a pencil and said, "While you write your letter, I'll unload the pelts and put your supplies on the porch. I'm sure you know how you want to place them on the drag."

"I'll just stand here at the end of the counter to write my letter, if you don't mind," said William.

"That will be fine," the shopkeeper replied as he started to carry William's supplies outside.

William went to the end of the counter and wrote:

Dear Pa, Ma, and Family,

Hope this finds all of you well. I am fine. Traveling a lot slower than expected. BR Mts. more difficult to cross than I planned. Decided to winter here near Sugar Creek, Tenn. and start again in the spring. Don't worry, Ma, I am eating well. Pa, there is plenty of wild game here in these mountains. You would love to hunt here. Tell all the family I miss and love them. Have found a friend who is helping me get through the winter. Hope to be with you next year this time.

Love to all, and Merry Christmas,
William.

William purposely did not mention his friend was an Indian girl. The idea of him spending the winter in a cave with a girl would have driven Ma to a state of anger. It would have been viewed as highly improper, and he would never hear the end of it.

When the storekeeper returned, William gave him the envelope addressed to "John Robert Daniel, Saulston, North Carolina." The shopkeeper looked at the address and said, "Never heard of Saulston."

William replied, "Not much bigger than Sugar Creek."

The shopkeeper said, "That will be three cents—one for the envelope and two for mailing."

William exited the store to load his drag. While loading, he noticed the grizzly man had departed. William suspected he had gone somewhere else, like the drinking building, to hang out for the rest of the day.

Once William had swung himself into his saddle, the storekeeper came out and said, "Thanks for coming by, and be sure to come back when you need more. Good luck this winter. Supposed to be a bad one, according to the almanac."

William thanked the merchant and headed Taz back in the direction from which they had come. He was anxious to get back to Aylana and the warmth of their cavern. Besides, the sky was beginning to look like more snow was in the forecast. Although going back up the mountain would be more difficult, William knew that once Taz was pointed in the direction of home, he would pick up his pace. With good luck he could make the cavern before dark.

About a mile out of the village, William encountered an unexpected obstacle. As he rounded a rock that jutted out into the trail, out stepped the grizzly man with his shotgun across his chest.

The grizzly man said, "Hold up there, young fellow. We got some business to do. And don't try to go for your gun, because I can blow you out of your saddle before you can touch it."

"What's our business?" asked William.

"That's fairly simple. You are going to give me your horse with the drag and whatever money you have left in your pocket. Or I'm gonna shoot you and take it…it's your call."

As the man was talking, William had turned Taz to where Taz's left side was exposed to the highwayman. He then said, "Well sir, I don't see you've given me much choice. I have no interest in dying today." With those words, William kicked his left foot from the stirrup as if he was dismounting from the right side of Taz.

"You're a smart young man. No sense in anyone getting hurt today."

William was smart enough to know that he was not going to be left alive to later identify this highwayman. So as William swung his left leg over the saddle with his right foot planted firm in the stirrup, and with his left hand having a solid grip on the saddle horn, he suddenly dropped from the sight of the grizzly man. As he dropped, he withdrew his revolver from its holster, an action the grizzly man never saw. Leaning under Taz's neck, William fired a single shot into the man's chest.

As the man staggered backward, trying to regain his balance and point his shotgun in William's direction, he quickly learned youth was much faster than the aged. William had already regained his seat in his saddle. Seeing the man was still intent upon firing at him, William fired a second round, which struck the stock of the man's shotgun with such force it knocked the gun from the man's hand. The force had also caused the man to completely lose his balance and fall backward.

When the grizzly man regained his presence of mind, he saw he was staring into the barrel of William's revolver with William standing astride him. His only words to William were "You kilt me!"

William responded, "Not quite. I think you will live to face a judge."

William placed the man's broken shotgun in the rifle sleeve on Taz and put the man across the drag. He turned Taz back toward Sugar Creek.

Upon returning to Sugar Creek, William took the man to the doctor's office and asked where he could report the incident. The doctor referred him back to the storekeeper, who also served as the town constable. The doctor said he would care for the man.

As William started out of the doctor's office, he spotted a wooden box in the corner. A large dog was lying beside the box, and the sound of puppies was coming from inside the box. William walked over and looked into the box. There he saw four cute puppies rolling around and barking at one another.

He then heard the doctor say, "I forgot to mention. I have a policy that whoever brings me a patient must take home one of the puppies."

"What kind of puppies are these?" asked William.

"Whatever you want them to be," came the reply from the doctor. "The bitch lying beside the box is mostly hound, but I think she may have bred with a wolf. I'm not sure."

William scanned the puppies for a moment and then reached in and pulled out a cute, fat puppy with a face that resembled a wolf. "I think I'll take this one," said William.

"Good!" replied the doctor. "And take one of those old towels lying beside to box to wrap him in to keep him warm until you can get him home."

William wrapped the pup in a towel, and two hours later, with all the proper authorities informed of what had happened on the trail, William, Taz, and the pup started back up the mountain. William had placed the pup, wrapped in the towel, in one of his saddlebags. He was now determined he was not spending another night on the trail. He was thinking,

"It's already going to be after dark before I make it home." Then it struck him. "I have now come to think of the cavern as my home, and I also feel an urgency and importance to get back to Aylana as quickly as I can."

CHAPTER 24

A MOUNTAIN WINTER

When William returned to the cavern, the evening was already shrouded in darkness. He thought it best he call out to Aylana. The last thing he wanted was to be shot in the doorway to his home. So he called, "Aylana, it's William! I'm back."

Aylana came running outside with a torch in her hand. The light from the torch reflected a glowing and thankful expression on her face. Although he wanted to embrace her, he thought it was best for her to make the next move. He could not help but wonder how his kiss upon his departure might have affected their relationship.

Then, hearing some rustling in a saddlebag, he was reminded of the addition they had to their unstated family. He reached into the saddlebag and pulled out the wrapped pup and handed him to Aylana, saying, "A gift from my trip."

Aylana took the moving towel, and as she tried to hold it close to her chest so as not to drop it, a small head emerged with a fast-moving tongue, which started licking her face.

She started to laugh.

William quickly said, "He's probably hungry. Hasn't eaten since this morning."

The excitement she expressed in her native tongue let William know she appreciated her gift and that he had been missed and she was glad to see him. But she made no move to greet him in the way had he bid her farewell.

She said that as soon as she took the pup inside, she would be right back to help unpack the drag and get everything inside. He knew she wanted to see what else he had brought back. He told her, "Let me get Taz in his shelter, and then we can carry everything inside."

But as he worked to unhitch Taz from the drag and remove his saddle, Aylana was already unpacking items from the drag and carrying them into the cavern.

By the time William had Taz bedded down for the night, the only thing left for him to do was to put the drag poles in their place beside Taz's shelter. Inside the cavern he found Aylana sitting by the fire, and the puppy was lapping water and chewing on a piece of meat. Aylana was examining all the items he had purchased. The only things she did not find were the two sticks of peppermint candy he had in his shirt pocket.

When she found the trousers he had bought, she spread them out on the floor of the cavern. She then went over to a stack of skins she had been working with and secured a roll of deerskin. She unrolled the deerskin and laid it beside the trousers William had purchased.

He could see she was comparing what she had been working on to what he had purchased. She had been making him a pair of deerskin trousers, which would be better for winter wear than the trousers he had purchased. They not only would be warmer but would repel snow and water.

He arose from where he was sitting, walked over, nodded his head in approval, and thanked her. He then reached into his pocket and withdrew the two sticks of peppermint candy. He gave one to her, and he licked the other. As she sat down next to the fire, the puppy bounced into her lap.

As usual, she first smelled the candy, but without hesitation she licked it in the same manner he did. She was having a little difficulty, as the puppy also wanted to lick. The fact she took to the candy without reservation was an indication to William that he had finally won her complete trust in him. Then, without warning, she took his hand and kissed it.

As far as William was concerned, she had now made the next move, and he could contain himself no longer. His arms went around her waist, and he pulled her body close to his, even as the puppy tried to squirm his way between the two of them.

Aylana lay her head on his chest and periodically would take a lick from her peppermint stick and then hold it in the air so the puppy could not get to it. The two continued to sit by the fire and lick on their candy while playing with the new addition to their unofficial family.

When the candy was halfway finished, Aylana suggested they save the remainder for another time. Prior to his arrival, she had prepared his bed on the other side of the fire. Standing up, they squeezed each other's hands, and William went to his bed and Aylana to her bed. The pup started his night with Aylana but by morning had joined William.

Both felt comfortable and secure as they drifted off into a deep sleep. Neither worried about the other on this night. William never mentioned to her his incident with the highwayman. It was best she not know how close she might have come to losing him. Besides, their winter survival was the most important thing to concern themselves with. The past was history, and furthermore, it lent no positive aspects to anything that required discussion. However, it did cause William to be ever more vigilant to what could lie around the next bend.

By mid-November Taz had a well-constructed stall. The interwoven branches around the side provided an excellent windbreak. The new tarp was placed on the top, declining from front to back. This would permit water or snow to run off the back of the stall. In short, Taz had a dry, wind-free stall. In addition, each evening his diet was being supplemented from the bag of corn William had purchased in Sugar Creek.

The pup, growing by leaps and bounds, was given the name Chewer because he wanted to chew on all the leather pelts Aylana had piled in the back of the cavern. He spent most of his days following William around to check his traps. Whenever a fish was pulled from the stream trap and William pitched it on the ground with it still flopping, Chewer was on it. He would hold the fish in his mouth until it stopped flopping.

The bonding relationship between William and Aylana continued with each's role more defined and their dependency upon each other growing. William's role was primarily providing the means for survival. He trapped the food and provided pelts for Aylana to make the things she believed the two needed. And while William gathered the wood and kept the fire burning twenty-four hours, seven days per week, Aylana prepared the meals. Using some of the salt he had acquired in Sugar Creek, William salted some wild boar hams like he had seen his father do at the farm. He hung them in the rear of the cavern to cure out. For now, and the near future, food and shelter were not issues of concern.

Again the skies were showing signs of more snow. Near the end of November, two feet of snow was dumped on the mountain. Chewer was excited and wanted to play in the snow, bouncing from one spot to another.

By now William was paying more attention to how the winds in the mountains could easily change directions, and there were times when it blew through the opening in the cavern. That problem was solved when William hung a deerskin flap over the entrance. With a leather strap, he could tie the entrance closed.

After that first big snow, William cut wooden strips and molded them with hot water into snowshoes. He found he could cross the snow quicker with snowshoes to check his snare traps and to gather fish from the stream traps. As the snows grew in depth, the less time Chewer wanted to play outside. With more time inside, the more time William and Aylana had to teach him commands. Soon he was responding to both Cherokee and English commands.

One evening in early December, Aylana surprised William with a completed bearskin coat that could easily be used as a winter blanket. And although the temperature in the cavern seldom got below sixty degrees, there were times when their secure and comfortable winter dwelling could use more warmth.

It was during this time that their bonding had grown to the point where they began to show loving feelings toward each other. The love was demonstrated through their holding hands as they sat around the fire at night or an occasional hand touch to the other's face. There was no intimacy between the two, although their longing for each other was growing stronger and more difficult to control.

The invisible wall between any intimate relationship was two-fold. First, William had grown up in a culture where intimate relationships occurred only after marriage. This was further complicated by his lack of knowledge of the Cherokee courting ways. He did not want to do anything that might be contrary to Aylana's tradition, customs, or faith.

On the other hand, in Aylana's world the woman never made an overt move toward the man. The Indian boy or brave normally consulted with the father before making any advances toward the Indian maid. When the father approved, the brave could be more aggressive in the courting ritual. It was as though the father had given his consent for any action the brave might want to take as long as the brave was faithful to the daughter. An unfaithful brave could easily find an arrow in his chest, delivered by the maiden's father.

Their courtship was made more difficult because she had no father with whom William could consult, and with William not making any aggressive moves toward her, she was beginning to think there must be something wrong with her. In her mind, she had done nothing to discourage William from making any moves toward her; therefore, he must not be interested in her. Maybe there was someone special waiting for him where he came from. She remained confused.

The longing for each other continued. But the invisible wall remained a barrier that could not be broken through, and there appeared to be no doorway anywhere along that wall. The love the two felt toward each other was felt in more attention being lavished upon Chewer.

In mid-December, Pa was seen galloping up the path from the main road. He had been to pick up some supplies Ma needed for the Christmas dinner she was planning. Contrary to his normal arrival, he tied Lucky Boy in front of the house rather than take him directly to his stall. He then bounced up the front steps; his cane had been discarded two weeks earlier. In one hand he held a cloth bag of Ma's supplies, and in the other, he held up an unopened letter.

Ma met him halfway along the hallway with "What has gotten into my spring chicken? Were you told the war is over?"

Pa was grinning. "Naw, something even better—got a letter from William. Haven't opened it yet, so round up all the kids so we can all hear what he has to say together."

When all were gathered around the dining table, Pa meticulously opened the letter, ensuring he wouldn't tear through any of the writing. He slowly read each word.

When Pa had finished, Ma sat back with a sigh of relief. "I'm so glad he has someone to be with during Christmas. I was worried he would be all alone."

Nancy said, "I wish he would have given us more details about his friend. Might be someone I would want to meet."

"Hush your mouth, Nancy! There is plenty of time for you to meet someone," replied Ma.

Pa spoke up. "I thought you were a little sweet on that Simpson boy over by Adamsville, Nancy Ann."

"Pa, how many times do I have to tell you my name is just Nancy? And the Simpson boy is okay, but he ain't special. I think he might be a little lazy, and he sure don't have much to say."

"That's just because he's a little shy," said Ma.

Pa then said, "Let's just change the subject. We just now got a letter from William, and we should be talking about him."

Fannie asked, "Pa, where is the Blue Ridge Mountains?"

"Fannie, they are on the far west side of our state. I've heard it's about five hundred miles," replied Pa.

The second-oldest boy, James Arrington, who was eight, said, "That sure is a long ways, Pa. Adamsville is just three miles, and that seems far to me."

"You're right, son. And when William gets home, he gonna tell you all about those mountains. I'm also glad he has found a friend with whom he can share Christmas. Hopefully, he will be back home by summer."

Ma, standing up to return to the kitchen, and with the bag of supplies John had brought her, said, "He's like his pa. He'll be home when he finishes the business he is about."

January 2, 1864, was one of the coldest days in North Carolina history. Several feet of snow was dumped onto the Blue Ridge Mountains. When William pulled back the flap to the entrance of the cavern, he saw he was going to have to step up to get out. By now Chewer's name had been shortened to just Chew. He didn't show any interest in going outside either.

William dropped the flap to return to get his snowshoes. Aylana asked, "Much snow?"

"Lots!" replied William. "I'm going to check the snare traps where the stream makes the sharp bend before going down the mountain. I shouldn't be long." Turning to Chew, he said, "Shake your body all you want, but you're also going. I know you need to go out for a while."

Once he had his snowshoes on, he said, "Come on, Chew. Let's go and see if we have a couple of mountain trout waiting for us."

Reluctantly, Chew followed William through the door into about three feet of snow. While the snowshoes kept William on top of the snow, Chew sank with every step. The snow was about four inches higher than Chew's back, which required him to jump for every advancement he made. However, his tail was wagging, so he was accepting the challenge.

Near the stream's edge, ice had begun to form. To avoid sliding into the stream, William had to be very cautious. Bending over the trap, he could see he had caught three trout. He carefully lifted each out, running a string through the fish's mouth and out its gill. Once he had all three on his string, he hollered, "Chew, let's go home." Chew was bouncing around in the snow enjoying his new experience.

Many of the trees were bent almost to the ground from the heavy snow. Some limbs had dropped so low from the weight of the snow that the ends of the limbs were buried in the snow. Having cleared the stream bank with no slips, William started backtracking to the cavern. After a dozen or so steps, he heard a loud bop and cracking sound. He looked up in time to see a large limb come crashing down on him. He was instantly buried facedown in the snow.

Momentarily dazed, William tried to take inventory of himself to see if anything was broken. And while he could move his feet and hands, the weight of the snow-laden limb precluded any movement of his body. Using his hands, he pushed the snow away from his face. He soon realized he might have some help because he could see the fast movement of paws near his face. Chew was trying to help dig him out.

After ten minutes of trying to dig himself out, he came to accept the fact that he just could not move. He was pinned down, and short of the large limb being moved off his back and hips, he was stuck there until there was a melting of the snow.

Above his head, he could hear Chew hassling. He then barked for William to get up, but that was not possible. William said, "Chew, go get Aylana! Go, Chew! Go!"

Chew must have understood, because William could no longer see his paws next to his head nor hear him hassling. But he could hear his barking fading in the distance.

Aylana, hearing Chew bark outside the entrance, assumed he wanted to be let in. So she went over to the entrance and held open the flap. But Chew would not come inside. He would only bark, bounce a short distance in the snow, and return to the entrance, only to repeat his previous actions.

His actions suggested to Aylana that Chew needed her to follow him. She then realized she had not seen William, and Chew was always with William when the two were outside. She quickly wrapped a deerskin around her and said, "Find William, Chew. Find William."

Chew started bouncing off in the direction of the bend in the stream where William had said he was going to check his fish trap. Without snowshoes, her trudge through the deep snow was difficult. And while her trudge might have been slow, it was not without determination.

About three-quarters of the way to the stream, she spotted a very large limb on the ground. Chew had made it to the limb and was barking and digging at it.

When she got to the limb, she could only see William's left hand above the snow. She began to throw snow off William's arm, then his head and shoulders. She asked, "William, are you all right?"

William replied, "I think so, but I can't move this limb to get out."

Aylana began to pull on the limb but soon discovered she could not budge it.

William said, "Aylana, go get Taz and a rope. I think Taz will be able to move the limb. And be careful. Walk Taz slowly so he doesn't accidentally step on your foot. He will want to walk slowly to ensure every step is on solid ground."

Aylana replied, "I understand. Chew! Stay with William."

Twenty minutes later Aylana returned with Taz. When William could see her, he said, "Put the rope around Taz's neck and slide it to the base of his neck so it's against his shoulders. Then tie the other end onto the tree just above my shoulders. I want you to walk Taz to the side so the limb will be pulled to one side."

Once all was tied, Aylana grasped the reins and started to pull on Taz while saying, "Pull, Taz! Pull!" At the same time, Chew was barking at Taz. Obviously, Taz got the message because Aylana heard William say, "It's moving! I can feel the limb moving!" Then Aylana heard the words "I'm free!"

Aylana said, "Whoa, Taz!"

She didn't have to repeat those words to Taz. Pulling that large limb in deep snow was a real challenge for him. He stood perfectly still, waiting for the next command.

Holding on to a branch from the tree limb and with the help of Aylana, William was able to stand. Knowing that Aylana could not get him through the deep snow by herself, he told her to bring Taz over to him while he maintained his balance with the tree branch. When Taz was close, William grabbed onto his halter with his left hand and put his right arm around Aylana's shoulders. Walking slowly through the snow, William made it to the entrance of the cavern. Chew had already gone inside, wagging his tail as if the mission had been accomplished.

After getting William settled by the fire, Aylana went back outside to put Taz back into his stall. Upon returning, she saw William was almost out of his shirt. After helping him get his shirt over his head, she could see his back was already turning blue. In addition to some serious cuts made by sharp branches, she suspected he had some broken or cracked ribs.

She got some of her paste for the cuts and some of the salve for the area that appeared to be bluish. Applying the paste and salve to Williams back from his shoulders to his waist gave her a sensual feeling.

She asked if he thought he might need some treatment on his hips. His response was "Probably."

She told him she would help him take off his trousers. Soon William was lying on his stomach, on a deerskin blanket, buck naked while Aylana ran her warm hands over his hips. To himself he admitted, "Having a tree fall on me was worth this sort of treatment."

When she finished applying the paste and salve, she covered him with the bearskin blanket that also served as a winter coat. She then restoked the fire and asked if William wanted anything to eat or drink. He replied, "I think I just need to rest for a while."

As the day turned into night, Aylana continued to keep a watchful eye on William. His restlessness was evidence of his discomfort. She believed him to be in pain, but she didn't know what she could do to help him. Periodically, she felt his head, and it felt very warm. Yet his body was shaking as though he was freezing. She watched as Chew pushed his body close to William. William was lying on his right side with Chew against his chest. She decided she must also help William become warmer. After throwing a few more logs on the fire, she went over and slipped under the bearskin blanket. Her chest pressed against his back, and her arms were around him. She place her left leg over his bare left leg. When she was as close to him as possible, she hugged his body close to hers. That night William was sandwiched between Aylana and Chew under a very thick bearskin. As his shaking began to subside, all went to sleep.

Sometime during the night, William's fever broke, causing him to wake at his normal time. He could not recall any time recently when he had felt so warm when he awoke. Then again, he had never awoke with two bodies pressed against his. To his front, Chew was stretched full length with his nose under William's chin.

To his back was the soft feeling of Aylana's body. He could feel her breathing on his neck and the warmth of her thigh across his bare left hip. He didn't dare move for two reasons. The first was the pleasantry of having her body so close to his. The second was that any movement was going to cause the burning sensation in his left rib cage to worsen. He was sure he had some damaged ribs, so he lay perfectly still so as to enjoy the moment the best he could.

Thirty minutes later, Aylana awoke. She raised up and peered over William's shoulder to see how he was sleeping, only to see his eyes open. She sat up and said, "Why you not tell me you awake?"

"Why would I, and ruin the moment?" he replied.

She scrambled from under the bearskin blanket and said, "I only try to keep you warm."

"And a very good job you did," replied William.

When William looked at Aylana, she appeared to be embarrassed that he had found her snuggled up to him. He said, "Thank you for helping me yesterday and keeping me warm last night."

Aylana made no reply as she busied herself in preparing them something to eat.

Chew took his time getting up and then gave William a big lick on the face. He then paced over to the entrance flap and whimpered at Aylana. This was a sure sign Chew needed to go outside. Aylana turned Chew out without any evidence that she was paying any attention to William.

Finally, William said, "If you will help me get up, I will put on my trousers."

"You wait for now," said Aylana. She then went to the area where she worked with the pelts and pulled out the deerskin pants she had made for him. She took them over and placed them on some rocks near the fire.

"When they are warm, I will help you. First, you eat."

Shortly, she brought him a tin cup of warm soup she had made with rabbit and flour. She had minced the rabbit meat to where it was as if it had been grounded. A few of the beans William had purchased at Sugar Creek floated in the broth.

After he had eaten, she helped him stand. Then she handed him his trousers and held on to him with her eyes closed. With her eyes still closed, she bent over to help him get his feet in each trouser leg. Once he had the trousers pulled up to his waist, he said, "You can open your eyes now. How do I look?"

Aylana replied, "Pants look good. Back looks bad."

Although it hurt, William could not help but laugh.

CHAPTER 25

A NEW BEGINNING

Over the next week, there was no mention of Aylana's action to help keep William warm, nor did she return to his bed. They continued to sleep with the fire between them and Chew changing bed partners during the night.

Even though there was some melting of the snow, the mountain continued to be covered as January changed to February. The first week after his injury, William, reluctantly and at Aylana's insistence, let her tend to the traps. He remained at the entrance of the cavern with his rifle in hand while she and Chew checked the traps. During the day Aylana saw that William remained comfortable and refused to let him do anything but feed himself.

Early into their move into the cavern, Aylana discovered in the rear corner of the cavern a triangle-shaped hole in the floor that dropped about four feet. Water could be seen flowing into and out of the hole, probably an underground stream that flowed into the main stream farther down the mountain.

Initially, they were excited about the prospects of having an inside source of water. But both became more excited when William suggested he could continue to collect their water from the main stream, and they could use the hole for their first-ever indoor toilet.

Aylana hung a deerskin in a manner where they could relieve themselves in private. Not having to venture outside for this basic necessity was one of the highlights of cavern living. And it proved to be especially beneficial to William as he recovered from his injury.

After a week of being pampered and trying hard not to show any discomfort from his injured ribs, William resumed the duties of checking traps and securing whatever was caught. Aylana would help him bring in water from the stream by hanging a bucket over a pole, and each would carry one end of the pole.

With the exception of an intimate relationship, William and Aylana were functioning as man and wife. By mid-February, each evening before going to their separate sleeping areas, they now kissed good night. However, that situation was slowly changing. Their kisses lasted longer than just a quick kiss before hurrying to bed. Neither wanted their kisses to end, their bodies were more difficult to separate, and the look they each gave the other continued to linger as they snuggled under their individual animal-skin blankets.

In late February, William took the initiate for a new beginning. As he and Aylana sat around their fire that evening, he told her, "Aylana, we need to have big talk."

She looked at him with a puzzled and questioning look and said, "You talk."

Looking at his left hand, William said, "William." Then looking at his right hand, he said, "Aylana." He then put his two hands together and said, "I want you and me to be one."

With an even more questioning look, she hooked her right forefinger into her left forefinger and said, "You and I be one." Then she extended her arms with her fingers still locked into his and said, "One together and make big family?"

William's face glowed as he repeated, "Yes, we become one and make big family."

She threw her arms around his neck and began to cry, saying, "Aylana, so happy!"

As William embraced her, he said in her ear, "William so very, very, happy."

Their embrace caused them to fall from their sitting position to a lying position on the floor of the cavern. Momentarily they rolled on the floor with one on top of the other as Chew barked and jumped around thinking it was going to be a big playtime.

With William on top of her, she saw the look in his eye and quickly shoved him back and said, "Not now!"

With a feeling of rejection, William said, "Why?"

After a period of time that included much broken English, Cherokee, and sign language, William came to understand they could not be married until the spring. She wanted to be married outside, under the sun god, with fresh flowers in her hair and wearing a new deerskin dress.

William was thinking, "All women must be alike. All want flowers and a new dress for a wedding. I wonder if I am supposed to give her a ring or a necklace. And are we to have vows for a marriage with no preacher or tribal leader?"

She then said they could be joined as one on the day of the first full moon in March. Without an almanac, William had no idea when that would be, but he was fairly certain she knew. He was thinking, "With my luck it will be the last day of March."

From that evening forward, it was a new beginning in the cavern. There was a more open display of love and affection for each other. Routinely, Aylana would slip up behind William when he least expected her and kiss him on the back of the neck. Likewise, he never entered or departed the cavern without first kissing her. At nights he would tease her by acting as if he was trying to get in her bed with her. They would then wrestle around with their bodies rubbing against each other while she was saying, "No! No! William!" He would then get up to go to his bed, smiling back he would say, "Soon, Aylana. Soon!"

As the end of March was drawing nearer, William became more worried that what had been a blissful new beginning would be changing when he finally told Aylana his purpose for being in the mountains. During all the time they had been together, she had not once inquired as to why he was there, although he had told her he was from a faraway place to the east. He thought the reason might be an Indian custom not to be inquisitive of one's past. But he also knew that when the weather became warmer, he would have to leave to find the Rouse brothers. He was thinking, "It will not be fair to Aylana for her to marry me and then shortly thereafter I leave to pursue what could be a dangerous journey. What will happen to her should something terrible happen to me? Pa went to war with the satisfaction of knowing I was at home to take care of the family. Aylana's only family, for now, is me."

Aylana had come to know William well now, and she knew he was conflicted by something. She knew of braves who had second thoughts after committing to marriage. They had always lived a free life, and a wife and a family meant that they would lose some of their freedom. And while she wanted to know the answer, she believed William needed to tell her in his time. So she continued to work on the dress she wished to be married in.

It was now March and William asked Aylana, "How many more moons before we are one?"

She thought for a few minutes and with a smile replied, "Nine more moons."

William knew he had to tell her now. She needed to know before they were married. Looking into her lovely face, no longer showing any evidence of the scratches and cuts it had received from the briar patch, he said, "We need big talk."

Aylana showed no reaction or concern. She just said, "What is big talk this time?" She was thinking, "William no longer wants us to be one."

William continued. "Aylana, you have never asked why I am in the mountains. You need to know because once you hear, you may not want to be one with me."

Now Aylana was truly confused. "How could he think that for any reason I could no longer love him?"

William said, "Before I found you, I was crossing the mountains to catch some very bad men who hurt my father. They beat him and left him for dead. He did not die, but he was hurt for a long time. He could not walk or talk. I promised myself that once my father had recovered to where I could leave home, I would catch the men and settle what they did to him."

"What do you mean by settle?" asked Aylana.

"Make the men pay for what they did to my father."

"What do you mean by pay?"

"I mean they must be put away so they cannot hurt anyone else, or they must die."

Aylana was stunned to hear such talk coming from a man she had come to love for his peaceful and loving nature. And while she had never thought of him as one who would seek revenge, she did see him as a man who would seek the right thing for his family.

William ended the big talk with "Not many moons after we are married, I will have to leave you to go after the bad men. I do not want to leave you alone, but this is something I must do. I will not be able to live with myself knowing my father sacrificed himself by going to the war so I would not have to, and then I do nothing to right the wrong that was done to him. Do you understand what I am saying?"

"I understand I love you, and I want to be one with you. I know a brave's wife must honor her man for doing what he believes is right. I know I will always wait for you, William."

Tears began to creep into William's eyes as he heard and saw the resolve of the face of this wonderful woman who still would be his wife. Without words, he embraced her, and she held tightly to him.

After several minutes of holding on to each other as each's life depended upon the other, William whisper into Aylana's ear, "I promise you I will come back."

"I know," she calmly stated. "I will always be waiting here for you."

CHAPTER 26

THE FIRST FULL MOON IN MARCH 1864

arch 28, 1864, was a beautiful day in the Blue Ridge Mountains in eastern Tennessee. The sun was shining bright, and the sky was blue and laced with pockets of cumulus clouds. The snow had all melted except in a few shadowy places. The air had a cold bite, and if weather history repeated itself, there would be more snow before the end of April. The most significant aspect of the day was that in the evening there would be the first full moon for the month.

Aylana was standing on a large flat rock at the bend in the stream that flowed down the mountain and away from the cavern. She was dressed in her recently completed deer buckskin dress. The neckline was made of brown and tan tassels. In her hair was a wreath made from a mixture of sprigs from winter green trees. Throughout the wreath were some colorful early-blooming wildflowers. Spread out on a rock beside her was one of William's bandannas, which covered an object on the rock. She was waiting for her future husband, who was to arrive ten minutes after she was in place.

Promptly at the ten-minute mark, William came, with Chew walking beside him. William was wearing the wool shirt he had purchased at Sugar Creek, washed clean. He also wore the deer buckskin trousers Aylana had made for him. His boots, which were well worn and in need of replacement, were as clean as he could possibly get them.

The two had briefly discussed the formality of the ceremony. They believed that outdoors in the presence of their gods, they could repeat their vows in their native tongues, and when they concluded, they would be just as married as if a pastor or a chief had presided over the ceremony.

William stepped up on the flat rock. Turning to Chew, he said, "Chew, sit!"

Chew immediately drop to a sitting position. Aylana had said the brave should say his vows first, since he had requested for the two of them to be one.

The two turned to face each other, and then William took both of Aylana's hands into his hands and said, "In the presence of our almighty God, I, William Henry Daniel, take you, Aylana, to be my lawful wedded wife, to honor, cherish, protect and defend, in both sickness and health, so long as the both of us shall live. So help me God."

Aylana, looking directly into William's eyes, slowly began a Cherokee chant, which William did not understand, but he knew it to be sacred to Aylana. The chant lasted for several minutes. She then removed William's bandanna from the small object it covered. It was a small knife. She first made a cut in the palm of her left hand, and then she made a small cut in William's right hand. As the blood ran from both hands, she grasped William's bloody hand with her bloody hand so the blood of both hands dripped to the ground as one. She then covered both their bleeding hands with William's bandanna. Together they tied their hands together.

She then reached inside a pocket of her dress and retrieved a wooden object carved into the symbol by which her tribe was known. It was tied on a leather string. She placed the object around William's neck and said, "My tribe is now next to your heart. It will protect you, keep you strong, and show all that you are one with the Cherokee nation because your wife is Cherokee."

William retrieved from his shirt pocket a leather bracelet embedded with colorful river stones, which he had made. He told her, "I will tie this to your wrist when the bandanna is removed. The leather represents the strength of the love you have shown me, and the colorful stones reflect the joy you have brought to me. Together they are strong and everlasting, as will be my love for you."

There, on the flat rock beside a winding stream, the two embraced and, with a deep and passionate kiss, sealed their marriage to each other.

Hands still tied together, they returned to the cavern. At the entrance of the cavern, they untied the bandanna. William then tied his bracelet to Aylana's left wrist. As Aylana entered the cavern, William picked up a rope that was outside the cavern and tied it around Chew's neck. He then led Chew over to Taz's stall and said, "Tonight, Chew, you are sleeping with Taz." He then tied Chew to a post inside Taz's stall.

William quickly returned to the cavern. Inside the only light was the flickering of the fire. There was only one bed, and it was on his side of the fire. He then heard a soft and seductive voice coming from under the bearskin. "What take you so long?"

๑

The month of April, for the newlyweds, was one of bliss and spontaneous lovemaking. Regardless of the time or place, all it took was a special look from one to the other for them to be united. On one occasion, the two were walking to one of William's traps, holding hands and enjoying the light snow that was beginning to fall when Aylana gave William the look that under the falling snow would be the perfect place to make love. Chew, not understanding, lay on the ground nearby and whimpered as if to be saying, "The traps are more important than for you to be taking the time to play."

There were two troubling aspects of the month of April. First, the month was only thirty days, and there was much to do before the end of the month. The second was that the day after the end of the month, William would be leaving to find the two men who had hurt his father.

The cavern was stocked with food and other supplies Aylana might need during William's absence. But there were still a few things he thought she might need before he returned. That meant another trip to Sugar Creek.

In the middle of April, William set out for Sugar Creek. Taz was attached to the drag carrying pelts for bartering, Aylana was in the saddle, and Chew was walking with William. They left a little before sunrise and arrived just as the sun was going down.

They made camp at the edge of the forest just on the outskirts of the village. Here they would spend the night. The following morning, when the storekeeper arrived, all were patiently waiting.

As the storekeeper stepped up onto the porch, he said, with a grin on his face, "'Peers to me, you brought reinforcements this time."

William laughed and said, "Yes sir. This is my wife, Aylana, and my dog, Chew."

"Pleased to meet you, Miz Daniel. Won't forget the name Daniel for a while. Your husband caused a lot of paperwork for me."

William quickly followed up with "I'll explain later, Aylana." The comment from the storekeeper reminded him he had never told Aylana all that had happened on his last trip to Sugar Creek.

"Y'all come on in the store to get what you need. I see you brought me some more pelts."

"Yes sir, I hope so." Turning to Aylana, he said, "You go with this man and get whatever you think you need, and take your time. I got some business I need to tend to. Chew, you come with me."

When Aylana entered the store, she was completely amazed and speechless as to all the different items she saw. She did not know where to start because there were items all over.

The storekeeper saw her shock and said, "Miz Daniel, you just take your time, and if you need some help, you just call me. My name is Draper."

William and Chew headed for the livery stable. The two big doors were swung open, and inside, a man in a leather apron was moving an anvil from one location to another.

William waited until the man set the anvil down and then said, "Looking for a well-broken saddle mule. Know where I might get one?"

The man looked at William and replied, "You look more like a horse man to me. Sure you don't want a good horse?"

"No sir! I want a mule my wife can ride. A mule is more sure footed in the mountains and more likely to identify dangerous places as to where not to go."

"Sounds like you might know your four-legged friends. Your dog looks more like a wolf than a dog."

"The dog is one of the pups the doctor had several months ago. He turned out to be a good one."

"And I think I may just have a good mule for you. Come and look in my corral."

William followed the man to the corral, where the man pointed out a mule that had the markings of a paint horse. It was white with large brown patches on his sides. "Now, that one is as good as you can get."

"Mind if I ride it?" asked William.

"Not at all. Hold on, and I'll get you a saddle."

William had already entered the corral and was walking toward the mule. As he walked, he said, "If he is as good as you say, I won't need a saddle."

William walked to the side of the mule. Its head never came up, which was a good indication the animal had been handled a lot by a man. Grabbing on to its mane, William jumped up and swung his leg over its back and was seated before the livery stable man could say anything.

When William settled on his back, the mule's head came up. William gave it a light kick in the side, and the mule started to slowly move around the corral. With a little harder kick, the mule went into a gallop. William found him easy to steer by pulling its mane in the direction he wanted it to go. After several laps around the corral, William pulled the mane back and stopped it in front of the man. Sliding off its back, he asked, "How much you want for it?"

"I can see you know about mules. I'll take sixty dollars and throw in a bridle and a lead line."

"Will you consider fifty?" asked William.

"Yes, if when you decide to shoe it, you bring it back for me to do."

"You got a deal!" said William. "I will also need a drag belt."

"That'll be a dollar," said the man.

After payment was made and William had a bill of sale, the drag belt was placed on the mule, and then William, Chew, and the mule walked back over to the supply store. He tied the mule next to Taz and entered the store with Chew following, wagging his tail.

As soon as Aylana saw William, she excitedly ran over to him and started pointing out all the things that were in the store. A lot of the items, she did not know what they were.

"Have you decided what you need?" asked William.

"If she has, she hasn't picked up anything," replied Draper. "I don't think she has ever been a general store before."

"Probably not," commented William. Then to Aylana he said, "Come with me, and I will help you get what you need."

An hour later they had all she needed and had bartered with Draper over the pelts. Draper was happy to get the pelts in exchange for the items they had selected.

Together, with the help of Draper, they carried the items onto the front porch.

"That sure is a fine-looking mule there by your horse, but I don't know who it belongs to."

William smiled at Draper and pointed in Aylana's direction and said, "I believe it belongs to her."

Aylana looked at William in disbelief and asked, "Me?"

"Yes, it's a wedding present," replied William. "Now we need to move the drag from behind my horse to your mule and put the supplies on it."

Aylana wanted to hug William for her gift but wasn't sure it was the proper thing to do in public.

As the two moved the drag behind the mule and attached it to the drag belt, Draper went back inside the store.

As they tied the supplies onto the drag, Aylana whispered to William, "I thank you later."

"Promise?" replied William. He then helped Aylana onto the mule's back.

As he swung into his saddle on Taz, he heard Draper say, "Wait one minute." He was coming out of the store. He hurried over to Aylana and handed her a small brown paper bag and said, "A wedding present from me."

"Thank you!" she said as she looked inside the bag. Inside were four peppermint candy sticks.

William waved to Draper and turned Taz toward home. Aylana followed, with Chew running along beside the mule. Now that both of them had transportation, William believed they could make the cavern before dark.

CHAPTER 27

POWDER SPRINGS

Back at the cavern, while William put Taz and the mule in Taz's stall, Aylana put the supplies they had acquired into their proper places and started their evening meal.

When William had settled down next to the fire to watch Aylana prepare their meal, she asked, "What problem you cause Draper?"

For a moment William didn't associate her question with the statement Draper had made about William causing him a lot of paperwork. But Aylana patiently waited for William's response as she studied his facial expressions. She was now to a point when she could tell by William's expression if he was only telling her what he wanted her to hear and not everything.

When William had connected her question with what Draper was referring to, he said, "Well, when I started back from my first trip to Sugar Creek, a man tried to take my supplies from me. Since I was much younger, I was able to get the advantage over him. I then took him back to Sugar Creek, where Draper is also the law. I had to tell him what happened, and he had to write it all on paper. That is what he was talking about."

"What happen to man who try to take supplies?"

"I'm sure he went to jail. But you should know that when he tried to shoot me, I shot him. It was not a bad hurt. He has probably recovered by now."

Aylana, said, "Thank you for telling me." As she handed him his pan containing some ham from the wild boar William had killed, slaughtered, and salted in early winter, she kissed him and said, "Thank you for the mule."

"What are you going to name it?" asked William.

Aylana went to the back of the cavern and brought back several pelts. She laid the tan deer hide on the floor and then placed the darker-colored pieces of other animal pelts on the deer hide. Pointing to the pieces of pelt on the deer hide, she asked, "What you call this?"

Looking over the display she presented, William replied "Patches."

Aylana smile and said, "I name my mule Patches."

Laughing at how she had conveyed her message to him, William said, "That is a very good name. From now on, your mule will be Patches."

The remainder of the month of April William spent ensuring that Aylana had all she needed in the cavern to last her two to three months. He watched her carefully as she practiced putting bullets in the rifle and firing at various objects he set up. He then took her hunting so she would get some practice at shooting moving objects such as rabbits and squirrels. She proved to be an excellent marksman.

He had her demonstrate to him how she could attach the drag behind Patches, in the event she needed to do so. And he instructed her that in the event she needed help or felt unsafe, she was to go to Draper's. He would inform Draper when he went back through Sugar Creek for Powder Springs that she might call upon him.

All the time Aylana continued to assure William she would be all right and that she was expecting him to return within two to three big moons. And he assured her he would.

Before either could comprehend how fast the month of April flew by, it was May 1. Before mounting Taz for his departure, William gave Aylana a goodbye kiss and Chew the command "Stay!" After swinging himself into the saddle, he didn't look back. He simply pointed Taz in the direction of Sugar Creek. It had been one year, to the month, since he had left his family in Saulston. Now he was leaving his new family.

A sense of pride overwhelmed Aylana as she watch her brave sitting straight in the saddle riding away to do what he must do.

Passing through Sugar Creek, William stopped at the general store and asked Draper to take care of Aylana if she should come looking for help. He said that he would adequately compensate him for any inconvenience she might cause. Draper said he welcomed her visit and would help her in any way he could.

William's only explanation for his departure was that he had business he must tend to and that he expected to return in two to three months. He then inquired if Draper knew the distance to Powder Springs. Draper said he thought it to be about fifty miles due west. William thanked him and was on his way.

The late afternoon of the second day, William arrived in Powder Springs. Once out of the rugged mountain and into more of the foothills, he and Taz made better time than he had expected. The greatest increase in their speed was attributed to the ability to travel on cleared trails and, in many cases, roads wide enough for a wagon or stagecoach.

Powder Springs was the largest town William had seen since he left Asheville, North Carolina. It had buildings on both sides of its main street. It had streets that merged from various directions into the main street. He walked Taz slowly through the town so he could take in all the sights. There were a couple of general mercantile stores, a bank, a clothing shop, a grocery store, and a barbershop, which reminded him that he hadn't had a real haircut in over a year. He had been cutting his own hair with a pair of shears.

When he saw the hotel, he was reminded that he had not slept in a real bed in about a year. He thought, "A hot bath and sleeping between some clean bed linens would be refreshing. The only thing that would make it better would be for Aylana to be here to share it with me. Maybe someday soon."

Approaching a man crossing the street, William reined in Taz and said, "Excuse me, sir. Could you tell me where I might find the livery stable?"

The man did not seem surprised by William's appearance. William was wearing his duster, which covered the revolver he was wearing on his side, and the coonskin cap Aylana had made for him. The man replied, "See that street down yonder that goes to your right? Well, if you uns turn on that street, you will run smack into the middle of it."

William touched his hat with his forefinger and said, "Thank you, sir!"

William arrived at the livery stable as the man was starting to move things inside to close for the evening. "Excuse me, sir. You got room for another horse?" asked William.

"Sure 'nuff do," replied the man. "You want him in a separate stall and fed?"

"Yes sir, I do."

"That will be forty cents…twenty-five for the stall and fifteen for the feed. The feed includes corn with the hay."

"That sounds good. You want me to ride him in?"

"Naw! You can just give him to me. I'll take him in, unsaddle him, and put him in his stall. Your saddle will be on the rack outside the stall and his bridle hanging on the side of the stall door."

As William stepped down from the saddle, he asked, "Do I pay you now or tomorrow?"

"Pay me now, in case you're in a hurry to leave before I get here tomorrow morning."

William thought, "I wonder if he thinks there might be a reason that I could be in a hurry to leave tomorrow. The town seems mighty quiet to me. Reminds me a lot of Goldsboro." William took his saddlebags off, threw them over his shoulder, and paid the man. He then said, "See ya tomorrow morning."

William started walking back down the street in the direction of the hotel. He had decided that he was going to spend the night there, get him a hot bath, and eat a real beefsteak dinner. But he would forgo paying for a haircut, and with no more beard than he had, he could still shave himself with his hunting knife. Tomorrow he would start inquiring as to the whereabouts of the Rouse brothers.

It was not long after William left that Aylana began to feel the loneliness of his absence. She had not felt lonely when he went to Sugar Creek because she knew he would soon be back. And while she was not sure when exactly this time he would be back, she refused to think the possibility of his not returning. William always kept his promises to her.

Either Chew also felt her loneliness, or it was his protective nature, because he never left her side. When she went to check traps, he was with her and never ventured out of sight. And if she was busy in the cavern, he was lying across the entryway. His constant presence made her thankful she had such a loyal companion and gave her a great sense of security. He would let her know if there was anyone or anything close to the cavern.

Checking the traps did not take up much of her time, since William, knowing the cavern was well stocked with food, had removed a number of them. He had left a couple of rabbit traps, a turkey trap, and the fish trap for her to routinely have fresh meat. But if for some reason, such as bad weather, she did not want to leave the cavern, she had sufficient supplies to meet her and Chew's needs.

Her only added chore was to take care of Patches. During the day she would take Patches to an open area a couple hundred yards from the cavern, put hobbles on him, and then leave him to graze. At night she would secure him in Taz's shelter. William had also stacked a sufficient amount of wood in the back of the cavern to keep the fire burning so she would not have to cut any. She prayed for the god of the Cherokee nation to watch over him, keep him safe, and return him home as soon as possible.

The morning after William arrived in Powder Springs, he awoke refreshed and ready to take care of business. When he checked into the hotel, he found the room for the night would cost him seventy-five cents, and the hot water for the bath with soap was twenty cents. After his bath, he had a large beefsteak dinner with potatoes, greens, and biscuits with water for fifty cents. His dinner was so filling that he thought he wouldn't need to eat again for a week. Never a coffee drinker, he passed up the complimentary morning coffee that he was offered to get to the livery stable by the time the owner opened the doors.

He needed information as to the location of the Rouse brothers. From his Pa he had learned the three best locations to get information were to start at the livery stable, then the local bar, and if there were more than two general stores, go to the post office. Those three places normally knew more than the local law enforcement and generally did not spend much time questioning why one might want the information.

William arrived as the doors to the livery stable were being opened. The same man from the previous day said, "You're a surprise! I figured you as one who would have gotten his horse and been gone by now."

William's immediate thought was "Did I give him the impression as one who might have run off without paying him? Is that the reason he wanted payment last evening?" But trying to be more hospitable, William replied, "Well, I've always been an earlier riser. However, before saddling up, I wanted to borrow a curry brush to brush my horse down from yesterday and a pick to check his hooves. There was a time yesterday when I thought he might have picked up a small stone."

William's real reason for an explanation of brushing and picking was to, in a more casual atmosphere asked some questions to the livery operator.

"Certainly! I think you uns find what you need on that thar table next to the horseshoe box," replied the man.

William brought Taz out of the stall and tied him to one of the stable support posts. After getting the brush and pick and having started to brush Taz, he asked, "You happen to know the Rouse brothers?"

"Who don't know them around here? But who's asking?"

"I'm William Daniel. My pa served with them in the army for a short time. When Pa learned I was coming this way, he asked if I would drop by and give them his regards."

"Don't mean any disrespect for your pa, but if he thought they were his friends, he would be in for a surprise."

"Why you say that?"

"I've known those boys all my life, and they never been anything but trouble. Thought joining the army might change them some, and it may have Herman, but there ain't no hope for Thurman."

"I don't understand. Mind explaining?"

"Well, both of 'um gave the town lots of problems. They had to go before the sheriff for stealing from one of our locals. Sheriff gave them a choice—join the army or go to jail. They chose the army."

"I appreciate you telling me that, but I promised Pa that I would say hello for him. Do you know how I might find them?"

"Can't tell you nothing about Thurman. He and Herman had a fallin' out when they come back here from the army. If you ask me, the army probably kicked them out, or they deserted. Anyhow, Thurman left from around here to only God knows where.

"Now, Herman settled down some. He married a local girl and moved out to the family's old home place. I think the girl might have been the wedge between the two boys, and if so, good for her.

"Well, like I said, Herman and his bride moved out to the family farm, where it appears he's trying to get some order in his life. Will surprise me if he makes a go of it."

"How do I find that family farm?" asked William.

"Go back to the main street and then go north for about three miles. When you come to a big oak tree that the wind has done broke in half, go east. You'll see an old farmhouse across a stream, needin' lots of repair work. Last time I saw it, the front porch had fallen almost clean off. That'll be the Rouse house." He laughed then like he had made a joke.

William had finished brushing Taz. He said, "Thank you, sir. I'll just take a quick look at Taz's hooves, and I'll be out of your hair."

"Take your time. Always glad to have someone to talk to. Now you be careful around Herman. I'd say pass on your Pa's howdy and get on down the road before Herman comes up with a way to take advantage of you."

"I'll keep that in mind," replied William.

In a short time, William saddled Taz and threw his duster across his bedroll. He had placed his Colt revolver in a saddlebag before coming to the stable. The man at the livery hadn't seen it yesterday, and there was no reason why he should see it today. Might lead him to thinking that William was up to no good.

When he was down the road at least a mile, he reined Taz to a stop and dismounted. He retrieved his Colt from the saddlebag and strapped it on, tying it down to his leg. He then put his duster back on to hide the revolver.

Within a short time, he spotted the half-broken oak tree. William thought, "Must have been strong wind to take that one down. I know I couldn't reach my arms around it."

Once he had passed the tree, he saw the stream and in the distance a house that had long ago seen its better days. With a slight chuckle, he said to himself, "Doesn't look like Herman has made much progress on repairing that front porch."

More surprising was seeing a man sitting in a rocker that was lisping to his left as he made the chair rock periodically. To William that was evidence of one lazy man. He would rather work to make the rocker rock than work on the porch so the chair would rock easier.

As William walked Taz within twenty feet of the porch, he said, "Excuse me, sir. I'm trying to locate a Mr. Herman Rouse."

"What the hell you want with him?"

William knew he was talking to Herman because he looked mighty close to the image on the wanted poster, minus a scar on his face. "Well, sir, he and my pa were in the army together, and when Pa knew I was going to be passing by this way, he wanted me to give him his regards."

By now Herman had gotten out of the rocker and walked to the edge of the porch. Once he was leaning against a post that was barely holding the roof up, he said, "What's your pa's name?"

William could tell from the way Herman asked about Pa's name he was suspicious as to how well his pa might know him. Possibly he thought he might have owed him some money.

William replied, "Mind if I get down and stretch my legs? Been riding for a spell."

Herman gave William a good look over, and not seeing any weapon, he said, "Yeah, you can get down."

When William dismounted, he made sure Taz's right side would block Herman's full view of him once he dismounted from the left side.

Once on the ground and looking over his saddle, he said, "His name is John Daniel."

As Herman rolled the name around in his head, William took off his duster and threw it across his saddle. Finally, Herman responded, "Boy, I can't rightly recall ever meeting your pa. Where was it that he and I met?"

William stepped around in front of Taz, giving Herman a full view of himself, and said, "Weldon, North Carolina's train depot."

"Now, boy, I never recall being there, and you best git yourself on down the road."

William replied, "Let me refresh your memory."

About that time a skinny, frail-looking woman came through the front door. She was wearing a dirty, faded, printed dress that had been made from cotton feed bags. She looked first at William and then at Herman and said, "What's a-going on out here?"

"Hush your mouth, woman, and git back in the house!" said Herman in an angry tone.

William spoke up. "Ma'am, you might want to stay and hear this story."

Herman quickly interrupted as he turned to his wife and said, "Mabel, git inside and git me my gun!"

Again, William spoke up. "Ma'am, you might not want to do that. I never shot a woman before, and I sure don't want to make you my first. For your safety, I think you should stay right where you are."

Herman stared back at William and said, "Boy, you don't tell my wife what to do!"

"Then you might think about giving her better advice. I think she needs to hear the story of how you met my Pa."

With a more brazen look than William expected and with her feet planted firmly in place, Mabel said, "Tell me! I want to hear how your pa met Herman."

"A sign of wisdom," said William. Then he continued. "My pa was shot in the war, and because of his wound, he was medically discharged. On his way home on the train, he got off at the Weldon depot. Herman led my father behind the train station, and Thurman followed. When they got to the back side of the station, Thurman hit my Pa in the head, and the two of them beat him almost to death. They robbed him of his military pay and left him for dead."

Herman interrupted. "I didn't do any of that. Thurman did it all. I was just there."

Mabel, with anger, said, "And you just stood there and watched Thurman beat up on a wounded soldier? What kind of man are you?"

Herman, realizing it was now two against one, said, "He's my brother! There was nothing I could do."

Mabel said, "I'm a good of mind to go in that house, git that gun, and shoot you myself!"

"Before you do that, Miz Rouse, please let me make the settlement for my pa. There are wanted posters for the Rouse brothers in both North Carolina and Virginia. In Virginia both are wanted for assault, robbery, desertion from the army, and murder. There is a five-hundred-dollar reward for each, dead or alive."

Herman, in defensive anger, said, "Boy, you ain't man enough to kill me. Hell, I bet you never killed a man in your life. I doubt you've ever been up against a real man. I think I'll just pick up that stick of wood leaning against these steps and come down there and give you a good beating."

As Herman reached for the fence post that was lying against the steps, William's Colt came out of its holster so fast that one would have thought the inside of the holster was greased. The round hit the post just below Herman's hand, splitting it in half.

Herman jumped back, stunned at what he a just witnessed. In all his life, he had never seen anyone so fast and so accurate. This was no ordinary boy; he was a gunslinger.

William calmly said, "Mr. Rouse, we can do this the easy way or the hard way. I don't really care as long as I get a settlement of what you did to my pa. When he came home, he couldn't walk or talk because of the damage you done to his brain. He was like a newborn baby starting at the very beginning of life. You did that to him.

"The easy way is for the two of us to ride back to Virginia, and you can tell your story of what happened to the proper authorities. Iffen a judge believes you, he may give you some leniency. Iffen not, you'll hang.

"The hard way is for me to put a bullet in your head and take you to Virginia draped over your horse. In either case, you are going back to Virginia."

"Why don't you take me to Carolina? I ain't wanted there for murder!"

"How do you know?" asked Mabel.

Sputtering, Herman did not know what to say. Mabel had just found out he knew more than he let on.

William, without raising his voice, said, "What's your answer? I ain't got all day."

Herman was staring into the barrel of a Colt pointed directly at his head. He believed this kid might do what he said he would do. "I'll go with you," replied Herman.

"Miz Rouse, could I call upon you to go saddle your husband's horse for him, and also be so kind as to throw a couple of biscuits in his saddlebag. He might git hungry on the trail. Iffen you would do that, I would be much appreciative."

⁊

William sat on Taz watching what he suspected to be Mabel's final words to Herman. The only thing she said in a somewhat elevated voice was "I can't believe you came back to Powder Springs leading me to believe you were some kind of hero in the war. That you and Thurman were discharged early because of your bravery. I believed you. I should have known you would never change."

Herman sat on a brown Morgan horse that was so thin from not receiving proper care that William wasn't sure he could make the trip. Herman's wrists were bound together so that he could still guide his horse and hold on to the saddle horn if the terrain became difficult to negotiate. He also had a rope tied around his waist that extended back to William's saddle, where it was tied to the saddle horn. The rope was sufficiently long to allow twelve feet from the rear end of Herman's horse to Taz's head. This allowed for Herman to have the lead in their parade to Virginia.

William had realized early on that, physically Herman probably could, if given the chance, overpower him; accordingly, he planned to keep distance between the two of them.

He had told Herman he had tied him this way for two reasons. First, he could steer him by pulling the rope to either the left or right when he wanted Herman to turn. Otherwise, he was to keep riding straight.

Second, if he attempted to get away, he would soon find himself out of the saddle on the ground. Should that happen, William was not going to chase his horse down, but, rather, Herman would be walking the remainder of the distance.

When it appeared all the talking between Mabel and Herman was over, William said, "Miz Rouse, iffen you got family or friends in Powder Springs you can stay with, I would suggest you go there. With the war going on, you never know when a scoundrel might show up at your door. And should that happen, he will be up to no good."

Looking from William to Herman she said, "Yeah, I know about scoundrels. I married one!" She then turned and started toward the house.

William said to Herman, "You lead out, and remember what I said. Virginia will take you dead or alive, and I don't plan to be troubled with you."

"Where in Virginia are we going?" asked Herman.

"Jonesville," said William.

"Never heard of it," said Herman.

That evening when they camped for the night. William tied Herman's back to a pine tree. He kept his wrists tied together, which did not prevent Herman from feeding himself the biscuits Mabel had placed in his saddlebag.

Before calling it a night, Herman asked, "How long will it take us to get to Jonesville?"

"Well, if the trail continues this smooth, we should make it by early morning day after tomorrow."

William decided with Herman trying to start a conversation, it would be a good time to press him as to the location of Thurman. "You know, Mr. Rouse, you could help yourself a lot by not only making the authorities know the details of how Thurman controlled all your misdeeds, but by also telling me where I could find Thurman."

Herman immediately seized upon the idea that he was controlled by his bigger brother. He thought, "I might just escape the noose if all the bad things we did were laid at Thurman's feet. I was a victim and was being pulled along. I can claim I had no choice. This here is a pretty smart kid to suggest I couldn't control our situation."

William said nothing, but he could tell Herman was giving the matter of blaming everything on Thurman some serious thought.

The following morning William gave Herman some jerky to eat with his biscuit. As Herman pulled on his jerky, he said, "Iffen I tell you where I think Thurman might be, would you put in a good word for me? You know, like I've been cooperative. Maybe something about me getting married and changing my ways when I was no longer associated with Thurman."

"While that's a possibility, I'm not forgetting what you did to my pa. I will ask that you be given the maximum punishment for hurting Pa, but fortunately for you, you didn't kill him."

"But your pa wasn't hurt in Virginia. That happened in Carolina."

"True, but it does show a continued pattern of violence after you left Virginia. And iffen you tell the location of Thurman, I'll tell the authorities that it appeared you had settled down to a farm life."

William was hopeful that with him agreeing to say something positive on behalf of Herman, he would be easier to travel with. He would find out with his next question.

"So, where do you think I could find Thurman?"

Knowing that Thurman would not be taken easily, Herman said, "When I last saw him, he said he was going to Yellow Creek, Kentucky. I don't know iffen he's still there. That was almost a year ago."

Those words ended the morning discussion, and both were back in the saddle within the hour with one more overnighter and then into Jonesville.

CHAPTER 28

JONESVILLE

Aylana was returning to the cavern from one of William's rabbit snares. There was nothing in it. William had now been gone three weeks, and although she initially experienced a trying loneliness, she was now adjusting to his absence and was set in her daily routines.

As she and Chew walked through the grass, grasshoppers and other insects would fly up, fly a short distance from her, and reposition themselves upon the grass or other foliage. A bird was chirping in a nearby tree, and periodically she would hear a woodpecker hammering away on some tree. Growing up in an Indian family, she had been taught to be attuned to the actions and smells around her. Correctly reading the signs and the smells could mean the difference in a life-and-death situation. Animals and humans gave off different smells. This was especially true with respect to their droppings. The smell of a campfire could be detected a great distance from the actual fire.

Not only had she been taught how to detect the activity of the creatures that could be around her, but she was also taught how the absence of activity might be a warning sign. The absence of birds chirping could easily be read as a sign that something had frightened them away.

One of the advantages of having Chew with her was his keen senses of smell and hearing could detect evidence of an abnormal situation much more quickly than a human could.

On this particular day in the latter part of May 1864, as she and Chew were returning from a rabbit snare, Chew, walking a few steps in front of her, suddenly came to a stop. His head went up as he sniffed the air, and his ears were working in various directions as if trying to pick up the direction from which he was hearing a sound.

Aylana froze in her steps. As she also sniffed the air, she strained her ears to pick up on any sounds unnatural to her surroundings. There were no birds in the air, and the forest was unnaturally quiet. She kept her eyes on Chew as he tried to decipher what and where the abnormal activity was coming from. It was then she noticed that the hair on the back of his head began to rise, his ears pointed to her front and right, and then she could hear a low snarl beginning to resonate from his throat.

The first thought that went through her mind was "Of all the days not to bring the rifle with me. Why did I choose this day to leave it in the cavern?"

Just as Chew planted his feet in a protective posture, two wild-eyed, snarling wolves came out of the brush onto her path. They studied Chew as he released a sinister snarl. Apparently the two were considering their odds.

Aylana reached to her side and slowly removed the hunting knife she used to cut captured animals from their snares. She knew that any use of the knife would have to be after one launched his attack at her. In a situation like this, one doesn't release their only weapon until they are sure it has done its job.

When the alpha wolf started to make his advance toward Chew, Chew issued a warning bark accompanied by a blood-curdling growl that only another wolf could issue. As his top lip rolled up, the full length of Chew's fangs were exposed.

The second wolf started to move in a flanking movement toward Chew. It was obvious to Aylana the two were going to attack at the same time from different directions.

Aylana slowly moved up to Chew's right side while quietly saying, "Stay, Chew. Stay!"

Chew didn't move, but his eyes rolled from one wolf to the other.

When the alpha wolf made his charge directly at Chew, and with Aylana between the second wolf and Chew, the second wolf raced toward Aylana. It all happened quickly. Just as the alpha was before springing, Aylana yelled, "Now, Chew!" Chew launched forward, grabbing the alpha wolf in the neck while he was still in the air. Both went to the ground.

The second wolf leaped for Aylana's neck, his mouth open and prepared to make the kill. Aylana threw up her left forearm, which entered the wolf's mouth. As she was falling backward to the ground, her right hand came up, stabbing the wolf in the chest with the hunting knife up to its hilt.

On her back, and with her forearm still in the wolf's mouth, she rolled the wolf off and continued repeatedly stabbing it.

Having a good grip upon the alpha wolf's throat, Chew had no intentions of releasing it as the two rolled on the ground in a growling frenzy. With the grip Chew had on the wolf's neck, the wolf could not get a bite on Chew. Its primary effort was to free itself from the death grip Chew had upon him.

Finally, in its last gasp of life, the wolf that had Aylana's arm released its grip and died. Standing up and somewhat dazed, Aylana was brought back to reality by the snarling of Chew and the alpha wolf.

Bleeding from her left arm, Aylana was looking for an opening to sink her bloody hunting knife into the other animal, but their rolling on the ground made it difficult. Finally an opening presented itself. Chew had the wolf on its side as he continued to sink his teeth into the wolf's throat.

Aylana entered the fray. With her legs straddling the wolf, she began to stab the wolf in the side and stomach area. Soon it lay limp. But Chew continued to hold on. Aylana commanded, "Chew! Let him go. You got him."

Chew was reluctant to let the wolf go. After hesitating for a second with a look of "You sure that is a good idea?" he released his grip.

Aylana sat down on the ground to take inventory of their injuries. She had a serious bite to her left arm. The bite probably went to the bone. And she had a number of deep scratches and cuts she received from the animal's claws. But other than that, she had survived.

Chew, after making several victory laps around the fallen wolf, came over and laid his head in Aylana's lap. She then examined him only to find he had fared better than she did. He only had some deep cuts from the wolf's claws. However, because of where Chew had seized his opponent, the wolf never had the opportunity to bite Chew.

Aylana stood up and said, "Chew, let's go to the cavern and doctor our wounds. We'll come back later and collect these two. Their pelts will make for good bartering with Draper." The two wounded warriors started back toward the cavern with Aylana holding her wounded arm.

William rode into Jonesville in the early evening of the second day. There had been a good trail all the way to Jonesville. As William entered the town, he found it amusing how the townsfolk stopped what they were doing at the sight of Herman riding in front with a rope around his waist and a young boy riding behind holding the rope.

Jonesville was much larger than Powder Springs, sizewise probably more comparable to Goldsboro. In addition to townsfolk moving along the streets, there were a number of Confederate soldiers. William continued down Main Street with the expectation that the sheriff's office would be there. Halfway along Main Street, William spotted a shingle protruding from over a door that read, Lee County Sheriff's Office. There were bars on the front windows.

William did not have to send a directional message to Herman by pulling on the rope, as Herman rode right up to the hitching post. William joined him and tied both of the horses. He then helped Herman out of his saddle. William opened the door and pushed Herman through.

A man with a bushy mustache and well-groomed hair and wearing a denim coat with a large silver badge stood up and asked, "What do we have here?"

"Sir, I have bought you Herman Rouse, for whom I have a Virginia wanted poster."

The sheriff reached out for the wanted poster that William extended to him. After looking at the picture on the poster and Herman's face, he said, "I believe you have. But you appear awfully young to be a bounty hunter."

"Sir, I'm not a bounty hunter. I'm just a son trying to settle a debt this man owes my pa."

"What debt does he owe your pa?"

"He and his brother, Thurman, robbed and near 'bout killed my pa in Weldon, North Carolina."

"So, why didn't you take him to North Carolina?"

"'Cause he's wanted for murder in Virginia and not in North Carolina. Furthermore, he's wanted dead or alive in Virginia, and I wasn't right sure which way I was gonna git him here."

"Don't reckon the difference in the reward made a difference, did it?"

"No sir! I just wanted him to pay the biggest price for what he done."

"Well, I think I got the right jail for him. Iffen you untie him, I'll show him where it is."

As William was untying Herman, Herman whispered, "Remember what you said about putting in a good word for me...me being cooperative and telling you about Thurman."

"I remember and will keep my word."

The sheriff escorted Herman to one of the jail cells.

After the door was closed and locked, Herman said, "Can I speak to the boy one more time?"

"Sure!" The sheriff walked back into his office and said, "Herman wants to speak to you one more time."

When William walked into the area where there were four cells, Herman motioned for him to come over to the bars.

Once William was close to the bars, Herman said in a low voice, "I need to tell you something about Thurman."

"I'm listening," said William.

"Boy, you be careful with Thurman. He ain't nothing like me. He ain't gonna let you git as close to him as you got to me. Second, he ain't gonna be sitting on no front porch on a farm. He'll be in the worst part of the town with the worst people, none of whom will be his friend. And he'll be worse than any of them. He'll just as soon kill you as look at you, and he ain't gonna do it face-to-face on some street. Iffen you uns don't git him first, he'll git you when you least suspect it. Thurman ain't got no heart at all."

William said, "Thank you, Herman, for that advice. And I'm going out there right now and write a statement to the sheriff on your behalf saying how cooperative you've been and how you got yourself married and was trying to make a go of it on your family farm."

"Thank you, boy, and…I'm real sorry about your pa."

William turned and walked back into the outer office, where the sheriff was waiting.

For the next hour, William explained to the sheriff what had happened to his pa and his efforts to bring to a conclusion a settlement for what had happened. He also told him how he thought Herman had made some effort to turn his life around, and while he wanted the maximum justice for his father, he asked that if there was any evidence that Herman had not personally participated in any murders, as he claimed, the court not order a noose around his neck.

William then took the time to write a similar statement to be read at Herman's trial. Finally, the discussion made the circle to when William would receive his reward money for Herman. The sheriff explained that first he had to file an affidavit with the states' attorney office advising that Herman Rouse had been apprehended and was being held for trial. The state's attorney office would then have to authorize payment. The process would take at least two weeks before he would be authorized to give William the reward money.

William assured the sheriff that would be no problem. Just hold the money until he returned with Thurman either dead or alive, and if he was not back within the month, forward the reward money to his father in Saulston, North Carolina.

When the sheriff had agreed, William asked, "How far is Yellow Creek, Kentucky?"

The sheriff replied, "About a two-to-three-day ride due west. Why? Do you think Thurman may be holed up there?"

"I have reason to believe that is to be the case," replied William.

As William started to leave the sheriff's office, the sheriff's final remarks were "Son, I wish I could discourage you from making this undertaking alone. But knowing you've come this far, I doubt I could be successful. So just remember that Thurman Rouse is a notoriously dangerous man. Of the Rouse brothers, he has the reputation of being the most violent. Don't trust anyone you talk to because, out of fear for their own personal safety, they will forewarn Thurman. And he will then either sneak up on you, or he will be prepared for your arrival."

"Thanks, Sheriff. I'll keep that in mind," replied William as he left the sheriff's office.

CHAPTER 29

YELLOW CREEK

Two days later William arrived in Yellow Creek. While in William's mind Yellow Creek was not exactly in the category of a town, it certainly was a thriving village with the energy to someday, in the near future, achieve town status. But today, he considered it to be more of a village.

His initial impression of Yellow Creek was that while it could satisfy the basic needs of its citizens, there was not a variety of shops or stores to provide choices of goods or services to address the wants of citizens from the bottom of the income scale to the top. The focus appeared to be on the needs of the average citizen of the community.

While on the trail, William had considered the advice he had been given by both Herman and the sheriff. He suspected, before ever arriving, that the village would be one in which a stranger, young or old, would be obvious and possibly the center of discussion. Furthermore, a stranger asking questions would attract enough attention to easily make him, if not a target of either physical or verbal abuse, certainly one of isolation. In order to locate Thurman without drawing attention to himself, he would need a strategy by which he could melt into and become accepted as a part of the community. And that would take longer than a couple of months.

His strategy was to find work and become a working contributor to the community. Hopefully, as he became more frequently seen, he would be accepted, and people would become less hesitant to share their thoughts and advice with him.

Since his pa had always said a livery stable was the best place to learn about a place and secure information simply by keeping one's ears open and mouth shut, it became his first stop.

He arrived wearing the most worn-out shirt he had; the buckskin trousers Aylana had made him, which had not been cleaned in weeks; and worn-out boots. He wanted to portray the image of a young man who was going through some very bad luck. His Colt was in his saddle-bag, and his duster was tied across his bedroll.

The livery stable's doors were open and latched back against the front wall. Through the doors he could see all the way through the stable to the corral that was behind the stable. Coming through the back doors was a bearded man with long hair and wearing a leather apron. He was bent over from the weight of the metal pail he was carrying.

William tied Taz to the hitching post outside the front of the stable. He was in touching range of the man before the man was aware he was there.

When the man looked in William's direction, William said, "Excuse me, sir. I was just passing through and have been down on my luck."

The man, who looked about the age of Pa, said, "Look a here, boy. If you're looking for a handout, you done come to the wrong place."

"Oh, no, sir. I'm not looking for a handout. I'm a-looking for a job."

The man looked at William from his head to his toes and said, "Do I look like someone who would pay a boy a salary to work for me?"

"Sir, I ain't looking for no salary. I'll work for a place to keep my horse, a haystack to sleep on at night, and just enough money to buy a little food."

The man gave William another look over and then seemed to let his eyes scan around the inside of the stable. He then asked, "Boy, how do I know you can do this kind of work?"

"Sir, if you uns will let me keep my horse here and sleep in the hay in that corner, over there, I'll work for two days without any pay. Iffen you're not satisfied, I'll be on my way. Iffen you are satisfied, then you pay me twenty-five cents a day beginning with the first day I worked."

The man was thinking, "The last boy I had didn't last a week, and I was paying him forty cents a day. What do I have to lose? At end of two days, if I'm not pleased, he's gone, and I haven't paid him anything."

The man said, "Boy, folks around here call me Benton. What do you go by?"

"William, sir."

"William, you appear to be too polite and smart to be from around here. Where you come from? And what brings you here?"

"Pretty near Sugar Creek, Tennessee. And with the war, things got poorly around the farm. So me being the oldest, I had to leave home to provide for myself. Pa gave me my horse and wished me good luck. I been to several other towns where I was told that with my horse skills, I might find work in Kentucky. So I'm in Kentucky."

Benton gave a big laugh. "Son, you sure 'nuff in Kentucky, but all the big horse places are farther to the northwest than Yellow Creek."

"Well, sir, I found I can't go much farther without food for myself. So I had to stop riding and start working."

"Tell ya what I'm gonna do, William. I'm gonna give you a two-day try. Now, iffen at the end of the days I tell you to git, I don't want to hear nothing about what I owe you for the two days you worked."

"Fair enough!" said William, with a big gratitude smile on his face.

"You can put your horse in the last stall on the right. Then you get water in all the stalls that have horses in them. Them that are in the corral, be sure they git some hay. There's a place at the end of the barn near your horse's stall where you uns can store your tack and sleep. And, know I'll be keeping my eye on you."

William said, "Thank ya, Mr. Benton. I promise I won't disappoint you."

"Just call me Benton, Boy. That what everybody else calls me."

The following morning, after a breakfast of eggs, bacon, grits, and biscuits, Benton, rubbing his stomach, walked out on his front porch. His unpainted house, small but adequate for him and his wife, was located behind his livery stable.

Looking over toward the stable, he saw horses were already in the corral, and the back doors to the stable were swung wide open. Pulling out his pocket watch, he saw the time was 6:30 a.m. He normally opened at 7:00 a.m. He was thinking, "That young fellow is getting an early start. Certainly not like the last fellow I had, who arrived for work between 7:00 a.m. and 7:30 a.m."

Benton put his arm through the right gallus of his bib overalls and started to walk toward the stable. Inside the barn, he could hear the sound of hammering. As he walked by the corral watering trough, he could see it had been filled to overflowing.

Upon entering the stable, he could see the boy was replacing boards that had been off for at least a week in one of the stalls. As he passed each stall, walking toward the boy, he peered inside only to see each one had already been cleaned, and fresh straw had been placed inside.

Tied near the unopened front door were the three horses that he had told the boy, the night before, needed to be saddled and ready to go before their owners arrived around 7:00 a.m.

When he walked over to the horses and ran his hand over their hips, he could tell they had been curry brushed before the saddles were put on. He had not told the boy that needed to be done. He casually walked around the horses and carefully lifted a hoof of each horse. The bottoms of the hooves were clean, and the hooves' rims showed evidence the hooves had been picked to preclude there being any stones or anything else that could impede the horse from being ridden. He had to admit that he was impressed by the boy's initiative and knowledge of horses.

The boy was so busy working on the stall that it appeared he had not seen him enter the stable. But unknown to Benton, the boy had seen every move Benton had made from the time he entered the barn.

Finally, Benton commented, "Hey, boy…I mean William. You sure are an early riser."

William feigned surprise and then said, "Living on a farm, I always got everything ready for starting the workday. I hope that didn't make for a problem," replied William.

"Hell no! I just never had a worker get to the stable before I did."

William laughed and said, "Since for now this is my home, I didn't have far to travel to go to work."

"Have you had breakfast?"

"Yes sir! Had some beef jerky left from my saddlebag."

"Well, you plan on having lunch with me. When you finish with that stall, you can start on repairing the corral fence. But watch for our customers who will be coming in to pick up their horses. I want you to meet them so they will know who you are should they bring them back and I am not here."

"Yes sir," replied William. William was thinking, "Things are going better than expected. Now he will be introducing me to people, which eliminates my having to inquire."

The three customers who came for their horses did so at staggered intervals. Benton signaled for William to come over to meet Dempsey first, then Abbot, and finally, Longfellow. None resembled Thurman. William knew he must bide his time, and hopefully he would never have to bring the subject of Thurman up to Benton. He was hoping that with time, either Thurman would come in or someone would mention his name. For now, he had to focus on retaining his job.

By the end of the second day, Benton had offered William full-time employment at thirty-five cents per day, told William he could set himself up a room in the loft of the stable, and his horse could continue to be stabled there at no charge. By the end of the week, William had received an invitation to have dinner with Benton and his wife.

CHAPTER 30

THE ENCOUNTER

By the end of the third workweek, William had been accepted by the Bentons and was now sharing lunch with them two or three times a week. While he had an offer every day, he respectfully declined because he didn't want to overextend his welcome, and Miz Benton asked far too many questions.

Miz Benton was a very cordial woman who had explained early in her first meeting with William that they were not able to have children due to an injury she had as a child. William estimated her to be around the same age as her husband. Because she and her husband had no children, she seemed to be exceptionally curious about his childhood and his family. This led to many questions.

He tried to minimize their discussions and his answers in a way that would not imply there was another motive for his being in Sugar Creek. He explained that he was the eldest of his family and that the war had made for difficult times for his father. That much was true, but the implication he made was that for his father, having to support five children was a heavy burden, with the most expeditious relief being William's search for ways to support himself. While William's explanations were not precisely true, they seemed to satisfy her curiosity.

Additionally, because Miz Benton took a liking to this very polite young man, she invited him to have supper with them twice a week. Those nights were Wednesday and Sunday. However, Sunday dinner had a condition attached. William had to accompany them to church on Sunday.

The condition for William was a true blessing because he got to meet more of the townsfolk, and as the preacher said, he could "separate the wheat from the chaff." In other words, those in church were probably not those who would associate with Thurman Rouse. Furthermore, the Bentons promoted him as a new young gentleman of their community. In turn, this diminished any idea one might have of his presence having an ulterior motive.

However, the negative affect of his "young gentleman" image kept him out of the places where Thurman might be found, and it was not the environment where the likes of Thurman would be a subject of discussion.

In the middle of William's fourth week, a different breeze started to blow. It all started when two unkempt men with mean and arrogant dispositions rode up to the livery stable. As William started out to see how he could help them, Benton, almost running, passed him to see to their needs. William slowed his pace but kept advancing.

The first man came out of his saddle with a menacing look. Shoving his reins in Benton's direction, he said, as he glared at Benton, "Old man, you best give this horse the best care possible. Rub him down and feed him well. And when I come back, I don't want to hear any excuses for him not to have been given the best of care."

For the first time, William heard Benton say, "Yes sir!"

The second man was now off his horse and handing his reins to Benton. He said, "And the same goes for my horse. Anything less than the best could result in unnecessary damages. Do you understand?"

Again, Benton replied, "Yes sir."

The two men paid no attention to the boy standing behind Benton. As they walked back in the direction of the main street, one said to the other, "Come on. Let's wash some of this dust out of our mouths. I think one bottle should do it." He slapped the other on the back as they laughed and continued walking.

Benton turned and handed the reins of the two horses to William. His face was ashen, and his hands were shaking. He said, in a somewhat shaking voice, "William, until the horses are gone, you are to devote yourself to their care and maintenance. Their stalls are to always be clean with fresh straw, no matter how many times they crap in their stalls, and their water buckets are to remain full. It is important that you follow my instructions. Do you understand?"

"Yes sir," replied William. "But can you tell me the reason?"

"William, listen carefully. They are two very dangerous men. They have a reputation for provoking incidents whereby people die and there are no witnesses that will come forth to tell what happened. They are the type that if they are not pleased with how we care for their horses, they will not hesitate to destroy my property or hurt one of us."

"Why doesn't the law do something?"

"Didn't you hear what I said? They will test a man's integrity, honor, and manhood to a point where a man feels he must react. And when he does, he is dead."

"Why doesn't the law intervene and put a stop to their actions."

"Son, listen to me. Stepping forward will result in the same misfortune as the man being defended. The law will not do anything under the claim there are not any witnesses who will disagree with what the two have said happened. They are always responding in self-defense. The survivors are the ones who have avoided confrontation until they ride out of the village."

"How long will they stay here?"

"Anywhere from two to four weeks, and then they move on to some other town. Normally, they are back here every four to six weeks. So don't do anything to rile them. If you take care of their horses, we'll be okay."

"Yes sir, Mr. Benton. I'll do whatever you say."

"One other thing. There is one more who will come in either today or tomorrow. He is the meanest of the bunch. He is easy to recognize because he has an ugly scar on his face. Rumor is he got it in the war while single-handedly fighting off a company of Yankees. Truth is, I think he's the only one who believes that rumor, and there ain't no one living to challenge the rumor. Now, take care of them horses."

William walked the horses to two clean stalls. While taking off their saddles and brushing them down, he was thinking, "Is my waiting nearly over? Could the man with the scarred face be Thurman? And if it is, when and where do I take him? Getting to him will be difficult with the other two providing him protection. But, iffen it be Thurman, he'll only leave here hog-tied or draped over his saddle. And that is a promise."

It was 6:30 a.m., the morning after the two riders arrived at the stable and created a noticeably frightened Benton. William was busy cleaning out stalls when there came a loud rap on the front door of the stable. Normally that door was not opened until 7:00 a.m.

The knock was heavy and demanding. William ran to the door and hollered through, "Just a minute while I unlock the door." He removed the large board that crossed both doors that secured them closed. Swinging the door open, he stood face-to-face with a man who was the spitting image of Herman. From the corner of his left eye to the bottom of his left chin was an ugly scar. The doctor who had done the job must have been in a hurry because there was no evidence of any attempt to preserve the face in its original appearance.

Apparently, the sight registered a shock on William's face because the man gruffly said, "Apparently you've never seen a man that survived such a serious war wound."

William, to his own surprise, stumbled with his words saying. "Ah, no sir, it's not your wound, but I'm here by myself, and we've never had anyone to arrive before our opening at seven."

"Well, kid, for your information, I am not just 'anyone,' and doors open when I arrive because I'm not on a fixed schedule. Did two men arrive here yesterday?"

"Yes sir. Their horses are in the two stalls near the back of the stable."

"Well, put mine near theirs, and you best take care of him. Otherwise, when I come back, I'll give you a whuppin' worse than anything your pa ever gave you."

"Yes sir. I'll take good care of him."

"Where is the old coot that's normally around here? I want him to know he is personally to see to the care of my horse."

"Yes sir, I will be sure to tell him. Will he know your horse, or would you like to leave your name?"

"Hell yes, he will know my horse. But so you don't forget who he belongs to, my name is Rouse."

"Yes sir, Mr. Rouse. I will take care to let Mr. Benton know exactly what you said as soon as he arrives, and I will see to your horse right now."

Rouse handed William his reins, turned, and started in the direction of Main Street.

When Benton arrived at 6:55 a.m., William gave him the full story of his encounter with Rouse.

Benton said, "I think I told you yesterday that the meanest one normally arrives the day after the others. He's always ill-tempered and begging for an altercation with someone. I'm glad you were here to handle the situation. With me, he's always testing me and trying to make me angry. Iffen he can get anyone a little riled, that's his excuse for a self-defense claim to murder. You stay wide of him, William."

"Yes sir" was William's reply as he went back to performing his duties, which included bedding down Rouse's horse in a stall near the other two horses with fresh straw.

Throughout the day, William worked hard so that he could ask Benton for permission to take off couple of hours early to take care of some personal business. Should Benton inquire as to his personal business, he would explain that he wanted to post a letter to his parents and take Taz out for an exercise run. Taz's movements had been confined to the corral for the last few weeks.

At three in the afternoon, with all his chores completed, William asked Benton for a couple of hours for some personal business he needed to take care of. Benton granted the time, and to William's surprise, did not inquire as to the nature of the personal business. However, the question might come up later.

Once Taz had been saddled with saddlebags in place and William was in the saddle, Taz began to show his excitement about being out of the corral. His ears were up, and his hips were moving from side to side, indicating he was ready to go. Once outside the barn, William relented and let Taz move into a slow canter. On his way to his first stop, the post office, he surveyed the streets in hopes of seeing either Rouse and his companions or, possibly, where they might be spending their time. He saw neither, but he could hear a loud ruckus coming from one of the side streets. For now he would not venture down the street but make his way to the post office. Once he had mailed the letter to his family to update them on his status, he and Taz picked up the pace as they departed the village.

For a short distance, he let Taz accelerate to a full run, which he seemed to enjoy. He steered Taz for the hills, hoping to find an isolated place where weapon fire would not be detected. Within the hour he had located the ideal place. It was surrounded by hills within a dense forest, which would buffer the sounds made by his Colt.

For the next hour, William practiced his fast draw and firing from the hip. He felt a lot better now that he had had the opportunity to confirm he had not lost his edge. He was confident that when he went up against Rouse, if he cleared his holster first, his round would go wherever he intended it to go. The problem that remained was, if he couldn't separate Rouse from the other two, how would he deal with them? Without his knowing whether they were wanted, they would have to make the first move so it would be clear that he had taken them down in self-defense. Of course, he still did not know how the local law would insert itself or its relationship with Rouse and his cronies. If they were not wanted in Kentucky, he might have a serious problem.

CHAPTER 31

THE PLAN

Over the next two weeks, there was a dramatic change in the atmosphere of Yellow Creek. The most obvious thing was the traffic within the village came to a standstill. Those who did venture outside scurried to and from their destinations. There appeared to be an element of fear that roamed the streets. Merchants who placed some of their items outside and in front of their stores no longer did so.

The reason, William learned from Benton, was that if Rouse or one of his hooligans was walking along the wooden sidewalk and considered an item to be an obstruction to their path, rather than walk around the item, they would throw it into the street. Even Benton was careful to make sure nothing obstructed the entrance to the stable. And, when he was in the stable, he nervously paced around as he kept an eye on the entrance. It was as if he might be expecting some form of trouble at any time.

Trouble did come to the village, but it was learned from another by way of rumor. The first incident occurred at one of the gambling and drinking establishments. Rumor was that a local gambler believed to be somewhat of a card shark got into a disagreement with Rouse. Rouse berated the man, calling him a cheater and a coward. It was said the man stood up and refused to gamble anymore. Common knowledge was he carried a pistol in his waistband. When he stood up and started to collect the money on the table, Rouse also stood up. And when the man started to put the money in his pocket, it was said, Rouse interpreted that movement to be the man going for his gun. At which point Rouse drew his pistol and shot the man dead.

Since those present either claimed they did not see what had happened or said nothing, and since the only witnesses to back up Rouse's story were his companions, the constable ruled the gambler's death was an act of self-defense on the part of Rouse.

The second shooting was of a local merchant. Allegedly, one of Rouse's companions was shopping in a local mercantile store. When he went to pay the shop owner, the shop owner reminded him of a box of ammunition he had picked up but did not present it for payment. Rouse's companion accused the shop owner of calling him a thief and shoplifter. After a lengthy verbal confrontation, according to Rouse's companion, the shop owner reached under his counter and withdrew a weapon. When he did so, the accused thief pulled his pistol and shot the shop owner dead. When the constable arrived, he found a gun lying on the floor near the shopkeeper. Although the wife claimed her husband did not own a gun and the one on the floor did not belong to him, the constable again ruled it was an act of self-defense on the part of Rouse's companion. No further investigation was warranted.

So the town folks continued to pray that Rouse and his companions would leave town soon. It was obvious to all that the constable had no intentions of taking on Rouse and his two companions.

This became more apparent to William when he decided to purchase a used rifle with the money he had saved working for Benton. After purchasing the rifle for fifteen dollars, William went to the constable's office to find out if there was any ordinance precluding the firing of a weapon within the limits of the village. The reason he would give the constable was that he wanted to target practice behind the livery stable. His primary reason was to get those living close to the stable used to hearing gunfire in the area. He believed that at some point, his showdown with Rouse would be at the stable, and should he have to fire his weapon when he confronted Rouse, his hope was that the locals would ignore the shot and assume he was just target practicing.

However, when he entered the constable's office, the only person present was the cleaning lady. She said the constable had to leave town on business and would be gone for about a week. When William asked who was assuming the constable's law enforcement responsibilities, she replied, "I don't have any idea. He doesn't tell me anything but what I missed cleaning."

William departed the constable's office thinking, "What a convenient time to have business outside of Yellow Creek."

🐑

John Robert sat on the front porch in his favorite rocking chair. He was wearing his bib overalls. A corncob pipe protruded from his mouth. For him, after putting in a good day of physical work, there was nothing more refreshing than the early-evening breeze that stirred the old oak trees in his front yard. There was something about the way the Spanish moss that clung to the tree branches swayed back and forth that provided a time of relaxation for him and the putting away of the challenges of tomorrow until tomorrow.

The gentle breeze reminded him of the days when he and William sat on this porch and discussed the subjects of fishing and trapping. Frequently the subject drifted to what William hoped for, for his future. While John had always hoped John would follow in his footsteps and become one of the most effective and efficient farmers in Wayne County, William always expressed his interest in the law. At a very early age, William had started a bank account in which he routinely put money for the day when he might be in the financial position to study law. Academically, he had the intellect to pursue such a goal. Now John sat alone, wondering where William might be and what he was doing. It had been some time since the family had received a letter.

As John puffed on his pipe, staring down the path leading to his house and pondering the health and welfare of his eldest son, he saw a cloud of dust racing up his path. The rider was in such a hurry John could not help but to wonder about his intent.

He was thinking, "In this day and time, one can never be too careful." John reached over and retrieved his rifle, which was resting against the door frame. He verified a round was in the chamber and that it was cocked and ready for firing. The war had emboldened scoundrels to the point where they were raiding unprotected homes and killing innocent people. The sad part was that most of those capable of countering such attacks were fighting the war. That left the defense of homes to the old folks and the women, none of whom were prepared to repel an aggressive attacker who was confident he held the upper hand. That was not the case at the Daniel farm, and William had done a good job of creating that reputation.

Soon the rider was close enough that John could identify him as one of the telegraph messengers. "God, I pray it's not bad news about William," thought John as he released the hammer on his rifle.

The rider came to an abrupt stop at John's porch steps. He said, "Pardon the dust, Mr. Daniel, but I'm trying to get back to Saulston before dark."

"That all right. Do you have something for me?"

"Yes sir! The postmaster knew I had to deliver a message to the Browns down the road and thought this letter might be important. He didn't know when the next time you would be in town. It's postmarked Kentucky."

"Don't recollect knowing anyone from Kentucky." Poor recollection for John was not out of the ordinary. While he had regained most of his physical abilities, he still suffered short-term memory losses. In particular, he could recall very little about his ever being in Weldon and the attack he suffered.

The rider leaned out of the saddle and handed the letter to John. Then he said, "Gotta be going, Mr. Daniel. Hope it's not bad news!"

And off he went back down the path, his horse in a fast run, kicking up clouds of dust.

John stood on the porch staring at the letter, also hoping it was not bad news. He could not decide if he should open it now or wait and open it with Becky. Then a sigh of relief came over him when he identified the perfection of the writing to be that of William. He quickly turned and headed into the house, hollering, "Becky, Becky, come quick! I think we have a letter from William."

Becky yelled back, "Don't you go and open it until I round up the kids. Come to the dinner table so we can all sit down to hear it."

Within minutes all were seated around the dinner table, anxiously waiting for Pa to open a letter that had come all the way from Kentucky.

James Arrington, eight years old and the fourth oldest in the family, asked, "Where is Kentucky, Pa?"

John answered, "I'll explain all that after we read the letter."

Becky reminded John, "You be careful opening the letter so as not to tear through some of his writing."

"I will," replied John as he withdrew his pocketknife and slowly cut open the letter. He then said, "Now, everybody be quiet, and let me read all of the letter before there are any questions. Can we do that?"

There was a simultaneous and unanimous "Yes, Pa!"

John opened the letter and began to read:

Dear Ma, Pa, and Family,

I hope this finds all of you doing well. I know you're surprised to see a letter from Kentucky, but I am now in Yellow Creek, Kentucky. Before I answer how I got here, let me tell you I am doing well, and the first part of my journey is over. Pa, H.R. is now in jail in Va. waiting for his trial. My catching him was not a problem. He told me T.R. was in Yellow Creek. When I got here, I learned T.R. returns here routinely about every three to four weeks. To await his arrival, I found a job at the local livery stable. You know I got plenty of experience cleaning stalls at home. Anyhow, I work for a good man who provides me a place to sleep, and his wife invites me to dinner several days a week and to supper twice a week. Ma, you will be happy to know I go to church with them every Sunday. As soon as I capture T.R. I will be coming home. All of you need to know when I come home I will be bringing a big surprise. Hope you will be happy with the surprise. Must close for now. Hope to see you all soon.

Love to all,
Your son and brother, William.

P.S. Pa, iffen you had been face-to-face with either H.R. or T.R., you could have handled yourself. They are known to be bullies who attack unsuspecting people.

Ma was the first to speak. "I'm so happy William is doing well and going to church! I just pray for his safety."

Pa said, "William is smart. He has already figured out these fellows, and he is not going to take any chances. I believe he'll be back here by harvest time this year."

"What do you suppose his surprise is?" asked eleven-year-old Fannie.

Thirteen-year-old Nancy replied, "I'll bet he has found a girlfriend."

Ma said, "Nancy, he wouldn't be bringing a girlfriend. Ain't no decent parents would let their daughter go trekking all the way back to Saulston with their boyfriend."

James Arrington returned to his first question. "Pa, where is Kentucky?"

Pa laughed and said, "Come on, son. Let's go into the sitting room, away from the women folks, and I will try to explain it to you."

As Pa stood up, Arrington came around and put his hand into his pa's hand, and the two of them walked together toward the sitting room.

The evening after William purchased his rifle and asked to do some target practicing behind the stable, Benton, lying in bed, was in a very restless mood. His, wife by his side, asked, "Benton, what is troubling you? Is it the Rouse gang being in town? I know it has everyone in a stir."

"No, it's William. I'm worried he's just about to leave us."

"Why would he do that? You haven't said anything to run him off, have you?"

"No, nothing like that. Besides, you know I've become very fond of William. He's a smart boy and can do well for himself right here in Yellow Creek. But he seems to have changed some since Rouse has been in town. As a matter of fact, today he went out and bought himself a rifle. I'm interpreting that to mean he's about to pull up stakes and move on."

"Well, I hope you're wrong. I like that young man, and so do many of the young girls in our church. They're always flirting with him. And while he's always friendly and nice toward them, he never encourages anything more than a casual friendship."

"I just have a feeling something is weighing heavy on his mind, and the very presence of Rouse and his gang has caused him to believe he should move on. You know that you and I are relieved when Rouse departs, but we know he will return in a few weeks. I think William is a person who does not like the idea of knowing a man like Rouse is going to show up every few weeks and disrupt the lifestyle of the citizens. And he has implied a lack of understanding as to why the law doesn't do something about our situation."

"I know why!" said Benton's wife. "Our law is afraid of Rouse, and we the citizens are letting the law get away with ignoring Rouse's meanest."

"Please don't say that beyond these walls; otherwise, Rouse could make it hard on us. He already makes my life miserable when he's in town."

Benton's wife said, "If you want to know what's ailing William, the best way to find out is to ask him. He's a good boy, and I know he would tell you. So put it out of your mind for now. Tomorrow is another day, so don't waste it on wondering. Ask William his intentions."

The following morning, around 11:00 a.m., when all was quiet in the stable and there were no customers, Benton said, "William, will you join me at the table where I keep my books. I have something I want to ask you in private."

A little puzzled because Mr. Benton had never suggested a private talk, William joined Benton feeling somewhat awkward.

Benton pointed to a chair in which he wished for William to take a seat. William did so and asked, "What can I help you with, Mr. Benton?"

"I'm going to be straight up with my question, William, and I hope you will be the same with your answer."

"Yes sir, I will."

"Thank you. Are you planning to be leaving us soon?"

"Mr. Benton, what I tell you must remain between just the two of us. I would prefer you not share this with Miz Benton. Do I have your word on that?"

A confused look came over Benton's face as he replied, "Yes, you do."

"Mr. Benton, when you gave me this job, I explained that I was only passing through and was currently a little down on my luck. I apologize for not being completely honest with you at that time. But I didn't know either the town's or your sentiment toward Thurman Rouse. I came here to get Rouse and was prepared to stay here as long as necessary to do so. But let me start at the beginning."

For the next thirty minutes, William related to Benton what had happened to his father and that the perpetrators were Herman and Thurman Rouse. He told of the oath he had taken to himself to bring the two to justice and to settle the debt he believed was owed his father. He told how Herman had warned him of Thurman's violent nature and the brother's understanding that Thurman had taken up residency in Yellow Creek. He knew that in order to get the information he needed, he had to become a resident of Yellow Creek. And for that opportunity he was deeply indebted to Mr. and Miz Benton.

William ended his story by saying, "Mr. Benton, I promise no harm will come to you if you will do what I say. As I understand it, Rouse's companions will ride out of town the day before he does. When Rouse comes to get his horse to depart, I will confront him. He is wanted in Virginia dead or alive. I will take him any way I can. My only request of you is, when Rouse enters the stable, you find a safe place and stay put. And while I may not leave here alive, I can promise you neither will Rouse. You and this town will no longer have to put up with the likes of him."

"But William, when I look at you I see a young man without the experience of Rouse. Rouse is a violent and angry man who will have no reservations about killing you. I have not seen anything in your character that would make you a match for Rouse.

"Mr. Benton please trust me when I say that sometimes looks can be deceiving. Rouse stands against those whom are frighten by him, which given him the advantage. I am not frighten by him; he will underestimate me and that will give me the advantage.

William, there must be something I can do.

"No sir, I could not live with the thought that your wonderful wife was made a widow by my actions. You must just remain safely out of sight. Let me do what I need to do. Will you do that for me?"

Benton, reluctantly nodded his agreement but added, "William, I know you have thought this through, but I still fear your lack of gun experience places you at a great disadvantage."

"Don't you worry about my taking care of myself. I promise my plans allow for me to remain within my limitations."

CHAPTER 32

THE TIME TO SETTLE UP

It was an overcast day in the Blue Ridge Mountains of Tennessee. It was just before sunrise, but there were no stars or moon visible. And while snow was no longer an issue, the possibility of rain and the smell of rain hung heavy in the atmosphere. Patches was hooked up to the drag, which was piled high with pelts from rabbits, raccoons, foxes, and two wolves. In accordance with William's instructions, Aylana did not have any big game pelts, such as deer. William explained he did not want her to try to kill anything as heavy as a deer. Hanging it for dressing it out was a strain for him, so she wasn't to do that. That request had been confusing for her to understand because she remembered that it was not an uncommon practice for an Indian woman to hang and skin deer. But she had promised to honor his request.

William had now been gone for over two months. As of now she wasn't worried because when he departed, he did say two to three months. However, the cavern was full of pelts that needed to be traded while they were still sufficiently pliable for making into hats, clothes, and boots.

Patches was ready to go, and Chew was sitting at Patches's front legs waiting for Aylana to make one final check on the security of the cavern. She ensured all the fires were extinguished and that the flap covered the entrance. In addition, she had piled limbs and brush around the entrance, making it difficult for anyone who might pass by to identify an entrance into the side of the mountain.

She untied Patches from the tree where he was waiting patiently. Holding the reins in her teeth, she grabbed Patches's mane with both hands and pulled herself up onto his back. Although a shorter mule would have been easier for her to mount, he would not have been as strong as Patches.

With a slight kick into his sides, Patches moved out, picking each step carefully as he started to move down the mountain. Aylana's plan was to make Sugar Creek before noon, conduct her trading business with Draper as quickly as possible secure a few supplies, and return to the cavern by no later than the edge of dark.

The trip down the mountain was uneventful. Chew remained about twenty feet in front of Patches. He seemed to understand his job was their security. Both Chew and Aylana had fully recovered from the injuries they had sustained from their fight with the wolves. And Chew gave every indication there would be no surprises on this trip. Furthermore, for the trip, Aylana had brought her rifle. She had tied one end of a rope on the barrel and the other end on the rifle stock. This permitted her to carry the rifle on her back, leaving both hands free to either provide guidance to Patches or fan branches from in front of her face.

Before noon Aylana arrived in Sugar Creek and rode Patches to the hitching post in front of Draper's Mercantile. After tying Patches, she and Chew entered the store.

Draper appeared very excited to see her and was very interested in the pelts she had on the drag. He told her to feel free to roam around the store and place whatever she needed on the counter. He would go outside and assess the pelts she had brought in.

She placed on the counter a few canned food items, flour, some apples and potatoes. She also included a roll of cotton fabric from which she could make William a shirt and her a dress. She had never had a cotton dress but all the women she saw in the village were wearing them.

When the bill was settled, Mr. Draper owed her some money, which was a surprise to her. She assumed it would be an even trade, but Mr. Draper was an honest man.

Mr. Draper helped her carry her items to the drag and helped unload the pelts. In the course of their work, she inquired if he had received any news from William. He said he had not but had every reason to believe William was safe and would return home before the end of the month.

As she was about to mount Patches, she saw a man approaching with a big smile on his face as if he had seen something enticing to him. When he drew near to Draper, he asked, "Hey, Draper, who is this pretty little thing you're helping here? She appears as if she might need my help."

Draper responded, "This here is Miz Daniel, and I'm pretty certain she does not need your help." By now Aylana was seated on Patches's back.

"Well, maybe I need her help," the man laughed in reply.

The man then froze in his steps. He looked down and saw he was staring in what appeared to be the snarling eyes of a wolf. Chew had taken a position between the man and Patches. His upper lip was curled up, revealing an evil grin. From within came a guttery growl that said, "One more step, and you are mine."

The man was starting to reach for his pistol when Draper said, "I wouldn't advise that. Before you clear your holster, this dog will have your throat in his teeth. And if that doesn't kill you, I suspect the lady on the mule will."

Without moving, the man looked up at Aylana, who had her rifle pointing at him.

The man, stuttering, finally got out the words "I was just trying to be friendly. Iffen you will call off your dog, I'll be going back toward the bar."

Draper counter with "Iffen you have any idea of following this lady, you might want to rethink that idea. There is no way you will sneak up on this dog, but he has a lot of ways he can sneak up on you. And iffen there is a next time, there will be no one to call him off you."

Chew was still braced in his position, never once taking his eyes off the man. Aylana in Cherokee said, "Chew, come!"

As Aylana turned Patches toward the mountains, Chew broke his stance and fell in trotting beside Patches. At the outer edge of the village and just before entering the forest to return up the mountain, Chew once again took the lead, and Aylana slung her rifle onto her back. By nightfall Patches should be back in his stall and Aylana and Chew back inside the cavern. As William would have said, quoting Shakespeare, "All is well that ends well."

஧

Two evenings after William had confessed to Benton his real intentions for being in Yellow Creek, one of Rouse's companions entered the stable just as William was locking up for the night.

Upon his entry he inquired as to the whereabouts of Benton. William explained that Benton was out by the corral ensuring all was secure for the night. The companion then announced, "Me and my partner will be pulling out tomorrow morning around seven thirty, and we want our horses saddled and ready."

William asked, "Do I need to have Mr. Rouse's horse ready?"

"No. He will be following us the morning after tomorrow. So be sure his horse is ready by the same time on that morning."

"Yes sir!" replied William.

After they had departed, William locked the front door and reported to Benton what Rouse's companion had said.

Benton commented, "Rouse is following through with his tradition of leaving town twenty-four hours after his companions. You may recall he arrived twenty-four hours after the other two arrived. I think he lets them come in first to see if things are the same as they were the last time he was here. If not, they have plenty of time to ride out to meet him and divert him to another destination. I guess that's one of his personal safety measures."

William thought that to be good information to know. He was thinking, "Now I don't have to concern myself with controlling the other two when I take Rouse into custody."

The following morning, just before 7:30 a.m., the two ruffians walked into the stable. William had brushed their horses down, saddled them, coated their hooves with liquid sealer, and tied them to a hitching post inside the front door. Benton was there to meet them. William remained in the background leaning against one of the stall doors. As a precaution he had his rifle resting against the wall inside the stall. If things started to get out of hand, he was prepared to take action.

As one of the men untied his horse, he said, "How much I owe you?"

Benton replied, "Your horses were here twenty-one days, and at thirty-five cents per day, it amounts to seven dollars and thirty-five cents each."

The man said, "I make it seven dollars even, because we're repeat customers."

Benton replied, "Okay."

Each counted out seven dollars and handed it to Benton.

The other called to William, "Hey, boy, come here."

William, hesitant to leave his rifle behind, walked cautiously toward the man.

The man, to William's surprise, flipped a quarter in the air toward him. When William caught it, the man said, "That's for doing a good job with my horse."

William replied, "Thank you!"

The other man showed no gratitude. He swung into his saddle and started out the front door with the generous man following along behind.

When they were out of sight, Benton exclaimed, "That has to be a first. I've never known any of them to offer a tip for services well done."

William replied, "I'll be glad to give it to you to make up for some of the loss you just took."

Benton said, "No sir. That being a first, you're entitled to it. As far as my loss, I would have been willing to take an even greater loss just to be rid of them."

"Let's discuss the plan for tomorrow when Rouse comes to pick up his horse. Now, Mr. Benton, I am requesting, for your safety and my being able to accomplish what I need to do, that you accurately follow my instructions."

Benton drew near to hear what William had to say.

"When Rouse arrives I will be in the back stall. Rouse's horse will be tied at that stall door. You are to greet Rouse and call for me to bring up his horse while you collect your payment. I'll be slow in coming, which will irritate Rouse and cause him to come looking for me. When he leaves you, you are to get out of sight in the first stall. My rifle will already be inside the stall with a round in the chamber and ready to fire. I want you to stay there until I tell you to come out. If there are any gunshots, I don't want you to get hit by a stray bullet. Do you understand what I need for you to do?"

"Yes, but I think you should let me help you with whatever you are going to do."

"If I need your help, I will call out with the words 'Move now.' If I call out, you are to exit the stall firing at Rouse as fast as you can. If I don't call out and anyone other than me sticks his head into your stall, you empty your rifle on him because it will be Rouse."

"That's your plan?" inquired Benton.

"That is my plan and my hand. I must be the one to play it."

The following morning around 7:30 a.m., Rouse swaggered into the stable. He was met by Benton, who said, "Good morning, Mr. Rouse. Your horse is ready for you."

"Well, where is he?" snapped Rouse.

"Oh! William just brought him out of his stall and tied him by the stall door. William is inside the stall."

Rouse looked down the stall walkway and saw his horse waiting patiently. "Tell him to get him up here. I ain't walking down there."

"William! Bring up Mr. Rouse's horse. Would you like to pay now, Mr. Rouse? That was twenty-one days at thirty-five cents per day, for a total of seven dollars and thirty-five cents."

"Hell no! I'm not paying again. My boys told me they already paid you."

"No sir, they didn't."

"Look ah here, you old bag of wind, I think you're trying to stiff me for seven dollars."

"No sir, I wouldn't do that."

"You sure as hell wouldn't, because I wouldn't let you. So now, I guess you're calling me a liar? And nobody, even an old man like you, ain't gonna call Thurman Rouse a liar."

Then a voice came from the rear of the barn. The voice said, "Mr. Benton is not calling you a liar, I am!"

Rouse's head snapped in the direction of the voice. He thought he was having a difficult time focusing because it appeared the stable boy was standing in the center of the walkway with a pistol on his side and the holster tied to his leg.

As Rouse was trying to get his eyes into focus, Benton backed slowly into the first stall and ducked out of sight.

By now, William had started a slow walk toward Rouse.

Benton had found a small crack between the boards where he could watch the interaction between William and Rouse. And he couldn't believe his eyes. William was no longer the boy he had known. He was now a man with piercing eyes and the look of a gunfighter he had once read about in the local news.

"Boy! You don't want to do this, 'cause you gonna git yourself killed," said Rouse in a higher-pitched voice.

William calmly replied, "Your brother, Herman, thought the same thing, but he is now in jail in Jonesville, Virginia. Iffen it makes you feel any better, he told me where I could find you."

"My brother? That son of a bitch! Why in the hell are you doing this?"

"Because you and your brother are scums of the earth, and someone needs to clean up the scum."

"Why do you think you have to be the one?"

"Because I have motive."

Rouse's hand moved closer to this pistol. "What is your motive?"

"Do you remember what you and Herman did to my pa behind the train depot in Weldon, North Carolina? Let me refresh your memory. My pa was a fellow soldier, and you and Herman took him behind the depot, beat him near death, robbed him of his military pay, and left him for dead. For that you have to be held accountable, and I'm here to make the settlement."

William could tell by the tone of Rouse's voice, the posturing of his body, and the twitching of his hand that he was just about to make his play.

William said, "Before you go for your gun, know that you can go like your brother, hog-tied over your horse to Virginia, where you are wanted dead or alive, or I will carry you back dead and strapped across your horse. It is all your choice."

Rouse gave himself away when a smirk crossed his face and he made a sudden movement for his pistol. A shot rang out. Rouse's pistol was half out of its holster when the round from William's Colt struck him in his right shoulder. Both the top of his arm and his shoulder socket were shattered. Rouse jerked back to his right in a stumbling motion, and his pistol dropped to the ground.

Rouse was not a quitter and was not about to be taken alive. With his left hand, he withdrew his Bowie knife from its sheath. With the look of a wild man, he started toward William. However, he never made two steps before there was a loud crack and Rouse suddenly went down.

William was shocked to see Rouse suddenly go down, but even more shocked to see Benton standing over Rouse with a bloody fence post in his hand. The back of Rouse's skull had been shattered.

Benton took a deep breath of relief and said, "I couldn't let you kill him. It was something I needed to do for the citizens of Yellow Creek. One of us should have done it before now, and I'm glad it could be me."

CHAPTER 33

UNKNOWN HERO OF
YELLOW CREEK

After confirming Rouse was dead, Benton rushed to the barn door and on the outside of the door hung a sign that read, "Will Return in 30 Minutes." He then closed the door and barred it.

While William placed Rouse's horse in a rear stall, hidden behind a pile of hay, Benton secured a large tarp. The two then rolled Thurman into the tarp and tied each end with a piece of rope. Together they placed Thurman in the stall with his horse.

After all evidence of Thurman having been in the stable was removed from sight, William said, "Mr. Benton, here is the story you must stick to, and it's a story in which you will not be lying. Should anyone ask you of the whereabouts of Thurman, you are to say he arrived around seven thirty a.m. to get his horse. After refusing to pay you what he owed you, he and his horse departed out of the rear of the barn. Since it was unusual for him to depart by way of the rear of the stable, you assumed he must have done something in town for which he did not want anyone to see him leave. I would also ask that be the same story you tell your wife. She may be worried if she knew the full story. And let's let that be the end of the story.

"When we close this evening, I will leave by way of the rear of the stable. We will place Herman across his horse, tie a box on each side of the horse, and cover all with another tarp. The shape will convey the appearance, should anyone see my leaving or meet me on the trail, of my having a packhorse in tow. I'm not telling you where I'm going. But I will tell you, for the help you have given me, half the reward money, two hundred and fifty dollars, will be deposited in the County Bank of Lee County, Virginia, in your name, Ira Benton."

"William, you don't have to do that for me."

"Mr. Benton, you sound like my pa. So the money is for Miz Benton but in your name. In the next couple of weeks, you're to close the stable for a few days, and the two of you take a few days of vacation and ride to Jonesville, Virginia. There the money will be waiting for you. It is only a small token of my appreciation for what you and Miz Benton have done for me. Now, I guess we best open our doors for a normal day of business."

After the front door of the livery stable was closed at 5:00 p.m., William and Benton resaddled Thurman's horse, threw him across the saddle rolled in the tarp, strapped a wooden box to each side, and covered all with a tarp. There was no suggestion that a body could be across the horse.

William then saddled Taz and placed his bedroll and saddlebags behind the saddle. His rifle was stowed in its sheath underneath his leg. He was in the saddle saying his last goodbyes to Benton when Miz Benton entered the stable carrying a small cloth bag. Looking up at William with tears in her eyes, she said, "Benton told me at lunch today you were leaving. I needn't tell you how sorry I am to see you go, but a young man must find his own way in this world. I brought you some home cooking for your travels. Please promise me that should you come this way again, you will stop to see us."

"Yes ma'am, I promise. Thank you for treating me like I was your son. I truly appreciate all you've done for me. I best git going. Ya'll take care of each other."

With that, William leaned over and gave Miz Benton a kiss on the top of her head. Then, without looking back, he turned Taz toward Jonesville with Herman's horse in tow.

$$\text{\ae}$$

At noon of the second day, William rode into Jonesville and directly to the sheriff's office.

When William walked into the sheriff's office, the sheriff said, "I see you made it back in one piece."

"Yes sir. And, I brought you a present."

"Have you got that other Rouse boy?"

"Yes sir, but not the way I had hoped to bring him to you. When I told him I was taking him in, he went for his gun. I got him in the shoulder before he cleared leather. The impact caused him to stumble backward, and he hit his head on something. It may have been the anvil, which was close by. Anyway, his head striking the object killed him."

"Damn! I really didn't believe you would be back. But I have your money for you for your delivery of Herman. It'll take another ten days to get you paid for Thurman."

The sheriff turned his desk chair around to his safe, spun a few dials, and pushed down on the handle, and the safe door sprung open. He withdrew a stack of money and counted out five hundred dollars to William for the delivery of Herman.

William said, "Thank you, Sheriff. Do you think when the other five hundred comes in, you can send it to my bank in Saulston, North Carolina?"

"I think we can find a way to do that. Now, iffen you're looking for a job, I can sure 'nuff use another good deputy."

"Thank you, sir, but I have someone waiting for me, and I best git to them. Iffen you will come out and look at your present, I got some business at the bank."

After William had placed two hundred and fifty dollars in the bank on hold for Ira Benton, he returned to the sheriff's office. There the sheriff had already confirmed the body to be Thurman and claimed it on behalf of the state of Virginia. He then said, "You sure 'nuff got him. One less thing the state of Virginia will have to worry with. For all the trouble you been through, I'm giving you Thurman's horse and saddle. You might need it before you get back home."

"Thank you. I can certainly use him."

"By the way, you are to be congratulated on getting your settlement. I'm sure your pa will be proud of you. And don't worry about that reward money; I'll be sure to get it to you."

The sheriff tied the reins to Thurman's horse around the horse's saddle horn and handed William a long lead line that was attached to the horse's bridle. William tied the end of the lead line around his saddle horn and said goodbye to the sheriff. His next stop would be the cavern nestled in the Blue Ridge Mountains of Tennessee, where his bride would be awaiting his return.

CHAPTER 34

THE NEWS

Her sides heaved; her throat burned; she had headaches and backaches; felt queasiness and fatigue. Into the privy William had constructed over the underground stream that ran below the floor of the cavern, Aylana lost everything she had eaten the night before. She felt so tired that she didn't think she would check the traps until later into the day.

At first she thought all the nausea she was experiencing was from having eaten some meat that had gone bad. Her sickness and the aches had been ongoing now for about two weeks. Each time she thought she was getting better, it returned. She knew William had said he would be gone two to three months, and to date it had been a long two and half months. She hoped so much that she would be recovered by the time he returned.

She thought, "Poor Chew. Each time I run to the privy to throw up, he runs with me. He patiently waits for me to wipe my mouth, and then I tell him I will be all right. I don't know what I would have done had I not had him here to watch over me and to keep me company. And for sure, no one is coming through that entrance unless I tell him it's all right. William, please hurry home."

William left Jonesville in a gallop. Now with two horses, he would make Sugar Creek faster. He would ride Taz hard for a couple of hours and then switch to Thurman's horse for a couple of hours. Although still in a gallop, Taz would be resting without carrying him. His plan was to ride straight through the night and arrive by early morning. He would make a quick stop at Draper's Mercantile to see if he owed him any money and then in daylight make his way back up the mountain to the cavern. While living in the stable had reminded him more of the life he had in Saulston, it was not home. That rocky cavern with Aylana and Chew was home.

He arrived in Sugar Creek around 6:00 a.m. He tied his two horses to the hitching rail and stretched out for a nap on the wooden porch in front of Draper's store. He would catch a quick nap before Draper arrived around seven.

It seemed he had just gone the sleep when he felt a gentle bump against his boot. He opened his eyes and glanced down at his foot to see the toe of a boot. Looking up, he saw Draper peering down at him.

Draper said, "You were in such a deep sleep, I'm sorry I woke you."

"I'm glad you did. Had you not opened your store today, I'm afraid I would have slept all day."

Draper laughed and said, "You must have been riding all night."

"Yes sir! Wanted to get home, but first wanted to know if you had seen Aylana, how she was doing, and if I owed you anything?"

Draper replied, "Your answers are yes, fine, and no. Now come on in and catch me up on how your business turned out."

William followed Draper inside and said, "Before I tell you how my trip went, tell me about Aylana."

Draper began. "Well, let me say, I wish I had gotten one of them pups when you did. That dog of yours is one protective dog. But before I tell you 'bout that, I saw Aylana 'bout a month ago, and she was doing just fine. She brought in some pelts to trade for a few items. The pelts were so good, I ended up owing her some money." He laughed about that.

"When she was ready to leave, some half-drunk trapper tried to be overly friendly in his approach to her, but he didn't get anywhere near her. That dog got between him and her, and that was when the wolf in him came out. I never heard such a growl, and when he grinned at the trapper, the man hastened back in the direction from which he came.

"As he left I reminded him that dog could smell a half a mile radius and rip his throat out before he even knew the dog was there. As fast as he left, I'm pretty sure he didn't follow her up the mountain.

"Of course, another thing that may have discouraged any trouble from him was she had that rifle pointed directly at him. She had that look of knowing how to use that rifle, and she wasn't gonna be hesitant about doing do so."

William smiled and said, "She is pretty good with it. Well, Mr. Draper, iffen we don't owe you anything, I'm gonna be heading back up the mountain. Mighty anxious to git home."

"Hold on a second, son. I have something for Aylana." Draper hurried back into his store. Returning a few seconds later, he had something clenched in his fist.

He handed William four peppermint candy sticks and said, "This will help celebrate your coming back home. And, by the way, I'm a-hoping you was gonna tell me something about your trip some time."

"Iffen you don't mind, I'll tell you the next time I'm here. I will say that I had to go as far as Kentucky, and all I set out to do, got done. Thanks, Mr. Draper, for helping Aylana and for the peppermint sticks. I'll see you soon."

After untying the two horses, William leaped up into Taz's saddle and said, "Let's go home, big fellow."

$$\mathcal{R}$$

It was now mid-July, and, by early afternoon, were it not for the trees providing shade to the entrance of the cavern, it would have been a hot day. The sun had crossed over the mountain and now was at the edge of the western sky. As the sun warmed the ground, the warmth crept to the entrance of the cavern. With the flap open, a breeze would periodically sweep through the entrance.

With her endless tired feeling and discomfort, Aylana had found an early-afternoon nap caused her to feel much better. After her nap she and

Chew would check the traps. They had not seen any more wolves, but both were more vigilant for the possibility.

When Aylana lay down for her nap, Chew took up his favorite position—across the entrance to the cavern. There he was fully stretched out so he could feel the warmth from the earth and enjoy the periodic breeze that rustled his fur as it blew through the entrance.

Suddenly, there was a familiar smell in the air. Chew's head came up from its sleeping position. His ears were up and switching back and forth trying to pick up any out-of-the-ordinary sounds. Then he was on his feet. He quickly looked back at Aylana to see if she was showing any indication of smelling or hearing anything. She was sound asleep.

Chew took a few steps outside the entrance. Now his ears were focused in the direction of the trail they used to go down the mountain. There was the sound of two horses, but one had a familiar smell. Then he caught the scent of man. He ventured farther from the cavern, straining to detect any motion. The familiarity of the smells caused him to restrain any of the aggression he was capable of initiating. Then the recognition of the smells produced a quick wagging of his tail as his excitement began to build. When the man on the horse raised up from ducking his head under a limb so Chew could see him, he could not restrain himself any longer.

With his welcome-home bark, Chew raced toward Taz, but his target was the man—the man for whom his loyalty and love were deep in his heart.

William saw Chew coming at full speed, and he wasn't stopping for Taz. William turned loose the reins and opened his arms, and none too soon. Chew leaped from the ground all the way into William's arms. Chew's front paws went across William's shoulders as Chew pushed with his back legs to climb up William's leg. Chew's tongue was working back and forth all over William's face.

William said, "I missed and love you also, Chew. Do you think I might get this kind of welcome from your ma?" Chew rode the remainder of the distance to the cavern in William's arms.

Upon reaching the cavern, Chew jumped from William's arms and bounded for the cavern, announcing that his pa was home.

Hearing Chew's barking, Aylana initially was alarmed, but when she saw his tail wagging and his racing back and forth to and from the cavern entrance, her only thought was "William must be home!"

Aylana reached the cavern entrance just as William entered. She threw herself into his arms, crying, "Oh! I have missed you so much. I so much love you. Promise me you will never leave me again."

Holding her as tight as he could, he said, "I promise!" And as they hugged and kissed each other, Chew raced around them barking, "All the family is together again!"

When they finally separated and Chew had settled down, William said, "Stand back and let me take a look at you."

Aylana stepped back with a happy smile on her face.

William then said, "Once I've put Taz and his new friend in the stall, I will be back for you to tell me all you've been doing since I have been gone."

Aylana replied, "And you must tell me what all you have been doing while you've been gone. But first you must tell me about that." She was pointing to the Colt strapped around William's waist.

William, being in a hurry to return home, had forgotten he was still wearing his revolver. He said, "I'll tell you all about it when I finish taking care of the horses. It would be nice if you would fix me something to eat. Other than jerky, I've been in too big a hurry to get home to stop to cook anything."

Aylana responded, "Take your time, because I am going to prepare a welcome-home meal for you."

William departed the cavern with Chew following, wagging his tail. It was almost as if Chew believed he had some relief from his protection duties.

After feeding and stalling the two horses with the mule, hanging the bridles, and putting the saddles across a wooden rail, he returned to the cavern. Once inside he asked, "Aylana, do I have some clean clothes here? I haven't had a bath in over a week. I think I'm going to the river bend and take bath. I must have an inch of trail dirt on me."

Aylana hurried to the back of the cavern and soon proudly returned with a new pair of buckskin trousers and a cotton shirt she had made. Although it was the latter part of July and a cotton long-sleeve shirt was going to be very warm, he excitedly accepted the new clothes and thanked her with a big kiss. "I'll be back shortly, looking like a new man," William said.

"Don't change! I like the man you are," said Aylana.

After a bath in the cool river water, dressed in his new clothes and his belly full of deer steak, corn, wild artichokes, and blueberries, William felt like a much-refreshed man. With Aylana snuggled up to him and Chew resting his head on William's thigh, Aylana insisted he tell her about his trip. However, he said she must tell her story first.

Other than her missing him, she said that while the ten weeks had gone by slowly, she and Chew had done well together. She told of their adventure with the wolves and how their pelts had brought a good price from Draper. She also told of how Chew had discouraged a trapper from making advances toward her.

With regard to the man making an advance toward her, William said, "Iffen you and Chew had not done such a good job of discouraging him, I might just get Taz, go down the mountain, and make a settlement with him."

When William's turn came to tell of his adventure, before he did so, he went over and withdrew something from his saddlebags. Handing Aylana the peppermint sticks, he said, "This might make my stories less boring." He then told her of the necessity for the pistol and that until the war was over and times returned to normal, it might be necessary for him to continue to carry it.

He then told her of his capture of Herman Rouse in Powder Springs, Tennessee, and the death of Thurman Rouse in Yellow Creek, Kentucky. He assured her he did not kill Thurman but that after being shot in the shoulder, his head struck something when he fell, causing an impact that killed him. He also told of Mr. and Miz Benton and their kindness to him. Finally, he told her of the reward money he had received and would be getting in the future.

When he spoke of the future, she asked, "What will we do now? While this cavern has provided us comfort from the winter elements, I was hoping that we could leave the mountains before the next winter."

With the warmth of her body next to his, the smell of forest outside, and the flickering light of the cooking fire, William suggested they wait on that subject for tomorrow. Tonight was meant for them to make up for the time they had not been together.

As they both slipped out of their clothes, Chew went around to the other side of the fire. He knew it was either that or he would have to go outside. He would not be sleeping next to his ma tonight…at least until the two were asleep, and then he could reposition himself next to her.

Just before daybreak, William was awakened by the sound of Aylana's bare feet striking the cavern floor as she raced to the privy. William raised himself to see if there was a problem. He saw Aylana leaning over with her head almost in the privy and her body retching as she began to throw up.

He jumped to his feet and raced to her side. With his arm around her, he asked, "Is there something I can do?"

She shook her head. Finally she stood up, and William handed her a cloth to wipe her mouth. She said, "I'm gonna be all right."

"How long have you been sick like this?" asked William.

"Off and on about six weeks," replied Aylana.

As she stood in front of William, without any clothes, he noticed that she appeared to have gained some weight, particularly in the area of her waist. A smile began to creep across his face.

Aylana, seeing his smile, asked, "What do you see that is so funny?"

"I'm not laughing, Aylana, and I certainly am no doctor, but I've seen your symptoms before. And what makes me happy is I am going to be the one to diagnose your condition."

"What are you saying, 'diagnose'? What do you mean, 'my condition?'"

"My dearest sweet wife, we are going to be parents…you are going to be a mama."

Shock came upon Aylana's face. "How do you know?"

"I know because I saw my mama have the same symptoms before my youngest sister and brother were born. She was sick in the mornings, tired all day, and gained weight in her stomach."

Aylana looked down at her stomach, patted it, and said, "I feel the same. I now have to take afternoon naps because I am so tired. Are you sure?"

"I think I am pretty sure."

Aylana's tears began to flow more as she asked, "Are you happy?"

"Very, very happy," responded William, as he embraced his pregnant wife.

An hour later, when the good news was finally accepted, Aylana wanted to talk about their future. Were they going to continue to live in the cavern or seek other dwellings before winter?

William, in a more solemn manner, said, "I have thought about our future a lot. And now, with a baby on the way, our actions have to be more immediate. I was going to suggest, if you were not pregnant, that we take some time to try to find your family. That is not the travel we should try to undertake now.

"My thought now is that we return to my home in eastern North Carolina. There, in the safety of my home, where there is a doctor nearby, is where we need to be. I can help my father during the harvest season, and then I want to go to law school. I want to be able to provide a good home for you and our child."

Aylana said, "I think we should do what you think is best. I don't think we will be able to find my family. There was talk the government was going to move all Cherokee farther south, maybe to a place called Florida. I don't know. How soon do we leave here?"

"I hope we can leave by the first of August. That is less than two weeks. I will sell all our pelts to Draper. All our belongings we will pack on the new horse. With you riding Patches and me on Taz, we should make Asheville, North Carolina, in two days. There we will board a train for Goldsboro. That trip may take three days. From Goldsboro we can be to my home on horseback in around two hours."

"What is a train?"

"It will be easier for me to show you than to describe it. But it travels much faster than a horse, and we sit in chairs to ride. We can even sleep while we ride."

Aylana's eyes became even wider when she heard she could ride faster than a horse while sitting and sleeping. It was decided that tomorrow they would start making ready for their trip.

CHAPTER 35

HOMEWARD BOUND

It was Friday, August 26, 1864. It had been fifteen months since William had departed from his family farm in Saulston, North Carolina. Now he was departing his second home near Sugar Creek, Tennessee. But this time he was not leaving a family behind but taking one with him. His immediate family now consisted of a wife with their unborn child, two horses, one mule, and a dog.

William looked over his traveling party. Aylana was riding Patches, the mule, and pulling a drag with all their pelts tied on it. The new horse was now a packhorse carrying all their personal possessions. The lead line to the new horse, still to be named, was tied around William's saddle horn. As normal, Chew was out front, scouting the trail.

The plan was simple. They would ride down to Sugar Creek and sell all their pelts and drag to Draper. From there they would make their way to Asheville, which William estimated would take, at the most, three days. In Asheville they would board a train to Goldsboro. There was no way William was going to permit Aylana to travel across North Carolina on horseback. The horses and mule would ride in one of the cattle cars. William, Aylana and Chew would ride in one of the coach cars.

William had also decided that since he was bringing such a large family home, he should not make it a surprise. Accordingly, in Asheville he would send a telegram to Saulston announcing their approximate date of arrival and the number his family could expect. William estimated the train ride should be no more than three days, depending upon any disruptions the war might have on rail travel.

When William concluded that all had been done at the cavern that needed to be done, he and Aylana said goodbye to their first home, and he gave the command to Chew, "Lead us to Sugar Creek, Chew!"

Chew started in that direction on an undefined trail. His nose was on the ground following the path that William used when he returned home.

Around midafternoon, the party arrived at Draper's in Sugar Creek. Draper had become somewhat attached to the young couple. The first thing he did was to give Aylana a hug and a stick of peppermint candy. He then said, "Aylana, honey, you just take your time shopping."

Aylana said, "William is outside. He has some pelts for you."

"Well, I guess I best get outside and see what they look like."

William waited outside while Aylana and Chew went inside. When Draper came out the door, William said, "Mr. Draper, I want to sell you the entire load, and I will throw in the drag."

"I see you now have a packhorse that appears to be all packed for a long trip. I hope you and Aylana are not permanently leaving us."

"The job I came out here to do is finished, and I'm ready to go back home to North Carolina. I certainly appreciate the kindness you've shown Aylana and me. But I need to sell what I have and try to get back home in time to help my Pa with the fall harvest."

Draper started to sort through the pelts. As he felt of their texture and saw how well they had been cured out, he said, "Mind telling me the business you had to take care of?"

William briefly went over what had happened to his pa and the promise he had made to himself to settle the matter the Rouse brothers had created with his pa. He told how both men had been returned to Jonesville, Virginia, because of the crimes they had committed there. He made no mention of the reward money or the fact that one was returned dead.

When William had finished his story, Draper said, "I sure hate to see you and Aylana leave us. I think the two of you could move down here to our community and help us grow this place into a nice town. But I understand that a man has to do what is best for him and his family."

William replied, "Yes sir, and now that Aylana is expecting, I feel we need to get back as soon as possible because it won't be much longer before she will not be able to make such a trip."

"Congratulations, William! Tell you what I'm gonna do. I will give you fifty dollars for all your pelts, including the drag."

"I think that might be a bit too much, Mr. Draper."

"Well, call the difference between what you think they are worth and what I'm a-giving you as a present for your soon-to-be addition to your family. Now, if you will unhitch your drag and leave it right there, I'll take care of it after I see if Aylana needs any help." Draper turned and reentered the store.

In a few minutes, Aylana and Chew came out of the store smiling. She was clutching a small brown paper bag.

William said, "Did you find something you wanted? I'll go in and pay Mr. Draper."

"No." Aylana replied, "Mr. Draper gave me a present to make my travels more enjoyable. He said our baby would like the taste also."

William then knew that Draper had given her a bag of peppermint candy. She placed the bag in her saddlebag and climbed up on Patches's back. She was now ready for their trip.

As William mounted Taz, Draper came outside to bid the couple a safe trip and expressed hope they would someday return to Sugar Creek. William replied, "I hope one day we will be able to return, if for only a visit."

William turned Taz in the direction of Asheville and led out, followed by the packhorse in tow and Aylana behind the packhorse. Chew, not sure exactly where he needed to be, was trotting along beside Taz.

The trip to Asheville was close to the time William had estimated. They spent two nights on the trail and arrived around midday of the third day. While they had spotted some troop movements, they encountered no problems.

Upon arrival at the train depot, William went inside while Aylana waited outside with the horses and Chew. In the depot William arranged for his two horses and mule to ride in a cattle car to Goldsboro. In order for Chew to ride inside the coach, where he would take up a passenger seat, William had to buy a ticket for him. The ticket clerk explained the trip would be in three legs, two of which would require a change in trains. While Aylana, William, and Chew would have to change trains, William would not have to concern himself with his horses because there was a crew at each station to move the animals to another car as required. However, their personal possessions on the packhorse would have to be placed in a freight crate. The depot crew would see that the crate was placed on the proper trains.

The three legs of the trip would consist of the departing train going first to Salisbury, North Carolina. There, William and his family would transfer to a train bound for Greensboro, North Carolina. In Greensboro they would board their final leg, which would take them to Goldsboro, and the train would continue to Wilmington.

When William asked how long the trip would take, he received a somewhat vague answer. The clerk said, "With this war going on, nothing is for certain. There could be lengthy delays. Trains could be rerouted. And worst case, all could be required to disembark for soldiers to get on. If all were to go as scheduled, your train will depart at six o'clock tomorrow morning and arrive in Salisbury by midafternoon. The train for Greensboro is scheduled to depart around eight p.m., arriving in Greensboro around three a.m. the next day. That train is supposed to leave around noon, arriving in Goldsboro somewhere around two p.m.

"What you need to know is that since about January, none of the trains have been arriving or departing according to their schedule. Just be thankful if you get all the way there by train. The only thing I can be certain of is that you will not travel according to the schedule. Now I'll give you a tag to put on your horse harnesses and one for your freight container. You are responsible for seeing they are in the right place to be put on the train."

William asked, "Where is the holding pen for the horses, and where do I get the freight box for our personal possessions?"

"The holding pen is behind the depot, and the freight box is located at the freight yard, which is clearly marked. You will see it once you get to the holding pen."

William, with tickets in hand, said, "Thank you!" and started out the door.

The clerk yelled after him, "You best be here by five tomorrow morning, because the train is subject to leave earlier than scheduled."

After William explained to Aylana all he had been told, he said, "You and Chew stay here with Taz and Patches while I take the pack-horse to the freight warehouse to pack our things in a freight container. Once I have the packhorse in the pen, I'll come back for the others. I'm putting the tickets in the saddlebag. You hold on to the saddlebag. And keep Chew at your side. I don't think anyone will bother you with Chew beside you. I'll be as quick as I can."

For Aylana this was all an interesting but somewhat scary experience. She was used to living in the forest, surrounded by no other people. Here people were pushing, shoving, and hurrying about. There were metal rails leading into and away from the depot. On one rail was a large iron machine with smoke puffing from its top. She remembered some of the braves in her tribe speaking of an iron horse that ran along iron tracks, but this was the first one she had ever seen.

William saw the frightened look on her face and sat her under a tree away from the depot. He reassured her she had nothing to fear. He and Chew would look after her. She tried to show bravery as she assured William she would wait for him.

Aylana, wearing her buckskin dress, sat with her back against a tree with her legs stretched out and crossed. Chew lay down beside her and placed his head in her lap. She sat there, eating a peppermint stick, in wonderment. Periodically, a man would pass by and tip his hat to her. Most, upon seeing Chew, who looked more like a wolf than a hound dog, skirted her presence with a wide path.

Within an hour William returned for Taz and Patches. He said, "All I have to do now is place the saddles in the freight crate and place Taz and Patches in the holding pen. Has anyone bothered you?"

"No. I've enjoyed watching all the people, but I already miss the forest."

"I know," replied William. "I should not be long. I'll leave the bedrolls with you because I plan for us to sleep under this tree tonight. We have to be ready to depart about sunrise. I won't be long." William departed with Taz and Patches in tow.

A short time later, a young Confederate soldier with a beard stopped near Aylana. He said, "Hey there! You pretty young lady. You been waiting for me?"

Aylana had become a very attractive young woman. Her pregnancy had added weight, which caused her face to be rounder, and her complexion was flawless. The weight she had added in other places had given her a mature appearance that most of the men who passed her could not help but notice.

Aylana made no reply. Chew moved to a sitting position with his eyes focused upon every movement of the soldier.

The soldier continued. "Iffen you'll send that dog on his way, I think we can have a good time together." He then started to move toward Aylana.

Chew's immediate instinct was to stop the man's advance. He rolled his upper lip up, exposing the fangs of a wolf. A deep, guttural growl rose from within him. His message was clear: "A step closer and you're mine."

The soldier's hand started to move toward his pistol as he said, "I think I'm just about to kill me wolf."

Then a voice behind him said, "Before your hand can touch the butt of your revolver, that dog will have torn your throat out!"

The soldier quickly turned around. Before him stood the body of a large boy, but the boy had the steely eyes of a man who probably knew how to use the Colt that was in the holster tied to his leg.

William continued. "My suggestion is you move on to join the other soldiers. My dog and I don't cotton to any man making an advance toward my wife."

The soldier sputtered back, "Sorry, boy. Didn't know this Injun was anyone's wife…especially a white boy! May have to come back to pay you a visit to explain that white boys don't marry Injun girls."

William said, "For now, I will consider this to be just an error in your judgment. So you best move on before my dog's patience expires."

The soldier turned and started moving in the direction of the depot.

William thought now was the time to explain to Aylana what she should expect in what was believed to be a "white man's world." He said, "Aylana, I am sorry for what that man did. He made unwanted advances and was most disrespectful of you. I can promise you that while the comments he made may happen again, I will always love and protect you from that type of person. My family will love you as I do, but we must be prepared for our love to be tested by characters such as that man. I am certain there will be times, even where we are going, where the feeling expressed will be the same as those expressed by that man. There are many who believe a white man should only marry a white woman. My family will join with me and stand up for the right of any couple to love and to marry whomever they wish. And together we will try to protect you from such people. Do you understand what I am saying?"

"Yes, I will try to understand. As long as I know you love me as much as I love you, we will be all right."

William leaned over and kissed Aylana and said, "Thank you. Now I must go send this message I have been writing for the last two nights to my parents, to let them know when they can expect us to arrive. You walk with me. Chew will guard our bedrolls."

Turning to Chew, William, pointed to the bedrolls and commanded, "Chew, stay!"

Chew stretched out on top of the two bedrolls that were lying side by side.

Holding hands, William and Aylana walked to the telegraph office, where William said, "I hope this message arrives in Saulston before we do."

CHAPTER 36

THE FAMILY

William, Aylana, and Chew were permitted to board the train at 6:15 the following morning. They had spent the previous evening under the tree near the depot. None slept any. William remained awake in anticipation the soldier might return with some of his friends, and he was prepared.

Aylana slept very little because of her anxiety regarding the ride in the large iron horse. The very idea this machine could transport them for several days without getting tired was completely beyond her comprehension. When it arrived at the depot around 2:00 a.m., she saw people getting off and acting as if the experience had been favorable. But, she still had reservations. What if once she was inside, and it started to move, she needed to get outside? What would she do?

Chew had sensed the anxiety of William and remained vigilant. His nose was constantly sniffing the air, and his ears were in constant motion as he tried to pick up any out-of-the-ordinary sounds.

When the time came to board, the only hesitation was from Aylana. But with William's reassurance and Chew bouncing on board with his tail wagging in anticipation of a new experience, she boarded.

The three worked their way down the aisle of an empty coach. William, with the tickets in hand, periodically glanced at the seat numbers on the tickets and the seats along the aisle. Finally, he came upon their three seats near the front of their coach.

He insisted Aylana take the window seat so she could look out at the countryside they passed through. Chew took the middle seat, and William took the aisle seat.

Slowly others started to enter the coach and to look for their seats. After all passengers assigned to the coach were seated, the coach was at about 50 percent capacity. Shortly thereafter, the conductor came by to punch all the tickets. As he started to punch William's tickets, he hesitated and then asked William if he could step outside onto the porch that separated their coach from the one in front of them.

Turning to Aylana, William said, "Don't worry; I'll be right back."

William accompanied the conductor outside, where the conductor said, "Sir, I'm sorry, but Indians are not allowed to ride in the front of the coach. She must go to the rear."

William squared himself in front of the conductor, which confirmed William was a few inches taller, and his shoulders were much wider. He calmly responded, "Sir, I think you have made a mistake. That is not an Indian with me. That is my wife. And with all due respect to you and your position, I have paid for those seats, we have been assigned those seats, and we have no intentions of moving my wife to any seat other than where she is currently seated."

The conductor shook his head and said, "Sir, I've had a complaint from the back of the coach from one of the soldiers."

"Mr. Conductor, you do your job and punch the tickets. I'll address the complaint from the soldier. Rest assured you will have no problem."

Smiling, the conductor punched William's tickets and said, "Have a good trip!"

Reentering the coach, William stopped by where Aylana was seated and said, "Everything is just fine. You and Chew sit here and keep watching out the window so you will know when the train moves. I'll be back shortly."

As William started toward the rear of the coach, he spotted the soldier who had made unwanted advances toward Aylana the previous day. William was confident he was the individual who had made the complaint.

As William approached the soldier, who was sitting with three other soldiers, William reached deep into his pocket and wrapped his hand around a wad of money. William was glad to see the soldier had an aisle seat.

When William was next to the seat where the soldier was, he said, "Excuse me, sir, but could I see you on the back porch of this coach. I think I can make it worth your while." He extracted his hand from his pocket far enough to expose the wad of money he was holding. He motioned to the rear with his head and started in that direction.

The soldier's first thought was, "The boy is going to try to buy my silence. And, he might just have enough to do it."

Leaning over to his traveling companions, the soldier said, "I have some business to transact with this boy." He then got up and followed behind William.

When the soldier exited the train, he felt a hand grasp him around his throat and slam him back against the back of the coach. He then felt the cold barrel of a revolver under his chin. Then he heard the words, "I understand you are not happy with the seating arrangements on this train?"

The man struggled to speak, as the grip to his throat was creating a problem. He finally muttered, "Injuns are supposed to sit in the rear of the coach."

William glared into the man's eyes and said, "Well, since that is not going to happen in this coach, I think you may want to try for another train."

Stuttering, the soldier said, "I'm to join my unit in Greensboro, for its movement to Front Royal, Virginia. I can only make it on this train."

The coach jerked slightly as the train started to move. The soldier tried to take advantage of the movement of the train, but he was too slow. When William's left hand lost grip of the soldier's throat, his left forearm slammed into the man's chest, knocking him back against the coach. At the same time, William holstered his Colt.

With a mischievous smile on his face, William said, "I'm sorry, but I think you just missed your train." Then William rammed his right knee into the man's left thigh, which caused the man to make a sharp turn to his right, and he was peering over the railing as the train began to pick up speed.

William's motion appeared to be synchronized as his left hand grabbed the man by the nape of his neck and his right hand grabbed the man's belt in the back of his trousers. And with a mighty heave, William threw the man over the railing and off the train. He watched as the man rolled away from the train and vanished from sight.

Reentering the train, William stopped by the seats where the soldier's companions were seated and said, "Your friend decided to take a later next train." He continued down the aisle and took his seat beside Chew.

Smiling at Aylana, he said, "My dear, this will be a great trip for us. It will give me the opportunity to tell you all about my family, and we can discuss the future for our growing family." With those words, he patted her stomach and kissed her on the cheek. Chew, having been awake all night, had curled up in his seat and was fast asleep.

John Robert was enjoying the late-afternoon breeze, puffing on his pipe and rocking in his chair while enjoying conversation and vivid memories with a man who had become a dear friend—Captain Julius Whitaker.

Whitaker had arrived the previous day and was quite surprised to see that John had recovered to the point where one would have never known he had been so severely injured. They talked about the contract John had insisted upon to keep William out of the army if John were to enlist.

Whitaker said, "That was the best contract I ever signed. You will never know how much your maturity in the camp helped the young soldiers. They viewed you as their father image, and to be honest, you could get them to respond to you better than I could get them to do what I wanted with an order."

John laughed and expressed how much he had enjoyed serving under Whitaker. John said, "When we worked together, there seemed to be an unspoken understanding between us. However, I must tell you, my being sent to Danville, Virginia, was not a pleasant experience."

Eventually, they returned to the subject of William. John explained to Whitaker how William had taken John's injury as a personal issue.

That he had set out to settle the score with the Rouse brothers and promised to return home as soon as that had been accomplished.

As John rocked, Whitaker got up out of his chair and lit a cigar. After blowing a couple of smoke doughnut-shaped circles, he cocked his head to one side and said, "I think you got company coming, and he's riding hard."

Instinctually, when John stood up to get a better look, he reached for his rifle, which was leaning against the door frame.

The rider was coming fast, but not so fast that John did not recognize him. Placing his rifle back next to the door frame, John said, "It's the telegraph messenger. He must have a message from William." John bounded down the front steps, without the slightest sign of a limp, to meet the rider. Whitaker followed.

As the horse came to a sudden stop, the rider said, "Mr. Daniel, I have a telegram for you from Asheville, North Carolina. Hope it's not bad news."

John replied, "I hope it's not bad news also."

The rider made no effort to leave, as he was hoping Daniel would share the message with him.

Whitaker watched anxiously as John tore into the message and began to read. He suddenly exclaimed, "William coming home! Before I read any further, I have to round up the family so we can all hear his message together."

Whitaker turned toward the house and said, "I'll get them, John. Don't you move."

The rider asked, "Mr. Daniel, may I stay to hear what William has to say?"

"Certainly, son! Get down from that horse, and stretch your legs while the family gathers."

Soon all the family, Whitaker, and the telegram messenger were standing around John waiting for John to read the telegram. One could have heard a pin drop, all were so quiet. The birds weren't even chirping.

John began to read. "Ma, Pa, and family, hope to be home within the week. Pa, settlement with RB is done…"

John paused for a moment to say to Whitaker, "RB refers to the Rouse brothers, the soldiers who attack me in Weldon."

Whitaker muttered in a low voice, barely heard by John, "Scum of the earth. He should have killed them."

John continued. "Explain details later.

Becky interrupted. "What's the date on the telegram, John? If it was long getting here, he could be here tomorrow!"

John looked at the postmark and said, "It's dated two days ago. Now, may I finish?"

All bobbed their heads in the affirmative.

John continued. "Ma, I wanted to surprise you but thought it might be too much of a surprise. Didn't want your surprise to be a shock to you. Ma, I married an Indian maiden, and you're gonna be a grandma."

Now John stopped reading and looked around the group. Becky looked stunned; some of the children stood open mouthed; Nancy and Fannie were jumping up and down saying, "We're gonna be aunts!"

Whitaker extended his hand and said, "Congratulations! Grandma and Grandpa!"

Becky said, "Finish the telegram, John! There may be more surprises."

It took a few minutes for John to regain his composure before he started to read. "Pa, I've added to our livestock. I'll be coming with two horses, a mule, and a dog. Hope you have room for us. Looking forward to helping you with the fall harvest. Love, William, Aylana, and ?"

Becky, the first to speak, as the others were trying to absorb what they had heard, said, "That William is not old enough to get married. Why…"

John quickly looked at Becky and said, "Now, just how old were you when you got married, Miz Daniel? As I recall, you were younger than William. Besides, William is more of a man than I was when I got married, and I was fifteen years older than you. He has more than proven himself a man. He looked after this farm as well as I could when I wasn't here, and now he gone and apprehended the men who attacked me. And for all of you, while he is your son or your brother, he is a man, and I expect him to be treated as such. And with respect to his wife, she will be loved as if she was born into this family."

By now the telegram messenger was back in his saddle. He said, "Thanks for letting me hear the message, Mr. Daniel. I best be getting back to Saulston." He gave his horse a kick in the side and was soon leaving a trail of dust behind him.

Whitaker reached over and put his arm around John's shoulder and said, "Well said, my true and dear friend. That boy of yours would have made a great soldier, but I'm glad he's having the opportunity to live a life that many of our young boys are not getting. I expect great things from him."

৯

In spite of the somewhat discomforting start of their trip, William, Aylana, and Chew found traveling by train an enjoyable experience. There were frequent and long stops that allowed time for all to stretch their legs, take Chew for a walk, and buy something to eat from one of the depot food vendors.

At no time did the train arrive at or depart from a destination as scheduled, which confirmed what William had been told before they departed Asheville. Nor were there any more instances where Aylana's seating was questionable. Most of the soldiers who had been on the train got off at Greensboro. Because of the delays between train departures, William had sufficient time to locate their next coach when they had to change trains. He assumed the horses and freight also made the proper changes. They soon discovered sleeping in the coach was much better than sleeping on the ground. Aylana laid her head against the window or across Chew to sleep. Chew had his head in either William's or Aylana's lap. William would sit straight up and sleep like he was stretched out on the floor of the cavern.

While Aylana enjoyed seeing the big towns of Greensboro and Raleigh, she longed for the open spaces, void of so many people. Her real comfort was the strolls in the forest, checking traps, and listening to the birds sing as she reclined against a fir tree. But she realized her world was changing, and she would have to adapt to the world from which William came.

Around noon of the third day after their departure from Asheville, William, Aylana, and Chew arrived in Goldsboro. Aylana and Chew accompanied William to the cattle car for the off-loading of the horses.

There were only six horses to be off-loaded. William showed his ticket stubs to the wrangler who brought the horses out of the cattle car. He matched them with the tags on the two horses and the mule and turned them over to William.

Chew danced around, happy to see his animal friends as they all went to the freight yard. There William claimed his crate and borrowed a pry bar to open it. Once it was open, he saddled Taz and Patches. Aylana helped him place their personal possessions on the packhorse.

Once he and Aylana were in their saddles, William commented, "Goldsboro looks the same as it did when I left. We're about two hours from my family."

Seeing a worried look on Aylana's face, he said, "Aylana, don't you worry about my family. You will soon see they will love you as much as I do. However, you must be prepared for three younger sisters who probably will ask you lots of questions. You will also have two younger brothers who will be a little shy until they get to know you. I can promise, without meeting you, they already love you."

Aylana replied, "I hope you are right. I am a little scared, but I know you will look after me."

The small party began its journey toward Saulston with Chew in the lead, sniffing from one side of the road to the other. William routinely pointed out the different crops growing in the fields. The most common crop she saw was tobacco, which William explained was probably the most-grown crop in Wayne County. Periodically, they would meet another traveler who would extend a friendly greeting or simply wave their hand.

Two hours later, the small party turned onto the path leading up to the Daniel farm. To William's eyes, although the valley on the outskirts of Boone was beautiful, home had the most beautiful terrain he had seen since his departure. In the distance he could see a small girl standing on the front porch. As soon as they made their turn, she disappeared into the house. Halfway up the path, William saw the front door swing open, and the entire family raced out through the door.

While most of the family remained on the porch with their arms wide open, his two youngest brothers never stopped running. As they ran toward William and his party, they were hollering, "William! William!"

Mindful that Chew could be aggressive, William said, "Chew, it's all right. They are family."

With tears in his eyes, he turned to speak to Aylana, only to see tears in her eyes. He then said, "Aylana, for now this is our home. I hope you will grow to love it as much as I love you. Here we will start a new life and begin a new adventure for our family."

Aylana smiled at William and said, "I know and I am ready for our new adventure."